A Sloop of War

A Sloop of War

by

Philip K. Allan

A Sloop of War by Philip K Allan
Copyright © 2018 Philip K Allan

ISBN-13: 978-1-946409-42-3(Paperback)
ISBN :13: 978-1-946409-43-0(e-book)
BISAC Subject Headings:

FIC014000FICTION / Historical
FIC032000FICTION / War & Military
FIC047000FICTION / Sea Stories

Editing: Terri Carter
Cover Illustration by Christine Horner

Address all correspondence to:
Penmore Press LLC
920 N Javelina Pl
Tucson, AZ 85748

Dedication

To my Jenny Wren

Acknowledgements

All authors need the help and support of those around them to make their vision a reality and I am no exception. The books of the Alexander Clay series start with a passion for the naval battles and campaigns of the Napoleonic Wars. Mine was first awakened by the works of C S Forester that I read as a boy and more recently those of Patrick O'Brian. That interest was boosted when I studied the 18th century navy under Pat Crimmin as part of my history degree at London University.

Many years later, when I first started on my way as a novelist, I received the unconditional support and cheerful encouragement of my darling wife and two wonderful daughters. I strive to make sure that my work is accessible for those without a knowledge of the period, or an interest in the sea, and the crucible of my family is where I first test my prose. This proved particularly valuable for *A Sloop of War,* with its need to portray a land siege. One chapter underwent three rewrites, until my sternest editor, my wife Jan, was satisfied. I would also like to thank my dear friend Peter Northen for his advice and support.

One of the most unexpected pleasures of my new career path is to find that I have been drawn into a community of fellow authors, who offer generous support and encouragement to each other. When I needed help and advice the most, I received it from David Donachie, Bernard Cornwell, Marc Liebman and in particular Alaric Bond, creator of the Fighting Sail series of books.

Finally my thanks go to the team at Penmore Press, Michael, Terri, Christine and Midori, who worked so hard to turn the world I have created into the book you hold in your hand.

Contents

Chapter 1 Arrival

Chapter 2 Barbados

Chapter 3 The Sloop of War *Rush*

Chapter 4 Micoud

Chapter 5 Punishment

Chapter 6 Chase

Chapter 7 Bridgetown

Chapter 8 Ball

Chapter 9 Convoy

Chapter 10 Vieux Fort

Chapter 11 Digging

Chapter 12 Siege

Chapter 13 Truce

Chapter 14 *San Felipe*

Chapter 15 Battle

Chapter 16 Departure

Chapter 1
Arrival

It was a perfect night to escape. Heavy rain beat down on the thatch and poured off the eaves in a liquid curtain. The air was thick with the hiss of falling water and the growl of thunder. No overseer would bother to patrol in such weather, and when his absence was noticed in the morning, the bloodhounds would have a scant trail to follow.

Inside the hut the other slaves were too tired to be disturbed by the rumble of the storm as it settled over the island. Bodies lay on the earth floor all around him. Some flinched in sleep from the occasional drop of water that penetrated the thatch, but most lay inert where exhaustion had overwhelmed them. He crept over to the wall and slipped his fingers under the bottom of a panel. After weeks of careful work, it was now only held in place by a smear of mud around its edges, and with a gentle tug it came away in his hands. The sound of rain was suddenly loud, and a cool rush of wind swept through the opening and into the hut. He looked around as a few of the bodies closest to him turned over, but none awoke. He slipped out into the compound, replaced the panel and stood upright. Once he was satisfied that no one had noticed him go, he eased his hands into the thatch, probing for the old machete he had concealed there. His fingers felt the cold touch of the metal, moved along the blade in search of the broken handle and pulled the knife free. He closed his fist around it and looked out into the night.

A flash of lightning seared across the sky. For a moment it caught a net of silver droplets hanging motionless as they bounced up from the packed dirt of the compound. In that splinter of light he saw the place on the outer wall he had chosen for his escape and the image remained with him as he stepped out into the dark. By the time his groping hands reached the far side of the compound he was utterly soaked by the rain.

He could feel that the surface of the wooden wall was now slick and treacherous but he was a powerfully built man and a confident climber. He thrust the point of the machete deep into the barrier with both hands and then used this as a foothold to scramble up. He pulled himself to the top of the wall and rested astride it for a moment. The ground outside was invisible in the dark, but he had chosen the spot with care. He knew it was flat, and free from any obstacles that might turn an ankle. He lowered himself down the outside of the wall until he dangled with his arms fully extended. Then he released his grip and dropped to the ground.

The slave paused for a moment, listening in the dark. Through the sound of the falling rain he heard the deeper gurgle of the stream that flowed past the slave quarters and down through the cane fields. He planned to use the water to wash away any scent trail that might survive the rain. He slipped down the muddy bank and stumbled along the choked water course, sliding over unseen rocks and fallen branches in the dark. The lightning helped his progress, and in the long intervals of black between each flash he tried not to think about the numerous snakes he knew to frequent the damp banks of the stream.

His original plan for the escape had been simple, if desperate. A universe away, across the ocean, he had been a skilled fisherman on a brown estuary near the sea. He knew how to handle a dugout canoe, and he knew that all streams lead in time to the sea. It would be strange if once he reached the coast, he could not steal a small boat to escape in.

But now he had another, better plan. After an overheard conversation between the plantation owner and one of the overseers he had changed his mind. He would leave the stream before it reached the water and make his way across country towards a village called Melverton. There he would search for Spring Hill Plantation, for he now knew that once he arrived there, all would be well.

*****

Next morning the tropical storm seemed a distant memory. The pouring rain and crash of thunder had been replaced by sunshine and a cool breeze. It sent small waves drifting across the indigo waters of Carlisle Bay to slap against the sides of the ships that lined the quaysides of Bridgetown, Barbados. The same sea breeze that had raised the little waves then pressed on inland, swaying the fronds of the palm trees and sending a scatter of points of sunlight dancing across the table top where George Robertson sat alone in the garden of Milton's coffee house, reading the latest newspaper from London.

It was not for want of possible companions that he sat alone. As was usual at this time of day, Milton's was thronged with the great and good of the Barbadian business community. Plantation owners from across the island, big florid men with calico waistcoats stretched over their ample bellies mixed with sharp featured sugar merchants and slave traders, their eyes aglitter at the prospect of the next deal. All of the places at the tables that surrounded his were taken and the busy chatter from their occupants filled the garden with noise. Mr Robertson did not sit alone under his palm tree because he was unsociable. He sat alone because, as usual, none of this fellow Barbadians was prepared to sit with him.

'Excuse me, sir,' said a cultured voice beside him. 'I am aware that we have not been introduced, but would it inconvenience you if I was to sit at your table?' Mr Robertson looked up in surprise. Standing over him was a well-groomed, sandy-haired young man in his mid-twenties dressed in the simple blue uniform of a naval surgeon. The man indicated the absence of alternative seating to be had in the garden with a sweep of his hand, before extending the same hand towards Mr Robertson.

'My name is Linfield, sir, Mr Jacob Linfield. I am the surgeon on the sloop of war *Rush*.'

'Pleased to make your acquaintance,' said Robertson in his gentle Scottish burr. 'Do you truly wish to sit here? Why if that is the case, pray take a seat by all means, Mr Linfield.' Robertson folded his paper and placed it on the table so as to be able to grip the young surgeon's hand. 'I am George Robertson and I reside here in Barbados.'

Robertson waved across one of the coffee house waiters to take Mr Linfield's order, and then returned his attention to his unexpected companion, who was now chattering away.

'I must say I had rather despaired of finding anywhere to sit,' said Linfield 'and then by chance I saw you seated here with no one else. A very happy coincidence for me, for I am quite fatigued with my morning's labours. I have been with an acquaintance of my father's, Mr Bradshaw, who was kind enough to show me around Bridgetown. I was surprised to find the settlement to be quite so extensive.'

'Bradshaw, you say?' asked Robertson, staring at the young man from beneath his bushy eyebrows. 'Do you mean 'Temperance' Bradshaw, the abolitionist?'

'Why I suppose so, although I have never heard him named as you have done,' said Linfield. 'He is certainly a committed Christian and I know he is not a drinker.'

'Upon my word, do you presume to make game of me, sir?' said Robertson, with sudden anger. 'Did you come to sit at this table in order to mock me in my isolation? If so you will find you have chosen to beard the wrong man! Or did that dog Campbell, or perhaps Haynes put you up to this?'

'Sir!' cried the surgeon as he recoiled from the table. 'I had no notion of offending you, and I am quite amazed by your uncivil reaction. I am no acquaintance of either this Mr Campbell or Mr Haynes you speak of. Indeed, until a few minutes ago the name of Robertson was one with which I was wholly unfamiliar. If I have provoked you in some way I am sorry for it, but it was certainly not my intention.'

Robertson glared at the surgeon for a few moments longer, but he could detect nothing but innocence in his frank blue eyes. After a few moments he extended his hand across the table in apology, and the men shook hands again for the second time in as many minutes.

'Your pardon, sir,' he said. 'I am not used to company here at Milton's of late, and the unexpectedness of your society, together with your naming of a leading abolitionist provoked some suspicion on my part that was not warranted by your behaviour.'

'I accepted your apology, sir,' said Linfield, his voice clipped. An awkward pause descended over the table. Linfield looked out at the waters of the bay, convinced that he had sat down at the table of a madman. He wished that his coffee was a little less hot so he might depart all the sooner. Robertson regarded the young man for a moment before he decided to speak again.

'Mr Linfield, would you permit me to offer you the comfort of an explanation of my behaviour? I would not want you to leave here thinking me to be quite out of my senses.'

'I assure you that will not be necessary, Mr Robertson,' said the surgeon, still looking out to sea. Robertson leant across and touched the naval officer's sleeve, forcing him to look around at him.

'I understand that I may have surprised you somewhat by the strength of my reaction, but it is on account of the manner in which some of my fellow Barbadians' have treated me of late. I was quite certain that they had put you up to provoke me, in which view I now realise I was wrong,' he said. 'Please do me the courtesy of at least hearing my explanation.'

'Oh, very well, if you must, sir,' relented Linfield.

'Do you read books, Mr Linfield?' asked Robertson.

'Naturally,' replied the surgeon. 'One can hardly follow my calling with any hope of success without diligent study.'

'Indeed,' agreed the Scot. 'For my part I am an enthusiastic reader. We are somewhat cut off here on Barbados, and books are at a premium. The island has no press, so we are reliant for our literature on books from abroad, chiefly from home, but also some from Boston or Philadelphia. So you will appreciate that when some six months ago a book arrived from Edinburgh together with a letter from a cousin of mine that recommended the brilliance of the writer's ideas, I was delighted. The book in question was by a Scottish philosopher named Adam Smith. Its title was *An Inquiry into the Nature and Causes of the Wealth of Nations*. Are you familiar with the work?'

'I have heard of it, sir,' replied Linfield, intrigued in spite of himself as to where this conversation was going. 'I cannot claim to have read it though.'

'Well, you are a more fortunate man than I,' said Robertson. 'For all my troubles began with the reading of that book. It is the principal reason why none of the gentlemen that surround us here will give me the time of day.

'I am a sugar planter,' continued Robertson. 'My father came from Dundee to Barbados and built up the plantation from virgin forest. My brother and I worked alongside him, though we were only boys, and when my father and brother succumbed to the yellow jack, I carried on alone. I flatter myself that I now own one of the best run plantations on the island, one that is a substantial enterprise by our standards. Much of my success I attribute to a combination of hard work, and my willingness to innovate. Unlike many of my neighbours who cling like limpets to the old ways, I flatter myself that I am open to notions of progress. So you will understand, sir, that it was with keen interest that I settled down in my favourite chair on the porch of my plantation house to see what observations my fellow countryman had to offer upon the wealth of nations.' Robertson sipped at his coffee for a moment, as if recalling that day in his mind.

'I must confess, Mr Smith's book does not make for the easiest of reading,' he continued. 'I found it to be hard fare, but I persisted, through all the tales of pin factories and his constant ranting upon the virtues of free trade. And as I read, Mr Linfield, the tiny bud of an idea left those dry pages and took root in my mind. I read on with increasing enthusiasm and as I did so, the notion grew and blossomed until by the time that I reached the book's end, I knew with certainty what course I would follow.'

'What had you resolved to do?' asked Linfield, his coffee now forgotten in its cup.

'I have over two hundred field slaves who work my land,' explained Robertson. 'Every one of those I have had to buy, and prime slaves do not come cheap. Having bought them I have to feed them, clothe them, house them, for every day of the brief ten years they might live before a combination of ill usage and hard work will cause them to perish. When that happens, why I have to buy yet more slaves to replace them, and so the cycle goes on. I also have to employ a large number of overseers, to keep those slaves productive in my cane fields. And what do I get in return? I get two hundred slaves who perform the bare minimum of work they can whilst, I am quite certain, they live for the day when they can escape from their compound and slaughter both me and my two daughters in our beds. You have doubtless heard reports of the ongoing slave rebellion the French struggle with in St Dominique? Mercifully that horror has not been visited on us here in Barbados, but I fear it is but a matter of time.'

'Sir, before you proceed further, it is only fair that I make my position clear,' said Linfield. 'As both a Christian, and a medical man, I am a committed opponent of slavery in all its forms. I hold the risk that you and your family are exposed to flows principally from your unwillingness to accept that those poor slaves are fellow humans in the eyes of our Creator.'

'I see,' replied Robertson. 'You will find that many of my fellow plantation owners are also Christians, and find little difficulty squaring their faith with the institution of slavery, but I will not battle with you over that. However, I do believe you may find my account of even greater interest than before. Shall I continue?'

'Pray do, sir. I am at your disposal,' said the surgeon.

'The idea I formed was this,' continued the planter. 'What if I was to grant all my two hundred slaves their freedom, and then re-employ them as agricultural labourers? I would naturally have to pay them wages, but that would be no great amount, for what alternative employment is open to them here in Barbados? Sugar is what we produce, throughout the island. Consider the costs of enslavement I would no longer have to carry, with the added benefit that my daughters and I would be able to rest easy in our beds.'

'Far be it for me to discourage any course that might lead to the emancipation of any slaves,' said Linfield. 'But will not the cost of wages, even if modest, be in excess of any potential savings?'

'I see you are an educated man,' smiled the planter. 'You believe you have put your finger on the principal flaw in my plan?'

'Yes, sir, that is right,' said the surgeon.

'No, sir! That is decidedly wrong!' insisted Robertson. 'For if Adam Smith is correct, I will have exchanged a reluctant workforce for a far more willing and productive one, and my plantation will thrive in efficiency as a consequence. It is that greater productivity that will make the whole scheme financially sound.'

'So what did you do?' asked Linfield.

'I confess that I am by nature an impulsive man, so no sooner had the idea come to me, then I was resolved to making it a reality. I freed them all. Oh, I lost some of my work force, naturally. There were those who chose to use their freedom to move elsewhere on the island, but the hundred and fifty who remained are quite as productive as the two hundred I had, so in that regard Mr Smith was quite correct.' Linfield felt compelled to shake Mr Robertson's hand for a third time.

'Sir, I congratulate you on your Christian humanity to your fellow man,' he pronounced, beaming at the planter. Robertson tried to shake himself free of the surgeon's hand.

'Christian humanity may go to the devil, sir,' he said. 'It played no part in my resolution. I did it because it was a superior way of running my affairs, no more and no less.'

'Oh, I see,' said Linfield releasing his grip on Robertson's hand.

'Regrettably there has been one facet of my project that I did fail to take into account,' continued Robertson. 'It has nothing to do with your Christian humanity, sir, and I do tire of receiving news from London that I am now the toast of Mr Wilberforce and his ilk. No, when I was pondering on the various advantages and costs of the scheme, I was somewhat focused on the pecuniary benefits. I gave scant consideration as to what effect the emancipation of my work force might have upon my neighbours.'

'Are they not inspired to follow your example?' asked Linfield.

'No, they are not, sir,' replied Robertson. 'Utter horror and alarm might be a more accurate description of their reaction. At a stroke I believe I have become the most hated man in Barbados, at least among the white population. Which, in a rather circuitous way, is the explanation as to why you find me seated here alone.'

'That is regrettable, sir,' conceded the surgeon. 'But will they not come round in time?'

'Aye, doubtless they might,' replied the planter. 'I am not overly burdened by the unpleasantness of my situation. One cannot have owned as many slaves as I have done without tending to become a wee bit thick-skinned. It is a shame for my two daughters, however. They are both of marriageable age but now find themselves quite cut off from polite Barbadian society.'

'Yes,' replied Linfield, 'I imagine that must be difficult for them.'

'No matter, sir, for it cannot now be helped,' said Robertson. 'For better or worse I have carried my resolution into effect.' Linfield felt that the plantation owner was probably a lot more philosophical about his family's exclusion from society than either of his daughters were likely to be. Perhaps it was with them in mind that he proffered his suggestion.

'I cannot help but observe,' he said, 'that the solution to your daughters' dilemma might not be staring you in the face.' Robertson looked at him blankly. After a while Linfield indicated his own coat.

'I am not sure that I follow you, Mr Linfield,' said the planter.

'I was indicating my uniform, sir,' explained the surgeon. 'Are there not a considerable number of Royal Navy ships now based at Bridgetown? It would be passing strange if there were not a few potential husbands for your daughters among their many officers.'

'Do you have any particular officer in mind?' asked Robertson, holding the younger man's gaze.

'No, no, not specifically,' replied Linfield, his face blushing a little. 'It was more of a general observation.'

'Hmm, I see,' said Robertson. 'Well I do believe it may prove to be a valuable one, perhaps a very valuable observation.' He gazed out into Carlisle Bay and pondered on what the young surgeon had said. At that very moment the willing sea breeze brought a further two warships around the headland. Doubtless both were crammed with eligible young men.

'What do you make of those two vessels, Mr Linfield?' he asked. The surgeon looked over to where the ships made their way across the water.

'I do not recognise them at all,' he said. 'They are both frigates, but they are in a very sorry state.'

As they beat up into the bay, Robertson could see what Linfield meant. The lead ship, the smaller of the two, lacked a proper mizzen mast. Her sides had numerous patched shot holes, and several of her yards had thickened sections like knuckles where they had been fished. Much of her quarterdeck rail was missing, the gash in the wood white and obvious like a bite from an apple. A long stream of silver pulsed out to one side, showing how her pumps worked just to keep her afloat. High in her remaining masts flew a battered looking Royal Navy ensign.

The second ship was a much larger frigate, and if anything it was in an even more battered condition. At her bows she lacked most of her foremast, and for a bowsprit she had little more than a stump that protruded from her beakhead like a broken tooth. Her long red sides were peppered with shot holes, with doubtless more unseen damage below the waters of the bay to judge from the pumped stream of water she too was emitting. Her stern was covered by an old sail stretched across it, the damage there presumably too significant to be patched at sea.

'Oh, but look!' cried Linfield, grabbing Robertson by the arm. 'The second ship is a prize! See how our brave navy ensign flies over the tricolour of France! Bravo, sir, oh Bravo!'

A Sloop of War

As the two ships approached the shore, both men could hear the sound of distant cheers from the warships at anchor, drifting up on the breeze. The sound was taken up on shore by the workers at the naval dockyard and spread outwards from there into the streets of Bridgetown.

Chapter 2
Barbados

Alexander Clay was the first lieutenant and temporary commander of the frigate *Agrius*, the smaller of the two damaged ships. He looked drawn and weary as he waited in the great cabin of the flagship *Princess Charlotte*. His calm grey eyes were bloodshot and rimmed in red. His normally tanned face looked pale and more gaunt than usual, while his best uniform coat still bore some of the scars of recent battle. One sleeve had a hastily mended rent and there was a dark patch on the back where his servant, Yates, had tried but not entirely succeeded in sponging out the last of a marine's blood who had been shot while he stood close to Clay.

In the last four days he had slept for no more than a few snatched hours, and had only washed and shaved for the first time prior to coming to make his report to the admiral. He had been through and won a desperate sea fight that had cost the *Agrius* a third of her crew, including her captain. For much of the battle he had thought his ship would lose, but after Captain Follett had been killed he had managed to out manoeuvre his larger opponent to win through.

The moment of his victory had been the start of his troubles. Only a hundred and sixty of the frigate's crew had survived the battle unscathed. With this number of men he had had to secure an even larger number of French prisoners, attend to the needs of a similar number of wounded from both sides, make vital repairs to two ships and then provide each with a skeleton crew for the three hundred mile voyage to Barbados. It was unsurprising that his normally tall frame was slumped down in his chair, on the verge of sleep, when the door of the cabin swung open.

'Lieutenant Clay, is it not?' asked Vice-Admiral Benjamin Caldwell, commander of the Windward Islands station, with a smile of welcome. Clay scrambled to his feet and shook the proffered hand. He found himself looking down into the kindly brown eyes of a brisk little man. The admiral was probably in his late fifties but it was hard to tell his exact age on account of the short horse hair periwig he wore, in spite of the tropical heat.

'Please retake your seat, Lieutenant Clay,' Caldwell continued, full of old world charm. 'Can I supply anything to fortify you after the rigours of your journey here—a glass of sherry perhaps?' Without waiting for an answer he waved forward his white-gloved steward, and a crystal glass of pale liquid appeared by his elbow, together with a fresh baked biscuit.

'My apologies that I kept you waiting,' he continued. 'I was issuing instructions for the removal of your many wounded to the hospital ashore, and for the dockyard to start work on repairs to your ship directly. I know that my clerk has your written report, but perhaps you would be kind enough to favour me with a verbal account of the *Agrius*'s actions? You might start with an explanation as to what has become of Captain Follett.'

Clay wondered for a moment if the admiral was always this polite, or did he reserve his most attentive behaviour for those that came with captured enemy ships in their wake. Gathering his thoughts he began.

'I regret to report that Captain Follett was killed during our recent action with the *Courageuse*. He was swept into the water when we lost our mizzen mast, and failed to resurface. We instituted a search for his body at the conclusion of the action, but without success.'

'That is very sad news, Mr Clay,' said Caldwell. 'I know the family, and his fall will come as a grave loss to them. But wait, do you not have his nephew on board, young Nicholas Windham? How has he taken the death?'

'Not well at all, I am afraid, sir,' replied Clay. 'He was close to his uncle, and I believe that he feels the loss keenly. Mr Windham survived the battle well otherwise—he escaped injury.'

'I will invite him over for dinner so that I can console him properly,' said Caldwell. 'Now, we have got in a sad muddle, starting your account with its ending. Let us hear of your actions from their proper beginning. Pray start with your departure from Plymouth.'

'We left Plymouth on the 20th of March, sir, and successfully convoyed the three East Indiamen we were protecting as far as Madeira,' began Clay. 'With the exception of one occasion off Lorient where we beat off an attack by a privateer, the voyage was largely uneventful.' Uneventful, thought Clay, what was he saying? It had only been uneventful from a naval point of view. There had been his meeting with the beautiful Lydia Browning on board one of the Indiaman, from which they had both fallen deeply in love with each other. Then there had been his violent dispute with the late Captain Follett when he had prevented Clay from meeting Lydia to propose marriage on the eve of her departure for India.

'Uneventful you say?' said the admiral. 'Excellent. What then happened after you arrived at Madeira?'

'As soon as your orders arrived we set sail, sir,' continued Clay. 'As instructed we sailed with all despatch in pursuit of the *Courageuse* with her cargo of reinforcements for the French island of St Lucia. We first sighted the enemy at about thirty-one degrees west. Regrettably it was close to sunset and we were unable to close with the enemy before the onset of nightfall. A dark night followed, during which we lost contact with the enemy.'

'That is very unfortunate, Mr Clay,' said Caldwell, his face unreadable. 'Was all done that should have been to re-establish contact with the French?'

'It was sir, but it was an almost moonless night, and in spite of our best efforts the enemy did evade us. The next day we resumed our pursuit of the French. We were becalmed for two days, which I believe allowed the French to get ahead of us somewhat. We next encountered them in fifty-two degrees west, during a storm. We again closed with them, bearing considerable sail at the time, when we were hit by a violent squall. That resulted in considerable damage aloft, and by the time we had made good our repairs, the French were out of sight once more.'

'One moment, if you please, Mr Clay,' said the admiral. A small v had appeared between his eyes and it had grown as the account went on. Clay found the admiral's expression reminiscent of the frown he had so often seen on the former Captain Follett's face during their time together.

'Are you saying that you overhauled the enemy twice and yet on both occasions they evaded you?'

'That is correct, sir,' answered Clay.

'Can you offer an explanation for this?' he asked. Yes, Clay felt like shouting, it was because the ship was under the commanded of an arrogant fool who refused to listen to any of my advice. But he also realised how important this meeting with Caldwell could be to his future career. He took a deep breath before he answered.

'Sir, the *Agrius* was under the command of Captain Follett at this time,' answered Clay. 'I am sure he had reasons for acting as he did, but I am afraid he did not share them with me. I will naturally provide you with all the information I have, but I do not believe it is my place to speak ill of such a recently fallen officer.'

Caldwell held his gaze for what seemed a long time to the waiting Clay, but he was able to return his look calmly enough, sure that he at least had done his duty.

'Very well, Mr Clay,' said Caldwell. 'I believe I understand. Pray continue.'

'We next encountered the *Courageuse* in the roadstead at Casteries in St Lucia. She came out to fight with us, and after an extremely hard-fought action we prevailed, with the loss of a third of our crew, including the captain who fell quite early in the action. I took command of the *Agrius* after that sad event.'

'Just a moment, Mr Clay,' said Caldwell, holding up a hand. 'I confess I am a little perplexed. When I saw the *Agrius* come in with her prize, I assumed that you had caught the *Courageuse* before she could complete her mission to resupply St Lucia as I had ordered. Are you saying that you failed, and that she was able to land her cargo?'

'I am afraid that is so, sir,' Clay replied. 'We fought her after she had unloaded.'

'But this is terrible news!' bemoaned the admiral. 'Do you realise that I am planning a descent on St Lucia with a view to her capture? It was essential for this endeavour that the island should have received no fresh encouragement to resist.'

'Sir, I do understand that this will come as a disappointment,' said Clay, aware that Caldwell's eyes had long since ceased to look kindly. 'I anticipated that you would at least need to ascertain the nature of the reinforcements that were delivered to the island. I have arranged some informal intelligence gathering among the surviving officers and crew of the *Courageuse* over the past few days using four Italian members of my crew who speak good French and have served aboard a French vessel. The details are in my report, but I believe I have obtained a reasonably full account.' Clay passed across a sheet of paper to the admiral.

Caldwell looked at the proffered sheet, and read out the list.

'2nd Battalion, 43rd Regiment, 520 men
2 companies of the 90th Regiment, 140 men
46 gunners from the Garrison Artillery

Arms additional to those borne by the above,
400 stands of muskets
200,000 rounds of cartridges
An unknown amount of powder taken from the *Courageuse's* magazine.'

'This is very impressive, lieutenant,' said Caldwell, looking up from the sheet. 'Are you quite certain as to the veracity of the contents?'

'Yes, sir, everything listed there comes from more than one source among their crew,' Clay replied.

The admiral rose from his chair and walked up and down the long line of stern windows that made up the back of the great cabin of the big three-decker. His silhouette was black and unreadable against the bright glare of mid-morning sunlight as it streamed in through the glass. After what seemed an age to the waiting Clay, he returned to his desk with a smile for the young officer.

'As I am sure that you are aware, it is customary in the service to promote the first lieutenant of a ship that has been successful in an action against a superior opponent,' began Caldwell, his eyes once more kindly. 'It is deemed to be a compliment to the captain, although I like to think of it as an acknowledgement that efficient ships win battles, and it is first lieutenants that make ships efficient. I will not hide that I am vexed that the *Agrius* did not stop those men from arriving to comfort our enemy in St Lucia, but I cannot hold you responsible for failings that happened under your previous captain. Since you have been in command, I am unable to find fault with your actions. So I shall go ahead and promote you to master and commander with immediate effect. It will at least serve as a reason for you to purchase the new uniform coat you so obviously stand in need of.'

'Oh, sir, you quite overwhelm me,' said Clay. 'I have been so engaged with the struggle to bring home the *Agrius* and our prize, I have not had the leisure to consider the possibility of promotion.'

'Well, it is done now, so let me be the first to congratulate you,' smiled the admiral, gripping Clay's hand.

A Sloop of War

'Thank you, sir,' said Clay. 'I have naturally worked and longed for promotion ever since I was posted lieutenant, and yet now it has arrived, I find myself quite ill-prepared. Thank you again, sir, although that phrase falls so very short of expressing the depth of my gratitude.'

'Shall we let matters rest at "thank you" then?' said Caldwell. 'But I am forgetting, you must at least let me be the first to wet your new swab. Price, more sherry here, and get Captain Miller to join us.'

The admiral's flag captain joined them, together with the other members of his staff, after which several toasts were drunk to the health of the newly promoted Clay, and his hand was shaken by one and all. Although his smiling presence was very much at the heart of the celebration, he found his thoughts leaving the great cabin of the *Princess Charlotte* and turning to distant India, where the woman he loved would soon be arriving. She had agreed to wait till he was in a financial position to marry her, and now he had taken a significant step along that road. He lifted his glass in silent toast. I am on my way, my darling Lydia, he promised. When his attention returned to the cabin, he found he was once again alone with Caldwell.

'Now to business, Captain Clay,' said the admiral, producing the unfamiliar title as a wedding guest might first produce the bride's married name, knowing it would draw a smile. Clay was not a captain yet, but commanders were called "captain" in the service as an honorific. 'I will also be promoting Charles Parker—commander of the *Rush*, a sixteen gun sloop of war. He will be made post, and take command of the *Agrius*. Which means I will need a new commander for the *Rush*—would that be of interest?'

'Yes, sir, it very much would,' replied Clay, trying and failing to keep a look of nonchalant gravity on his face, as if promotion combined with the offer of his first command on the same day was a normal occurrence.

'Excellent, I will get the relevant orders drawn up,' continued Caldwell. 'Parker will doubtless have some followers he will want to take with him from the *Rush*. One is sure to be the ship's only lieutenant, who I know to be a great friend of his. Are there any men you would want to transfer across with you?'

'I would be grateful if I could have my particular friend John Sutton as my lieutenant on the *Rush*. He is currently third lieutenant on the *Agrius*, and my servant Yates,' said Clay, after a moment's thought. John Sutton was his best friend, and an excellent officer. 'There may be a few others who will want to volunteer to come with me. Would it be best if I resolved the particulars directly with Captain Parker?' He would like to have some other familiar faces with him in his new command, but the compliment of a sloop was tiny when compared with the *Agrius*.

'Yes, I can agree to that. I will give you a few days to settle into your new command, and then I will need you at sea. I am cruelly short of handy little sloops like the *Rush* for blockade work, and these French Islands are thick with inlets and little ports to watch. But for now you must attend to your own health. You do look as if you stand in want of much needed rest. Get some tonight, and be prepared to take command of your new ship in the morning, Clay,' concluded the admiral, as he shook his hand in farewell.

*****

Two days later William Munro and James Fleming returned to the frigate *Agrius*, arm in arm with each other. It was long after midnight, and both men were contentedly drunk, having spent the evening celebrating the promotion of their former first lieutenant Alexander Clay, and the departure of their friend John Sutton to be his sole lieutenant aboard the *Rush*. Munro was the taller of the two men. He was an Ulsterman, with a fine head of red hair that sadly clashed with the magnificent scarlet of his marine lieutenant's uniform. His pale complexion was all the paler as a result of the blood he had lost from a nasty head wound sustained in the ship's recent victory. The wound's dressing, however, served to give him a dashing, piratical air as it swept around his head and down low over one eye. Fleming was a less imposing figure. A sandy-haired Scotsman, he was the purser of the *Agrius*, and had spent the battle below the waterline in the cramped little cockpit helping the surgeon to treat the wounded.

'It seemed strange to hear the general discourse on our triumph over the *Courageuse* tonight,' said Fleming, as they made their way towards the wardroom. 'It felt as if I was not present at the battle at all. You all had such engaging tales to tell of broadsides fired, and manoeuvres performed, but for me the engagement largely consisted of sitting in the gloom of the cockpit holding down yet another poor wretch while Wynn removed one of their limbs.' He shuddered for a moment as he recalled the horror of what he had witnessed that day

'You were very busy at times, I collect?' asked Munro.

'Ha! Busy you say?' said the purser. 'At the hottest part of the action the wounded were being stacked like logs as they waited treatment.'

'But were you truly not aware of the battle at all,' asked the marine, 'apart from by the flow of your patients, that is?'

'We were conscious of the roar of the cannon above our heads for sure,' said the purser. 'And naturally we felt the shock of the enemy's fire coming home through the timbers of the ship, but as for if this was for good or ill, we had very little idea. The flow of wounded made it clear that the affair was a particularly savage one, but the fall of the mizzen mast, for example, quite passed me by. It was only when I eventually came back on deck many hours later that I noticed it was absent.'

'How very strange,' said Munro, as he held the door of the wardroom open for his friend.

The cabin was almost wholly dark when the men entered it. A single horn lantern swung on a hook next to where the butt of the destroyed mizzen mast still ran through the centre of the table and up into the captain's cabin above their heads. The lantern's shutters were closed, allowing only a few rays of light to escape and illuminate the lines of officers' cabins that ran down each side of the wardroom.

'What a sad, quiet place this is now, William,' said Fleming. 'Not so long ago we were a community of seven in this very room.'

'Well, Booth may perhaps return from his sick bed ashore, although he was sore injured in the battle,' said Munro. 'But Wynn will definitely be back, once he can do no more to help the injured in the hospital, and of course our former first and third lieutenants who have abandoned us for this saucy little sloop of theirs will doubtless be replaced. Which only leaves you, me and our gallant second lieutenant.'

'And here he is,' whispered the purser, opening the shutters on the lantern. 'Nicholas Windham himself, in all his pomp, asleep like a lamb amongst the clover.' Both men stood looking at the slumped form of Windham. He was seated at the end of the wardroom table, asleep on his arms with a half empty bottle at his elbow. As the light fell on him, he stirred, his head dropped from his arm, and he jerked awake.

'Ah, the carouser's make their happy return,' he said without a smile for them. He pushed himself upright and blinked in the light as he got his bearings. His dark hair was tousled, his soft young face marked with red where the buttons of his uniform cuff had pressed into one cheek.

'Indeed we have,' replied Munro, taking a seat near to Windham. 'You should have been there, Nicholas.'

'The loss of my uncle is yet too raw for me to be able to take much joy in conviviality. I would have been but indifferent company, William,' said Windham. 'I trust you made my excuses to the rest of the party?'

'Rest assured that I did,' replied Munro. 'But you did miss a most pleasant gathering. In addition to our former shipmates, some of the *Rush*'s officers came too. Regrettably the swab in question was absent from Alex's shoulder, a local tailor having yet to finish attaching it to his new coat, but we certainly wetted it most thoroughly, with a bumper too.'

'Aye, that we most certainly did,' agreed Fleming. 'One of the *Rush*'s officers, a tolerable fellow named Linfield, introduced us to a most capital acquaintance. He was a sugar planter by the name of Robertson, a fellow Scot of course. We celebrated in a tavern called the Morro Castle, and he very handsomely collected our bill for the evening to express his thanks for our glorious victory over the French.'

'A glorious victory, was it?' said Windham. 'And hasn't our first lieutenant covered himself with glory as a result? My uncle barely a week in his grave, and Clay has been promoted and assigned his own ship. One doesn't need to look very far to see who has gained the most through all of this.'

25

'Oh come now, Nicholas,' laughed Munro. 'You are hardly in a position to complain about that. Your uncle used his influence and connections to see you promoted to lieutenant when you were but nineteen years old!'

'Well that may be so,' said Windham. 'But it is the last preferment I shall get from him. Now he is no more I must shift for myself.' He sloshed some of the rum from the bottle into three glasses, and took a long pull from his own.

'None more for me, I thank you,' said Fleming. He left his rum in its glass and rose from the table. 'I am for my bed. I meet with our new captain tomorrow at two bells in the forenoon watch, and would not have him think of me only as a drunken sot. I bid you both a good night.' Fleming made his unsteady way over to his cabin.

'You might take a leaf from his book, Nicholas,' said the marine, pointing his glass towards the purser's back. 'We shall find matters under Captain Parker will be a good deal tougher. The officers of the *Rush* were saying that he is a hard taskmaster.'

'Brilliant!' spluttered Windham. 'So Clay and Sutton are away on their cursed sloop of war, while I find my dear uncle is to be replaced by some bloody tartar.'

'Come on, Nicholas,' urged Munro. 'You do Alex an injustice. I do sympathise with your loss, but I fail to see any connection between that and his promotion. You know as well as I that it is the custom in the service to promote the first lieutenant after a single ship action. He would have got his step whether your uncle lived or not.'

'Oh is that what you believe?' sneered Windham. 'My uncle shared much with me you know. What if I was to tell you that I know he had resolved to break Clay when we arrived here in Barbados? I believe that Clay knew it too.

And had it not been for his death, your friend would have been on the beach by now.'

'But why,' protested Munro. 'Clay was an excellent first lieutenant, why would Follett want him broke?' Windham turned his bloodshot eyes on the Ulsterman, pointing towards him with a swaying glass of rum but instead of answering the question, he posed another.

'How did my uncle come to die, William?' he asked.

'Come, come, Nicholas,' said Munro. 'We have been over this already. He was swept into the sea when the mizzen mast fell, that is all.'

'Please, indulge me with the particulars,' persisted Windham. 'I was down on the main deck with the guns when it happened, so I have only the vaguest of reports to go on.'

'Oh, very well,' said Munro. 'It was at the hottest part of the action, when matters were not going well. It is hard to relate exactly what occurred, for the quarterdeck was thick with gun smoke. Booth had been taken below sometime earlier. I recall that Lieutenant Sutton was stood by the wheel, the captain was over by the rail, looking across at the French ship. We were hit by another broadside, and one of the shots must have struck the mast a few feet above the deck. The whole mizzen came down, and the quarterdeck was smothered with debris, including the block that lay me low.' Munro indicated the bandage on his head. The wound seemed to throb under its dressing in sympathy with his memory.

'When I at last regained my senses I perceived that the mast was down and trailed over the side. The line of its fall was almost directly where your uncle had been standing earlier,' he continued. 'The afterguard were all engaged in cutting at the shrouds to free the ship of the wreckage. I remember Lieutenant Clay had appeared from somewhere, and was talking to Sutton, near where your uncle had been. Mr Knight then came running up from the bows with his men to aid the effort to free us of the last of the wrecked mast, after which Lieutenant Clay took command of the ship. I hope that gives you some comfort, Nicholas, but it is truly all I know.'

'Does it all not strike you as very convenient, William?' asked Windham. 'The mast comes down. Smoke and confusion is everywhere. My uncle goes over the side, and Clay and his close friend Sutton are there at the scene, the two men who have gained most through all this.'

'Have a care what you are saying, Nicholas,' warned Munro. 'I understand you to be upset by your loss, but you are bound for very dangerous waters here. I was there on the quarterdeck, and I discerned nothing wrong.'

'But you were out of your senses for much of the time,' said Windham. 'What if the deed took place then? I can still remember when I first learned of my uncle's death. It was Clay who told me. I remember quite distinctly how he spoke to me, how awkward and distracted his manner was. I have reflected on it since, and am convinced he did not speak like a man with nothing on his mind.'

'Nicholas, see sense,' urged Munro. 'He spoke in the heat of battle. Naturally he had much on his mind, not least how to avoid defeat at the hands of a superior opponent. Think man! The quarterdeck was crowded with people, none of whom saw anything wrong. You were not even there.'

'I know what I saw in Clay's eyes that day, William, and it was not the look of a guiltless man,' replied Windham. 'No, I am resolved to get to the bottom of this, if only for the sake of my uncle. I shall not let it pass.'

'Well, you must do as you see fit, Nicholas,' replied the marine, getting up from the table and stretching his arms out as he yawned. 'I truly don't think it will answer, but in any event I must go to my bed. I should have turned in when Fleming did. He will be asleep by now, the dog. I would urge you to do the same.'

But Munro was wrong about James Fleming, for he was not yet asleep. In the dark of his cabin he mouthed a silent prayer as he lay in his cot, asking to be spared from any more of the dreams that he had had each night since the day of the battle. Before sleep took him, he ran his hands over his arms and legs, trying to show his mind he was uninjured. Perhaps tonight, for the first time, he would not wake up convinced that each of his limbs ended in a bleeding stump.

*****

Lieutenant John Sutton stretched out his legs in the back of the carriage and looked across at his commanding officer as he adjusted the unfamiliar gold epaulet on his left shoulder. Sutton was a pleasant looking young man, of medium build with dark eyes and hair, and was a year younger than his friend. He nudged Jacob Linfield, the third occupant of the carriage who sat next to him, and drew his attention to Clay. Clay noticed the gesture, and left his epaulet alone.

'I daresay I shall become accustomed to it in time, but for now I am quite conscious of the extra weight on one side,' said Clay, by way of excuse. 'Perhaps I shall even things up and purchase one of those parrots they sell in Bridgetown market to sit upon the other shoulder.' Both his companions laughed at this. Sutton for the shared pleasure in his friend's promotion, Linfield because he did not yet know the *Rush*'s

Philip K. Allan

new commander well, and thought it prudent to laugh at his superior's jokes.

'My, what a whirl these last three days have been,' sighed Clay. 'You have no notion how difficult it is to take over a new ship, and prepare her for sea in such a short time, Mr Linfield. The habits of a settled crew to understand, a fresh group of petty and warrant officers to become familiar with, and all this on top of revictualling a ship with which both Mr Sutton and myself are wholly unfamiliar. That we have got there at last seems little short of miraculous.'

'I must confess there were occasions when I did despair of our being ready on time, sir,' added Sutton. 'Yet here we are, ready to depart at dawn and with a free last evening to spare.'

'We sail to St Lucia, I collect, sir?' asked the surgeon.

'Indeed, to blockade one of the smaller ports,' replied Clay. 'A place called Micoud, on the east coast. Admiral Caldwell is busy sending out most of the squadron. He wants nothing to be permitted to go to or come from the island, while he prepares for his invasion. Has the *Rush* been to those waters before?'

'Not since I have been with the ship,' replied Linfield. 'Under Captain Parker we have chiefly been employed patrolling the waters close to Martinique.'

'Now, Mr Sutton,' said Clay, leaning forward. 'I do not propose to discuss matters pertaining to the *Rush* for all of this evening, but before we arrive at our destination it has just come to mind that you have yet to tell me which members of the crew of the *Agrius* have followed us onto our new ship?'

'Apart from his first lieutenant, Captain Parker wanted to take both of his midshipmen with him,' replied Sutton. 'I

30

have persuaded Mr Preston and Mr Croft to come across to the *Rush* in exchange.'

'A sound choice,' said Clay. 'They both have much to learn, but I believe we may make tolerably good officers of them, particularly Preston. How old are they now?'

'Both seventeen, sir,' said Sutton. 'They are but a little older than you and I were when we joined the midshipman's berth on the old *Marlborough*.'

'I hope they may enjoy happier surroundings then we did in that ship,' said Clay, shivering at the recollection. 'Did any of the hands volunteer to join us?'

'Plenty, sir,' replied Sutton. 'Unfortunately there were only four from the *Rush* who wanted to transfer the other way to serve with Captain Parker. He seems to have a reputation as a harsh disciplinarian.'

'Who did you fill those spaces with?' asked Clay.

'The best four I could find, all from the same mess in the larboard watch. Sean O'Malley, Sam Evans, Joshua Rosso and Adam Trevan. Rosso originally volunteered, on condition the others came too.'

'Did he now? That is interesting,' said Clay. He considered for a moment telling his lieutenant that on the *Agrius,* he had discovered that Rosso had embezzled funds from a previous employer. Rosso was an excellent seaman, and as many of the crew had criminal pasts, he had decided to turn a blind eye. No, he thought, the fewer that knew that the better.

'An excellent choice, Mr Sutton,' said Clay. 'Although O'Malley is something of a hot-head, and I am not sure how we will fit Evans into the *Rush*. Wait till you see him, Mr Linfield, he was quite the largest man on the *Agrius*. Why he must be all of six foot six and a good two hundred and forty pounds.'

'Goodness,' said Linfield. 'He will find the headroom on the lower deck a challenge.'

'Now for the less good news,' continued Sutton. 'I am afraid that I could not persuade Captain Parker to allow Lloyd to be your steward. Apparently his reputation as a cook has reached even here. Hart volunteered to take the post, and with a lack of alternatives I was forced to accept him.' Clay groaned. He had hoped to escape from the *Agrius*'s ill tempered wardroom steward at last.

'Oh well,' he said with resignation, 'at least the post is filled.' He turned next to the *Rush*'s surgeon. 'Now, Mr Linfield, we have just time for you to tell us a little about our host for tonight. Apart from the very civil way that Mr Robertson funded the wetting of my swab the other evening at the Morro Castle, I know very little about him.'

'I cannot claim Mr Robertson as an acquaintance of long standing,' said Linfield. I only met him myself on the day that the *Agrius* first arrived at Bridgetown, but I know him to be a substantial planter with some rather unorthodox views of his labour force.'

'Why, Mr Linfield,' exclaimed Sutton. 'You have not known Mr Robertson a week! Yet he is prepared to fund us in our cups and now host a dinner in our honour tonight. I do declare that you are wasted as a surgeon. Have you considered serving your country as a diplomat?'

'Well, we shall soon see what fate has in store for us tonight,' said Clay looking out of the carriage window, 'for I believe this must be the place. It was very handsome of Mr Robertson to provide us with his carriage to collect us from the quayside, and bring us here to Melverton. We will doubtless spend an evening with a number of his rather dull neighbours, and then we can make our excuses and leave.'

But Clay was wrong about the evening. To his surprise no other guests had come, and instead the three young men were in for a rather more intimate evening with their host and his two daughters. Both girls must have got their looks from their mother, for unlike their father they were fair. They had tresses of blond hair piled up on their heads, and both had hazel eyes which they lowered to the floor as they stepped forward to be presented to the officers. Miss Elizabeth Robertson was both the older and plainer of the two, and assumed the role of hostess from her long deceased mother. When they went through to dinner, she had placed herself in the position of honour, between her father and the principal guest. Mr Robertson had asked Clay for a full account of the *Agrius*'s battle with the *Courageuse*, but Clay was at root a shy man when he was with unfamiliar company, and his account needed diligent questioning from his host to tease out the details. As the account wound on, Miss Elizabeth found her attention wandering with a degree of envy towards her younger sibling's end of the table.

All of this had served to free her younger and prettier sister Emma to indulge in flirtation with the two other young gentlemen lured to the house by their father. Emma had a languid eye for the dark looks of John Sutton in particular, which was a shame. Had she given a little more of her attention to his lighter haired companion, she might have detected a flicker of interest in Jacob Linfield's pale blue eyes.

'Might that be a cannon ball tree I can see at the edge of the lawn?' asked the young surgeon.

'I daresay it might,' replied Emma. 'I am no great expert on flora.'

'I must congratulate you on what charming grounds you have here, Miss Emma,' said Linfield, indicating the waterfalls of pink hibiscus that cascaded down either side of the dining room's large bay window. Emma glanced at the display with an indifferent eye.

'They are tolerable this year, Mr Linfield,' she conceded. 'Last year they were better tended. Do you like flowers at all, Mr Sutton?'

'I regret to have none of my colleague's expertise, Miss Emma,' replied Sutton with a smile. 'The only cannon balls with which I am familiar do not grow on trees.'

'Oh, Mr Sutton!' smiled Emma. 'How droll you are.'

'Look, now there is a hummingbird in your flowers!' enthused Linfield.

'Were you long in the navy, Mr Sutton?' Emma asked, turning towards her neighbour, her back to the window.

'Why I should say about fourteen years, Miss Emma,' he replied. 'I was only a boy when I went to sea. My father is a lieutenant in the navy, and he got me a place in a friend's ship. How about you, Mr Linfield?'

'I am far from the veteran mariner that you are, Mr Sutton,' Linfield replied, one eye still on the shimmering green bird. 'I joined at the start of the war, directly I had finished my medical training. The *Rush* is only my second ship.'

'You must have travelled very extensively in all those years, Mr Sutton,' asked Emma. 'Were you ever in the West Indies?'

'Regrettably not,' replied Sutton. 'This is my first visit to Barbados, and after only a few days here we depart in the morning.'

'What a shame,' exclaimed Emma. 'There is some very

agreeable countryside around here, and I had wondered if you might care to ride over it?'

'Alas I am no horseman, Miss Emma,' said Sutton. 'Although I believe Mr Linfield rides. With his enthusiasm for your native flora and fauna, I am sure he would make a much more diverting companion.'

'Would he now,' said Emma, appraising the surgeon through her almond-shaped eyes.

As dinner proceeded, Mr Robertson perceived that things were not going as he had planned. For one thing Clay did not seem to be very interested in his older daughter. He was perfectly polite, but their talk had increasingly strayed towards the war and the politics of Barbados, subjects that did little to show Miss Elizabeth at her best. Looking down the table he could see that all was not going his younger daughter's way either. Miss Emma was drumming the tip of her closed fan on the edge of the table in the hope of regaining Mr Sutton's attention, while the object of her desires was in animated conversation with the young surgeon. He coughed into his napkin with just enough force to silence the room.

'My youngest daughter has a considerable reputation on the island as a performer of attitudes,' said Robertson.

'Attitudes, sir?' asked Clay. 'I am not familiar with the concept, what pray might they be?'

'Are you not aware of them?' asked their host. 'Well, perhaps we might persuade Miss Emma to a short performance. Emma, my angel, would you oblige these gentlemen with a wee demonstration?'

Miss Emma, it transpired, could be persuaded. She stood up in front of the party, and adopted a curious stance. Legs a little apart, her back arched, she placed one hand on her forehead, and extended the other arm in front of her, while she simultaneously composed her face into a frown. Once in position her body froze into statue-like stillness, her eye fixed on a point somewhere close to the chandelier. The three officers exchanged glances. Clay and Sutton's faces wore the glazed expression of persons determined not to laugh.

'There, sir,' breathed their host. 'Have you seen anything to match it? Naturally you can tell what the attitude is?'

'Eh, discomfort?' speculated Clay.

'No, sir! It is Perseverance!' said Robertson. 'Surely you can see it now? It is one of Miss Emma's more celebrated attitudes. Elizabeth my dear, could you assist Mr Sutton. He seems to be choking on something.'

*****

'There was another matter of a certain delicacy I wanted to discuss with you, captain,' said Mr Robertson when his daughters had retired, leaving the men to their rum and cigars.

'I am of course at your disposal, although I should tell you that I am engaged to another lady,' said Clay, hoping to pre-empt what he thought might be on his host's mind.

Robertson paused for a moment, the decanter motionless in his hand. He looked at Clay with surprise, before he continued.

'No, that was not what I wanted to speak to you about, although you naturally have my felicitations for your engagement. I wanted to explain the reason why no other guests accepted my invitation to dinner tonight. Spring Hill Plantation has something of a notorious reputation on the island. Did Mr Linfield provide you with any detail as to how matters are arranged here?'

'I have not had that opportunity, Mr Robertson,' said Linfield.

'No matter,' continued Robertson. 'I can leave Mr Linfield to apprise you of the particulars. Suffice it to say I took a decision some months back to free my slaves and re-employ them as labourers. As you can well imagine, this has made my neighbours somewhat furious with me, although the more charitable among them are prepared to consider me as simply mad.'

'You amaze me, sir,' said Clay, 'and has your project delivered success?'

'Well, it is early days,' cautioned the planter, 'but my former slaves are certainly more productive, and obviously happier than they were before. No my principal problem is that Spring Hill is now considered to be a haven for every slave who has run on the island. They arrive here in hope that they too may become free, but of course I can only offer freedom to my own slaves. Under the law here in Barbados a slave is the property of their owner. I therefore have to hand them back to their masters, which my workers find very distressing, knowing how brutal will be their punishment.'

'I sympathise with your predicament,' said Clay. 'That does sound most unfortunate, but I am not sure how I can help you, Mr Robertson. I make no claim to expertise of the law, whether Barbadian or otherwise.'

'Nor would I expect it of you, sir. Perhaps I might offer you a summary of the position?' continued his host.

'By all means,' said Clay.

'Well, here in the islands of the West Indies we have laws passed by our own legislatures that permit the institution of slavery. In England, or indeed in my native Scotland, no such explicit legislation exists. Thus if a slave can get himself to a territory where English law applies, there is generally considered to be sufficient ambiguity for him to become a free man,' explained Robertson.

'Ah, I think I see where this trail may lead, sir,' said Clay. 'Would a location falling under English law include the deck of a Royal Navy ship?'

'Precisely so, captain,' beamed his host. 'In consequence the navy have numerous black sailors in their ranks, many of whom are former slaves,' concluded Robertson. Clay shook his head as he replied.

'That may well be so, Mr Robertson, but the navy has also need to be careful. If we were thought to be encouraging slaves to run it would be seen as a mischievous interference in the running of this colony. I am sure you understand that after the American war that is not a path we can lightly take.'

'I understand, captain,' continued Robertson. 'I do not propose a general flight of slaves to your ship. I have in mind a single exceptional individual. He is a person of considerable intelligence, having learnt to speak English to a level that far exceeds that which I have encountered in any other Negro. Haynes, his owner, was training him up to serve in his house, but found him to be too rebellious an individual, so returned him to work in the fields. He was a fisherman before he was enslaved so he has some knowledge of the sea, and wishes to volunteer to serve. I can confirm that he is a fine strong young man, and must have an uncommonly resourceful character to have evaded his pursuers and arrived here. I believe he would make an excellent hand, and knowing how the navy is often short of men I wondered if you might take him as an exception. He could ride back with you hidden in the trunk of my carriage, and it would be passing strange if he failed to get on board the *Rush* unobserved.'

Clay exchanged glances with Sutton and Linfield. Linfield was leaning forward in his chair with a look of eagerness, while Sutton seemed more ambivalent.

'It is true, we are a little short of compliment, sir,' said Sutton. 'If this hand is as good as Mr Robertson believes something might be made of him.'

'That is as may be,' said Clay, turning to their host. 'Mr Robertson, I do understand your predicament. I am not an unkind man, but I am perplexed as to what this poor individual has to do with me. Unlike Mr Linfield here, I have no particular views on slavery. It is a matter that I have hardly given any consideration to. At best I regard it as an unpleasant necessity that happens far away, out of the general sight. I suppose I might regard it in the same way as I do hanging. I know that some criminals must hang, but I have never felt any desire to witness the actual execution.'

'Sir, it is true, I make no secret of my abolitionist views,' said Linfield. 'For me it is an abomination that this man should have ever lost his freedom. But might I appeal to your natural sense of justice? In the little time I have spent with the officers who know you best, they say you are an honourable man. They speak of you standing up to your previous captain on several occasions when you believed you had been wronged. Might you not extend such moral fortitude to one who stands in dire need of your help?'

'I am not sure that any notion of extending my moral fortitude will help me much if I get hauled up before Admiral Caldwell, Mr Linfield,' said Clay, feeling a flush of annoyance. Damn Robertson, he thought, confronting him in this way. Until he had mentioned this man, Clay had been enjoying a pleasant evening, still warmed by the comfortable afterglow of pleasure from his recent promotion.

'What will become of him if we refuse to take him, Mr Robertson?' asked Linfield. Their host's face grew grim.

'I will have to return him to his owner, Mr Haynes. He is not a man to be trifled with. I believe he would seek to make an example of this individual as a warning to his other slaves. I will spare you the details so soon after we have eaten, but let me say that slaves who run from Mr Haynes are seldom able to work again.'

'Sir, I appreciate that this is a matter of some delicacy,' pleaded Linfield, 'but I must urge you to assist this poor negro, if only from a motive of Christian charity.' Clay shifted in his chair, steeling his heart to say no, but then he looked into Linfield's eager face and felt a little ashamed. The young surgeon would offer this poor slave his freedom in an instant and damn the consequences, he thought.

'Oh, very well, Mr Robertson,' he said. 'I will do what you ask, but only this once and only as a particular favour to you. Mr Linfield, not one further word from you if you please, or I shall change my mind again.'

Chapter 3
The Sloop of War *Rush*

The following morning the *Rush* left Bridgetown with the first glimmer of dawn, and was out at sea when the sun climbed up from behind the lush hills of Barbados. Inside the little sloop, Robertson's runaway slave was being read in by Taylor, the captain's clerk. He slowly recited out loud the Articles of War that would now govern the new recruit's life. Each article listed an offence, followed by the punishment that would follow if it was committed. The offences were to be punished with a savagery oddly reminiscent of that meted out to slaves, often death and never less than a flogging. The new recruit met each article with an ever wider grin of delight. At last he was free.

'Now then, let us get you properly entered in due form,' said Taylor, when he had reached the end of the list. He pulled the ship's muster book towards him and dipped his pen into the ink well.

'Name?' he asked. It was a proud moment for the former slave. Five long years ago he had been forced to leave his name in the cages of Bridgetown market as part of the dehumanising process he had gone through. Today he would reclaim his true name once more.

'Ablanjaye Senghore,' he said, struggling a little to roll his tongue around the unfamiliar Ashanti syllables, now rusty with lack of use. Taylor's pen stopped in mid-air, a droplet of ink forming on the nib.

'Beg pardon?' he queried. 'What was the name again?' Senghore repeated his name a little more slowly to the clerk.

'I am sorry, but that will never do,' said Taylor, laying down the pen.

'But it is my name!' protested Senghore. 'It was taken from me when I was made a slave. I had to use the name the master gave me.'

'Well, that is as may be, but it will never answer for the navy,' insisted the clerk. 'Can you imagine the boatswain or Lieutenant Sutton calling such a name? No, no, we will have to put down something more regular.'

Taylor was a kind man, and he noticed the look of trembling disappointment in Senghore's face.

'I tell you what, I will try and set down a name as close to yours as I can find,' he offered. 'I can't say fairer than that now, can I? Come on, let me hear it again.' Ablanjaye Senghore repeated his name for a third, and as it turned out, final time. Taylor wrote down *Able Sedgwick, landsman* with care in the muster book.

'All done, Sedgwick,' he continued, once he had collected the recruit's mark in the ledger, 'Welcome to the navy. Now this here is Mr Croft. He is the midshipman in charge of your division. He will take you to the purser to be allocated a hammock and your clothes, and will show you where you will mess.' The newly christened seaman turned to the thin figure of the teenage midshipman.

'Shall we go, Mr Croft,' he suggested. Croft bristled at the familiarity in Sedgwick's voice.

'First let me acquaint you with the correct mode of address to an officer,' he shouted up at the powerfully built man. 'From now on you only speak to a superior officer when asked to do so and secondly you address me as "sir". Is that clear, Sedgwick?'

'Yes... sir,' said Sedgwick.

'The correct way of expressing your comprehension is to reply "aye aye, sir",' barked Croft.

'Aye aye, sir,' replied the former slave, a little bewildered. As he followed his new officer he had much to ponder. He was not sure what he had been expecting from freedom, but so far it did seem to be turning out to be a bit of a disappointment.

*****

Free at last, thought Clay to himself, as he stood on the quarterdeck of the *Rush*. He had breakfasted that morning in the captain's cabin of the sloop, and had thought it to be a room of infinite space and light. True, the deck was uncomfortably low, with at least four inches too little headroom for a man of his height, but the room spread across the whole twenty-six feet of the sloop's beam. As captain he was allocated every pane of glass that the ship possessed - five sash lights in a sweep across the stern, and a further one on each side of the ship in the quarter galleys. Off the main cabin he had his own sleeping quarters and better still, for the first time in his life, he had a privy just for him. Compared to the dark seven foot square box that had been his cabin for so long on the *Agrius,* it was close to paradise.

He felt free in other ways. His time was now his own, to do with as he would. He knew that in Sutton he had a competent officer who would ensure the *Rush* was a well organised and efficient ship, without too much input from him. Best of all, he had his own ship, and was setting out on his first independent mission, away from the watchful eye of any senior captains or admirals. Everything feels wonderful, he thought, as he stared over the stern rail of his sloop at the slowly retreating island of Barbados, now little more than a green line on the horizon.

The slowly retreating island of Barbados, he repeated to himself. He frowned for a moment, looking first up at the spread of bulging white sails and then down at the sloop's wake. He strode forward to inspect the traverse board that recorded the ship's speed, shaking his head at what he read. The officer of the watch was the sloop's master's mate. He was still getting used to such junior warrant officers keeping watch. In the *Agrius* it was only senior sea officers that did so, but the little *Rush* boasted but two of those, Sutton and Joseph Appleby, the ship's sailing master. The more competent of the warrant officers would have to keep watch too.

'Ah, Mr Wardle,' said Clay, recalling the unfamiliar name with difficulty. 'Would you pass the word for Mr Sutton and the boatswain, if you please?'

'Aye aye, sir,' Wardle replied, touching his hat in salute.

George Carver, the boatswain, was the first to arrive on the quarterdeck. He knuckled his forehead at his new captain rather than saluting, betraying him as a former seaman who had worked his way up. He was young for a boatswain, probably no more than late thirties. His pigtail was relatively short, with barely a grey hair among the brown. He was also one of the few men Clay had met in the service who was taller than him. Sutton arrived slightly later, apologising for the delay, but he had been down in the hold looking over some damage that the carpenter was keen to show him.

'No matter, Mr Sutton, you are with us now,' said Clay. 'Gentlemen, how fast do you think we are going?' The boatswain and the lieutenant both looked up at the sails, and then down at the wake in a curious repetition of the process that Clay had gone through a little earlier.

'Five knots?' speculated Sutton. The boatswain signalled his agreement, not wanting to disagree with his new lieutenant.

'You are wrong, Mr Sutton. We have not touched three knots all morning,' said Clay. He pointed across at the distant island. 'When we departed Bridgetown it was dawn. We have been favoured all morning with a good stiff trade wind that any Christian ship would fair delight in, yet here we are, almost noon now, and yet the wretched island is still in sight.' He turned to the boatswain.

'Mr Carver, I had always been told that these Swan class sloops are well founded vessels capable of a tolerable turn of speed. With the sail we have set, should we not expect a little more from her? Or did the Navy Board play a cruel trick on us when they named the ship *Rush*?'

'No, sir, by rights she should be much swifter than this,' replied the boatswain, 'but I am afraid she is long overdue to be careened. Her bottom is all foul with weed, some of the bigger fronds are as much as a cable long. You can see them in her wake sometimes. Did Captain Parker not mention it when he handed her over to you?'

'He most certainly did not,' fumed Clay. 'Fronds of weed two hundred yards long! I have never heard of the like! No wonder she shows a shocking want of speed.'

'But Mr Carver, why has this not been addressed before?' asked Sutton.

'Well sir, I know that Captain Parker did request she be careened a few times, but there are precious few facilities at Bridgetown, and there always seems to be another ship as needed it more, like. By rights she should have been sent to one of them proper dockyards at Jamaica or Antigua, but what with the squadron being so short of ships I imagine the admiral was never able to release her. We did try to get some of the weed off by giving such members of the crew as can swim large knives, but what with the sharks hereabouts....'

'Our duty is to blockade Micoud. How shall we intercept any French craft if we can barely muster three knots?' demanded Clay. 'I doubt if we could overhaul a rowing boat! No, gentlemen, it will not do. I need you to deliberate with each other and devise some proposal to address matters. With your intimate knowledge of the ship, Mr Carver, and I know from my experience of Mr Sutton's resourcefulness, I have every confidence you can produce a solution that will answer to provide some immediate improvement now. For my part you can rely on me to insist that the ship is properly careened when I next see the admiral, but alas we shall not now be back in Bridgetown for several months.'

*****

Able Sedgwick was finding that his time handling his dugout canoe on the west coast of Africa had not prepared him well for the bewildering life ahead of him as a seaman aboard the *Rush*. The only other ship of a comparable size he had ever been on was the slaver that had brought him to Barbados, but he could draw little of any use to him now from that appalling experience. Although he did not know it, he was in many ways fortunate that his naval career was to start aboard such a small ship. He could have been posted on

46

board a second rate like the admiral's flagship the *Princess Charlotte*, lost among a crew of almost eight hundred strange faces spread across her many levels of deck. The *Rush* was at least a manageable size with her single gun deck and with only a hundred and twenty souls aboard.

Two of those souls now stood in front of him. One was his petty officer Tom Green, a barrel-chested man whose deep bass voice was so rich with the accent of the Welsh valleys, that Sedgwick found it a struggle to follow more than one word in three. The other was a pleasant looking man in his late twenties with long blond hair and penetrating blue eyes who held himself with the swaggering self assurance of a trained top man. He was every inch the sailor. The same shapeless clothes that had been issued to Sedgwick seemed to hang well on his muscular frame. His long hair was neatly plaited down his back, a well used marlinspike hung around his neck and a single thick gold hoop glinted in his left ear.

'Now look you, Sedgwick,' Green boomed, 'this here man is Adam Trevan. You will be one of his mess mates. Just you keep right close to him for now, do as he tells you, and keep your nose clean. He will show you your duties, like. Right, carry on the pair of you.'

'Aye aye, Mr Green,' replied Sedgwick to the retreating Welshman's back, before turning to face Trevan. The seaman held out his hand towards him with a smile. Sedgwick was familiar with the gesture. He had seen white men shake hands before, in the slave market, on the plantation, but no man, white or otherwise had ever shaken his hand before. After a moment he touched Trevan's hand uncertainly, felt his own hand gripped firmly and responded in kind.

'Right there, Able,' said Trevan, 'now that sheep buggerer is out the way, let's get you sorted. Starting with your kit.'

'Sorry, Mr Trevan,' said Sedgwick cautiously. 'My English

is good but I find you and Mr Green's accent a little difficult. What was that about sheep buggery? This morning Mr Taylor read me the Articles of War, and buggery I think is very bad. Is it not punished with death?'

To his surprise, Trevan started to laugh.

'Oh dear me,' he chuckled. 'Him with his Welsh, and me being Cornish like, that must be vexing for'ee. I will try and talk a mite slower. First up, I ain't no Grunter, so you can stow the Mr Trevan. Call me Adam.'

'Thank you, Adam,' said Sedgwick.

'The part about him buggering sheep is not really true,' explained Adam. 'We hands tend to be a bit saucy-like, you know, a bit rude when we are talking about the Grunters and all. We don't mean anything by it most times. Didn't you slaves do something similar with the overseers on your plantation, when they couldn't hear you?'

'Yes, we did,' replied Sedgwick, a little disturbed by the parallel Trevan had found between the hard faced, brutal overseers he had left behind, and his new ship's petty officers. Before either man could say anything more, seven clear strokes of a bell sounded from the forecastle.

'Right Able,' said Trevan. 'We need to hurry. Seven bells means we are on watch in half an hour. Let's get your kit stowed, starting with that hammock.'

*****

When Trevan and Sedgwick came on deck at the start of their watch, the former slave's head buzzed with all that he had learnt. The Cornishman led the new recruit to their watch station up on the forecastle of the *Rush*, and Sedgwick was instantly entranced with the delightful free flowing wind and the sweeping motion of the ship. The sloop's speed through the water may have been a matter of shame for its new captain, but to him the towering white pyramids of canvas spoke only of raw power. Ahead of him the long bowsprit thrust towards the distant horizon, holding out a broad fan of overlapping triangular head sails that soared up high above his head. Beneath his feet the *Rush's* round bow seemed to be constantly busy, shouldering aside the deep blue water with muscular ease and throwing an ever renewing wash of white foam to either side. He smiled with pure joy. This was closer to what freedom should feel like.

'Now then, Able,' said Trevan, drawing the new recruit's attention back on board. 'Let's see how much you can remember. Whe're you going to find your hammock tonight?'

'On the larboard side, abaft the main mast, three rows over, second from the top,' recited Sedgwick, 'I will hang it at place number thirty-seven on the lower deck.'

'That's very good, mate,' said Trevan. 'You even said "abaft" like a proper tar. Now, can you tell me what all the ship's bells mean?'

'The day starts at noon, when we get our grog,' answered the new recruit. 'The bell then counts out each half hour, and when it gets to eight bells, the watch changes and the bell starts afresh.'

'Well I never did,' marvelled Trevan. 'You sure you never been to sea before? You must be a right deep one, or maybe I am just a proper good teacher, like. You are now ready for your next lesson. What do you reckon them two Grunters are up to?' Trevan pointed towards the quarterdeck where Sutton and the boatswain were engaged in a lengthy discussion, with much pointing, and peering over the side.

'I am not sure, Adam,' said Sedgwick. 'How would I be able to tell?'

'I haven't got a clue, mate,' said Trevan. 'I only knows that when the Grunters are doing a deal of thinking it generally leads to trouble and work for us next, you mark what I say. See now, them two have just disappeared off in the direction of Pipe's cabin.'

'Pipe's cabin?' queried Sedgwick. 'Is that another of your seaman words?'

'No, not this time, mate,' chuckled the Cornish man. 'Pipe is what we used to call the captain back on the *Agrius*. Clay pipe, see, like what you smoke—you get it? Mind, that's just for us like, don't you go letting the Grunters hear you call him that. Steady now, they're back. That was right quick,' he continued, looking past Sedgwick.

Down on the main deck Sutton and Carver had reappeared, and were calling over some of the petty officers, including the hulking figure of Green.

'Told you so,' said Trevan, as Green came towards them. 'Here comes that Welsh bugger.'

'You forecastle men!' rumbled the petty officer up at them from the main deck. 'Come with me down to the cable tier.' Sedgwick and Trevan followed the other seaman down first onto the main deck, then down ladder ways through the ship to the low, cramped orlop deck, deep below the waterline. As they descended through each layer they saw parties of men busy removing the gratings that covered the main hatch way, to create a large square opening running up through the ship. Trevan looked around at Sedgwick in surprise.

'This is mighty strange,' he said. 'It's almost as if we are about to rouse out a cable to anchor with, but that makes no sense right out at sea like.'

As they descended the light became weaker till they were in semi-darkness. Green took a lantern from its place by the ladder way, and bent double as he disappeared into the gloom. The bright sunlight and clean air of the Caribbean seemed a distant memory now. They were surrounded by sharper vapours, rising up from the dark hold below them, bilge water and damp, vinegar and the sweet smell of something half rotten.

At the foot of the lowest ladder way, Sedgwick stopped, unable to follow the other men under the low beams and along the dark deck.

'What's the matter, Able,' asked Trevan. 'You ain't scared of the dark, are you?' Sedgwick shook his head. In the dim light Trevan could see beads of cold sweat blistering his face. He was once more that terrified and bewildered young Ashanti fisherman, being forced onto the slave deck of the ship that had brought him to the Caribbean. Claustrophobia seemed to flow in a fog from the narrow space ahead, threatening to overwhelm him.

'Does this ship carry slaves?' he whispered.

'No, mate, nothing down here worse than rats and damp,' Trevan reassured him. 'It's a narrow, dark spot I grant you, but there is little for you to fear, except for one very angry Welshman if we don't look lively now. Come on, you stay good and close to me.' Sedgwick felt the Cornishman's hand once more in his. This time it was leading him forwards as if Trevan was a mother, and he a child.

They made their way through the coils of huge cable that filled the space, following the light of Green's lantern as he searched. Strange bars of yellow and black flowed over the stacked cables and the bodies of the other men who crouched around the cable tier.

'Stretch of eight inch cable he said, not used for years he said,' muttered Green, peering around the coils of rope. He paused at last at one lost in a far corner. 'Right, over here lovelies,' he ordered. 'Get the end of this cable out to the main hatch and feed it up to the party on the deck above. Look lively now!'

*****

Once the cable was laid out in long loops across the main deck, Lieutenant Sutton explained what he wanted the men to do.

'Take a yard of cable each and cut at it with your knives,' he explained. 'Not all of the way through, but frayed so that the fibres bristle, as if it were the tail of an angry cat. Do you all follow?' The men exchanged glances at the strange order. Slowly at first, they started to stab and rip at the thick rope, but under the encouragement of Sutton and the boatswain they soon worked with increasing enthusiasm. Trevan indicated a space where Sedgwick should sit on the deck, next to a large savage-looking seaman with dark hair and eyes.

'No, not here, Trevan,' he muttered angrily. 'You take your fucking monkey somewhere else.'

'Easy there, Josh Hawke,' said Trevan. 'This here's a shipmate now.'

'No negro bastard is ever going to be a shipmate of mine, do you hear me?' Hawke snarled.

'All Right, Josh, keep your temper like,' said Trevan. 'We will find us another spot. Come on Able, let's go over there.'

The two men moved to another section of the rope, and sat cross-legged next to each other working away at the tough hemp. After a while, Sedgwick spoke up.

'Adam,' he said, 'who was that man, and why is he so angry?'

'I shouldn't take no notice of him,' said Trevan. 'Hawke's

a strange bastard. He's not got many mates on the barky, to be honest. Most of us will be just fine with you, but he was pressed off a slaver. I reckon that might be why he is a bit hot about having you as a shipmate.'

Sedgwick looked across at Hawke. He well remembered the sailors who had manned the ship that had brought him to Barbados. They had been pitiless, cruel men who had cowed their cargo with unremitting savagery. He could still feel the hot pain from the bull hide whips they had used to lash the slaves and the casual way that the sick and ailing had been tossed overboard alive to the waiting sharks.

'Steady there, Able,' cautioned Trevan. 'You're stabbing at that cable like you be trying to kill someone!'

When the cable was butchered to the satisfaction of their lieutenant, the ship hove to into the stiff breeze and the call went out for all hands. The small deck was soon thronged like a market day crowd with both watches gathered. The crew were agog to know what the strange hairy rope was for. Under Sutton's supervision it was looped under the bowsprit and lowered down until it disappeared beneath the hull like a belt. Each end of the cable rose out of the sea and came over opposite sides of the ship. The crew were split between the two ends and encouraged to pull in opposite directions as if about to take part in a tug-of-war match.

Backwards and forwards the cable sawed, as first one half of the crew and then the other heaved on it, scrubbing the hull of the *Rush* in much the same way that a bather might towel his back dry. Sutton and Carver each supervised an end as they progressed slowly back down the ship, carefully working their way around the various chains, port lids and swivel guns as they went. Up on the quarterdeck Clay looked with satisfaction at the clumps of dislodged weed that bobbed to the surface all around his ship. At the end of two hours of the back-breaking work that Trevan had feared, the cable was pulled back on board, and the men dismissed. The *Rush* still needed to be cleaned properly, for the curious scrubbing would have missed much, but at least she would be able to go a little faster now.

*****

'Hey, Adam,' called a voice as Sedgwick and Trevan walked past on route to their mess table. The sailor had to shout to be heard over the hubbub of the lower deck, where discussion of the afternoon's strange activity combined with anticipation of their coming evening meal, made for a noisy combination.

'Evening, Tom,' replied Trevan, shaking his fellow sailor by the hand. 'This here is Able Sedgwick, just joined our mess today. Able, that be Tom Wilson, ordinary seaman in the afterguard.'

'Good to have you on board, Able,' said Wilson with a smile, before returning to Trevan. 'Them two Grunters you followed across are rare deep ones, and no mistake. Fancy scrubbing all that weed off with a cable! I never heard tell of such a thing, but it's given the barky a good couple of knots, according to my mate Ben, him being a quartermaster an' all. I tell you that arse Parker would never of dreamt of such an idea.'

'You're not wrong there,' enthused Trevan. 'Why do you think me and my mates was so keen to follow them across from the *Agrius*? But I tell you, Tom, you ain't seen the half of it. Pipe is a rare good fighting captain an' all, and you knows what that means?'

'Prize money!' they both said together, their eyes wide with greed.

'You got it,' laughed Trevan. 'Now just you let me and Able get away to our dinner. God I could eat me a horse.'

'Lads, this here is our messmate, Able Sedgwick,' he announced to the sailors seated around the table once they had pushed their way through the caldron of noise. 'Like us, he is new to the barky.'

'Would you be one of the Galway Sedgwicks, at all?' asked the seaman on his right, to general laughter. He was a man of medium build with dark curly hair, brown eyes and the thick accent of central Ireland.

'That jester is Sean O'Malley,' explained Trevan. 'He is a papist sod, but him plays the fiddle well, so we keep him in the mess, like.'

'Pleased to meet you, Sean,' smiled Sedgwick. Inwardly he groaned at having yet another tricky accent to master.

'Your man there be Joshua Rosso,' said Trevan, indicating a swarthy-looking sailor seated next to O'Malley. 'Only we calls him Rosie. He's the brains in the mess, having his letters and all.'

'Delighted to meet you, Able,' said Rosso, his educated voice contrasting with those around him.

'And the big bastard over there is Sam Evans,' continued Trevan. 'Like you he's a volunteer landsman. He knows little of the sea, but he can be quite useful in a mill. He saw off a gang of Yankee sailors in a grog shop back in Madeira when we was all on the old *Agrius*.' Evan's smiled at Sedgwick and shook his hand.

'It will be nice to have some other bleeder fresh to the sea who can help me deal with all the nautical bollocks this lot spout,' said the huge Londoner.

'I know I am rated landsman,' said Sedgwick, 'but back home in Africa I was a fisherman, so perhaps I will have some new nautical bollocks for you?'

To his delight his new mess mates roared with laughter at this. Rosso and O'Malley both thumped him on the back as they settled him onto a stool between them. Sedgwick felt himself warming to his new companions. The friendly faces and easy laughter was a delight to someone so long starved of those simple pleasures. In this alien environment, these were the most welcome of the many strange experiences he'd had that day.

The next strange experience was about to unfold, in the shape of the meal that had been slapped down in front of him in the square wooden plate he had been issued with earlier. On it appeared to be a large piece of leather in a steaming, gelatinous mess of gravy. Next to it was a pale green swamp, while on the side were some hard white discs. His mess mates all set to with keen appetites. Most of them tapped one of the white discs absently on the table with one hand while they spooned food into their mouths with the other. Sedgwick stared at the disc that Evans was tapping opposite him, transfixed by the small white worms that fell from it to wriggle amongst the crumbs.

'Ain't you hungry, shipmate?' asked Trevan, observing his hesitancy.

'No, I am, Adam,' replied Sedgwick. 'I am just a little unsure of what nature of food I have here.'

'Well, I make no doubt it will be a while since you have had any good Christian food set before you,' said the Cornishman, slipping back into teacher to the new recruit. He began by pointing at the green swamp.

'That there is pease, which we get most days. It is right good, especially when hot. On the side is ship's biscuit . You best leave those for now, till I can show you how to tap out

the weevils, and that is your pound of pork, you know pig.'
Trevan supplemented his explanation by wrinkling up his
nose and making squealing noises.

It was small wonder Sedgwick was unable to recognise
the lump of salt pork, almost a year in its barrel and barely
softened in the cooking process, as something edible. Meat
had been a rarity in Africa and unknown during his time as a
slave. The thought of a whole pound of it just for him was
profoundly new. As he started to eat, he found that the
quantity and quality of the strange looking meal was far
better than he had been used to as a slave. The pork was very
salty and required considerable chewing, but was tasty for all
that. The pease was very good, and easy to eat, and towards
the end of the meal he even tried his hand at some biscuit
tapping. He was famished after his first day at sea, and found
himself eating with much of the relish of his new mess mates
around him. When he at last glanced up from his meal, his
hunger sated, he felt hostile eyes on him. Looking back down
the ship, through a gap between bodies on the crowded deck,
he saw that the brooding gaze of Josh Hawke was fixed on
him.

*****

A few days later, Clay contemplated his own meal with
similar suspicion to that shown by Sedgwick as the plate was
slid in front of him with panache by his steward.

'God bless my soul, Hart, what manner of remove is this?'
he asked, pointing at the steaming dish. It appeared to
contain a thick, folded beige sheet, glistening wetly.

'Tripe a La Poche, sir,' announced Hart proudly. 'Mr
Lloyd was good enough to let me have some of his recipes
before we left Bridgetown. Now that I am a captain's
steward, rather than serving the needs of the wardroom, I

have resolved to produce some superior vittles than previous, like.'

'Well, that is very admirable of you,' said Clay, prodding the section of tripe with his knife. The tip punctured one of the folds, and it slowly collapsed with a hiss of escaping fluid. 'But you do perhaps need to advance by stages. Mr Lloyd was a chef of considerable ability. His talent was built up over several years apprenticing in Paris before the start of the war, you know.'

'Ain't I experienced too, sir?' protested Hart. 'I done four years in the kitchen of the Ox and Bush on the Guildford road before I joined the navy.'

'Quite so,' agreed Clay. 'Perhaps the fare you learnt to prepare in that inn might prove a more fruitful starting point than some of Mr Lloyd's more extravagant dishes. Do please try not to let your culinary ambition soar too far above your actual cooking ability, Hart.'

'Aye aye, sir,' grumbled the steward, his arms firmly crossed. 'Would you be having some potatoes with that at all, sir?'

Clay was destined never to discover if Hart had, in fact, pulled off a rare culinary triumph. Just as he struggled to cut off his first mouthful of tripe, he heard a cry from the deck above.

'Deck there! Sail ho!' yelled the lookout, the sound clear through the open skylight above Clay's head.

'Where away?' came the officer of the watch's reply, louder and much nearer. The voice was pure Devon. Mr Appleby, the ship's rather overweight master must be on watch, thought Clay.

'Three points on the starboard bow, and making for the coast, sir.'

Clay was about to dash on deck when he remembered that he was now the captain, with a certain gravitas to uphold on board. He decided to ignore the dangerous looking tripe, and quietly stuffed as many of the potatoes into his mouth as he could before the expected knock came.

'Come in,' called Clay, his voice rather distorted with food. The marine sentry outside his door opened it to allow the midshipman to enter.

'Mr Appleby's compliments, sir, and there is a sail in sight off the starboard bow.'

'Thank you, Mr Croft,' Clay replied. 'Please tell Mr Appleby that I will be on deck shortly.'

*****

When Clay came up onto the quarterdeck he could sense the excitement all around him at the prospect of action. The *Rush* had been standing off from the east coast of St Lucia, out of sight of land so as not to alert the French to her presence. She was patrolling the approaches to the small port of Micoud in the hope of catching any ships that tried to enter or leave. It would seem one had now slipped into her net.

'Mr Croft, take this glass and go aloft. Tell me what you make of her,' said Clay to the midshipman.

'Aye aye, sir, aloft it is,' replied Croft. He rushed to the mainmast shrouds and scampered up them with the facility of a gibbon. Clay looked on with admiration for a moment. His fear of heights would never have allowed him to climb at such a speed. He turned to the officer of the watch.

'Mr Appleby, kindly put the ship on the other tack and have the topgallants set. I want to head her off before she can reach safety.'

'All hands! All hands to make sail!' The boatswain's calls shrilled through the ship, bringing the watch below up on to deck. The top men raced up the rigging only marginally slower than Croft had, while the other hands crowded around, ready to sheet home the newly set sails and brace round the yards. Looking forward, he noticed the bulky figure of Sedgwick as he ran to his place on the forecastle without any apparent hesitation. He is learning fast, thought Clay to himself.

'Deck there!' came a girlish squeal. Croft's adolescent voice had recently started to break, and when forced to shout tended to reverted to its pre-pubescent pitch. 'She is a square-rigged merchant brig, on the port tack under easy sail. Should be visible from the deck soon.'

Clay took his glass and stared across the brilliant blue sea at where the brig would appear. There was nothing visible yet, but with their two tracks converging he should be able to see her soon. He looked farther forward. The blue strip of sea was cut now by a greenish smudge topped with bulging cloud as the island of St Lucia appeared on the horizon.

'I think I can see her now, sir,' said Sutton's voice at his elbow. Clay focussed back towards where Sutton was pointing, and he saw two tiny white squares, flecks of something more solid than the pale sky. Top gallant sails, lifting just into view. He raised his voice up towards the masthead.

'Mr Croft, what sail does she carry?'

'Topsails and now topgallants, sir, same as us,' came the falsetto reply.

'Mr Appleby, can you shake out the courses and take a cast of the log, if you please,' Clay ordered.

With her big lower sails set, the *Rush* heeled over under

the press of canvas, her round bow dipping into each wave with a crash of spray before she lumbered up again ready for the next one.

'Oh dear, oh dear,' said Clay. 'How laboured she is! The *Agrius* would have fair sliced through this sea with half the top hamper we carry, would she not, Mr Sutton?'

'Indeed so, sir,' lamented his lieutenant. 'We may have removed some of the longer fronds, but I fear we still have a mass of weed as thick as grass for the sea to grip upon.'

'Well, there is little we can do about it now. Kindly take a bearing on the chase and see if the main sails have made a difference.'

'There is not much in it, sir,' said Sutton, after a period of careful observation, 'but I believe her to be head-reaching on us.' As Clay digested this news the master joined them, fresh from casting the log.

'Six and a half knots, sir,' he reported proudly. He touched his hat with one hand in salute, while with the other he clung to the mizzen shrouds to keep his footing on the steeply sloped deck. 'Mr Sutton here and Mr Carver have improved things markedly with their scrub of the hull.'

'And yet, gentlemen, it would seem we are out-paced by a merchant ship that carries a third less canvas than us,' said Clay. 'This is a sorry state of affairs to find upon a King's ship, I must say.' He looked up at the bulging pyramids of canvas on the masts, and down at the sloping hull. A line of ugly green weed, dense as a mat, was visible on the windward side of the hull, testament to how far the ship was heeled over. He sighed to himself. She could bear no more canvas than she had.

'Deck there!' came the latest hail from Croft at the masthead. 'The chase is setting more sail now.' Clay looked across at the brig, now visible on the horizon as their courses drew closer together. He watched a large sail billow out from her foremast, before being sheeted home. It was less smartly done than it would be on a Royal Navy ship, but it would still mean that the brig would be able to show them a clean pair of heels.

Two hours later, and Clay's first pursuit of an enemy as a captain in his own right had ended in failure. The *Rush* had done her valiant best, trailing along in the wake of the brig in the vain hope that something might carry away in the Frenchman's rigging. They were standing into the Bay of Micoud and the emerald coastline of St Lucia was folded close about them, rising up from the brilliant blue of the sea. They were so close in that they could see stretches of white coral sand, and catch the occasional glimpse of red mud roads and terracotta roofs dotted in among the thick green of crops and forest. Ahead of them the ship they pursued was taking in her sails. She had made the tricky turn around the large sand bank that lay across the entrance of the bay, and was ghosting into the sheltered water beyond. Clay watched as she dropped anchor with the sand bank between her and the *Rush*.

'The town of Micoud is directly behind the brig, sir,' said Appleby beside him. 'You can just see the church tower and some of the roofs.'

'Yes, I see,' said Clay, looking through his telescope 'Tell me a little about the bay, Mr Appleby.'

'The entrance is blocked as you see by that spit of sand,' said the master. 'To the south of it there is no clear passage for ships on account of a coral reef. Do you see where those waves are breaking? The only navigable route is round the north end, the way you saw the brig enter the bay. That approach is protected by a battery marked on the chart. We should be able to see it soon. Ah, here we go.'

As the ship glided through the water, a puff of smoke appeared on the top of the low cliff at the northern end of the bay. Moments later a line of splashes rose out of the sea as a cannon ball skipped towards them, each jet of water progressively shorter as the shot lost momentum. The final small splash was several hundred yards short of them. Clay glanced round and called back towards the quarterdeck.

'Close enough, Mr Wardle,' Clay ordered. 'Kindly bring her to the wind, if you please.' The *Rush* turned through the water and with her topsails backed she came to a halt. As the ship swung, Clay and Appleby moved along the forecastle rail to keep the bay in view.

'No batteries covering the southern end of the entrance then?' said Clay.

'That's right, sir,' said Appleby. 'No real need for any. You couldn't pass anything bigger than a ship's boat through the channel between the reef and the sand bar.'

Clay continued to stare after the brig with the longing of a cat outside the bars of a bird cage, before he closed his telescope and turned away. If only this wretched ship had been careened, they would have caught the Frenchman easily, he thought. He began to pace up and down the weather side of the ship in search of inspiration. Then he stopped, almost mid-stride, a look of determination spreading across his face.

'Mr Wardle, take us back out to sea, if you please,' he ordered. 'Mr Appleby, can you join me below with the best chart you have of this coast. Mr Sutton, will you come too.' He strode down the quarterdeck ladder and disappeared in the direction of his cabin.

Chapter 4
Micoud

In the warm darkness of the tropical night, the *Rush* slipped back towards the land once more. As she moved across the calm water, her wake stirring a faint trail of milky phosphorescence that disappeared moments after it formed. The ship showed no light to the world outside, only on the main deck did her two battle lanterns provide enough faint light for the members of the cutting out expedition to assemble, the marines with their stamped tread, the seamen with their bare-footed patter.

Up on the quarterdeck Joseph Appleby conned the ship. The island ahead was a black bar dotted with the occasional light from dwellings on shore. Where the town of Micoud lay the bay was illuminated by a faint wash of light which gave him a navigational mark to aim at. He ordered the ship to heave to, and the sound of her gentle passage through the water was replaced by the slap of waves against her stationary hull.

'We are in position now, sir,' he said to Clay. 'Four cables east of the sand bar.'

'Thank you, Mr Appleby,' replied Clay. He turned to the group of officers around him. 'Well, gentlemen, do you all understand your parts?' He turned first to the officer in the group he had never served with before.

'Lieutenant Macpherson, what role will your marines play?' Clay heard the soldier stroke his bristling sideburns in the dark before he answered.

'My men will be with Mr Preston in the cutter, sir,' he replied, in his soft Highland accent. 'We are the second boat, and are to board the brig from the larboard side.'

'Very good. What about you Mr Sutton?' he asked next.

'I am in command, sir,' he replied. 'I also have the launch. We attack the starboard side at the same time as the marines make their assault. Having secured the ship we signal to the *Rush*, slip the anchor, and bring the prize out by the deep water channel.'

'And finally Mr Croft?' said Clay.

'I am to take the jollyboat in last of all,' recited the midshipman. 'I wait till the other boats are engaged, then I board over the bows and fall on the French from an unexpected quarter.'

'And for my part I wait for Mr Sutton's signal, and then stand in to distract the battery,' concluded the captain. 'Very well, gentlemen, that is all quite clear. You may depart at your convenience. Good luck to you all.'

'Aye aye, sir,' they replied, turning away.

The blocks of men dispersed to the sides of the ship, and clambered down into the boats alongside. Those left behind quietly wished their departing shipmates well. The line of boats formed up next to the ship, and then slipped away into the night, heading for the unprotected southern entrance to the bay ahead. Clay watched them go, feeling for the first time in his career the true loneliness of command. Before now he would have been in one of those boats, controlling his own destiny, able to make his own decisions. Now he felt the utter powerless of having to trust on others to perform well without him. He had sent more than half of his crew off into the night, and now, if the whole attack was a disaster, he would barely have enough men to limp back to Bridgetown to report the calamity to Admiral Caldwell. He felt a cold prickle of sweat on his neck as he stared out into the dark.

*****

In the cutter, Evans and Rosso pulled in steady time with the other oarsmen, propelling the boat through the black night. Not yet trusted with an oar, Sedgwick was in the centre of the boat, squashed against the double file of marines who sat with their muskets upright between their knees. He fingered the unfamiliar weapons he had been issued with. He first looked at the thick bladed cutlass, which weighed and felt like a much longer version of the machetes he had used to cut sugar cane on the plantation. The other weapon he had been given was a pistol. He had received a brief demonstration of how to cock, point and fire the gun, but he had never seen one used in action before, let alone discharged one himself. 'You just stick it against one of the Frogs, and pull the bleeding trigger,' Evans had explained to him. Thinking about that now in the dark, he was unsure if he would be able to bring himself to do that. Best leave the pistol alone, he concluded, and stick with the big machete.

'Easy oars,' whispered Preston, and with a gentle hiss the way came off the cutter. To one side Sedgwick could see where the waves splashed against the coral edge of the lagoon, the faint starlight flickering off the broken water. On the other side they had slid level with a darker shadow on the water. They were next to the launch, which had also stopped.

'Why have we halted, Mr Sutton?' asked Macpherson in a stage whisper from the stern of the boat.

'Guard boat ahead,' came the whispered reply from the launch. Sedgwick looked around towards the bow. He could see the masts of the brig now, a web of black lines silhouetted against the faint rind of light from Micoud. Then he saw the guard boat as it splashed busily across the water of the bay, a trail of phosphorescence in its wake. The sound of a conversation in French, followed by a burst of laughter drifted across to them. The boat disappeared behind the low dome of the sand bank that stretched away like the back of a whale, having apparently seen nothing.

'Give way all,' came Sutton's murmur from beside them, and the launch started to move. A few moments later the cutter was moving too, slipping towards the dark mass of the brig. Closer and closer they came. The hull of the ship loomed up above them, shutting out the light from the shore.

'Qui va là?' The shout from the deck of the brig was sudden and loud after the hush of their careful approach.

'Put your backs into it!' shouted Preston from the stern sheets of the cutter, and the boat surged forward. Up on the side of the brig a chain of flashes lit the night as muskets banged at them. Sedgwick heard the rip as a musket ball flew over his head, but the ragged volley seemed to have missed everyone in the boat.

'Easy all!' shouted Preston. 'Larboard oars in! Hook on in the bows there.' The men just managed to get their oars into the boat in time as the cutter swept alongside the brig. Macpherson was quickly on his feet. He swept out his sword, the polished blade silver in the night.

'Marines, follow me!' he ordered. 'Mr Preston, kindly come after us with the boat crew.' The cutter rocked as the marines swarmed up the side of the brig. Sedgwick saw Macpherson above him clinging on to the main chains with his left hand while he thrust at someone out of sight with his sword.

The resistance on deck was fiercer than expected, Sedgwick thought. He had imagined that the marines would have swept onto the deck of the brig, but they were being held up at the ship's side, and seemed to be locked in a frantic struggle with the French crew. A firearm flashed above his head and one of the marines fell backwards from the ship's side. His body crashed onto the gunwale of the cutter, before it slipped into the dark water. With the marines blocking their way up the ship's side, the crew of the cutter looked around at each other, desperate to help, but unsure what they could do.

Sedgwick stood in the boat, close to the side of the brig. Next to his head he could just make out the solid square of a port lid, hinged at the top, and was reminded of the panel he had used to escape through on the rain sodden night when he had taken his freedom back on the plantation. He slipped his fingers under the lip of the port and just as before, he tugged at it. The heavy wood moved a little under his hands.

'Mr Preston, sir!' he called. 'This port lid is loose. If we could prise it open, we can get onto the brig this way.' Moments later Preston had swayed his way up the rocking boat to stand next to him. He saw instantly what Sedgwick meant.

'Good man, Sedgwick,' he enthused. 'Slip the flat of your cutlass under that side. Evans, get your boarding axe under the other side. Now, three, two, one, heave!' Sedgwick was a strong man, Evans even more so. After a moment of creaking resistance the port lid came free with a splintering crack. Evans held it open.

'After you, me old cock,' he said to Sedgwick. 'This was your bleeding idea, after all.'

Sedgwick stared through the opening at the deck beyond. The light from some shaded lanterns faintly illuminated the space. He could just make out the doors of store rooms or officers' cabins opposite him. He pushed his head through into the ship and looked forward where he saw lines of unoccupied hammocks slung under the low deck beams. Beyond them was the foot of the ladder way to the deck above, down which the sound of fighting flowed.

Satisfied with what he saw, Sedgwick pulled himself through the square hole and dropped down onto his hands and knees. His cutlass spilt from his grip as his hand jarred against the deck. Glancing up from his prone position he saw a streak of movement. A shadowy figure loomed out of the dark, the faint light of a lantern glistening off a long steel edge. He heard a deafening explosion just above him, and in the orange light the image of a French sailor, his face distorted with fury, cutlass raised, flashed into existence. A moment later it was dark once more, and he was crushed to the deck by a heavy, warm weight.

He shook himself free of the body, and looked behind him as he stood up. Evans had one arm and a shoulder pushed through the port, a smoking pistol in his hand.

'You all right, mate?' he asked. Sedgwick nodded, still shocked by the ferocity of the Frenchman's attack.

'Fuck me, I thought you was gone there, Able,' said the Londoner as he squeezed his huge frame with difficulty through the opening. 'That would have made for a bleeding short career if he had stuck you. I've barely had time to learn your name!'

Evans and Sedgwick pulled the body of the French sailor

Philip K. Allan

out of the way, and the rest of the cutter crew slipped through the port to join them. Sedgwick remembered just in time to recover his cutlass from the deck, and joined the growing group of sailors at the foot of the ladder.

'Right, you men,' said Preston. 'Follow me up the ladder way. First we fall on the men holding up Mr Macpherson and the marines, then we can help the launch crew.'

They ran up the ladder way, and spilt out onto the deck of the brig. It was almost as dark as it had been below. The struggling figures along both sides of the brig were difficult to make out, except when the flash of a pistol or a musket lit the scene, freezing the action in a strobe of time.

'Come on *Rushes*!' shouted the midshipman as he dashed across the deck. Sedgwick followed him with Evans on one side and Rosso on the other. In a moment they were upon the enemy. A French sailor in front of him spun round to meet this new assault, but he was just too late to avoid the savage blow from Sedgwick's cutlass. For an instant the man's face was close, his mouth wide open, his eyes filled with horror. Sedgwick had just time to register how young the face was before the teenager crashed at his feet, dragging his cutlass down with him.

Behind the first Frenchman another sailor turned to face him with a snarl, his cutlass swept back. Sedgwick ripped his own weapon free from the young man at his feet and managed to get it up in front of him in time to parry the blow. The blades crashed together with a shriek of edge on edge. Over the Frenchman's shoulder Sedgwick saw the cross-belted figure of one of the marines. The Frenchman followed his look, but turned too late to avoid the thrust of the soldier's bayonet. He spun away with a scream of pain, and fell down on deck too. Moments later the battle was over.

A Sloop of War

The remaining French sailors threw down their weapons, the fight knocked out of them by the surprise attack in their rear. An officer in a naval uniform reversed his sword, and handed it to Preston with a stiff bow of his head. The battle persisted for a little longer on the other side of the deck, but then those French defenders surrendered too as Macpherson and his marines tramped up behind them with muskets levelled, threatening to fire a volley at point blank range. Just at that moment Croft led his jollyboat crew over the bows of the brig with a cheer, to find that the fight was over.

'Better late than never, Mr Croft,' glared Sutton. He was in considerable pain from a sword cut on his left forearm, but this had not stopped him noting the late arrival of Croft and his men.

'Mr Macpherson,' he said. 'I would be obliged if you and your men would secure the French prisoners.'

'Aye aye, sir,' the Scotsman saluted smartly, and marched away to bark orders to his men.

'Mr Preston, kindly set the fore topsail and let slip the anchor. Mr Croft, have the wheel manned, and arrange for the signal to the *Rush*. Then get the ship's boats in tow behind us.'

'Aye aye, sir,' came the replies from Preston and Croft. The two midshipmen departed, both calling to their boat crews.

Up in the bows of the captured brig, Preston organised his men quickly.

'Top men, lay aloft and set the topsail,' he ordered. 'Evans and Harrison, get below with your axes and cut the anchor cable. The rest of you are to man the sheets.'

Sedgwick joined the group of men on the portside of the bow, lined up ready to sheet home the large topsail once it

Philip K. Allan

had been released from the yard above them. In the faint light coming from the port of Micoud off to his left he could just make out the top men as they swarmed up the rigging and ran out onto the yard high above his head. Across the water came the sound of a tolling church bell, clashing out in alarm.

'Well, if the clods up in that battery have missed all the clamour down here, that will tell them something's astray,' muttered Rosso next to him, nodding ahead. 'They are up there on top of that cliff, and we've got to sail right up towards them before we can turn round the end of this here sand bar to slip away.' He looked around and sniffed for a moment. 'Wind's all right, mind, to carry us out,' he added. Sedgwick turned his face towards the shore, and felt the cool breath of the land breeze starting to blow.

From under his feet the steady pounding of axe blows stopped abruptly, and he heard a loud splash over the side. Evans and Harrison ran up on deck.

'Anchor cable is cut, sir,' reported Evans.

'Thank you, Evans,' replied Preston. 'Can you let Mr Sutton know, please. You will find him by the wheel.' While Evans lumbered off, the midshipman glanced up into the rigging above his head, just in time to see a large square of white canvas tumble down from the topsail yard.

'Brace the yards!' he ordered. 'You men, sheet home and belay.'

The big sail began to draw and the brig moved forward through the water. Out at sea, Sedgwick saw a sudden line of orange flashes, tongues of fire shooting out. For a brief moment he saw the shape of the *Rush* as she slipped towards the entrance of the bay. The roar of canon fire arrived a few moments later, rolling back off the surrounding cliffs.

'Ah, just in time,' muttered Rosso next to him. 'Now that will set them French buggers a vexing problem. Do they oppose the ship firing at them, or try and hit us, now we have shown we have the brig by setting sail?' Sedgwick thought about this for a moment.

'Which do we want, Rosie?' he asked.

'Well, it would be good if they dally so long they resolve to do neither,' replied Rosso. 'But failing that, we want them to fire at the barky. She is better built to take the punishment, she is farther away, but chiefly coz our arses aren't in her.'

Rosso's faith in French indecision was short lived. The *Rush* had just fired her second broadside at the battery, when a line of six orange flashes lit up the top of the cliff.

'Ha, see!' said Rosso with satisfaction. 'They are firing at the *Rush*. Long may that last.'

The brig was almost at the end of the sand bank now.

'Ready to go about, Mr Preston,' yelled Sutton from by the wheel.

'Man the braces,' ordered Preston.

Too late, the battery on the cliff realised they had chosen the wrong target. As they made their turn towards the open sea, the gunners finally shifted their fire onto the brig. The sound of the passing shot was like fabric tearing in the air all around Sedgwick. A backstay parted with a crack, and swung free through the air.

'Mr Preston!' called Sutton. 'Kindly set the foretopsail, if you please. Then have that stay spliced.'

The next salvo of fire from the battery was a little better aimed. One shot crashed into the hull of the brig, leaving a large hole in her port quarter. But with both sails drawing and no lights showing she was now quickly vanishing into the night. By the time that the next salvo was fired, she was all but invisible to the gunners on the cliff. Where their shots fell, none could tell.

*****

'She is the *Olivette*, an armed brig out of Martinique, sir. One hundred and forty tons burden,' explained Sutton to his captain, pointing across at the prize as she followed the *Rush* under easy sail. They were seated opposite each other in the main cabin of the sloop and were sharing a much needed pot of coffee after their largely sleepless night. It was morning now and the sea outside the sweep of glass was tropical blue once more. The two young men were tired but exhilarated by their night's work.

'She was carrying various supplies of food and munitions for the garrison at Micoud, none of which she had been able to unload, sir,' continued Sutton. 'She had a crew of seventy, which is why she was able to put up such a good fight. We lost four killed and nine wounded, seven of whom Mr Linfield is tolerably confident of saving.'

'I hope you included yourself amongst that number, John?' asked Clay with a smile. Sutton flexed his left hand under the large bandage that swathed his lower arm.

'I shall be fine, thank you, sir,' his friend replied. 'It really is but a scratch. It is my pride that is truly wounded. The brig's master turned out to have some considerable skill with the short sword for such an elderly gentlemen. I was lucky Macpherson and his marines arrived to put an end to his fencing exposition before he was able to run me through.'

'What state is the prize in?' asked Clay.

'Some little damage to the rigging, which Mr Carver has in hand, sir,' said Sutton. 'Only one shot struck the hull. It did a cruel amount of damage to the quarter. Chips is working on it now and says it should be patched by six bells in the afternoon watch.'

'Good. Now, tell me how you perceived that the officers and men performed?' asked Clay.

'On the whole with much credit, sir,' answered Sutton. 'I should say that Mr Macpherson appears to be a most steady officer who knows his duty well. Mr Preston did his part with particular dash. It was his men that broke in through the gun port, which allowed the cutter crew to fall on the defenders from the rear. That was crucial to our ultimate success for without it I fear it might have been a much bloodier affair. Neither my launch crew nor Macpherson and his Lobsters were making much progress up to that point. On the other hand, Mr Croft made a sad hash of his role. He arrived on board after the fight was quite over. With regard to the men I have few concerns. They fought with good pluck and spirit against a much tougher opponent than we had expected to find.'

'So in summary, a very creditable first action for the *Rush*,' said Clay. 'Apart from Mr Croft, who we brought with us, and we already knew can show a want of initiative on occasion.'

'Yes, I agree, sir,' said Sutton. 'It was also a very creditable action in the matter of prize money. I am sure you will have calculated the progress last night's little affair will have made towards advancing your position where Miss Browning's hand is concerned?'

'Not at all,' replied Clay, a little too abruptly. He had been making that very calculation before Sutton had arrived. 'It was our duty to prevent our enemies receiving the comfort of the delivery of the supplies the *Olivette* was carrying.' Sutton continued to grin at Clay, forcing his friend to do likewise. 'Although I will own that my three-eights of the capture's value are not unwelcome,' he added.

'To that end can you tell off a prize crew for the *Olivette* to see her safely conveyed to Barbados?' Clay ordered. 'I will have my report on the action ready shortly, together with some private correspondence for them to take with them to Bridgetown. You might also see if any of the officers and men have letters they wish dispatched too. And I would like to invite the officers who took part in the action to join me for dinner later. I believe a celebration is in order.'

Once Sutton had left the cabin, Clay completed the report he had been writing for Admiral Caldwell, and then pushed the sheets of stiff paper to one side for Taylor, his clerk to seal later. After a moment of reflection, he pulled a fresh sheet of paper towards him and began to write again.

My Darling Lydia,

I live in hope that you will have received my previous letters, but I fear that my efforts to date may have been in vain. Sir Francis and your aunt, Lady Ashton, have forbidden my correspondence with you, and if this injunction is still in place I am sure they will have had the means to intercept any openly directed approach. So today I am resolved to attempt a subterfuge. I will include this letter within one to my dear sister and your firm friend Miss Betsey Clay, with the request that she should forward it to you within one of her own letters. Like Odysseus within his wooden horse, I shall trust that her package too will conceal this letter till it should reach your hand.

If this is truly the first letter that you have

received from me, then my first obligation is to provide you with an explanation of the events and disappointments of the last day you were in Madeira, even though the recollection will cause me as much pain as I am sure it will cause you. That morning I awoke resolved to formalise the understanding we had reached when we were last together aboard the East Indiaman Devon. *My intention was to seek you out, and to make an unambiguous declaration as to how fervently I admire and love you. Although in my heart I knew that you felt the same as I did, only learning of it from you directly would have fortified me for my next intended action. With your encouragement, I would have resolved to demand an immediate interview with Sir Francis, and requested your hand in marriage.*

I am still pained by the recollection of the events of that sad day, when I was prevented from putting any of this into effect. Sir Francis had been alerted to my intentions, and prevailed on my superior officer, Captain Follett, to forbid my absence from the Agrius *until such time as your ship had departed for India. Captain Follett was all too willing to play an active role in this intervention in affairs that should have been of no concern of his, and his actions were the source of a most bitter dispute and rift between us thereafter.*

Thankfully I am blessed with the dear friendship of Lieutenant Sutton. His actions in seeking you out during your uncle's farewell dinner, and his initiative in contriving to speak with you alone are testament to what an admirable friend to us he is. While I was held as an impotent bystander aboard the Agrius, *he was able to make the declaration to you on my behalf that same evening. Although it was delivered in haste, and in an unsatisfactory manner, he was at least on hand to reassure you as to my true feelings. He also brought back to me your reply, which gave me such renewed hope as to our future happiness then, and continues to provide me with comfort now that we are apart. I have the note you wrote with me here.*

Clay reached behind him to slip a hand into the inner pocket of the uniform coat that hung on the back of his chair. The piece of paper crackled less now then when Sutton had first pushed it into his hand all those months ago. It had become soft and pliable with repeated handling. He held it briefly to his nose, but the last trace of her long remembered perfume had vanished altogether now. He opened it once more, and read the twelve words it contained. *To my dearest Alexander, I promise to wait for you—Lydia Browning.*

He stared for a moment out of the sweep of glass at the rear of the cabin. The moving ocean was quite the colour of her eyes, the foaming wake echoed her creamy white skin. He remembered their last meeting on the forecastle of the *Devon*, how the wind had teased out strands of her dark hair from beneath her hat, and sent them flying in the warm tropical air. Most of all he remembered the look of desire in her eyes, and how she had bent her face up towards his, willing him to kiss her. With a smile of pleasure he returned to his letter.

I hold no ill will towards Sir Francis for his views. If he loves you but a small part of the manner in which I do, and has your best interests at heart, his

78

actions are quite understandable. I am sure that he must live in fear of penniless fortune hunters praying on his niece and ward—if I am ever favoured with a daughter as beautiful and as clever as you, I have no doubt that I will be possessed of similar feelings. I understand that he will have objections to an approach from a naval lieutenant with few prospects. But here, my darling, I can perhaps bring you a little hope, for my situation has improved materially since we were last together.

The Agrius *left Madeira a week after you did, and embarked on the pursuit of a substantial French frigate called the* Courageuse. *The chase lasted the entire breadth of the Atlantic Ocean, with the ships finally coming together off the west coast of St Lucia. Our enemy had been well named courageous by her French builders, and the battle was a ferocious affair. Our opponent was quite superior both in the number and calibre of her guns, and her people proved to be spirited and resourcefully led. We eventually prevailed, but with grievous losses on both sides. Captain Follett was killed, Mr Booth, our ship's master badly wounded, and a third of our men were casualties. I am happy to report that myself and Mr Sutton survived intact, and that your friend Lieutenant Munro of the marines was but lightly wounded. Mr Munro has subsequently made the fullest of recoveries, and indeed now flatters himself that the resulting scar on his brow can only serve to make him yet more attractive to the fairer sex!*

As a result of the action and my part in our eventual triumph, I have been promoted to the rank of Master and Commander by Admiral Caldwell. I now have my own ship, the sloop of war Rush, *with Mr Sutton ably serving as my lieutenant. We are engaged at present in the blockade of St Lucia along with other ships of the Windward Islands command. Last night we successively cut out and captured the French armed brig* Olivette, *and it is via this vessel that I am able to send my letter. My share of the prize money for this capture, together with any others in the future, will do much to remedy the want of fortune that lies at the root of your uncle's objections to me. I live in hope that one day soon I will be in a position to be able to claim you for my own.*

Oh my dearest Lydia, how very far away you are! The West Indies and India are almost as distant to each other as any two points could be on the globe. With the most favourable of winds possible, I still know that this letter will take near four months to reach you in far Bengal, and any reply from you will take much the same time to find me here. I do so long to hear how you are. Have you persisted with your resolution to continue with your writing? Perhaps your first novel shall be set in India?

You spoke with such passion about India when we were together, so much excitement in what sights and diversions it might afford. I hope the reality has lived up to the country you hoped to find, and that all your diligent study before you left England has prepared you well for the experience. I shall imagine you reading this letter in some private situation all of your own, in the oriental garden that surrounds your house. It will be quite full of exotic flowers, huge colourful butterflies and strange birds. The garden I hold before my mind's eye is walled in red sandstone, with palm trees framing the tops of the temples visible in the distance. You will read this letter, and I hope smile with pleasure, sure in your heart that though I am far away, my love is all about you. I can picture you now, in a sky blue riding habit. You will put aside my letter, and go off on your ride, preferably upon an elephant!

Until we are together once more, believe in me.

Alexander Clay

Clay read the letter again, and then sealed it with care. He addressed it with her name, and then wrote *Commander Alexander Clay, at sea on board His Majesty's Sloop of War Rush* on the back. He slipped it into the letter he had already written to his sister, and then sealed this letter too, wondering if Lydia would ever get to read it, all those weeks later, on the far side of the world. Clay thought again about how remote the possibility was of them ever being together one day. Even if they could somehow defeat the geographical divide, there was still the gulf between them in situation and background. He looked again at the note, and drew hope from its firm reassurance. She would wait. Wait till he had bridged that gap. So I must have a fortune, thought Clay, and prize money is the quickest route to one of those.

*****

'Ah, fecking prize money!' said O'Malley, with a large grin on his face. 'Ain't it just the finest thing in the world!'

'What I don't get,' said Evans, 'is how come you and Adam get the same as Rosie, Able, and me? We were the ones as risked our bleeding necks seizing the prize, while you

81

and Adam were safe and sound on the ship, far as I can tell.'

'Sure, but that was because of the need for calmness and reason back here on the barky,' continued a sanguine O'Malley. 'Any fool can run around like Uncle Dermot's hens waving a cutlass. But cannonading an enemy battery at night? That is an occupation as takes some of your real skill.'

'But they didn't even hit the *Rush* once,' protested Rosso.

'And doesn't that just prove what I am fecking saying?' replied the Irishman. 'Any fool can let himself get hit, but it takes real accomplishment to evade the beating in the first place.'

The seamen were off duty, and took their ease around their mess table. O'Malley idly plucked at the strings of his fiddle, picking out some variations on a familiar hornpipe. He had been asked to accompany some of the starboard watch who planned to dance later. Rosso was in the middle of a letter he was writing on behalf of one of his new shipmates on the *Rush*, word having spread that he could both read and write. Sedgwick was seated next to Trevan, who was teaching him how to sew. The shapeless clothes he had been issued with when he first joined were gradually being adapted by the two men into something that would fit properly. Sedgwick concentrated hard on his work, the curved yoke of his shoulders bent around the patch of cloth, the pink tip of his tongue protruding from the corner of his mouth. With an exhalation of breath he finished his line of stitching, cut the thread with his clasp knife, and joined in the conversation.

'So will I get some of this prize money, Sean?' he asked.

'Sure you will, Able,' enthused O'Malley. 'We all will, equal shares like. It may not be a fortune, but there will be enough to drink Bridgetown dry, and find some willing doxies after.'

'Fact is you did more to win it for us then most,' said Evans, slapping him on the shoulder. 'If you hadn't found that loose gun port, we might not have had a bleeding prize at all.'

'Did you ever hear tell of the crew of the old *Indefatigable*?' asked Trevan. 'She was the guard ship in the Western Approaches when the war broke out like. Well, all the inbound French commerce had no notion of any war, so she was taking prizes easy as picking fruit. Trading brigs, Guineamen full of gold dust, French East Indiamen packed with indigo and spice. I tell you Black Beard weren't in it. When she was paid off in Plymouth, the crew was that rich, they all went down to the harbour and were skimming guineas into the water.'

'Why the hell would they do that?' asked Evans in horror.

'Because they bloody well could, Sam!' replied Trevan.

The others all cheered at this, their eyes alight with greed. Trevan noticed that Sedgwick smiled at his friends' delight, but had not joined in.

'You all right, mate?' he asked, his voice pitched below the loud chatter of the others.

'I am well enough, Adam,' he replied. The Cornishman looked at him for a moment, understanding the place he had gone to.

'You know, boarding a ship is proper strange,' he explained. 'When you are busy doing it, it's all rage and pluck and give a cheer, lads, and that sort of answers to pull you through it. Then it's all over, and we be right pleased to have won, and happy to be alive like. Everyone hallos, and slaps your back. But then that comes to an end, and it all quietens down. We get back to the barky, back into life here, watch on, watch off and then you gets to thinking on it. On them dreadful things you might have done, or maybe how you got through, but your mate didn't, and then away down you slip. I tell you, there won't be a person on the barky who was there who ain't feeling right down, just like you does now. But it will pass, lad. Trust me, it will pass.'

'I still see the sailor I killed,' said Sedgwick. 'His face was so close when he died, I felt his last breath on me.'

'Would that be the first man you killed, like?' asked Trevan.

'That's right, Adam, but he was no man, little more than a boy really,' said Sedgwick. 'I make no doubt that he would have killed me if I had held back a moment, but it still feels bad.' Sedgwick sighed before he continued.

'You know, all my time as a slave I would dream of killing,' he said. 'I would practice it in my sleep. In dreams I would kill the tribesman who sold me to the white traders. I would drown the slavers who brought me across the ocean to Barbados. Many was the time I killed Mr Haynes and his overseers on the plantation. But all that practice in your head doesn't prepare you for what it might truly be like. Nor for the empty feeling inside after it is done.' He looked up to find that the others around the table were now silent and listening to him. He thought he might expect to see contempt on the faces of his messmates, but he detected only sympathy.

'There is not one of us who didn't feel like that the first time,' said Rosso. 'Now I might tell you that it will become easier the next time, but that won't answer, for it is not true. But I hold that to be a decidedly good thing. For if killing might be swabbed away as easy as the blood stain we leave behind on the deck, we might grow over fond of doing it, and where might that take us?' The mess mates sat for a moment and looked at each other, the silence companionable.

'Well, I am still going to get fecking drunk when we get our prize money,' said O'Malley after a while, puncturing the silence.

Sedgwick pushed back his stool and rose from the table. He walked towards the bows, where the heads were positioned either side of the bowsprit. When he emerged a few minutes later, Josh Hawke was walking in the other direction. His face darkened when he saw him.

'That is all I fucking need,' he sneered, blocking Sedgwick's way. 'Using the same privy as a savage. You need to find somewhere else to shit, boy, 'cause I ain't sharing with no bleeding monkey.'

He tried to walk past Hawke, but he blocked his path once more, trapping him against the side of the ship, his face so close Sedgwick could smell his breath. 'Your sort ain't nothing but trash,' he continued. 'In the middle passage, I used to pitch filth like you over the side. I probably chucked your sister, or your mother to the sharks.' Then Hawke laughed. His mouth was full of broken teeth and his breath was foul.

Sedgwick recoiled from him, his mind full of unwanted images. He remembered that he had been one of those cowed wretches, weeping and filthy, packed like spoons on an excrement-sodden deck. He had seen family and friends, too sick to survive, tossed over the side of the ship. He had been a victim of brutal men like Hawke for much of his life. The last few weeks of freedom seemed to have been an illusion. He felt he was still a slave inside, who had to bow to whatever injustice the Hawkes of this world chose to impose on him. He bowed his head in submission, and went to push his way past, but then he stopped.

Another image came to him. The other face that had been pressed so close to his, not Hawke's but the young French sailor he had killed. He straightened up and looked Hawke in the eye for the first time. Why did he need to cower before this man? He was a member of the crew, just like Hawke. Hadn't he broken free from his plantation? Hadn't he fought beside his new companions? If he allowed men like Hawke to push him around, would he ever truly be free? He thought that he had won his freedom already, but he had been wrong. He needed to win his freedom again, now, here.

'Were they in chains?' he asked, his voice low with menace.

'What?' asked Hawke, confused by the change in Sedgwick's manner.

'The people you pitched over the side, in the middle passage. Were they in chains?' repeated Sedgwick.

'Course they fucking were,' laughed Hawke. 'What of it?' Sedgwick held out his hands, wrists together, palms up.

'Look, Hawke,' he growled. 'No fucking chains on me. Shall we see how brave you really are?'

*****

'We were exceedingly fortunate to have had a shoal of flying fish pass over the ship but a few hours ago,' explained Clay to his guests, indicating the plates that had appeared in front of each officer. 'A significant number fell to the deck after they had struck the rigging, and Hart reacted swiftest, so for once we are to be treated to a fish course.'

'If you were of a religious inclination, sir, you might consider it to be manna from heaven,' suggested Macpherson, to polite laughter.

'Quite so, Mr Macpherson,' replied Clay with a smile. 'Do

please all begin. I am sure it is delicious.' Clay was quite sure it was nothing of the kind. He knew his steward's limitations, but for once he was wrong. With fish so fresh, not even Hart had been able to wholly ruin them, and his guests were soon eating with obvious pleasure.

There were only seven officers grouped around the table in the main cabin of the *Rush*, yet with a servant behind every chair, they had managed to fill the space thoroughly. Clay sat at the head of the table, with Sutton on one side of him and Macpherson on the other. In the middle of each side were two ship's officers that had played no part in the successful attack on the *Olivette*, but Clay had invited them because he had yet to spend any time with them informally. One was the purser, Charles Faulkner, a haughty aristocratic man in his early thirties with a shock of auburn hair. The other was the *Rush*'s sailing master Joseph Appleby. With his red cheeks, rich Devon accent and very overweight body that threatened to burst free from his bulging uniform, Appleby had the look of a farmer who had chosen the wrong calling.

At the bottom of Clay's small dining table, as befitted their low station in the *Rush*'s pecking order, sat Preston and Croft. Both teenagers were conscious of their august surroundings, and tried their best to avoid the forms of behaviour that would be normally tolerated in the gun room. Croft kept placing his elbows on the table, only to hastily remove them in response to a significant glance from Preston opposite him. Preston, for his part, seemed congenitally unable to eat with his mouth closed. Clay suppressed a smile as he glanced at them, reminded of the many occasions when he and Sutton, at a similar age, had struggled to behave correctly through this very situation back on board the *Marlborough*. At least the captain's table had been rather longer on a ship of the line, allowing distance to conceal many of their behavioural flaws.

'Upon my word, this is capital fish, sir,' enthused the ship's master. 'Why this is better than a plate of Torbay joeys.'

'I am glad to hear you say it, Mr Appleby,' said Clay. 'That sounds like high praise indeed, although I confess I am not familiar with the expression.'

'Baby mackerel, sir,' explained Appleby, through another mouthful of fish.

'It seems strange to be dinning without any music,' said Sutton. 'On the *Agrius* we had the benefit of four Italian string players of some repute who served amongst our idlers. They would play most agreeably during dinner.'

'How did they come to be on board?' asked Faulkner, his interest piqued.

'Well, we had had the good fortune to capture a privateer off the coast of Normandy, and among the crew were these four,' explained Clay. 'The captain of the privateer had a considerable passion for music, and had placed them on the ships books. They carried out no maritime duties, but instead performed for him. When we captured them, they offered to join the *Agrius* on the same terms, and the late Captain Follett agreed. They are still aboard her now, doubtless performing for Captain Parker.'

'We could always call for O'Malley with his fiddle, and one of Mr Macpherson's marines with his drum,' suggested Sutton. 'Although I fancy it would not quite answer.'

'Speaking of captured ships, gentlemen,' continued Clay. 'We must toast the health of the conquerors of the *Olivette*.'

'Hear him!' called out Appleby, raising his glass. The four conquerors sat modestly by while Clay, Appleby and

Faulkner drained their glasses.

'It was a most savage fight, I collect, Mr Sutton?' asked the master, deftly moving the conversation along.

'It was indeed, Mr Appleby,' answered the first lieutenant. 'She had a prodigious large crew for such a vessel. Mr Macpherson and I were struggling to board her, for they matched us in force, and the crew were alert and waiting. It was fortunate that Mr Preston was able to enter via a gun port and catch them at a disadvantage.'

'Well then,' said Clay. 'We have our next toast. The endeavour of Mr Preston, may we long be blessed with it.' The others drank the midshipman's health noisily as the wine started to take effect.

'In truth, sir, it was actually Sedgwick who came up with the idea,' said Preston.

'I call that very handsome on your part to say so, Mr Preston,' said Clay smiling at the young officer. 'But it is still to your credit that you made such good use of Sedgwick's valuable suggestion. There are many officers who might have thought themselves too superior to take advice from a rating.'

'Would Sedgwick be the new negro volunteer, sir?' asked Macpherson. 'The hand who joined us in Bridgetown?'

'That is so, Mr Macpherson,' said Clay carefully. 'He was recommended to us by a friend of Mr Linfield's, and it would seem he is fast becoming a valuable addition to our crew.'

'A word of caution, sir,' said Sutton. 'Sedgwick has just been reported to me by the Master at Arms. It would seem he was caught earlier today fighting with Hawke. There is some suggestion of provocation, but it appears that it was Sedgwick that initiated the disturbance.'

'Well, that is a pity,' sighed Clay. 'Just as I am resolved to praise Sedgwick, I find I must now punish him. I make no doubt that Hawke was behind this. He was at the top of a list of potential troublemakers among the crew that Captain Parker left me. But let us not allow such matters to ruin our appetites, I pray gentlemen, for here comes our main course.'

Hart came into the cabin at that moment, bearing a huge steaming pie.

'It may not be as exotic a remove as flying fish,' continued Clay, 'but it is a favourite of mine. Hart does a very tolerable steak and kidney pie.'

'Shall we attack Micoud again, sir?' asked Appleby, accepting a large slice. 'I understand there was other shipping still in the port, including a brace of schooners.'

'Well, Mr Appleby, we must be a little cautious there,' replied Clay. 'I am as fond of a prize as the next man, but I fear the French will be rather better prepared for us next time. Having just stuck our hand into the hive and robbed it of its honey, it might be best to let the swarm settle before we do so again.'

The conversation was now flowing around the table, allowing Clay to look over his officers as he spread his portion of pie out to cool. He was reasonably satisfied with what he saw. Sutton was talking to Macpherson about backgammon. Both men, it would seem, had a passion for the game, but had been unaware that the other had any interest before now. Appleby was talking to the two midshipmen, telling them a story from his time in a merchantman before the war. All his guests seemed animated, except for the purser who was sitting aloof, sipping at his wine. Clay sighed to himself. It was time for him to be the good host.

'Mr Faulkner!' he called. 'A glass of wine with you.'

'Why thank you, sir,' replied the purser, coming out of his reverie at the sound of his name, and draining his glass.

'So tell me, Mr Faulkner, how did you come to be in the navy?' asked Clay.

'I am but a recent member of the service,' he explained. 'By the time I decided to go to sea I was already in my late twenties, so rather too old to follow the tarpaulin route of learning to reef and splice and what not. Could you imagine my abiding in the gunroom with Mr Preston and Mr Croft?'

'No, I am not sure that I could,' said Clay, exchanging glances with Sutton. Clay wondered if the purser was aware that this was precisely the route that they had both followed. He listened for and thought he heard a hint of distain in Faulkner's voice.

'I have always had a facility with numbers,' he continued. 'So my father bought me a bond as a purser, and I joined the *Rush* two years ago.'

'I collect then that your father is a man of substance?' asked Sutton. 'I had wondered why your uniforms were so excellently tailored. It will be a relief to find that they have not been funded at the expense of the ship's finances.' The others all laughed at this, and after a moment Faulkner joined in.

'He is tolerably well off, to be sure,' he said, as the laughter died away.

'Well, I am delighted to have you on board, Mr Faulkner,' said Clay with a smile. There is more to you than meets the eye, Charles Faulkner, Clay thought. I wonder why you really came to sea?

Chapter 5
Punishment

It was raining. In a steady patter it drummed on the sails and collected in beads of silver that flowed down the lines of rigging. It dripped down onto the normally gleaming white deck and turned the planking to a dull shade of grey. It fell on the ranks of sailors, rolling off their tarpaulin hats and soaking their pig tails as they stood in a box around the upturned grating that had been lashed to the main mast. It splashed off the officers' oilskin coats.

Clay stood by the quarterdeck rail, staring towards the horizon. The low cloud that hung over the ship had turned the sea from its usual deep blue to jade. Over the horizon was St Lucia, and the bay of Micoud. The *Rush* was once more positioned just below the horizon, out of sight of land, but ready to pounce on any shipping that tried to enter. Assuming they could catch them, Clay reminded himself, glancing down towards the weed that still encased the hull below the waterline. Sutton marched up to him and saluted smartly.

'All hands assembled to witness punishment, sir,' he said. Clay looked at his friend, his expression blank.

'Thank you, Mr Sutton,' he replied. 'I shall come directly.'

With a final glance out to sea, Clay turned from the rail and walked past the scarlet lines of the marines drawn up at the front of the quarterdeck. He went down the ladder way and out onto the main deck. In the centre of the box of men stood Hawke and Sedgwick, each between a pair of marines. The master at arms stood to one side, together with Miller, one of the boatswain's mate. Clay noticed with distaste he was fingering the red cloth bag that held the cat-o'-nine tails.

'Carry on, Mr Honeyman,' said Clay.

'Joshua Hawke, ordinary seaman and Able Sedgwick, landsman, sir. Both men are charged with fighting contrary to article twenty two of the Articles of War,' bellowed the master at arms, as if his captain was somewhere high in the rigging, rather than three feet away.

'Will you be so good as to read that article to the accused, if you please,' said Clay.

'If any person in the fleet shall quarrel or fight with any other person in the fleet, or use reproachful or provoking speeches or gestures, tending to make any quarrel or disturbance, he shall, upon being convicted thereof, suffer such punishment as the offence shall deserve.'

'Thank you, Mr Honeyman. What have you to say for yourself, Hawke?' asked his captain. Hawke stared out past Clay's shoulder. His lip had been cut badly, and one eye was closed and purple with bruising.

'Nothing, sir,' he growled.

'Does anyone wish to speak on this man's behalf?' Clay called out. No one moved. After a pause he carried on. 'Very well,' said Clay. 'Your disciplinary record is poor, Hawke. In the last twelve months Mr Honeyman tells me you have been punished for fighting on two separate occasions before today. You need to endeavour to control your temper in future, is that clear?'

'Aye aye, sir,' replied Hawke, his face bearing not the faintest trace of remorse. Noticing this, Clay steeled his heart and added a dozen lashes to the punishment he had already decided on.

'Three dozen lashes,' he ordered, and then turned to the next prisoner. 'Now Sedgwick, this is all very vexing. I had thought you to be adapting to your new life in a satisfactory way, and now I find you have been fighting with a shipmate. What have you to say?'

Like Hawke, Sedgwick stared out past Clay's shoulder. His expression was one more of sadness than anger. His face, too, was bruised and cut.

'Nothing, sir,' he replied.

'Does anyone wish to speak on this man's behalf?' Clay called again. This time Croft left his place in front of his division and marched over.

'Sedgwick is new to the service and our ways, sir,' he began. 'Apart from this incident, none of his officers have found him wanting in the diligence with which he performs his duty. Mr Preston also wishes me to commend his actions in the recent attack on the *Olivette*.'

'Thank you, Mr Croft,' said Clay. He then turned to the prisoner.

'As this is your first offense, and taking into account the handsome fashion in which Mr Croft spoke up for you, I am prepared to be lenient. I shall live in the hope that you will mend your ways, and I shall not find you come before me again. A dozen lashes.'

Hawke was punished first. He was stripped to the waist, and tied by his wrists to the grating. The first few dull thwacks of the cat just reddened his already scarred back, but soon cuts began to appear, and he writhed in agony. The rain washed a steady stream of blood down his back, onto his trousers and eventually down to the deck.

'Three dozen, sir,' said the boatswain's mate, once the punishment was complete. He stood to one side of Hawke and washed the fragments of his skin and blood from the leather tails of the cat in a bucket of sea water.

'Thank you, Miller,' replied Clay. 'Cut him down if you please, Mr Honeyman.' Hawke staggered a little as he made his way below, helped by two of his mess mates, but his head was held high and defiant. That punishment will have done no good at all, thought Clay.

Sedgwick's shirt was removed, and he too was lashed onto the grating. A gasp went up from the assembled seamen. Several men pointed, and an angry murmur rolled along the ranks.

'Silence there,' ordered Sutton, and the sound petered out. Clay strode forward to see what the men were looking at. Sedgwick's skin was a webbed mass of scar tissue, pink and red in contrast with the brown of his arms. The wounds ran in all directions and covered every inch of his back. In all his time in the navy, Clay had never seen the like before. It was the back of a man who must have been flogged dozens, perhaps hundreds of times.

'Mr Linfield!' called Clay. 'Kindly examine the prisoner, and confirm if he is fit to receive punishment.'

The surgeon walked across, and ran his hands over Sedgwick's back, looking closely at his scars. After a while he came back to where Clay stood.

'Physically he is fit,' began Linfield. 'But surely simple Christian charity dictates that this man has been punished enough in his life...'

'Thank you, Mr Linfield,' interrupted Clay. 'Miller, proceed with the punishment, if you please.'

Another angry mummer rolled around the deck, quickly silenced by Sutton once more. Soon all that could be heard was the steady sound of leather on flesh.

*****

The wardroom of the *Rush* was a cramped space at the very stern of the ship. It was tucked underneath the captain's suite of cabins on the deck above, but had no natural light at all, placed as it was on the waterline of the ship. Down each side of the space were the officers' cabins. They were tiny dark boxes just big enough to contain a cot, a desk and a wash stand. The space that remained was filled by the wardroom table, around which the officers were now seated.

They had grown accustomed to speak a little louder than was normal in order to be heard. The wardroom was never quiet, and the officers were in constant competition with the groan of the ship's timbers and the creak of the rudder positioned just behind the room. Over all was the endless churn of the ship's wake as it boiled past them like a millstream just a matter of feet from where they sat. It was the ship's surgeon who was trying to make himself heard today.

'I still hold that Christian decency demanded that the captain should have commuted the punishment in some way,' said Linfield to his fellow officers as they waited for their dinner to appear.

'But Jacob, you gave him no choice,' said Charles Faulkner, sipping at his wine. 'He had already passed sentence. Once you pronounced that the blackamoor was fit to be punished, there was very little that Pipe could have done.' Sutton looked up sharply.

'Mr Faulkner,' he protested. 'Kindly do not refer to the captain with such a want of respect. I am aware that the crew call him by that name, but even they have the delicacy not to do so in front of their officers.'

'Your pardon, sir,' replied the purser. 'I was not thinking.'

'The point you make is sound though,' continued Sutton. 'Unpleasant as the state of Sedgwick's back may have been, he was guilty of the offence. There are many ships where he would have received a much harsher punishment. I doubt if Captain Parker would have been so lenient, were he still in command. I know the captain well, and he is no friend of the cat. When he was first lieutenant on the *Agrius* he would endeavour when he could to use other punishments. You would be surprised how effective a couple of hours of cleaning the heads can be as a deterrent.'

'Why do you hold he used the cat to punish this case then, John?' asked Macpherson.

'Because it was fighting, Tom,' replied Sutton. 'And a disturbance hot enough for knives to have been drawn. No captain can allow such an act to be tolerated on his ship.'

'That is true,' replied Linfield, running a hand through his sandy hair. 'But I cannot but reflect upon the savage way Sedgwick must have been treated during his time as a slave. The state of his back bears shocking witness to that truth. I have rarely seen such a profusion of lacerations.'

'Well, for better or worse it is done now,' said Sutton, looking towards the wardroom door for the arrival of their meal.

'But is this episode concluded?' persisted Linfield. 'I understand that it was Hawke who provoked the fight by goading Sedgwick about his past. I observed his countenance after punishment, and it did not look to me as that of a penitent determined to change his ways.'

'Sadly that is probably so, Jacob,' said Sutton. 'Ne'er do wells like Hawke seldom respond to yet another flogging. But if it is any conciliation to you, these matters have a way of resolving themselves on board a ship, particularly a small one like the *Rush*. I would not be at all surprised if I was to receive a request for a transfer to another ship from Hawke before too long.'

'Really?' said the surgeon. 'But he has served on the *Rush* for years. Why would he ask for a transfer?'

'I suspect he will be given little choice,' replied Sutton. 'I have spent most of my life among sailors. They may not conform to your notions of Christian decency, but a ship's company can display a sense of natural justice every bit as strong. You heard the men's reaction earlier when they saw Sedgwick's back. They have little love for Hawke and his bullying ways - consider how not one man among them was prepared to speak up for him. They will not come to their officers for a solution, for that too would be against their code, but I expect matters to be resolved none the less.'

'Well, I for one will be pleased if that poor man obtains relief,' replied the surgeon. 'The sooner slavery is abolished in all its forms the better, I say.'

'Do you now?' replied Faulkner. 'Yet who will then work on my father's plantation in Jamaica if that was the case?'

'Upon my word!' exclaimed Macpherson. 'You have kept that very quiet, Charles.' The purser shrugged before he replied.

'Mr Linfield has very decided views on slavery,' he said, 'and I have not wanted to cause undue friction in the wardroom by expressing my opposition to them, but my point remains. My father does have an interest in a plantation in Jamaica. I understand that it is a well regulated concern, in which the slaves are under the protection of a kind master. It is my belief that they enjoy as great, if not even greater advantages than they would have done when under their own despotic governments back in Africa. For one thing they are exposed to Christian teaching that is like to save their souls from damnation.'

'Your father's plantation sounds unusually liberal in its regime,' said Linfield. 'If it is as well run as you claim, it would be quite the exception. But why does it require the plantation workers to be slaves? If the plantation is so attractive, let the slaves go free and work for your father voluntarily.'

'That will not answer. I have always understood slavery to be the natural condition of the blackamoor,' replied Faulkner. 'Back in Africa it is quite endemic. Most of those that are transported to the West Indies are handed over to the slave traders by their black masters.'

'Oh come, sir!' said Linfield, becoming angry. 'You cannot truly believe such things to be correct. It is your fellow man you speak of! Just because he may have been ill treated in Africa by leaders ignorant of all notions of civilisation cannot be justification for further ill treatment by we that claim to be civilised. No, the whole trade should be stopped without delay.'

'Ah,' said Sutton, with considerable relief. 'Here is our dinner at last. Might we perhaps move the conversation on to a less contentious subject, gentlemen, before words are said that might be regretted later? Mr Linfield? Mr Faulkner? A glass of wine with you both.'

*****

'Good morning, Sedgwick, please come in,' said Linfield, rising from his chair in the cramped little cabin that served as a dispensary on board the *Rush*. 'What is it that ails you?'

'Mr Green said I was to come and see you, sir,' said Sedgwick, his frame filling the dispensary door. 'It's them wounds from my flogging. Most are healing just fine, but I have one that keeps opening. Mr Green says he is done with me coming on duty with blood on my shirt. He says he will have me flogged again, if I don't get it seen to.'

'Yes, I imagine that would vex most petty officers, even one who is less particular than Mr Green,' smiled Linfield. 'Come in, Sedgwick. Take off your shirt, and let me have a look at this deficient wound.'

Sedgwick stripped off this shirt and Linfield looked again at his scarred back. In the light of the single lantern each ridge and trough of scar tissue was thrown into sharp relief, making the former slave's back look even more disfigured than it had when he had last examined it on the main deck.

'Yes, I believe I can see where the problem may lie,' said Linfield as he ran a hand over the rutted flesh. 'The cat has cut a little more deeply here, and with so many previous wounds the skin has failed to renew itself. I shall apply a brace of sutures to close the wound. That should answer.' Linfield reached for a bottle and a cloth.

'I shall first swab the area with some spirit of wine. It may hurt a little,' the surgeon warned.

'I doubt it, sir,' said Sedgwick over his shoulder. 'I don't really feel much in my back anymore.'

'No, I don't suppose you do,' said Linfield, reaching for his needle and gut. 'Which may be most fortunate, for my needle's prick generally hurts rather more than the spirit. You would be surprised which burly stoics among the crew squeal when they feel it press.' He applied the stitches to the wound, his patient quite inert as the needle went in. 'You really cannot sense this at all?' he asked.

'I can feel the tug, sir, but nothing more,' said his patient.

'Well I'll be damned,' muttered Linfield. 'It is as if I was mending a shoe.'

Once Sedgwick had pulled his shirt back on, and had thanked the surgeon, he started to leave.

'Sedgwick, come back for a moment,' urged Linfield. 'Take a seat again, I would talk with you.' The sailor returned and perched on the edge of the cot.

'I wanted to say how sorry I was for your punishment,' said Linfield. Sedgwick shrugged his shoulders.

'Wasn't your fault, sir, nor the captain's,' he said. 'I started the fight with Hawke, so I needed to be punished. Captain had no choice in the matter.'

'But I could have prevented it,' said Linfield. 'When I examined your back, I should have told the captain not to go ahead.' Sedgwick shifted himself uncomfortably on the bed.

'I don't blame you for that, and certainly not the captain, sir,' he said. 'I owe him everything. If he had not taken me when Mr Robertson asked him to, I would have been handed back to Haynes, and that would not have ended well. He is as cruel a man as the devil. Twelve lashes is a cheap price to escape what that bastard would have had prepared for me.'

'I might have stopped even that punishment,' said Linfield. Sedgwick saw the frustration in the young surgeon's face, and smiled at him.

'Thank you for that, sir, but I am doing just fine,' said Sedgwick. 'My new life grows on me, and I have some mates now amongst the crew. All I truly want is to be accepted as part of the lads. Some of those around me are mates because they pity what has been done to me, like you did when you saw my back. Others they hate me because of my race like Hawke does. But I want to just be seen as me, once a slave, yes, but now a sailor and a fellow *Rush*. That has to mean no special favours. When I do wrong, I need to take my punishment like one of them too.'

'God bless you, Able Sedgwick,' said Linfield. 'That was very well said indeed. You make me feel quite humble.' He paused for a moment as another thought came to him. 'The eloquence with which you speak has put me in mind of what an asset you could be for the abolitionist movement. You might tell me your story, and I could write it up as a pamphlet. It could be most effective in influencing the debate.'

'Perhaps later, sir, once I feel I truly belong among the crew,' replied Sedgwick. 'In truth, being closeted with an officer writing away at books and the like won't answer for doing that at all. May I go and rejoin my muckers now?'

Chapter 6
Chase

The *Rush* had just gone about on the other tack when the sail was first sighted. She had ploughed up and down the same empty stretch of sea for several weeks now, like a prison guard patrolling a section of wall. St Lucia was over the horizon and the clouds that sat above the island were visible from deck most of the time. More concrete evidence of land came from the numerous frigate birds, hanging like black crucifixes in the sky, which drifted far out to sea on the wind to inspect the lonely little sloop. Occasionally the tops of St Lucia's highest green hills were just visible as tiny green teeth, proud of the horizon at the extreme end of one run.

'Deck there! Sail ho!' bellowed the lookout.

'Where away?' yelled Sutton as he craned his head back to look up at the sailor standing high up on the royal yard.

'Two points forward of the larboard beam,' came the reply. 'Royals just proud of the horizon, sir.'

'Mr Preston,' said Sutton to the midshipman of the watch. 'My complements to the captain, and a ship is in sight off the larboard beam.'

Clay came on deck, and sniffed at the air. The wind had been dropping for most of the morning, and now only a gentle breeze remained.

'Any sign of her from the deck, Mr Sutton?' he asked.

'Not yet, sir,' replied the lieutenant.

'What do you make of her, O'Neil?' Clay yelled up at the masthead.

'Royals of a man-of-war for certain, sir,' the lookout replied confidently. 'A big one I should say, her being so clear this far away an all.'

'Hmm, a large warship,' muttered Clay. 'Probably one of ours, Mr Sutton.'

'Shall I put the ship about to close with her?' asked his lieutenant.

'No, we need to maintain our position watching Micoud,' he replied. 'Besides, on her current course we will learn more presently.'

After an hour, the sail of the ship was visible from the deck. Slowly it grew as the two ships converged, the *Rush* slowly hauling herself into the wind, while the strange ship flowed towards them with the wind behind her. As more and more sails lifted over the horizon it became clear that the ship was moving as fast as she could in these light airs.

'What do you make of her now, Mr Sutton?' asked Clay as the two men studied the approaching ship.

'Warship for sure, sir,' said Sutton.

'Which means nine chances in ten she is one of ours,' said his captain, 'what with most of the French and Dutch navies bottled up in their home ports by our squadrons.'

'Unless she is a blockade runner, sir,' suggested Sutton. 'She might be a lone ship that has broken out in poor weather perhaps and headed across the Atlantic?'

'She might indeed,' said Clay. 'What makes me a little nervous, Mr Sutton, is what will follow if you are correct and she proves to be a more powerful enemy. Let us be frank, to our tiny little *Rush* almost all enemies are more powerful. In which case how will we evade her with this damned foul bottom of ours?'

'Well, let us hope she is indeed one of ours, or perhaps a neutral, sir,' he replied. 'For good or ill we shall know soon.' The two men settled their glasses to watch the approaching ship once more. After a while Sutton spoke again.

'She carries a fair press of sail, sir,' he said, 'All her plain sail, as well as studding ones, aloft and alow.'

'Yes. She is a big ship too,' added Clay, 'Judging from the spread of her canvas, and her masts look very tall.' He called up to O'Neil once more.

'Masthead there! What do you make of her now!'

'Deck there!' yelled O'Neil. 'I can see her hull. Looks like a ship of the line to me. Two decker I should say.'

'Any colours visible?' asked Clay

'None flying, sir,' came the answer.

'Kindly bring her up into the wind, Mr Sutton,' ordered Clay. 'I am very uncertain of this ship.'

'It is curious that she shows no colours, sir,' agreed Sutton. 'I can't imagine one of ours doing that.'

Gradually the strange ship's hull rose up over the horizon, a solid dark block beneath the pyramid of white sails. Clay studied her with care, looking at her bows. He hoped to see if she had the round bows of most enemy ships of the line, or the open beak head of a British designed vessel, but the angle was wrong. He really needed to see her in profile.

'Mr Preston,' called Clay. 'Please make the private signal, if you please.'

'Aye aye, sir,' replied the midshipman, hurrying over to join the rating by the mizzen halyard. A few minutes later the signal was flying.

'She is taking a deuced long time to reply, sir,' muttered Sutton. 'Ah, here it comes. What do you make of the answer, Mr Preston?'

'It's the wrong response, sir,' replied the midshipman. 'I think it may have been the correct response once, but not for a good eight months. Excuse me, sir, but Wilson here thinks he knows her.'

Clay and Sutton both turned towards the signal rating, who had Preston's glass in his hand. He had the look of a solid, intelligent seaman.

'Beg pardon, sir, but we was berthed next to her in Port of Spain last winter, when the Dons was still on our side in the war,' he said. 'I reckon she is the *San Felipe*, seventy-four guns, from her rig.'

'Well that comes as a relief,' said Sutton. 'At least the Spanish are neutral.'

'They were neutral two months ago when we were last in Bridgetown, Mr Sutton,' said Clay. 'I doubt if they are now. If that ship is entirely innocent, why does she show no colours, and why is she attempting to signal to us using an old private signal? No, I am quite satisfied that ship wishes us ill. Kindly put the ship before the wind, if you please.'

The *Rush* paid off, turning round till she had her stern towards the approaching ship. As she settled on her new course, the boatswain's call trilled through the ship.

'All hands! All hands to make sail,' bellowed Carver, urging the top men up the rigging.

'Every sail we own in the world, if you please, Mr Sutton,' ordered Clay. 'Let us see if we can outpace this Spaniard in these light airs, even with our foul hull.

Sail followed sail as the Rush gathered speed. With the

wind so light, there was no risk to the ship from such a mass of canvas. The huge main courses were set below her usual topsails, requiring the combined manpower of half a watch to sheet them home. Her small topgallant sails were deployed at the top of her masts, with her tiny royal sails added above those. Finally the long studding sail booms extended out from the yard arms, adding even these sails to the profusion.

'Every square sail set, sir,' reported Carver with satisfaction when the last studdingsail was drawing.

'Thank you, Mr Carver,' said Clay. He returned to watching the Spanish ship following in their wake. She was now well up over the horizon bearing down on them under her own mountains of canvas. Clay could see her tall, wide hull, ploughing through the sea. He could now even make out where her black hull was striped with two pale yellow layers, one for each of her gun decks. Sutton joined Clay at the stern rail, and pulled out his own glass. Both men were quiet for a moment.

'She's a seventy-four for sure, sir,' said the lieutenant. 'Dons carry thirty-six pounder cannon on the lower deck, eighteens above. She could sink us with a couple of well aimed broadsides.'

'Well, we must hope her aim is off, Mr Sutton,' replied Clay. 'Or keep well ahead of her. Do you believe she is still gaining on us?' Sutton watched her for a moment.

'Yes, sir, I believe that she is,' he said.

'That is what I believe too,' replied Clay. 'Thank you for confirming it.' He turned to Preston.

'My compliments to Mr Appleby, and would you ask him to join us please,' he said. 'Mr Sutton, will you kindly order a cast of the log. I would like to know what speed we are making at present.'

While the log was cast, the ship's master came struggling up the ladder way and across to join Clay. He was even more dishevelled and breathless than usual.

'You wanted me, sir,' he asked. Clay paused to look Appleby up and down. He adopted a look of particular severity, largely to prevent himself from laughing. The master's neck cloth was wound loose around his collection of florid chins before it hung down the front of his shirt, his hair stuck up wildly and his waistcoat had been sadly mis-buttoned, so that one was spare at the top of the garment, and a hole was spare at the bottom.

'Sorry, sir, I was asleep in my cabin, and thought it best to come as quickly as possible,' Appleby added to fill the uncomfortable silence.

'In future, Mr Appleby, I would rather you appeared on the quarterdeck attired in the manner to be expected of a King's officer,' replied Clay. 'I am content to wait for you a little longer if needs be.'

'Aye aye, sir,' replied a chastened Appleby, re-buttoning his waistcoat. 'Only Captain Parker was a rather less patient man.'

'Well, I will forgive you on this occasion, then,' replied Clay. 'We are currently doing....' Clay looked towards Sutton, who had just completed the cast of the log.

'Two knots and one fathom, sir,' he said.

'Two knots and one fathom,' repeated Clay. 'I need you to lay me a course for Bridgetown, and let me have an estimate as to how long it will take us to arrive.'

'Aye aye, sir,' said the master, raising a hand to touch his hat in salute, and realising just in time that he had neglected to put one on. After a moment of confusion he turned away and went below.

When Appleby returned to the quarterdeck he was as well dressed as his ample frame would allow. He marched over to Clay and Sutton and touched his hat. Over Clay's left shoulder the Spanish ship had grown noticeably closer.

'The course you need is east by half south east, sir,' he said. 'If what little wind we have holds we should be there sometime tomorrow morning.'

'Thank you, Mr Appleby,' replied Clay. 'Mr Sutton, make it so please. Let us see if we can outpace the *San Filipe* with the wind on our quarter.'

The *Rush* swung towards distant Barbados, and settled on her new course. She was now broad reaching, with the wind flowing in from forty five degrees to one side, her fastest point of sailing. Like an obedient dog, the *San Filipe* turned onto the new course too.

'Well, sir,' said Sutton after a while. 'I believe we may be going a little swifter, but I fear that the Dons are too. I am quite certain she continues to gain on us.'

'Very well, Mr Sutton, let us lighten the load a little,' said Clay. 'Can you start the fresh water over the side. Just retain enough for two days.' A jet of silver soon pulsed over the side as the men pumped away the excess water that the ship carried, but all too soon the jet came to an end.

'Is that all, Mr Sutton?' asked Clay, disappointed.

'I fear so, sir,' replied the lieutenant. 'We have been on station for some ten weeks already.' Both men turned back towards the Spanish ship. Starting the water had done little to stem the remorseless approach. She was now close enough for them to see more details, the catheads that stood out to each side of her bows like a pair of horns on a charging bull and the elaborate gilding as it winked in the sun around her figurehead.

Clay felt a strange unreality about the situation they were caught in. All seemed well at the moment because the danger to his ship was unfolding so slowly. Yet unless he could check the remorseless approach of the Spaniard, the *Rush* was ultimately doomed. He trawled his memory for ideas, times in his past when he had faced similar dangers. It needed to be something that might give them an edge, something the Spanish could not respond to. After a moment he turned back to his friend.

'Do you recall the time we became becalmed on the *Agrius,* chasing the *Courageuse*?' he asked.

'Yes, sir,' replied Sutton. 'We towed her for most of the day with the ship's boats. But that will not answer today, sir. We have too much way on us to launch them, and I doubt we have enough time to hove to and do so. The Dons would be on us in a flash.'

'But we also used sweeps,' said Clay.

'So we did!' exclaimed the lieutenant. 'And the *Rush* is a much lighter ship than that lump of an *Agrius*. Sail and oars together, that might just do it, sir. Shall I put it into effect?'

'If you please, Mr Sutton,' replied Clay. Behind him the red and gold flag of Spain broke out from the masthead of the *San Filipe*, and rippled against the blue sky. The Spanish were preparing for their easy victory.

*****

'Look lively, you lot,' said Petty Officer Green, his voice gravel, 'Three men to each sweep. Go and collect them from Mr Carver.' The sweeps had been brought up from the hold where they had long lain unused and were now stacked on the deck. They were odd looking oars, relics from the bygone age of galleys, thin, with tapered spoons at their extremities. There were twelve in all, six to a side. Sedgwick, O'Malley and Evans lifted one from the top of the pile, and then Evans and Sedgwick looked around, uncertain what to do next.

'Over there, lads,' said O'Malley, trying to point with his head as both his arms held the handle of the sweep. 'Between the fecking guns in the waist. Can't you see the sweep port, at all?'

'What, the little square hole, down by the deck?' asked Sedgwick, peering between the guns.

'The very same!' said O'Malley. 'Were you never after noticing them little holes? Well, I suppose you being new an' all, you can't have stood by them above a hundred times.'

'I have seen them, Sean,' replied Sedgwick. 'I have just never known what they were for.'

'Well, Able old fruit,' said Evans, 'I think you are about to discover a whole new type of slavery. You've done yer time as a field slave, now you're about to try being a bleeding galley slave.'

'Only marriage still to come,' said O'Malley, with a significant look towards Trevan, the sole member of the group with a wife.

'Pipe down there, O'Malley,' shouted Green. When all was quiet, Clay walked down the middle of the deck and stood in front of the main mast.

'Men, the enemy behind us is a Spanish ship of the line,' he said, indicating the tall pyramids of sail looming up behind the *Rush*. 'Provokingly, she is a little too powerful for even you lions to be sure of beating in a fight, so we need to show her a clean pair of heels.' The hands grinned at this, a few chuckled. 'The sails won't answer on their own, which is why we need to use the sweeps. Most of you have never used them before, but they are not unlike an oar in a boat, just bigger. Listen to your officers, who will tell you what to do. We will change crews every hour, and no one will be spared. You will shortly see some of the more reluctant idlers in the crew taking their turn at some honest toil. Carry on, Mr Sutton.'

'Aye aye, sir,' said the lieutenant. 'When I give the order, you will push the oar out through the sweep port, that will act as your rowlock. You row standing up and facing forward. You walk backwards towards the stern, catch the oar in the water, and then walk it forward to take a stroke. Take your timing from Mr Green, and row long and strong. Ready? Out oars!'

The oars extended out from the side of the ship, bending into gentle arcs under their own weight. When everyone was in position, Sutton gave the next orders.

'Walk aft! Catch the water, and stroke! Walk aft and stroke! Stroke! Stroke!' Up on the quarterdeck Clay watched the oars swing through the air, and then foam through the water. Like some huge bug the *Rush* started to move a little faster. Clay turned and took a careful bearing on the *San Filipe*, lining the bow up with a ring bolt on the deck. He looked away for forty strokes of the sweeps, and then looked back. The Spanish ship was in exactly the same position. Sutton came up to join him.

'All sweeps deployed, sir. How do we fare?' he asked.

'Well, Mr Sutton, the welcome news is that thanks to your efforts the Spaniard no longer gains on us,' said Clay. 'But I fear that our speed is sure to slacken a little as the men at the oars tire, and we will lose more time when we come to change the crew over, so we are very much still in the woods.' The lieutenant looked at the sun as it hung over them.

'At least seven hours till nightfall, sir,' he mused. 'Although with a clear sky and the moon close to full, that will provide us no relief.' Both men were quiet for a moment, deep in thought. After a while Clay spoke.

'At the very least we need to arrange the crew change, formulated as well as can be, so we lose no momentum,' he suggested. Sutton considered this for a moment.

'I could have the men told off in advance, with a mix of idlers and marines with seamen at each oar,' he said. 'Then we could change the crews over oar by oar, so as to lose no time through the confusion of all changing at once.'

'Excellent suggestion, Mr Sutton,' said Clay with a smile. 'Kindly make it so.'

*****

Hour after hour the two ships travelled across the calm blue water as the sun swung ever higher in the sky. It beat down cruelly on the men at the oars. They were not just seamen now, but a ragbag assortment of crew members. Stiff backed marines attempted to row in step, to the jeers of the sailors. Coopers mates and sail makers, cooks and clerks, any pair of arms would do in the *Rush*'s increasingly desperate struggle to escape from her remorseless pursuer. The sweat ran down the faces of the men, soaking their shirts, while those who had completed their stint lay in whatever patch of shade they could find, knowing it would be their turn again all too soon.

There was many a weary glance towards the quarterdeck where the lone figure of the captain stood. He had been staring hour after hour at his approaching enemy. The sun was now sinking towards the west, almost touching the tops of the *San Filipe*'s huge masts. Clay kept his face calm and impassive for the benefit of the crew, but inside he felt the first tug of despair. Was it only a few months ago he had congratulated himself on being the commander of this little ship and delighted in his pathetic little prize? He had written to Lydia to boast of his growing fortune, encouraging her to believe in him. But now look at me, he thought. I could be dead in the next few hours, or more likely a prisoner of war, rotting in a Spanish gaol for years to come. Lydia would never wait for me then, her uncle would persuade her to move on before age and grief marred her suitability for marriage until no suitor would consider her.

The Spanish ship seemed to fill his vision now, she was so close. He could see individual seamen as they clambered about her rigging, tiny figures against the white sheets of her sails. He could make out her figurehead, the mass of gilding had resolved itself into the royal arms of Spain, clasped by two enormous gold cherubs. To one side of the figurehead, high on the forecastle, his eye was drawn to activity. He focused his telescope on the spot, but he was already sure of what he had seen. A moment later there was a puff of smoke, followed by a series of splashes as the cannon ball skimmed like a stone towards him. The final splash fell two cables short, just at the moment that the sound of the gun's roar reached him.

He turned around from the rail with a look of renewed determination.

'Mr Croft,' he called. 'Kindly ask the boatswain and the gunner to join me, along with Mr Sutton.'

'Aye aye, sir,' said Croft, before rushing off. Clay returned to his contemplation of the Spanish colossus bearing down on him, just in time to see the next shot fired from her bow chaser.

*****

'It will not be long now,' moaned O'Malley. 'Not now they are firing at us and all. Christ, I am fecking knackered.' The mess mates had just finished their third stint at the sweeps, and were flopped around under the forecastle, watching the fresh crew that had replaced them work away at the oars.

'We may be up to our shanks in shit, but it is right good to see old Lardy Coppell do some honest work for a change,' said Evans, indicating the very fat gunner's mate who was grunting noisily as he sweated over his oar.

'Why are we not firing?' asked Sedgwick. 'Surely we need to fight back?'

'Well, aren't you the fearsome gallowglass?' said O'Malley with a smile. 'Now you've killed your first Frenchman, you all for spilling some Spanish blood, is it?'

'Unfortunately it ain't so simple, Able,' said Evans. 'Adam explained it all to me when I was in my first sea fight. See how all the guns on the ship point out to the sides? That's fine if we are alongside the enemy, but it don't answer when the enemy is behind us. Some ships have stern ports where they can fire a couple of cannon backwards, but the *Rush* ain't one of those. Even if we could, firing our little six pounders at that monster of a ship would be like chucking pebbles at a charging bull.'

'A moment if you please, Admiral Samuel Evans,' said O'Malley, pointing towards the quarterdeck. 'The Grunters are up to something.' The others followed the Irishman's gaze. Close to the quarterdeck rail they could see the cluster of officers around Clay, who was busy issuing his instructions and pointing about him.

'Looks to me as Pipe has a plan of some kind to swipe the Dons in the eye,' said Evans with satisfaction. 'About bleeding time, too.' The group around Clay dispersed in the evening light. Sutton and Carver came down the ladder way on to the main deck, and called over several of the petty officers, including Green.

*****

'Haul away, Mr Green,' called the boatswain, as he stepped back from the fastening that he had tied himself.

'Aye aye, Mr Carver,' replied the petty officer, turning to the line of men tailing at the rope. 'Haul away now,' he ordered. 'Handsomely does it!' The line of seamen all lent back in unison and threw their combined weight against the rope. There was a groan from the heavy block and tackle as the strain came on, and the six pounder cannon rose jerkily up off the deck till it hung suspended over the ship. Another party of hands swung the gun out over the ship's side. It turned in a slow circle for a moment, while the boatswain checked that the massive weight was clear of the still working oars. When he was satisfied he jerked hard on the line running from his fist to the hitch that secured the canon. The rope released, and the huge mass plunged into the sea, throwing up an enormous burst of water. Carver looked around from the ship's side.

'Next cannon, if you please, Mr Miller,' he called, and with a squeal of gun trucks another six pounder cannon was heaved along the deck on its dull red carriage until it was under the heavy duty block , and the process of attaching it began again.

The seamen lined up alongside the rope took a welcome break. O'Malley winked at Sedgwick before he turned towards Evans.

'So, my Lord Admiral,' he asked, attempting to put on an affected English accent. 'Pray tell, was the throwing of all our guns away part of yours and Pipe's plan to defeat the Spanish, at all? I must say, it is a master stroke Drake himself would have been proud of. How shall we defeat the Armada, your Majesty? Why, I shall toss me cannon over the side, just as soon as I've finished this game of fecking bowls!' O'Malley gave a sweeping courtly bow, and Evans had to join in the general laughter of the men around him.

'I were thinking of something a touch more aggressive,' he conceded. 'But if it speeds up the barky enough for us to slip away, I am all for it. Watch your back, Able.' Evans pulled Sedgwick out of the path of a line of the ship's boys, each bearing a single six pounder cannon ball. When they reached the side, they pitched them into the sea, before they disappeared to collect a fresh load.

'Well if throwing away our guns faster than a congregation of fecking Quakers doesn't answer, we should move to ditching some of the crew,' said O'Malley. He looked the huge Evans up and down. 'Course we would have to start with the heaviest first.'

'Clap on there, look you!' called Green, and the men spat on their hands, and picked up the heavy line, ready to haul the next cannon skywards.

*****

Clay stood at the stern rail and looked at the *San Filipe* as he had done for hours now. The sun slid towards the horizon, turning the clouds in the west to blooms of rose and yellow. The Spanish ship had become a thing of beauty, her backlit sails great scoops of coral, her rigging a fretted web of black, silhouetted against the sunset. The gentle evening light flattered the scene and robbed it of much of its menace. Then the *San Filipe*'s bow chaser roared out again, the stab

117

of orange flame bright in the fading light, reminding Clay of the terrible danger his ship was still in.

'The last of the great guns is going over the side now, sir,' reported Sutton from behind him. 'Mr Carver will then get the hatchways opened so we can sway up the rest of the shot. Do we gain on them any?' Clay judged the distance between the two ships for the umpteenth time that day.

'Perhaps a little,' he conceded. 'She makes indifferent practice with that bow chaser, thank God. Do you know she has only hit us twice?'

'That is poor, even for the Dons, sir,' said Sutton. 'Mind you, we have managed to hold her at extreme canon range so far. Doubtless if the distance were to shorten, she would start to knock us about more cruelly.'

'Doubtless, so let us avoid that at all costs,' said Clay. 'She also shows no sign of giving up the chase. I believe we must prepare ourselves to row through the night to avoid her.' Sutton considered matters for a moment.

'We had best change to two hour stints at the oars,' he suggested. 'That way at least those not rowing can get some sleep.'

'I agree, Mr Sutton,' said Clay. 'Kindly make it so. Also we should drop all the anchors bar one over the side. That will be another few tons of weight saved.'

'Aye aye, sir,' said Sutton. 'I will have them jettisoned directly.'

*****

It was now dark night over the calm tropical sea. As the distance had lengthened a little, out to beyond the range of her bow chasers, the *San Filipe* had stopped firing, but she still chased them onwards through the night, a grey mountain in the gloom always just behind them. On the main deck of the *Rush* the space looked strange, empty and uncluttered without the rows of cannon down each side of the ship. Battle lanterns had been lit, and hung under the forecastle and the quarterdeck, their light projecting the figures of the rowers into huge ghoulish shadows on the sails that still bulged in the steady but light wind. The moon had slipped below the horizon now, leaving the sky as a bowl of infinite beauty, studded with countless stars.

At the sweeps no heads lifted from the unremitting watch to look at the heavens. Nothing existed for the rowers but the reality of the hard wooden shaft in their painfully sore hands. Back three steps, catch, heave forward three steps, wrestle the oar free of the water. Back three steps, catch, heave forward three steps, free the oar. And again,... and again,... and again.

Even as a slave, Sedgwick had not known a day of work like it. He had taken his first stroke of the oar some eighteen hours ago. In this last stint he had been working for almost two hours now. Next to him on the sweep was O'Malley, beyond the Irishman the figure of Evans. Sedgwick's arms and shoulders were on fire, his chest was raw and tender where the shaft of the sweep pressed against it as he pushed forward on each stroke. Somewhere on the deck he was aware of a voice. He dashed the sweat from his eyes and looked to one side towards the vague figure.

'Well done, lads,' urged Clay. 'You're nearly at the end of your toil. Come on, O'Malley, show the others how unwearied you are. Well done, Sedgwick, keep those strokes long.' The figure moved on to the next oar with fresh encouragement and Sedgwick returned to his private world of pain.

'Easy for his honour the Pipe to fecking say,' muttered O'Malley.

'God's teeth, this is like the final round of a mill,' added Evans, his words slurred. 'Last bleeder standing wins.'

'All right, lads,' said Green, a few minutes later. 'Pass your sweep over and go and get some food up in the bows.' Sedgwick looked up in disbelief. Was it over at last? Could he really stop? A dishevelled marine took his place at the oar, and he stumbled after Evans and O'Malley. Under the bows, the men were given a cup of water and some ship's biscuit and cheese. They wolfed these down where they stood, and then looked around for somewhere to rest. The deck resembled the aftermath of a savage battle. Bodies lay strewn across the planking. Most were asleep. Linfield and his assistant moved among the men, treating the worst of the blistered hands. Sedgwick spotted Rosso waving them across to a patch of free deck near the head of the ladder way, and he led the others across. They all flopped down to rest. Sedgwick lay on his front, the way he had learnt to sleep as a slave, after years of punishments inflicted on his back. He pillowed his head on his arms, and fell quickly asleep.

An instant later, he was shaken awake.

'Come on, Able,' said Evans, his voice for once sounding shrewish and nagging to Sedgwick's ear. 'We're back on the sweeps.' Sedgwick forced his eyes open, to find that the night was over and grey light washed across the deck. He pulled his aching body upright and looked around him. Away to the east a tiny sliver of fire showed where the sun was rising. Behind the ship he could still see the wide span of sails of the *San Filipe*, perhaps a little more distant, but still following closely, poised to overwhelm the sloop if she should slow.

He shuffled across to take his place back at the sweep. He reached for the oar, forcing his hands not to recoil from the harsh touch of the wood as he gripped it and immediately he started to row again. All around him were the haggard, grey faces of people pushed to very edge of exhaustion. After a few strokes with the oar, a call came from somewhere high above him.

'Deck there! Land ahoy!' yelled the lookout from the masthead.

'Don't break rhythm there!' shouted Sutton, as the oarsman looked about them with sudden interest.

'Where away?' called Clay from the quarterdeck.

'On the starboard bow, sir,' came the reply. 'A large island.'

'Barbados to be sure,' muttered O'Malley.

'Doesn't that mean other British warships?' asked Sedgwick.

'If we ever make it, like,' said Evans. 'Just keep rowing for now, till we got that Spanish bastard off our arse.' The men settled back into the steady to and fro of rowing with a renewed purpose, in spite of their exhaustion. Barbados was in sight. At last there was now some end point to their torment, instead of this ceaseless rowing across an empty sea.

'Sir, sir!' came the sound of Midshipman Croft's excited falsetto from the quarterdeck.

'Ain't that lad's voice broke yet?' muttered Evans.

'Back on the old *Mars* one of the cooper's mates was after being a eunuch we captured from the Turk,' said O'Malley. 'Massive fecker, so he was, but when he talked he squeaked like a mouse.'

'The *San Filipe*, sir!' continued Croft excitedly. 'She has hauled her wind!'

'Don't break rhythm there!' shouted Sutton, as the men all began to cheer.

Clay watched as the *San Filipe* swung round in the early

morning light and showed her long yellow and black sides, studded with her two rows of gun ports. She settled on her new course, and the two ships started to diverge. For the first time he saw her gilded stern, far more elaborate than any British warship. Glass windows flashed in the early morning sun, and he could see panels of scarlet and indigo, all framed by twining gold figures. Inside he felt the warm glow of triumph. That huge ship had finally been defeated by his stubborn little sloop, and her refusal to give up her flight. There had been a time when he had felt despair, when the chase had seemed hopeless, and their remorseless pursuer certain to overhaul them. He patted the oak stern rail with affection. They had fired no shots, no cutlasses had been swung, and yet this felt almost more like a victory than the cutting out of the *Olivette*. When the Spanish ship was a healthy distance away he turned from the rail.

'Mr Croft,' he called. 'My complements to Mr Sutton, and the men can stop rowing now.'

Chapter 7
Bridgetown

Outside the hull of the *Rush* the bright sun shone in the porcelain blue sky. The little silver waves of Carlisle Bay lapped once more against the side of the sloop as she rode to her sole remaining anchor. Her sides were strangely lofty. Relieved of the weight of her guns she rode lightly on her reflection, a wide band of olive green weed visible all around her waterline. On board a minimal anchor watch rested in what shade they could find, which allowed her exhausted crew and officers to sleep.

But not all of her crew slept. Deep in her hold, a man knelt in the centre of a ring of hostile faces. His hands were tied behind his back, and a sailcloth bag hung loose over his head. The space would have been pitch black, were it not for the orange light of a small lantern placed in front of the hooded man. Light and shadow flickered against the barrels and stores that surrounded the group, and reflected back from the low beams above their heads.

'You are all fucking bastards!' came a muffled shout from the man in the centre of the ring. The voice was hot with indignant anger, but the men that surrounded him could also detect that beneath the bravado lay a strata of fear.

'No, Hawke, you're wrong there,' said one of the figures in

the ring, his voice calm and patient. 'Bastards would have dropped you over the side one night, nice and quiet like, with a sore head and pockets full of grape shot.'

'When I get out of here, I am going to have you,' snarled Hawke's muffled voice. 'I am going to have you all.' The figures in the ring laughed at that, no one bothering to respond to the threat.

'Is this about that fucking monkey?' said Hawke's exasperated voice. 'Is the sod giving you all one up the arse?'

No one laughed at this. Instead one of the figures in the ring rose silently to his feet and walked towards the centre. He stood over the kneeling figure, drew back his fist and smashed it into the bag. With no chance to avoid the blow it crunched into Hawke's unprotected face. He let out a howl of pain and then was quiet. His assailant returned to his place in the ring.

'You're going to go and see Pretty Boy Sutton,' said the first voice. 'You will do it later today, and you will tell him that you wants to transfer to another barky. You can choose which one. Is that clear?'

'Like fuck I will,' muttered Hawke. A fresh figure left the ring, and delivered another crashing blow.

'Why are you doing this?' groaned the kneeling man. 'He's only a bleeding negro.' A trickle of blood appeared from under the hood and made its glistening way down Hawke's chest.

'So are you going to do it?' asked the first voice again. The hooded figure was silent, the shoulders shaking a little.

'Let's just end it here,' said a fresh voice. 'Pipe's off the boat, Grunters are all in bed, even the Lobsters are asleep. No one will ever know who slit his throat.'

'No, no!' cried Hawke, the hooded head turned this way

and that as his fear overcame his anger.

'So will you do it?' asked the remorseless first voice. The hooded head was still for a moment, and then bobbed in agreement. No one moved. The hold of the ship was almost as silent as a tomb. The only sound that could be heard was a slight dry guttering from the lantern and the muffled sound of Hawke weeping.

*****

Across the waters of the bay, in the great cabin of the *Princess Charlotte*, Clay was once more seated opposite Admiral Caldwell. The cabin was unchanged from when he had last been there. The panelling was painted in the same shade of dove grey. It was still Price with his white steward's gloves who placed a glass of pale sherry by his side, and murmured something incomprehensible close to his ear. The same kindly brown eyes regarded him across the large desk.

'So captain, you have discovered that the Dons are at war with us, I collect?' said the admiral as he settled himself into his chair and took a sip from his own glass. 'We only heard ourselves on Monday last. Of course they do make a curious pair of allies. On the one hand we have the new regicidal French republic and upon the other the most corrupt monarchy in all Europe.' Caldwell shook his head in disbelief, his periwig wobbling with the gesture.

'I had deduced war might have broken out, sir,' said Clay, 'when the *San Filipe* chased us from St Lucia practically into Carlisle Bay.'

'Yes, I see you do look rather haggard once more,' said Caldwell with a smile. 'Upon my word, I am not sure if I have the ill fortune to only see you after sleepless nights, or if this is your natural condition, what?' Clay laughed dutifully at his superior's joke.

'No matter, for I was planning to recall the *Rush* shortly in any case,' said the admiral. 'As you have doubtless noticed from the growing mass of shipping in the bay, our long awaited descent on St Lucia is in preparation. I expect General Abercromby and his soldiers to arrive from Jamaica any day soon. Now tell me, what have you been about?'

'The blockade of Micoud has gone tolerably well, sir.' began Clay. 'The French have made little attempt to get any shipping in or out of the port. The exception being the *Olivette*. She was able to slip past us. Rather vexingly I found the *Rush* to be so encumbered by weed that even a brig loaded with a full cargo was able to give us courses, and yet still outpace us. However we sent in the boats to cut her out the night she arrived, before she was able to unload, so no harm was done.'

'No harm indeed. She is a fine little prize, duly condemned by the prize court shortly after she arrived here, both ship and cargo,' said Caldwell with satisfaction. 'Pray continue, captain.'

'The balance of our time on blockade was uneventful until yesterday, sir,' said Clay, surprised to find his first encounter with the Spanish ship had been so recent. 'We were approached by a strange sail that we identified as the Spanish seventy-four *San Filipe*. She came on in a most threatening manner and was so superior in force that we were driven from our station. The wind was very light, under which conditions she was able to head reach on us. We deployed our sweeps, and started our water, but it wouldn't answer, she was still the swifter ship. When she had closed to a position where she was able to open fire on us, I ordered the guns to be pitched over the side.'

'By Jove! Are you saying that you threw all of your great

guns into the sea?' asked Caldwell, his eyes growing wide in disbelief.

'Yes, sir,' replied Clay, 'and when this dire expedient also failed to address our want of speed, I ordered all of our six pounder shot and most of our anchors to follow them. Once that was done, we were able to hold her just outside long cannon shot by rowing continuously for some twenty hours. It was only this morning, when we were within sight of Barbados, that the *San Filipe* at last gave up the chase.'

'I shudder to think what the Navy Board will make of this profligacy, captain,' said the admiral.

'I would welcome any enquiry into the matter you might care to convene, sir,' said Clay. 'Naturally it would need to also look into the particulars behind why the *Rush* was sent to sea in such a lamentable condition that she was unable to avoid capture by any other means.' Clay held his superior's gaze, sure of his position.

'Well, perhaps I may be able to smooth matters over with the Navy Board,' he conceded at last. 'I do have a certain amount of credit in that quarter. This does mean that the *Rush* will require something of a refit before she can put to sea once more.' Caldwell rose from behind his desk, and paced up and down the cabin. The admiral seemed to brim with energy. Clay remembered from their first encounter that he had not managed to remain seated for the whole of that meeting either.

'Replacing your anchors should not prove overly taxing,' said Caldwell. 'But I doubt if the dockyard will have as many as sixteen spare six pounder cannon.' He pressed on to the quarter galley before turning on his heel and heading back towards Clay. Suddenly he halted in mid-stride. 'What is your view of carronades?' he asked. Clay thought for a moment.

'We had them on the quarterdeck of the *Agrius*,' he said. 'They are powerful weapons, and they can be discharged rather more briskly than cannon, but they also have a very short range, sir. I would not want only carronades in my armament.'

'Indeed,' said Caldwell. 'Fact is I know that the dockyard have taken delivery of a batch of new twelve pounder carronades. They weigh much the same as the long six pounders you had committed to the deep. You could have a couple of long nines in the bows for range work, and a broadside of carronades. It would give the *Rush* quite a punch. Upon my word, it would come as decided shock for anyone unfortunate enough to come up close alongside you, what!'

Clay had a moment of intuition as he realised the position he was now in. Although Caldwell as a vice-admiral was infinitely superior to a lowly commander, Clay was a commanding officer in his own right to be negotiated with regarding the armament of his ship, not to be simply ordered. He used his new found power at once to get what he wanted.

'Will this refit of the *Rush* include a thorough careening of her bottom, sir?' he asked.

'Yes, I believe that would be in order,' replied the admiral.

'I think the carronades will answer very well, sir,' said Clay. 'Thank you for making such a valuable suggestion.'

'Good, that is resolved then,' said Caldwell, returning to his seat behind the desk. 'I will get matters in motion directly. The fact is, Clay, I need you and the *Rush* back at sea soon, especially as I now have a rogue Spanish ship of the line to worry about too. As I said, we will soon be mounting our attack on St Lucia, and I need you to play your part in it.

I have in mind a role for you operating under Captain Parker's command, now that the *Agrius* has at last finished her repairs. That was a shocking amount of damage she suffered in your battle with the *Courageuse,* don't you know? The yard have had to practically rebuild her.' The admiral took a sip of sherry and stared out of the stern window towards where the frigate swung at her moorings.

'How long do you anticipate the refit of the *Rush* will take, sir,' asked Clay.

'Oh, I should say a good week,' replied Caldwell. 'Which I fear means that you and your officers will be unable to avoid receiving invitations to the Governor's Ball on Saturday next. A ball, I ask you! Any one would think that war had never broken out, what!'

*****

'My thanks, Mr Croft,' said Sutton, as he followed Jacob Linfield out of the *Rush*'s jollyboat and up the stone steps that led to the top of the quayside. Behind them lay the waters of the bay, now seeming to glow with its own amber light in the last rays of the dying sun. Ahead of them were the delights of a run ashore in Bridgetown.

When they reached the top of the steps, the two men set off to stroll along the cobbled street that ran on top of the harbour wall. They had to weave their way through the early evening crowds. Residents taking the air greeted the two young officers politely, the men touching their hats, the women smiling from beneath their bonnets. The many hawkers raised the volume of their calls, hoping to supply them with tropical fruit, large fluted sea shells, sprays of dazzling feathers or small captive animals.

'Where are you bound for this evening, Jacob,' asked

Sutton, pushing from his path an arm bearing a large parrot.

'I sup tonight with Mr Bradshaw, an acquaintance of my father's who now resides here in Bridgetown,' replied Linfield. 'But before that I thought I might venture out to Melverton to pay my respects to Mr Robertson.' Sutton gave the surgeon a shrewd glance.

'And doubtless to Miss Emma as well?' he asked.

'Eh, well naturally if she is there,' he answered, his face colouring. Sutton chuckled to himself. He masked the side of his mouth with the flat of one hand.

'Fear not, Mr Linfield,' whispered Sutton. 'Your secret is safe in my hands.'

'I assure you there is no secret,' said Linfield. 'I do admire Miss Emma's character, but there is no understanding between us. The summit of my ambition was to remind her that when we last dinned at Melverton she made a very handsome offer to take me riding and show me a little of the island. I was hoping to take advantage of her invitation tomorrow.'

'Well, I wish you every success in your design,' said Sutton. 'Pray give my regards to Mr Robertson and do try and resist the temptation to engage his daughters for all of the dances on Saturday.'

'Oh, as for that I am but an indifferent dancer,' replied the surgeon. 'But what of you, Mr Sutton? What are your plans for tonight?'

'I dine with Lieutenant Munro of the marines, who you will have met when we wetted the captain's swab. I served with him aboard the *Agrius*,' replied Sutton. 'In fact, if I am not mistaken that is his scarlet jacket over there.' Sutton waved his hat in the air, catching the attention of the Irishman, at the cost of generating some alarm among the exotic birds on a nearby stall.

'John, top of the evening to you,' said Munro as he strode up and clasped his friend's hand. 'And Mr Linfield too, if I am not mistaken. What a pleasant surprise. Will you be joining us, sir?'

'Alas no, Mr Munro,' replied Linfield. 'I have a previous engagement, so I will leave you gentlemen to your revels.'

'My loss, I am sure,' said the marine. 'Before you depart, I must caution you to prepare yourself for a busy day with the mercury ointment tomorrow. I have just witnessed a number of the *Rush*'s crew heading towards one of the town's more notorious bawdy houses in a most determined fashion. Sean O'Malley and Sam Evans were leading the charge.'

'I thank you for the intelligence, Mr Munro,' sighed Linfield. 'And now I really must go. Good evening to you both.'

The two friends watched the surgeon disappear down the street, before turning to each other.

'So where shall we go, William?' Sutton asked. 'I take it that while I have been away fighting our country's enemies, you have not spent your months here wholly in idleness while waiting for the repair of the *Agrius* to be completed. Are you at least able to recommend a satisfactory place for us to dine?'

'Quite so, my dear Mr Sutton,' replied Munro. 'Rest assured I am no truant. After extensive research, at no small cost to myself, I can tell you that we have a table arranged at the Crown. It has decidedly the best wine to be had on Barbados, on account of the landlord having some connections with a French wine merchant in Martinique. It is said on moonless nights, in spite of the vigilance of the excise men, the odd barrel has been landed in a little cove around yonder headland. Shall we go there for a jug of bishop?'

'With all my heart, William,' said Sutton, linking arms with his friend as they set off up a side street.

The Crown proved to be a little way back from the harbour, in the district of Weymouth. As the two officers walked, Sutton gave the Irishman an account of the *Rush*'s various actions since they had last been together.

'And how has it been to serve under Captain Clay?' asked William.

'Do you know, I find it perfectly agreeable,' said Sutton. 'We have served together so long, I now find that like a long married couple we are quite accustomed to each other's ways. He makes a very good commanding officer, and I believe we may yet turn the *Rush* into a tolerably efficient little ship.... What the devil is the matter, William?'

As Sutton had been talking, he had noticed that the Irishman's attention had been caught by something past his shoulder. As he turned to follow his gaze, Munro pulled him back behind the corner of a house.

'Direct your attention towards that tavern across the street,' he hissed. 'Do you see Lieutenant Windham is seated by the window, having a most animated conversation with another gentleman?'

'Why yes, so I do,' said Sutton, peering in the direction Munro was pointing. 'In fact the other gentlemen is our purser, Mr Faulkner. That is interesting. I had no knowledge of them being acquainted. But why all this subterfuge? Why should we not greet them openly?'

'Do you have no notion why not?' asked Munro. 'Let us hasten to our tavern by a different way. There is much I have to tell you.'

*****

When they arrived at their destination, Sutton found the Crown to be both comforting and yet unfamiliar. The building was new and its design was that of a Georgian coaching inn that might be found in any English market town. The colour of the walls, a deep yellow, was a little unusual, as were the lofty palm trees that bent at various angles over the rear of the building. Its construction had used local materials with tropical wood taking the place of oak, and thatch on the roof in place of slate. The staff, all of whom were black house slaves, wore the mop caps, skirts and aprons of home. In place of mutton stew, the officers dined on goat, with plantains on the side.

'So come, William,' said Sutton, when they were settled into one of the Crown's more comfortable booths. 'Why should I avoid an encounter with Lieutenant Windham in the street?'

'You need to have a care with him, John,' said Munro. 'He has always had an ill character, and Captain Parker has brought out the worst in him. No one could ever accuse Windham of being a diligent officer, but his uncle was quite willing to indulge his nephew. That has changed with the new captain who is a brute to those who he finds wanting in the performance of their duties. I am compelled to share a wardroom with Windham. I see him every day, and what I observe is not very edifying.'

'You have my sympathy,' said Sutton, 'but I still do not see how this should bear on my relationship with him.' Munro glanced around him before he replied.

'Our friend Mr Windham has never been quite reconciled with the accounts that he has heard of his uncle's death, and since you have been away it has been playing on his mind.'

Philip K. Allan

'What has he to say about the death of Captain Follett?' asked Sutton, maintaining a calm exterior, his appetite quite gone.

'It started on the night we last met, to celebrate Alex's promotion,' began the Irishman. 'You collect that he made some excuse to avoid coming. When Fleming and I returned to the ship, we found him sat in the wardroom, quite drunk, brooding over his uncle's death. He said much that was regrettable, about how you and Clay had done so well out of the death. How convenient it was for you both that the captain should have fallen.'

'But this is madness!' exclaimed Sutton. 'It is quite normal for a first lieutenant to get his step after a successful action, whether the captain should survive or no.'

'Not according to friend Windham,' said Munro, leaning closer over the table and dropping his voice. 'You recall he spent plenty of time alone with his uncle in the days before the battle. He maintains that that Captain Follett was resolved to break Clay when we reached Barbados. Then he went on to ask me again what I had seen, since I was on the quarterdeck when the mast came down. Well, I thought it was just a matter of the wine being in and the wits being out, but he is proving to be just as persistent on the issue when sober.'

'But Clay was not even on the quarterdeck when his uncle went over the side,' said Sutton.

'That is true. But you were there. You were standing right on the spot,' said Munro. Sutton held the Irishman's gaze for a moment. He felt empty inside as he wondered what Munro really knew. After a few moments, his companion continued.

'John, you are Clay's closest friend. You have made no secret of your admiration for the man, and all of us were

134

aware that the captain and Clay were quite estranged. Do you remember that time on the *Agrius* when he told us he was going to apply for a transfer, but he was worried that Captain Follett would blacken his name?'

'Yes, I remember,' answered Sutton.

'So, Follett is bent on ruining your friend's career,' continued Munro. 'The day of the battle comes, and the captain is making a decidedly poor fist of things. It was common knowledge to all the officers on the *Agrius* that Follett was no swimmer—he told us as much himself at dinner in his cabin, the day that Danish seaman drowned. Thick gun smoke everywhere, then the mizzen mast comes down and all is confusion. The captain is knocked over the side, but perhaps he manages to clap on to a rope? Everyone is engaged in cutting at the rigging to clear the ship of wreckage. What more perfect cover could you conceive of for someone standing by the ship's rail over which the captain fell to choose the wrong rope, and solve a hat full of problems with a single sword cut?'

'You describe the scene almost perfectly, as if you were there, William,' said Sutton. And then he gasped, as he realised what he had said. 'But of course you were there!'

'John,' said Munro, 'I may have been struck on the head by a falling block, but I had rather more of my wits than I latter made out. Yes, I saw what transpired between you and the captain, and I did nothing to stay your hand. That blackguard deserved it, and there is not a man on board the ship that day, save perhaps Windham, who was not heartily pleased that you did what you did. We were on the brink of defeat until Clay took command. I give you my word that I will hold my peace till the earth covers me over. No, your problem is not that I may betray you. It is that if I saw what you did, I may not be the only one.'

'Who do you suspect knows?' said Sutton, his meal congealing on his plate.

'There could be any number who might have seen something,' said Munro. 'And our friend Windham is persistent in his enquiries. Not only those who were on the quarterdeck at the time. I know he has spoken to most of my marines, in particular those that were sharpshooters positioned in the main mast. Then there would have been ship's boys scurrying to and fro bringing up ammunition for the quarterdeck guns.'

Sutton felt trapped. He looked around the tavern and began to read significance into the glances of the other customers. His act had never been planned. The moment had presented itself, and he had seized at the opportunity. He looked back at Munro.

'What would you council me to do?' he asked.

'Nothing rash, John, but you must be on your guard,' the Irishman said. 'Your foe has an unpleasant and bitter character, and wishes you ill. I do not believe Windham has any conclusive proof of what he suspects, for if he had he would already have acted. He will get no such decisive intelligence from me. My purpose in speaking to you of this is to warn you to be careful. I can watch what Windham is about on the *Agrius*. You need to do the same on the *Rush*. There are those who have volunteered to move from the *Agrius*, one of whom may know something, and now there is Mr Faulkner who you need to regard with suspicion. It would seem he is an associate of Windham.'

Sutton reached across and gripped the Ulsterman's hand.

'You are right, brother. You have my eternal thanks.'

'I know it,' said Munro as he patted his friend's arm. 'But you must be careful. A ship has many eyes, John, and not all are friendly.'

*****

Able Sedgwick sat alone at the mess table, his shore-going rig spread out in front of him. By his side he had his small sewing kit, a few borrowed needles stuck into a piece of cork and a skein of thread, with his large clasp knife lying next to them. It was the same knife he had drawn on Hawke, and would have used if friendly hands had not seized his wrists in time. Hawke may have drawn his knife first, but he had quickly followed him. Thinking back on the fight, he was still shocked by the violence of the anger he had felt. He knew with certainty that he would have used the knife, pushed the blade deep into Hawke's soft white belly if he had not been stopped. He shivered with revulsion at the thought of what he might have done. When his hands were steady once more, he returned to his needlework.

He was now growing accomplished at altering his clothes. At first he had found sewing difficult. His large hands, calloused by years of manual labour, first on the plantation, now on board the *Rush*, had lacked the required dexterity. But in Adam Trevan he had a patient teacher. The Cornishman had spent many hours with him, sewing the same two pieces of cloth over and over until at last he began to produce stitches sufficiently tiny, and in a straight enough line to meet with even Trevan's grudging approval.

He had just finished unpicking a seam of his best linen shirt. Along one lip of the gaping mouth he had produced in the garment he positioned a length of bright blue ribbon. Having done so, Able began to sew closed the seam again, pinching the ribbon between the two sides of shirt so it ran like a soft crest, a quarter of an inch of bright colour, proud of the milk coloured cloth.

The mess deck was almost empty now, with most of the crew ashore. A scatter of men sat at some of the tables, some played cards in groups or chatted to friends, but most were solitary like Able. Those left behind were either shortly due on duty or notorious deserters who could not be trusted, even on an island with no obvious means of escape. Able was not in either of those categories, and his friends had tried their best to persuade him to come ashore with them.

'Come on, Able,' Trevan had said. 'You been nearly three months on this damned boat, like. Don't you want the feel of honest soil beneath your feet?'

'The devil can take the honest soil beneath your feet,' O'Malley had laughed. 'A dishonest whore between my thighs is what I am fecking after.'

'I am sorry, Adam, but the risk is too great,' Sedgwick had answered. 'What if I am spotted by my former owner?'

'He would have to come with a pack of traps to nab you,' Evans had growled, patting one open hand with the balled fist of the other. 'It would be good sport to see him try.'

'No, he has the right of it, Sam,' Rosso had said. 'We can talk bold now, but after we have all had a few mugs of knock-me-down, they could come and take him as easy as a newborn lamb.' He had turned towards Able. 'You best stay safe on board, lad. This must seem like an odd breed of freedom, what with you not able to leave the ship and getting flogged an' all. They do say that a man who would go to sea for pleasure would go to Hell for a pastime.'

He had had to sit to one side as the lower deck bubbled with excitement. Everywhere he had looked seamen had been preparing themselves to go ashore. Embroidered best shirts, the seams bearing all the colours of the rainbow, were being pulled over pale torsos that were webbed blue with tattoos. In front of him O'Malley had been plaiting Trevan's long blond pig tail for the third time, determined on achieving perfection. Evans had been trying to lever his large feet into a pair of thin, shiny leather shoes. Like all the seamen he went barefoot on board, and either his shoes had shrunk, or his feet had widened in the months since he had last worn them. With a roar of triumph he had got the second shoe on, and had tottered around the deck for a while, trying to accustom himself to the unfamiliar feeling. Then, as if a plug had been removed somewhere, the deck had drained of men, and the sound of animated chatter had now been on the outside of the hull, receding from him at the speed that the ship's boats could row.

Able added the final run of stitches to the shirt. He then worked back over the last few and pulled it tight. With a slice of his knife he cut the thread, and worked the stitches flat with his strong fingers. He held the shirt up to admire it in the dim light. Not bad he thought and a glow of satisfaction ran through him. Then he dropped the shirt back onto the mess table as loneliness took over. What was the point of a shore-going rig if he was unable to leave the ship? He wondered where his friends would be now. Still drinking in some grog shop, or would they have moved on to the bawdy house? He felt a stir of desire in his own loins. With a shake of his head he returned to his needle work, cutting open another seam on the shirt, and beginning the process of adding a fresh length of ribbon.

Later that night Able felt himself being shaken awake in his hammock. He opened his eyes and stared about him in the gloom. He had been expecting to be woken up with the return of the drunken revellers from ashore, but the deck around him seemed to be quiet and empty.

'At fecking last!' muttered O'Malley from just beside his ear. 'You sleep sounder than a drunk parson.'

'He be awake yet?' came the sound of Trevan's voice from the other side of the hammock, his breath laden with rum fumes. 'Ah, that's good.'

'Now, Able,' continued O'Malley from the first side. 'Me and Adam are after giving you a little surprise. You will need to be quick, mind, the boat we came back on will not wait beyond six bells.'

'What... what surprise?' whispered Able, still groggy with sleep.

'Well telling you will not answer!' said Trevan, shocked. 'What manner of surprise would that be? Just close your eyes, and you lay back down.'

'An' be fecking quick!' added O'Malley. 'If the Grunters catch us will be in a world of trouble.'

Able relaxed back in his hammock, and closed his eyes. From beside him came the sound of rustling, accompanied by suppressed drunken laughter from Trevan and O'Malley. The hammock sank lower as a considerable weight was added to it. Able felt the press of a warm body on top of him. He opened his eyes in surprise, and found himself looking into the heavily made up face of a girl.

'Hello there, my lover,' she said, with practiced ease. 'I hear from your mates that you're feeling lonely. We can't have that now, can we?'

*****

Jacob Linfield had nothing but admiration for Emma Robertson's display of horsemanship. He had been pleased that, when he had mentioned the vague suggestion of the horse ride made so many months before, she had readily agreed. The offer had really been directed at the handsome Sutton, but it had been made in an open enough way for him to take advantage of it. Now they were making their way along a narrow trail that ran like a canyon between walls of lofty sugar cane. The ground was slick with red mud, yet Emma, riding side saddle, and her mare had bounded ahead of him. He could only catch the occasional glimpse of her rose coloured ridding habit as it flashed like a distant butterfly from farther up the path.

'My word, but you are an accomplished rider, Miss Emma,' he gasped as he clattered up to where she waited at the top of the rise. 'I know I am in want of practice, but even were that not the case I doubt if I could keep up with you.'

'Thank you, Mr Linfield,' she smiled. 'I have ridden most days since I was a child, and know these paths well. Am I inconveniencing you by going too fast?'

'Perhaps a little,' he said, mopping at his brow.

'Well, we shall go rather slower for the next part,' said Emma. 'You expressed a desire to see a little of our fauna, and the woods ahead have a family of monkeys in residence which we may chance to see if we approach with care. Would you like that?'

'Above all things,' said Linfield, looking where she pointed. 'What manner of trees are those?'

'They are mahogany trees,' said Emma, urging her horse into a walk.

It was cool in the dappled shade of the wood, and Linfield soon found himself surrounded by new and delightful wildlife. Where the canopy thinned there were sunlit glades, draped with flowering vines. Large butterflies were busy among the flowers, and hummingbirds flashed and shimmered in the light. He took such a child-like wonder in all that he saw, gasping at each new discovery, that Emma found it hard not to smile with him.

'Pray, what is that bird there, Miss Emma?' he asked. 'The one above us who calls so insistently.'

'People here call it a blackbird, although my father tells me it is quite different from the one with which you will be familiar in England,' she replied.

'I collect you were born on the island, Miss Emma,' he said. 'Have you ever been home?'

'If by home you mean Scotland, I have not,' she said. 'Home for me is really Melverton. Ah, be still, Mr Linfield! There is your monkey, high in the next tree. Do you see him?'

They watched the animal in companionable silence. To Emma it was charming in an everyday sense, while Jacob watched its antics with open delight. She found herself increasingly looking at her companion rather than at the wildlife. Under the ridiculous straw hat he wore, he did have quite an attractive face, she thought. After a while the monkey slipped away deeper into the wood, and Emma urged her horse back into motion.

'Will you attend Sir Richard's ball on Saturday next, Miss Emma?' asked Linfield.

'We do normally go to the Governor's ball,' she replied. 'But this year may be difficult, given the decline we have had in our relationship with our neighbours. I know that Papa is not minded to attend.'

'The officers of the squadron have all been invited,' said Linfield. 'We will depart for St Lucia shortly afterwards, so it may be the last occasion to see us for a while.'

'Then I shall tell my father we must go,' said Emma, urging her horse into a trot.

They crossed the top of the ridge, passing a boundary stone as they did so, and started to descend through more delightful forest.

'We have just crossed into a neighbouring plantation,' explained Emma. 'I do not normally come this way, but there is a tolerably fine cascade of water you might like to see on this side of the ridge, after which we will return to my father's land.'

'That sounds quite magical, Miss Emma,' said Linfield, entranced by all the beauty around him, not least his young companion.

A little while later they left the trees and skirted once more along the edge of a cane field. This one was being cut by a line of slaves, their machetes flashing in the sun as they worked. Behind the slaves stood the overseers, long whips coiled in their hands. As Linfield looked he saw one of the whips flash through the air. A slave suddenly arched up in pain, and the sound of the crack followed a little while later. Emma looked across at her companion, and saw that his face had been transformed. Gone was the boyish delight in all he saw, replaced by tight lipped fury.

'I apologise, Mr Linfield,' said Emma. 'It was a mistake to come this way. I had not thought that they might be cutting these fields so soon.'

'There is nothing to apologise for, Miss Emma,' said Linfield. 'I am heartily pleased to have witnessed slavery first hand. It shall serve to strengthen me in my resolve to oppose it in all its forms.'

They were close to the end of the line of workers now. The nearest slave looked up at them, his face blank with exhaustion, empty of any emotion. Emma urged her horse to go forward, and after a moment of hesitation Linfield followed. They continued in silence along the track. Emma looked across at her companion, a little concerned.

'Do you still wish to view the cascade, Mr Linfield?' she asked.

'Perhaps on another occasion, Miss Emma,' he replied. 'I take it this track will serve to return us to your father's plantation?'

They were now screened from the line of slaves by uncut sugar cane, and Emma had just begun to relax, when they rounded a fresh turn in the path and came across another open patch of field. Here a wooden tripod had been set up, and a slave had been tied to the uprights. Two overseers were whipping his naked back, while a further group of slaves looked on. The man being whipped appeared to be unconscious, but still the punishment continued, a steady flow of blood dripping from his back and onto the ground.

'Mr Linfield!' cautioned Emma. 'We must ride by. Come on.'

'I agree, this is certainly no sight for a lady to witness,' said Linfield, pulling up his horse and swinging down from the saddle. 'I shall see you back at the house, Miss Emma.' Emma hesitated for a moment, but Linfield brought the flat of his hand down on her horse's rump, and the animal shot off up the path. He watched her depart for a moment, and then ran across till he stood in front of the slave, his arms spread wide to block any further blows.

'In the name of all Christian decency, you will stop this barbaric punishment!' he yelled, his eyes blazing with rage. The two overseers looked at each other, unsure what to do next, while the watching slaves raised their heads with sudden interest.

'What in all damnation are you about, sir?' shouted a furious voice. Linfield turned to see a red faced man on a horse approaching.

'This man is in need of medical attention, and I am a surgeon, sir,' explained Linfield.

'This slave is none of your damned business!' roared the man. 'He is my property, and he will receive the punishment that I have instructed for him. I see you have come here with one of that negro-lover Robertson's brood. You are trespassing, sir! Get the hell off my land, before I have my dogs set on you.'

Chapter 8
Ball

Clay was sitting in a chair in his cabin while he waited for Sutton to join him for their regular morning meeting. This was when his lieutenant would normally update him on the state of the ship and crew. Together they would work through all the dozens of matters, great and small, that governed the life of the little wooden world that was the *Rush*. Their usual pot of coffee waited in its battered pewter pot and Sutton's chair was set for him on the far side of the desk. What was less usual were the three small matching blue books that lay on the desk, together with the canvas package they had come in. Clay started to reread the letter that had accompanied the books once more.

The desk and the two chairs were virtually the only items of furniture that were left in the cabin. Hart had long since arranged the removal of the dining table and chairs. Samuel Yates, the ship's boy that had been Clay's personal servant for two years now, was down on his hands and knees packing the last of his clothes into his sea chest. Clay returned to the letter from his sister Betsey, and read the final paragraph once more. In it she reassured her brother that she was in regular correspondence with Lydia in Bengal, and that she would gladly send her brother's letters on to her within her own. She had confirmed that the first letter he had sent had been despatched, and she would forward any reply when it eventually came. He put down the letter with satisfaction and glanced towards the cabin door. Beyond it was the main deck of the *Rush*, curiously empty now with the crew gone and every movable object cleared away. As if in response to his gaze, someone knocked on the outside of the door.

'Come in,' called Clay. The door swung open, and in came Lieutenant Sutton.

'Ah welcome, John, I was wondering what time it must be,' said Clay. 'With no one manning the ship's bell it is difficult to tell.'

'It is five bells, sir,' replied Sutton, sitting down in the chair. 'Or perhaps we should say half past ten in the morning, as we are shortly to move ashore. You seem very pleased with yourself?'

'I have received a most engaging package from home,' replied Clay as he poured the coffee. 'What do you make of these?' Sutton took one of the proffered books. It was a single slim volume bound in leather. He flipped it open and read from the title page.

'*The Choices of Miss Amelia Grey. A novel in three volumes, by A Lady,*' he read out loud, before looking at his captain with mock gravity. 'May I say how refreshing it is that after so many years of friendship, you still have the power to surprise me, sir. I had never suspected you of being a connoisseur of romantic fiction.'

'Before you are overly censorious, my dear John,' said Clay, 'you should know that what you hold in your hand is the first published work of my sister Betsey. She is the anonymous lady author.'

'God Bless my soul!' exclaimed John, looking at the book

with renewed interest. 'Is she really now?'

'Yes, she has had an inclination to become a writer for some time,' said Clay. 'Her friendship with Lydia Browning was at first based on their mutual love of literature.'

'By Jove,' said Sutton. 'I had no idea. Has Miss Browning been published too, then?'

'Not to my knowledge, no,' replied Clay. 'I understand her aunt and uncle object to her doing so, although if she were to publish anonymously, as my sister has now done, they might never learn of it.'

'Well, I have always considered Miss Clay to be among the cleverest ladies of my acquaintance, but I had no notion that her accomplishments stretched so far,' said Sutton, returning the book to Clay. 'Would you have an objection to my reading her work, once you have done so yourself?'

'By all means,' said Clay with a smile. 'We might develop our connoisseurship of romantic novels together. Now perhaps let us return to the state of the ship.'

'I have tolerably good progress to report where that is concerned,' began Sutton. 'The *Rush* is now empty of everything, including the ballast. It is all in storage in the dockyard. Mr Carver had already completed stripping the ship of the rigging, masts and yards by yesterday evening. All that is left on board now is this desk and chairs, the cabin bulkhead and that chest over there.' Clay followed Sutton's glance towards where Yates added the last of his shirts to the top of the sea chest. He frowned as he looked at his servant.

'Yates, stand up, boy,' he ordered. Yates rose to his feet and turned to look at his captain.

'What is that wriggling in your pocket?' asked Clay. A look of dismay filled the thirteen-year-old's face.

'Please, sir,' he replied. 'It is only William Pitt.'

'William Pitt, in your pocket!' roared Clay. 'Do not presume to make game of me in my own ship, boy.'

'No, sir, that's what I calls him,' said Yates, producing his pet from his jacket and holding it out on a trembling hand. The mouse regarded the two officers through uncertain eyes, and to Yates's huge relief, both Clay and Sutton burst out laughing.

'Who was that volunteer back when we served on the old *Marlborough* who had a pet mouse, sir?' asked Sutton. 'He got flogged for it, I collect.'

'Yes, I remember,' said Clay, looking at the horrified Yates. 'His name was Hewett and he received twelve lashes. Mind you, if I remember aright, there were aggravating circumstances. Did he not allow the mouse to escape during divine service, and in his haste to recapture the animal he dropped the newspaper he had been reading?' Clay let Yates tremble a little longer, before he pronounced judgement.

'I will permit you to keep Mr Pitt,' he said, 'on condition that you undertake to keep him properly caged. Also you are not to appear on duty with the mouse on your person. Is that clear?'

'Yes, sir,' said Yates with a grin of relief. 'Thank you, sir.'

'So, Mr Sutton,' said Clay, taking a sip from his coffee. 'Now we have resolved the secure housing of the Prime Minister, we might return to the state of the ship. When does she get handed over to the dockyard?'

'Noon today, sir,' said the lieutenant. 'Once we are finished here, I have a party on deck ready to remove the last of your furniture and clothes. The dockyard will then careen her fully and renew her copper. Once that is done they will warp her against the gun wharf, and bring on board her new armament. That will all take them a few days, as they need to fit slides for the carronades, and the gun tackle fixings are different from the gun carriages we are familiar with. With a following wind, we should have her back by Thursday, ready to load everything aboard her once more. I believe we will have her ready for sea with the crew back on board shortly after the Governor's ball on Saturday.'

'What of the men?' asked Clay. 'Where will they be quartered while the work goes on?'

'The dockyard has a spare sail loft where they can sling their hammocks, and we can use the dockyard kitchens to feed them. Officers are to be billeted at that tavern we went to celebrate your promotion, the Munro Castle, where I have secured rooms for you as well.'

'This is really capital work, John,' said Clay. 'I am most impressed. You seem to have it all arranged very well.'

'Thank you, sir,' said Sutton.

'How are the men behaving, with all these changes?' asked Clay.

'Passing well for now,' said Sutton. 'I believe they rather enjoy the novelty of being ashore, although I plan not to let them be idle. Oh, and Josh Hawke has requested a transfer. I have arranged for him to join the *Princess Charlotte*.' Clay was on the verge of asking how this convenient move had been engineered, but thought better of it.

'That is good news. I am sure that it will be for the best,' he said.

'I think so too, sir,' said Sutton. 'And last, but by no means least, I have this morning arranged some carriages for seven bells in the dog watch on Saturday to take the officers from the Munro Castle to the governor's ball.'

'Oh yes, the ball,' groaned Clay. 'I really do struggle in such gatherings.'

'Come now, sir, that is precisely what you said about dinning on the *Earl of Warwick* last year,' said Sutton. 'You remember, the night you first met Miss Browning. With luck, Saturday may prove similarly diverting.'

*****

General Sir Richard Nugent, Governor of Barbados, was well aware of the Royal Navy's obsession with punctuality. Having issued an invitation for a ball due to commence at eight o'clock in the evening, it came as no surprise to him or to Lady Nugent that of the twenty or so guests who had arrived as the clock struck the hour, every one of them was either a naval or a marine officer.

'Admiral Caldwell, what an unexpected pleasure,' he said, with a glassy stare towards his wife. 'I see you and your officers have seized the field of battle. Again.'

'Sir Richard, your ladyship,' beamed Caldwell. His freshly laundered periwig bobbed towards his hosts. 'Doubtless the officers of the garrison will eventually dribble in to even matters up, what? In the meantime may I name some of my officers to you? Captain Parker you know I think, but you will yet to have had the pleasure of meeting Commander Alexander Clay of the *Rush*.'

'Ah yes, the gentleman who brought in that captured French frigate earlier this year,' rumbled Sir Richard. 'Upon my word, that was a damned fine show, Clay.'

'Thank you very much, Sir Richard,' said Clay, colouring a little at the praise. 'Might I introduce you and Lady Nugent to some of my officers?'

From long years of practice the governor was used to being presented to rows of junior naval officers, and managed a smile and a nod with good grace as the stream of names flowed past him, until he was introduced to the *Rush*'s purser.

'Did you say Charles Faulkner?' he said, eyeing his guest with interest. 'Sir Christopher Faulkner's boy? I believe we may be acquainted already.'

'Sir Christopher is my father, sir, but I am not sure...' began the purser.

'Yes, yes,' persisted the governor. 'I seldom forget a face. Now let me see... Ah! I have it! You are a member of Whites, where we have played at cards before. In fact I seem to recall having bested you quite soundly in many a skirmish across the baize, what?'

'Of course, Sir Richard,' said Faulkner with a weak smile. 'Good to renew your acquaintance. Your ladyship.'

'I always thought there was more to our Mr Faulkner than met the eye,' muttered Sutton into Macpherson's ear

'Aye, me too,' replied the Scot. 'But did you ever truly suspect him of being a rake?'

Once the introductions had been completed, the officers made their way through into the residency's ballroom. An expanse of wooden floor spread out before them, the deep burgundy of the polished mahogany contrasting pleasingly with the pale lemon of the walls. Above their heads hung a double line of chandeliers, their blazing candles already adding their heat to the warm tropical air. Down one side of the room was a series of glazed double doors that looked out onto a veranda, and the residence's garden beyond. All stood open to allow the sea breeze in. The wall opposite was lined with tables heavily laden with food and drink, while at the far end of the room was arranged a small orchestra, mainly dressed in black, but with four brightly coloured figures in their midst. Clay looked at them with interest.

'You have doubtless recognised the *Agrius*'s little troop of musicians?' said Captain Parker at his elbow. He was a dark haired man, almost swarthy in complexion, with eyes that were close to black. 'Sir Richard was struggling to find enough players on the island, so I volunteered them. I must say that carrying them on the ship's books was one of Captain Follett's more inspired innovations. They play well, and their music is a most pleasant diversion.'

'Indeed, sir, we took them from a French privateer in the channel last year, together with a large black tomcat,' said Clay.

'You mean Robespierre?' said Parker. 'I did think it a little strange that the ship's cat had such a French name. Would you like him back on the *Rush*?' Clay thought for a moment, remembering the numerous times he had had to remove the cat from his cot late at night, and all the hairs he had found on his uniforms.

'I believe the hands think he brings good fortune to the ship, sir,' he replied. 'I would not want to interfere with that. You know how superstitious the men can be.'

'Champagne, sir?' asked a footman, his white powdered wig contrasting with his black face. Parker and Clay both helped themselves from the tray.

'Damnation to the French,' said Parker, clinking his glass with Clay's. 'Hmm, this is rather tolerable.'

'I am always surprised by the facility with which champagne is to be obtained, in spite of our having been at war with France for over three years now, sir,' said Clay, sipping at his wine. Parker looked surprised.

'Do you truly not know where this batch came from?' he asked. 'Why, it was on board that brig you captured. Once the prize court had lawfully condemned it, Sir Richard pounced and purchased every bottle. The admiral was furious.'

Parker and Clay were having to raise their voices to speak now as the ballroom filled with ever more guests. The blue of the navy no longer predominated. Looking about him, Clay could see plenty of scarlet jacketed army officers from the garrison, and a growing number of civilians, the men mostly in black coats, but some in green or various shades of blue. Many of the women were in white, but others had dresses in all of the colours of the rainbow. Most of the gowns were cut to conform to the latest European fashion, the material gathered into a high waist with a coloured ribbon, and the sleeves short and puffed, leaving a tantalising cylinder of bare arm above the wearer's long white gloves.

Two young ladies flowed past the captains as they stood talking. One had on a white dress with sky blue ribbons, the other was all in very pale yellow. Both had added a spray of tropical bird feathers to their piled up hair, and the one in blue and white favoured Clay with a dazzling smile. For a moment he was reminded of Lydia, the girl's dark hair and blue eyes were so very similar, and he automatically smiled back. The ladies swept on, leaving Clay with an empty sense of loss.

'I think I may try a little of the food, sir,' he said to Parker. 'Will you excuse me?'

*****

'Ladies and gentlemen!' called the Master of Ceremonies with a voice that might have reached the masthead in a gale. 'Pray take your places for the first dance, which shall be The Plough Boy's Reel.' This announcement was followed by an instant buzz of anticipation. Those ladies with partners were led out onto the floor, while those without scolded their mothers over their failure to obtain the services of one of the choicer gentlemen.

Two lines formed down the centre of the room, one of ladies, the other of men. Both rows tweaked at their clothing, and smiled about them a little awkwardly, aware of the unbroken circuit of watching guests around the ballroom. The Master of Ceremonies strode down between the couples, straightening the dressing of the lines with the pedantry of a sergeant major. When he was finally satisfied the dancing began.

It was an uncomplicated routine with which to start the ball and the sets were well understood by the dancers. Alternate couples crisscrossed the floor, while those on either side of them stood still so as to form human poles around which those dancing could turn. When the set was complete, the roles were reversed, with human poles becoming animated and former dancers frozen into stillness.

The dance may have been performed well, but the ladies that had failed to obtain partners observed the efforts of their more favoured colleagues with waspish hostility.

'Oh, do look at the lack of poise with which Miss Morgan moves,' hissed one from behind her fan. 'Why, even old Mrs Galbraith with her truss is a superior dancer.'

'And what an ill choice of colour Miss Brown has selected for her dress,' replied her companion. 'What consequence her figure may have, is quite lost by that revolting shade of green.'

As the dancing continued, the party of the *Rush*'s officers gathered at one end of the room found covetous eyes upon them. Like sharks around a wounded mariner, various wives of plantation owners closed in on the group, intent on

obtaining dance partners for their daughters. Charles
Faulkner, the broadcloth of his uniform picked out for its
superior weave by those with a nose for money was an early
victim. He was followed shortly after by Macpherson,
conspicuous with his dashing sideburns and scarlet tunic.
Linfield and Sutton had escaped the first onslaught by
locking themselves into an animated conversation with the
recently arrived Lieutenant Munro. Only the corpulent
Joseph Appleby was left, rejected as an undesirably gross
figure to pair with their delicate offspring. This was a shame,
for the *Rush*'s sailing master would have been a very willing
dancer, if only he had been approached.

Towards the end of the first dance, a ripple of movement
traversed the room, centred on a group that had just entered
the ballroom. Conversation faltered and died around them,
causing the Master of Ceremonies to peer over the heads of
the dancers to see what was amiss.

'Well really,' said a florid lady to her daughter standing
nearby. 'What are they doing here?' Linfield broke off from
his conversation with Munro, and craned his neck to see
what had caused the commotion. Walking towards them, in
the middle of a ring of turned backs came the figure of
George Robertson. On his right arm was his oldest daughter
Elizabeth, looking grim. On his left arm and close to tears
was Emma.

'Come on,' he said to Sutton. 'There are two damsels in
need of saving. If you will dance with Miss Robertson, I will
partner Miss Emma.' Sutton looked over at the group,
unsure of what to do. The hostility towards them in the room
was palpable. 'Come on, John,' urged Linfield. 'I suggested to
the poor girl that they should come tonight, against her
inclination. Surely common decency requires us to intervene.
If I can't persuade you to stir, I shall have to do so alone.'

'What's this hesitation, John,' said Munro, with a smile. 'You were never so shy facing the French.'

'I should happily opt for a shot-torn deck over the risk of exposing myself to the censure of the company at a ball,' muttered the lieutenant. He hesitated for a moment longer and then gave in. 'Oh, very well, Jacob, lead me into the lion's den.'

'Mr Robertson, Miss Robertson and Miss Emma; a very good evening to you all,' said Linfield, as if the resolute wall of guests' backs around them was quite normal. 'I trust I find you all in good health?'

'Tolerably well, Mr Linfield, I thank you,' replied Robertson. 'And how are you and Mr Sutton enjoying your enforced time here in Bridgetown while your wee ship is put to rights?'

'Mr Sutton, I know, has been somewhat harassed by all the work involved in restoring the *Rush*,' replied the surgeon, 'But happily that is now complete. I must thank you for your hospitality this week sir, and for the loan of Miss Emma. She took me on a most diverting ride and introduced me to some of the island's fauna. My only regret is that I shall not be able to repeat the experience. The squadron is held on notice to depart now. We shall go the moment the army arrives from Jamaica.' Emma was still too upset to speak, but she smiled in acknowledgement with downcast eyes and her face blushed a little. She wore a dress of apricot silk, and Linfield thought how pleasingly the colour in her cheeks contrasted with the warm tone of the material.

'I did hear of your ride over my neighbour's land and of your intervention in the punishment of one of his slaves,' said Robertson. 'He sent me a rather furious note threatening legal action, which I must say I regard as pleasing progress. The last time we spoke he swore that he would never communicate with me again!' The men joined in his hearty laughter, while the ladies fanned themselves and smiled.

'May we advance to more pressing matters, sir?' asked the surgeon. 'Mr Sutton and I were wondering if either of your daughters had yet made any commitments as to the next dance.' Robertson smiled at the two young officers, and indicated the turned backs with a wave of his hand.

'I believe I can confirm that no prior engagements have yet been formalised,' he said, just loud enough for those around them to hear.

'Then might I request the pleasure of this next dance, Miss Emma,' said Linfield, bowing his head towards the younger daughter.

'Why yes, Mr Linfield,' she said, smiling with relief. 'That would be most acceptable.'

'And might I have the pleasure of this next dance with you, Miss Robertson?' said Sutton, speaking for the first time. Elizabeth looked at her father with concern.

'Go ahead, my child,' he said. 'I will be quite fine on my own.'

*****

'What a very poor figure John Sutton cuts with that rather plain girl he is dancing with,' said Lieutenant Windham of the *Agrius*, with an air of satisfaction. 'They really are a most undistinguished pair.' He was lounging against one of the pillars on the veranda in the now dark garden. Golden light spilt out from the large open windows, through one of which he could see the dancing in the ballroom. Sutton and Elizabeth had just completed their set and were processing down the outside of the double line of dancers. As they disappeared from view, Windham glanced across at his companion, visible in the shadows only by the glow from the tip of his cigar.

'Have you made any progress with him?' asked Windham, his words a little slurred. 'Have you discovered anything useful?' The man took a long draw on his cigar before he answered. The nose and one eye of Charles Faulkner were briefly visible in the red glow.

'Not a damned thing, Nicholas,' he replied. 'I am frankly surprised. He is not a very close cove, don't you know. His character is tolerably open, with very little conceit. Are you quite sure he is guilty of what you accuse him?'

'Oh I know he is,' said Windham. 'He and Clay had a complete want of respect for my uncle. They both knew that once the ship reached Bridgetown, he would have broken Clay like a straw.'

'But how can you be so decided in your opinion that there was foul play?' queried Faulkner. 'You were not even present when Captain Follett fell.'

'No, I was down on the main deck, doing my duty at the guns,' said Windham. 'Then Clay came down, interfering with everything as usual, demanding to know why the guns were not fired more briskly. He sent a midshipman up with a message to the captain telling him to break off the engagement while we reordered ourselves. Naturally Uncle Percy was not going to tolerate that sort of damned impertinence. He sent the same fellow straight back, telling him we fight on, whatever the Wondrous Clay thought, damn his eyes. I saw the look of utter contempt on his face. "You carry on here," he said, and then stormed off up to the quarterdeck.' Windham drained his glass, and looked around for a refill.

'So why do you not hold that it was Clay who killed your

uncle?' asked Faulkner.

'Oh, he has more low cunning than that,' said Windham, his face red with anger. 'He used his creature Sutton to do it for him. Probably didn't have the bottom to do it himself.' Windham looked about him once more. 'Where are all the damned servants? Ahoy! What has a man got to do to get a bloody drink here?'

'We will go in directly, old boy,' said Faulkner. 'First tell me how you know all this to be so?' Windham looked about him before answering.

'Because, my dear Charles, I have found a witness,' he said. 'One of the powder monkeys on the *Agrius* who was there when the mast came down. He says Sutton ordered the afterguard over to the larboard side to clear the wreckage, which left him all alone on the same side that my uncle had fallen from. He remembers Sutton looked over the broken rail, then he drew his sword to cut away at some strands of rigging. He thought nothing of it at the time, given everyone was hacking away to free the ship of the fallen mast.'

'That is pretty thin, Nicholas,' said Faulkner, shaking his head. 'The word of a ship's boy won't answer against that of an officer, and in any case what did he truly see? Lieutenant Sutton cutting free some wreckage.' Windham drew Faulkner close to him, till the purser could smell the alcohol fumes on his breath.

'That is why, old boy, I need you to come up with something more incriminating,' he said, his voice thick with menace. 'My family were very generous to yours over your debts. I don't think you would want the attention of your new friends brought to your colourful past, would you? They might wonder if you were really the sort of person to have put in charge of the ship's wherewithal, what?'

A Sloop of War

*****

In the ballroom, Emma Robertson was growing ever fonder of Jacob Linfield. They were now dancing for the fourth time in a row, and as they whirled around one another, she was able to study his face. It was the only unmoving object in her vision, against the kaleidoscopic backdrop of the ballroom moving past. When they had first met she had been drawn to John Sutton's dark colouring, but now that she was forced to take notice of the fair haired surgeon, without his straw hat, she saw that he was really quite handsome too. The pale blue eyes that held her gaze were kind, and his mouth carried a broad smile of simple pleasure in the dance, much as it had as he watched the butterflies on their ride together. With another turn they were back at their places in the line, puffing with effort and grinning at each other while the other couples completed their sets.

With a long final chord the orchestra brought the dance to an end. The men all bowed to their partners, while the ladies dropped into curtsies, their dresses spreading around them on the floor like opening flowers. A polite patter of applause came from those watching the dance, and the lines broke up as couples went this way and that. Jacob leant forward to take Emma's hand, and helped her up from her curtsy.

'My word, Mr Linfield, much as I am enjoying your society, you must let me defer the pleasure of another dance for a moment,' she gasped as she fanned herself. 'It is never cool here in Barbados, but with all this press of persons, it is really too warm to be endured.' Linfield looked up at the blazing chandeliers that hung from the ceiling of the ballroom.

Philip K. Allan

'I fear the candles are not helping matters either. Allow me to procure for you some refreshment,' he said, waving over a footman with a loaded tray of drinks. 'What will you have?' Emma accepted some fruit juice, and he took a glass of wine.

'Shall we see if a turn about the garden will not answer to restore our composure,' he suggested, once they had finished their drinks. He indicated the open double doors that led out onto the veranda, and through which a delicious sea breeze could be felt on their faces. 'Unless you fear you may get a chill, Miss Emma?' he added.

'Well, you are the medical man, Mr Linfield,' she said with a mischievous twinkle. 'Do you council me against it?'

'Not in the least,' laughed the surgeon as he led her towards the door. 'If sea air were in anyway a harmful vapour, I would have a decidedly full sick bay to deal with.'

Outside in the garden they both breathed in the warm tropical air with delight. The moon had now risen, dusting the waves of Carlisle Bay with silver. Behind them the noise and light of the ball spilt out into the night through the open windows. Ahead of them the garden was velvety dark and inviting, full of the heady scent of tropical flowers, and the rustle of the breeze amid the tree tops.

'When I arrived here earlier, I believe I saw a pathway over here,' he said, holding out his arm. 'Shall we venture out and see where it leads?' Emma linked a gloved arm through his, and they set off into the night.

'Mr Linfield,' she said after a while. 'I must tell you how grateful I am for your intervention when we arrived. I knew that my father's actions had made us disliked, but I had but little notion of the depth of the contempt in which we were held. I was willing him to turn about and leave, but he can be

162

a most determined man.'

'And are you now pleased that he was so persistent, Miss Emma?' he asked, his face invisible in the dark, but the tone of his voice clear.

'Yes I believe I am, Mr Linfield,' she replied, enjoying the warm contact of his arm. 'I will confess that immediately before you approached us, I had been hoping that the ground might open and swallow me up, but I am now content that it remained solid.'

'As am I,' he said. 'It is strange, but I had told Mr Sutton that I was but an indifferent dancer, yet with you as my partner I felt distinctly fleeter of foot than I can remember. You really do have many talents, Miss Emma.'

'Really, Mr Linfield?' she replied. 'I always thought of myself as generally deficient in the accomplishments that a young lady of quality should possess.'

'By no means, Miss Emma,' said the surgeon. 'You are a most able horsewomen, you dance very well, and you are agreeable and quick in discourse.'

'That is very obliging of you to say so. But I cannot help noting that you did not mention my performance of attitudes, such as the one I demonstrated when we first met, Mr Linfield?' she queried.

'Ah, well, yes....' he stuttered. 'I am, eh, perhaps not the best person to comment on refinements such as those.' Emma laughed aloud at his obvious discomfort.

'Shall I let you into a secret, Mr Linfield?' she whispered. 'It is my father who is chiefly fond of seeing them performed. I believe it is because my late mother was much taken by them, and it reminds him of her. Between us, I think they are rather absurd.'

'Oh, thank God,' he said. 'That is a relief.'

'Miss Emma,' he continued, after a few moments of companionable silence. 'It has been difficult for me to understand how distressing the social isolation that has followed on from your father's act of emancipation must be for you and your sister. Perhaps after tonight, having witnessed the cruel way your family were treated, I can comprehend it a little better. But I need to inform you that I believe in my heart that what your father has done is right. Oh I know that he was motivated by other notions than human decency, but I still hold the course he has followed to be the correct moral one, even if it was not the easiest one for you and your sister.'

'Thank you for your candour, Mr Linfield,' she replied, her voice serious for once. 'My father had warned me that you were somewhat hot in your views on the matter of slavery. Indeed, you demonstrated that quite fully when you intervened with that poor wretch when we rode together. If I may be frank in my turn, I would have thought your views absurd a year ago. I have spent my whole life among sugar plantations. To me slaves were as necessary a part of such enterprises as cattle are to a farmer. In many ways I had regarded our slaves in a not dissimilar light. To my mind they were never persons in any meaningful sense of that word.'

'Miss Emma, I must ask if you still hold such views now?' he asked, his voice neutral.

'No, Mr Linfield, I confess my ideas on the matter have changed somewhat,' she said. 'I will not deceive you. I am still far from being the committed abolitionist, but perhaps I have travelled a little way along that path. Would you like to hear my present views?'

'Very much so,' he said, 'if you do not consider it overbearing of me to enquire?'

'By no means,' she said, trying to read his expression in the dark. 'I know how important a matter this is to you.' They walked on a little farther, becoming silent as they passed another couple.

'I had assumed that when my father freed our slaves,' she continued, once they were alone, 'they would slide into a life of dissolution. The wages that my father paid them would be squandered on drink and vice, if only through ignorance of any better manner of living. In some cases this has happened, but most of them have not followed that route. The land that my father made available to them has been divided intelligently among them. They have arranged it into plots where they can grow vegetables, and some of them now even keep chickens. They have built themselves dwellings as well, together with a little furniture. In many ways they seem to be establishing themselves into a well regulated community. One couple have even approached the local parson with a view to formalising their relationship into marriage.'

'Have they indeed?' he said. 'That is encouraging. Will you show me this community when I return next to Barbados, Miss Emma? I should very much like to see it for myself.'

'Why, yes, if you wish me to,' she replied. They were now deep into the garden. It was some time since they had last seen any other couples enjoying the night air. Emma stopped in a patch of moonlit ground between two stands of trees and turned to face her companion.

'Mr Linfield,' she asked. 'There is something I too must ask you. Was it only pity for my situation that made you approach me earlier tonight?'

'Oh Emma,' he said, his voice suddenly passionate. 'My actions were not driven by pity. Had you been the most

165

popular lady here tonight, I would still have wanted to dance only with you. I admire you very much indeed, and I hope you now regard me with a little more favour than before.'

'Jacob, of course I do,' she said. He looked into her face, and saw she was crying, the teardrops pearls in the moonlight. He tentatively took hold of her other hand, and gently, little by little, drew her into his arms. Neither of them had any experience of this situation. With great uncertainty at first, but soon with growing confidence they kissed.

Chapter 9
Convoy

'Back home at last,' said Appleby. He spread his arms wide as if to embrace all of his fellow officers gathered around the wardroom table. The sailing master of the *Rush* had long arms and he seemed to fill the space as if a large bird had suddenly opened its wings. To his fellow officers it served only to emphasise how cramped and dark their accommodation was when compared to the rooms they had now relinquished in the Moro Castle.

'Back home, and yet soon to be on our way, to judge from the armada gathered in the bay,' said Faulkner. 'Do you have any more intelligence for us yet, John?' Sutton looked up from the game of backgammon he was playing with Macpherson and shook his head.

'None yet, but I trust I shall have some soon. The captain is away at a conference on board the flagship now, and with the *Rush* fully restored I hope we shall shortly play our part in whatever is afoot.'

'Do you have any notion to which part of St Lucia we will be heading?' asked Macpherson, rattling the dice in the cup and spilling them onto the board. 'Ah, double four. Excellent.'

Philip K. Allan

'All I know for certain is that we are to operate alongside the *Agrius*, Tom,' replied Sutton. 'Beyond that I have no certain knowledge. My turn I believe.'

'Yet the arrival of all those troop ships from Jamaica in the night must signify a departure of some immediacy?' persisted Faulkner.

'Perhaps, Charles, but if so the captain has not yet taken me into his confidence. Seven again for me, Tom.' Several turns of backgammon passed in companionable silence, before Faulkner spoke again.

'I am intrigued by this game you play,' he said, indicating the board. 'Tell me, when does one place a wager?' The two players exchanged glances.

'This is principally a game of skill, Charles,' Macpherson replied. 'It needs no pecuniary element to give it savour.'

'You don't say?' said Faulkner. 'Yet the main activity would seem to be the casting of dice. Surely it is therefore also a game of hazard?'

'There is a degree of chance, for sure,' conceded the Scotsman. 'But over a run of games that will even itself out. In backgammon the more skilful player almost always wins.'

'I regretfully have to agree,' said Sutton. 'Tom soundly beats me eight times out of ten. I for one am pleased we play only for honour. Have you loaded these dice, Tom? I have thrown yet another seven.'

'Does it lose its interest for you if it is not played for money, Charles?' asked Macpherson. Faulkner looked a little awkward at this.

'Not entirely, no,' he replied. 'Although I will concede that I have found that a financial risk does add materially to the ability of a game to divert.'

'Did Sir Richard not say that you are a member at

Whites?' asked Sutton, his eyes fixed on the board as he moved his counters.'

'I was once a member, but that was some time ago. I have not been back there for several years,' said Faulkner. Appleby whistled at this from his end of the table.

'From reputation they game with some proper lucre there. Did you ever witness any fortunes change hands, Charles?' he asked. The purser was about to answer when Linfield came in to the wardroom, carrying his large straw hat.

'Ah, Jacob,' said Faulkner. 'Have you made yet another visit to Melverton? You must prepare yourself for them to cease. The captain is aboard the flagship with Admiral Caldwell as we speak, doubtless learning of our fate.'

'No, not this time, Charles,' said Linfield. 'With our departure imminent I was making some calls to friends here in Bridgetown. I did have coffee with Mr Robertson at Milton's, however.'

'How did you find him?' asked Sutton.

'He is very well, thank you, John,' said Linfield. 'He had a most unexpected visitor this morning. A fellow plantation owner by the name of Walker came to call. Apparently he was so ashamed by the manner in which the company treated the Robertsons at the governor's ball that he has decided to renew contact with the family. Is that not splendid?'

'That is very good news. And was Mr Robertson accompanied by the lovely Miss Emma?' asked Sutton with a smile.

'Regrettably not,' replied the surgeon.

'Is that the lady you spent most of the night of the ball dancing with, Jacob?' asked Appleby.

Philip K. Allan

'Yes, that was Miss Emma, although I might not term it quite like that. We danced not above six or seven times,' replied Linfield evasively, twisting the straw hat in his hands. Sutton and Appleby continued to look at Linfield, waiting to see if he would say any more. A dry cough sounded from the other side of the table.

'I believe it is your turn, John,' said Macpherson, the game very much shaping in his favour. Sutton picked up his cup and had begun to shake the dice when there was a knock on the wardroom door.

'Come in,' he called. The door opened and Midshipman Preston stepped into the wardroom.

'Mr Wardle's compliments, sir, and the captain's barge has just shoved off from the flagship,' he said. 'Mr Wardle also asked me to say that he believes the boat is making for the larboard side of the ship, so that no ceremony will be required to greet his return.'

'Please give Mr Wardle my compliments, and tell him that I will be up directly,' replied Sutton. 'Mr Appleby, you had better come too. If he has orders he will want a course to be laid off for sure. My apologies, Tom, we will have to carry on our game some other time.' The two officers hurried out, followed shortly after by Linfield who needed to see how his few patients were doing in the sick bay. That left Faulkner and Macpherson as the only two officers in the wardroom.

'Perhaps I might take Mr Sutton's place in the game?' asked Faulkner, moving across into the vacant chair opposite the marine officer.

'By all means,' said Macpherson. 'But let me set the board up afresh. I would not wish my worst enemy to adopt the hopeless position that the good lieutenant has got himself into.' With practiced ease the Scotsman swept up the pieces,

170

and arranged them again on the board. 'Shall I acquaint you with the manner of play, Charles?' he asked.

'If you will,' said Faulkner. 'I have had the benefit of watching you and Mr Sutton, but I have doubtless missed much.' Macpherson paused for a moment, as if gathering his thoughts, but when he spoke it was not to explain any rules.

'You recall that earlier I implied backgammon is not played for money,' he said. 'I was not being entirely truthful with you, for it can be. Perhaps it might have been more accurate if I had said that I no longer choose to play the game for money. Oh, I could do right enough, and doubtless I would make a handsome return playing against the likes of Mr Sutton, but alas, I know it would not end there.'

'I see,' said Faulkner. 'So I collect that have you have played the game for money in the past?'

'I have, Charles,' the marine officer said, 'obsessively so at one time. I have found in my life that there are certain persons who have appetites that can never be fully sated, no matter how they may gorge themselves. There are plenty in the service who have such a weakness for drink, for example. My brother serves in a John Company regiment in India, and tells me there are many among his men who are quite enslaved to the milk of the poppy. The indulgence that once had possession of me was playing backgammon for money. But now that I know from bitter experience that I cannot restrain myself within modest and temperate limits, I am resolved not to wager a farthing. I now play purely for pleasure.'

'Thank you for your candour with me, Tom,' said Faulkner.

'I am not candid with you for any desire to confess my failings, Charles,' said Macpherson. 'I do so because I believe you and I may be fellow travellers.' Faulkner looked at him with surprise.

'Is it really so obvious?' he asked.

'Aye, I think that it is,' said Macpherson. 'It has always been clear from your demeanour and your dress that you are not the normal run of purser to be found in the service. Add to that the rather indiscrete manner in which Sir Richard greeted you at his ball, and the rest is not difficult to fathom. No the really interesting question is not the detail about your past, but why you have chosen to make such a secret of it?'

'Can you not tell?' asked Faulkner. 'It is not chiefly that I feel any shame in my past, although that is part of it. You have me at a disadvantage where candour is concerned, Tom,' Faulkner said. 'Such a failing as you describe might be tolerated in a marine officer rather more easily than in a purser, with responsibility for the financial running of a man-of-war.'

'That is true,' conceded the Scotsman. 'Is it that which the creature Windham holds over you?'

'How the damned hell do you know...' the purser stuttered. Macpherson chuckled at his discomfort.

'Do you not know that marine officers are worse than old wives upon the village green when it comes to their love of gossip?' he said, holding up a reassuring hand. 'And William Munro of the *Agrius* is a particular friend of mine.' There was an awkward pause while Faulkner took all this in, after which Macpherson carried on.

'Charles, you have not asked for my counsel, but if it's not too overbearing I would give it to you anyway,' he said. 'You are a fine purser. Your record in the service is good. As far as I can see, you no longer gamble. If you could bring yourself to be a wee bit more frank with the captain and your brother officers, I believe you might well find that this Windham fellow would lose much of the grip he has upon you.'

*****

On the deck above Faulkner and Macpherson's heads, Clay took off his heavy full dress coat with relief. He handed it together with his hat and sword to Yates, and sank into the chair behind his desk. Opposite him in the main cabin of the *Rush* sat Sutton and Appleby, both eager to discover the outcome of his meeting on board the flagship. Through the spread of glass behind their commander's back they could see the waters of Carlisle Bay, quite full of shipping now. Long lines of troopships swung at anchor close in to Bridgetown. Farther out was a single row of warships, a combination of hulking ships of the line, their big rounded hulls squat and heavy, and graceful frigates with tall, delicate masts. Dotted across the bay were many small, insect-like boats, moving between the various vessels.

'It was quite the gathering,' said Clay as he leafed through his notes. 'I cannot recall when I last saw so much gold braid in one place. Besides the admiral and Captain Miller, Parker and myself, there were the captains of the *Princess Charlotte*, the *Majestic*, the *Beaulieu*, the *Madras*, Totty of the *Alfred* plus a couple of others. As for the army, there were even more of them. General Abercromby freshly arrived from Jamaica of course, together with a veritable herd of colonels and majors, all of them spoiling for action. Oh, and Sir Richard with some of his aides. I tell you for crowds, Bartholomew fair ain't in it.'

'So are we on the move against St Lucia at last?' asked his lieutenant.

'Indeed we are, Mr Sutton,' confirmed Clay. 'We set sail at

dawn tomorrow. And if Mr Appleby would be good enough to spread out that chart, I will outline the plan of action.' He moved the inkstand from his desk to one side, making enough space for the master to unroll the map.

'Now, here is our friend St Lucia, of course,' he said, indicating an egg shaped island about thirty miles north to south, and perhaps half that wide. 'There are only two places that are fortified to resist assault. The first is the principal city, Castries, up here on the northwest coast. It will be to the attack on Castries that the bulk of the expedition will direct itself. The admiral and most of the squadron will descend on the coast and land the army, who will then invest the city, while the fleet bottle up the seaward side. Is that all clear so far?'

'Perfectly, sir,' said Sutton. Appleby nodded in agreement.

'Excellent,' said Clay. 'Now to our part in the enterprise. The second fortified place is right down here on the southern coast, the bottom of the egg if you will. Do you see this peninsula here?' Clay tapped the chart with his finger, and both men leant forward to look at the map more closely.

'Vieux Fort,' read Appleby out loud. 'I am no scholar of French but I deduce that means old fort?'

'Bravo, Mr Appleby,' said Clay. 'At the end of the promontory is a small fortress that dominates the town of Vieux Fort at its feet, and the waters to either side of the peninsula. We will operate under the command of Captain Parker of the *Agrius*, and we will escort a small force there under the command of a Colonel... ah Gordon,' he concluded, referring to his notes.

'What manner of force does Colonel Gordon command, sir?' asked Sutton.

'I do not have the particulars here, Mr Sutton,' said Clay, 'but I do know its general character. It is a mixed force of infantry and some engineers, together with a small siege train. It has all been fitted into four of the transporters, so I doubt that it can be much above a thousand men.'

'Do we know the detail of our role yet, sir?' asked Appleby.

'We are to escort our four troop transporters to St Lucia, enter the bay the lies to the west of the Vieux Fort peninsula where there are suitable beaches convenient for the landing of troops,' replied Clay. 'Once the army are established on shore, our task then will be to provide what support Colonel Gordon deems he may require that will tend to the success of the expedition. Perhaps our marines, a shore party to help with the siege and I have pledged some gunners to man the siege train. When we have seized Vieux Fort, and the general has captured Castries, the rest of the island should capitulate as easy as kiss my hand. Any further questions?'

'No, sir,' said Sutton. 'That all seems clear for now. The primary step is for us to be ready for a prompt departure.'

'Precisely so, Mr Sutton,' said Clay. 'Mr Appleby, kindly have the relevant sailing instructions prepared for tomorrow. Gentlemen, we are part of a powerful strike force, we have a prime crew, and at long last a ship with a creditably clean hull. The French on St Lucia will shortly be in receipt of what I trust shall be the rudest of shocks.'

*****

In all the excitement of the expedition's departure, Clay had forgotten that the next day was a Sunday. But not withstanding their captain's memory, the rhythm of the ship swept on as steady and predictable as the motion of the planets. Because it was Sunday, the crew of the *Rush*, along with every other crew throughout the navy, had plum duff for lunch; and because it was Sunday, they had 'make and mend' in the afternoon that followed. The bare minimum of hands that were needed to sail the ship, which was a much easier task now that her newly coppered hull slipped so readily through the water, had been posted after lunch. They had only to keep her on station exactly two cables distance behind the *Agrius*, and watch for the approach of any enemy. The four heavily laden troop transporters could be seen by anyone who cared to look, wallowing along in an untidy gaggle close under the lee of the two warships. The rest of the fleet had diverged from them all morning, and was now only visible as a distant forest of mastheads, the hulls of the ships having slipped below the horizon.

All of which left the rest of the men free from duty. The afternoon sun was warm, the trade wind fresh. As a result the forecastle of the *Rush* was as crowded and as noisy as an Arabian bazaar. The foremast rigging was alive with clouds of drying clothes, while most of the men had also taken the opportunity to unwind their pigtails, and wash their hair too. Trevan was the owner of a much admired head of hair, the pigtail of which reached to his waist. Freed from its normal constraint, it billowed free in the wind.

'You still be teaching Able his letters there, Rosie?' he asked, looking up from the piece of scrimshaw he was working on.

'That I am, Adam,' replied Rosso. 'And he is making very pleasing progress. He may even pass for a scholar by the time I have finished with him.' Trevan looked at the piece of paper Rosso and Sedgwick were bent over, and puffed his cheeks out in wonder.

'How you make any sense of all them squiggles is beyond

me,' he said, his head angled to one side like a chicken. 'I can make out them letters as is in my name, like, but all the other ones? God bless my soul, no!'

'I could teach you too, you know, Adam, if it was something you wanted,' suggested Rosso to his friend.

'A vynn'ta y skrifa Kernewek, Rosie?' he asked in his native Cornish. 'Now, let me see you set that down in a right and proper fashion.'

'All right, Adam, you win,' said Rosso laughing with him, before returning to his more willing student.

'Now then, Able, let's try some simple words,' he said, looking about himself for inspiration. The mass of multi-coloured clothing flapped over his head. The blue sea stretched away in every direction. Behind Trevan's back was the side of the ship, the interior painted a dull red.

'How about some colours?' he suggested.

'All Right,' agreed Sedgwick. He pointed towards the sea. 'How do you write blue?' Rosso showed him, and Sedgwick traced the shape of the letters several times to fix them in his mind. 'Is it the same word for the wind?' he asked. 'The wind blue?'

'Eh, actually no,' admitted Rosso. 'We set that down thus.' He wrote "blew" on the sheet. Sedgwick looked confused, but faithfully copied out the new word.

'That's very good, Able,' enthused his teacher. 'Pick another colour.' Sedgwick pointed at the ship's side behind Trevan. 'Red' he said.

'That's my name! Rosso means red in Italian. Oh, but don't you go worrying about Italian just yet,' he added. 'Let's stick with a right Christian tongue like English. See, R E D - red.' He wrote down the letters, and Sedgwick traced them again.

'Rosie,' he asked, once he had finished. 'Red also means something to do with reading, yes? When I joined the ship I was "red" in?'

'Oh dear, oh dear,' muttered Rosso. 'It does, but that's not set down the same way either.' He wrote down "read", and swivelled the paper towards Sedgwick, who looked at the new word for a moment.

'It seems to be very difficult, this English of yours,' he sighed. 'I think I now start to see why so many of my shipmates have not bothered to learn their letters, Rosie.'

'You're fecking right there, Able,' said O'Malley as he came up, having picked his way across the crowded deck to join them. 'Now your Irish, there's a noble tongue for you, and very convenient to write, or so I have been told.' Like Trevan, his hair hung loose too, a river of dark curls that gave him the look of a Restoration aristocrat. 'Will you tie my hair up first, Adam, or are you after me doing yours?' he asked.

'Do me first, Sean,' said the Cornishman, sitting upright and staring past Able's shoulder to make the Irishman's job easier. 'You will need to find a tie-mate soon, Able, rate your hair is growing,' he said. Able ran his hand into his hair, noticing for the first time how bushy it had become. As a slave it had been regularly clipped for him, to prevent lice and other parasites.

O'Malley knelt down behind Trevan and gathered his hair into his strong hands, pulling and teasing it into tresses.

'So why are you looking to learn your letters any road, Able?' asked the Irishman as he worked.

'I sort of want to improve myself,' explained Sedgwick. 'I may not always be a sailor, and knowing my letters will help me with other callings. But also it is to follow a notion what

178

the surgeon had. He thought if I was to set down my story it may help with ending slavery.'

'Well, that all sounds right noble, so good luck to yous. None of us can read, apart from Rosie, and he learnt as a child. Even big Sam over there can barely set down his name straight.' Able followed O'Malley's look to where Evans stood on the forecastle rail, recovering his freshly washed clothes. With one hand he held onto the foremast shrouds while he stretched up with the other.

'Hoy, Sam,' shouted O'Malley. 'Mind out for the sharks!' The others laughed and heads turned to watch the big man. Evans flapped a dismissive hand towards O'Malley and the gesture unbalanced him a little so that one foot slipped from the rail. The ship rolled under him at that moment and the wave of his hand became a frantic attempt to regain his balance. For a long moment he beat at the air like a bird before he fell from view. Everyone on the forecastle froze in disbelief. A moment later the sound of a heavy body striking the sea came up from over the side.

'Sam!' shouted O'Malley, jumping to his feet. Rosso dropped the sheet of paper, and ran to the ship's side with Sedgwick at his heels.

'Man overboard!' yelled Trevan, coming to life at last, and turning to bellow towards the quarterdeck. Rosso and Sedgwick arrived at the forecastle rail just in time to see the thrashing figure of Evans slip below the surface. He was soon back up again, his eyes wide with panic as he retched and coughed up water. The struggling figure drifted ever sternward as the *Rush* sailed on.

'Can he swim, Rosie?' asked the former slave.

'I doubt it, Able,' said Rosso. 'Few of us can, and he comes from Seven Dials.' Sedgwick pulled his shirt over his head, and let it fall to the deck. He dropped his clasp knife on top, and climbed up onto the rail.

'Keep an eye on my stuff, Rosie,' he said.

'Hold fast a moment,' called Rosso, but he was too late. Sedgwick tumbled forward, his body stiffening into an arrow just before it speared into the water. Moments later a head of black hair broke the surface and swam towards Evans, whose struggles had become increasingly laboured.

John Sutton had been watching the four transporters through his telescope, tutting to himself at the poor way that they kept station when he heard Trevan's shout. He looked forward, saw the crew clustered on the starboard rail, and ran across the deck just as the struggling figure came level with him.

'Mr Croft!' he yelled. 'Get that life buoy in the water. Quartermaster, helm a lee! Bring her up into the wind.' As the ship's way came off her, Sutton rushed to the front of the quarterdeck. 'Mr Carver, jollyboat crew away!' he called. The order was picked up quickly by those on the main deck. Satisfied that the boat would soon be launched, he returned to the rail to see how the sailor fared. To his surprise he saw a second figure in the water, almost up to Evans and swimming well.

'*Agrius* signalling, sir,' said Croft. 'Why have you left your station?'

'Reply "*Rush* to *Agrius*, man overboard," if you please Mr Croft,' ordered Sutton, 'and kindly pass the word for the captain.'

'I am here, Mr Sutton,' said Clay as he climbed up the quarterdeck ladder to see why the ship had flown up into the wind. 'Who is in the water?'

'I believe it is Evans, sir,' replied the lieutenant. 'But now

Sedgwick appears to have joined him. He would seem to have some skill as a swimmer, unlike the unfortunate Evans.'

'I suppose he might be able to swim,' mused Clay. 'Did not Robertson say he had been a fisherman back in Africa before he lost his liberty?'

In the sea Sedgwick was close to Evans now, but it was clear that the big man was becoming exhausted. The water was colder than he had expected here in the deep Atlantic channel between Barbados and the crescent arc of the main Windward Islands. Ahead of him Evan's head slipped below the surface. His shirt ballooned up with trapped air for a moment, and then collapsed. Sedgwick took a deep breath and dived down.

He could see Evan's now, a struggling figure beneath him. His face was white in the wash of sunlight that filtered down into the water, his dark eyes wide with panic. He swam down, grabbed the big Londoner around the waist and drove powerfully up, forcing his head above the surface. Then he released him and came up for air himself. Evans clutched at him, forcing him under in his desperation to push himself up. Sedgwick circled below him and came up behind his friend. He slipped his arm round Evan's chin and lay back in the water, his mouth close to the drowning man's ear.

'Sam!' he gasped. 'Stop struggling! I have you now, just lie still and let me chiefly do the swimming.' Evans flayed around him with his arms, but Sedgwick held him firmly by the chin until the realisation gradually came to him that he was no longer drowning. Sedgwick felt Evan's body start to relax a little, melting into his grip. He kicked out with his legs and slowly towed the Londoner towards the approaching jollyboat. Evans coughed a few times, spitting salty phlegm onto Sedgwick's arm, then lay still. His rescuer glanced behind him in the water, judging how far away the boat was.

'How did you wind up in the water too?' gasped Evans.

'Saw you was after a swim and thought it might be a lark, so I jumped in after you, you great lump,' he replied. 'Try to keep your mouth closed.'

'Wasn't you worried about them sharks an all?' asked Evans, ignoring his advice.

'Are there sharks here abouts?' said Able. 'If I had known that I would have left you to bloody well drown.' Evans laughed at this, took in a mouthful of water, and his body arched in Able's grasp as he coughed.

'Keep your mouth shut, you idiot, and just lie back,' hissed Sedgwick.

Chapter 10
Vieux Fort

Late evening, and the sun drifted ever lower into the purple clouds that formed a towering hedge along the western horizon. Beams of light, thin shards of gold, spilt out across the velvet blue sky for a moment, and then with tropical quickness the light in the main cabin of the *Rush* faded. Clay was entertaining his officers once more, and they were seated around his dining table, their faces cross lit in the last of the daylight. Those who faced towards the stern windows were flushed with colour; those with their backs to the sunset were highwayman dark. Hart hastened forward with candles for the table, and lit the lamps that hung about the cabin, till the space glowed warmly once more. The officers talked among themselves, sipping at their wine, and waited with keen appreciation for the arrival of their meal.

'So have Sedgwick and Evans made a prompt recovery from their ordeal?' asked Clay.

'Indeed they have, sir,' said Linfield. 'I had instructed both men to rest for the balance of the day, but I understand that they ignored me and went on to take a full part in evening gun drill. Is that not so, Mr Sutton?'

'Precisely so,' replied the lieutenant. 'They are both very

sound. I have high hopes of Sedgwick in particular, sir. He must be given the chief credit for saving Evans's life, for I am most uncertain that the boat would have reached him in time. Mr Carver tells me he is a quick learner, and has already progressed much of the way to becoming a valuable seaman. Once he can show that he can hand, reef and steer, I believe we might rate him as ordinary.'

Clay was about to respond to Sutton's suggestion when Faulkner caught his eye. He closed his mouth again, picked up his fork and tapped the side of his glass to gain the attention of his other guests.

'Gentlemen,' he said. 'Earlier this evening Mr Faulkner came to see me to explain a matter of a certain delicacy. He also asked if he might be permitted to address a few words to the company tonight before we commence our meal. Mr Faulkner, pray continue.' All eyes turned towards the purser. Most were indifferent but those of Macpherson, seated opposite him, brimmed with encouragement.

'Ah... gentlemen,' he started. 'I hardly know where to begin. I wanted to tell you that I have been guilty of a sin of omission with regard to my past, and this has caused me to fall short of the necessary candour that should exist between fellow officers amid the perils of war. I would like to correct that now, and to ask for your understanding as to how it may have come about.' He paused for a moment, to gather his thoughts. The cabin was silent.

'In my youth I became enslaved to a love of games of hazard,' said Faulkner, looking down. 'My devotion to such practices brought me into contact with an unsavoury and rakish part of society, among whom I was to become a most active member. I was a young man then, and had I been checked by the council of friends or family, I might have avoided the excesses to which I later succumbed.

Unfortunately the converse was the case. Most of my acquaintances were like minded. I became a sad creature, virtually nocturnal in my habits, and I practiced gambling to the exclusion of almost all else.' Faulkner's tale stuttered to a halt, the purser unsure what to say next.

'What was the result of this obsession, Charles?' encouraged Macpherson.

'Why the virtual ruin of my family's prospects,' replied Faulkner, looking at the Scot. 'I accumulated such debts that had my family not been favoured by the consideration and generosity of many of their acquaintances, the Faulkners might have quite ceased to exist.'

'I see,' said the marine officer. 'So how was it you came to join the service?'

'I have always had some facility with numbers, Mr Macpherson,' replied the purser. 'My father was generous enough to give me another chance by purchasing for me the bond of a purser, and was able to command sufficient preferment as to find me my position here on board the *Rush*. Thanks to the level of my debts, it is the final act of support of which he was capable, and I will be eternally grateful for it. And now I must make my own way in the world.'

'Are you still tempted to gamble?' asked Appleby.

'I am sorely tempted,' replied Faulkner. 'But as yet I have been successful in not succumbing.'

'You will all understand that I did have some concerns about Mr Faulkner's tale,' said Clay. 'It is a rare thing to place a ship's finances in the hands of a self-confessed rake. I am somewhat reassured by his candour. We have discussed matters at some length and I have received such reassurances as to his future conduct that I am now quite satisfied that they will be safe in his hands.'

'Mr Faulkner, might I have a glass of wine with you?' said Macpherson. 'I consider the openness of your address to your brother officers in its way to be quite the match in bravery to Sedgwick's rescue of Evans.'

'Hear him,' called Linfield, banging the palm of his hand on the table top.

'Thank you, Mr Macpherson,' said Faulkner, smiling with relief as the weight of his past eased a little from his shoulders. He raised his own glass, and the two men drained them together.

'Well, gentlemen, that was very handsomely done by Mr Faulkner,' said Clay. 'Now, do we have any further confessions to hear? No active pederast, or undiscovered murderers amongst us? Capital, shall we proceed then to dinner?' The company cheered at this, Appleby a little too loudly, while Sutton spluttered over his wine. Hart and his assistants came in from the coach, carrying in a large rib of beef.

'Fresh meat at sea, gentlemen,' said Clay. 'A rare treat even when we are only a day out from port. Barbadian beef is not something which I can claim any familiarity with, but in the absence of a fortuitous shoal of flying fish it will sustain us, I make no doubt. Yes, I will have some of the vegetables thank you, Hart.'

With roast beef, Hart was on safer culinary grounds than normal, much to his captain's relief. Clay had recently had to be firm with his steward, insisting that he should stop adding sugar to every dish, even if it was a luxury that was freely available in the Caribbean.

'Are we all served?' he asked, looking at the heaped plates around him. 'Splendid, into battle we go.' The officers of the

Rush were all active young men, with keen appetites, and the novelty of fresh meat had not worn off after only ten days in Bridgetown refitting. In consequence a companionable silence descended over the table, punctuated only by the clink of glass on glass, and flatware on plate.

'Ah,' said Clay, the first to come up for air. 'That is considerably better. Mr Appleby, I see your trencher is clear, would you care for some more? Hart, would you oblige Mr Appleby? While we eat, perhaps I might tell you a little of the plans for the morrow?' Heads came up from plates along both sides of the table, and Clay had all of their attention.

'I am sure Mr Sutton will have told you the general situation,' he began. 'Our particular task is to descend on Vieux Fort in the south of the island. We will approach that place tonight, and land Colonel Gordon and his men at dawn, so as to give the French as little notice as we can. Once the troops are ashore, we are to provide what assistance they may require to invest and capture the small fortress we shall find there. I am expecting that the colonel may ask for the support of Lieutenant Macpherson and his marines, perhaps some men to help dig trenches and the like, and he will certainly call on us for gun crews for his siege pieces thereafter. He may also require your assistance, Mr Linfield, if the siege proves to be a bloody affair.'

'How is the landing to proceed?' asked Faulkner.

'We land in the bay to the west of Vieux Fort, which is called Black Bay,' Clay answered. 'We will anchor as close inshore as we dare and unload the transporters using our ship's boats.'

'Are there any navigational hazards to consider, sir,' asked Sutton. Clay looked across to Appleby to respond.

'Nothing on any of the charts,' replied the master. 'This

Philip K. Allan

being the Caribbean proper, there will be precious little tide to detain us.'

'Why is the bay called Black Bay?' asked Linfield, almost to himself. The others around the table looked at him quizzically. 'It is a French island,' he explained. 'All the names are French. The island itself is called St Lucia, not Saint Lucy. Micoud Bay, Castries, Vieux Fort; all these names are French, but not this Black Bay. I was just wondering if there might be an explanation as to why?'

'Well, it is a little strange now you come to mention it, Mr Linfield,' replied Appleby with a smile. 'I have heard an explanation which I can share with you, but I am not sure if I can give it much credence. The story goes that Blackbeard, the notorious buccaneer, used the bay to hide his ill gotten gains, and it bears his name in consequence.'

'Where is old Abrahams when you need him? He might have known,' said Sutton. 'You remember him, sir, sail maker's mate on the *Marlborough*.'

'I believe I do remember him, yes,' said Clay. 'One of the older hands, long scar on his arm. He had been in the service for years.'

'The very same,' said the lieutenant, turning back to the general company. 'I was a youngster in those days, but newly come to sea, and I did love to hear some of his fund of tales. He had served in most parts of the world over the years, always in the navy. During the Seven Years War he was here in the Caribbean under Rodney when he had the Leeward Islands command. He always said that many of the veteran seamen were former pirates, pardoned in their youth and then recruited into the navy. He had no end of yarns about sea fights and bloody encounters he had heard as a young man, all happening in these very waters a couple of generations ago.'

188

'It seems strange to think of men passing from piracy to the navy with never a backwards glance,' mused Faulkner. 'One wonders if they contrive to pass the other way with the same facility. It may help explain why the crew seem so obsessed with prize money.'

'I hope you are not considering a further change in career, Mr Faulkner,' said Macpherson. 'Done being a rake, how about a little buccaneering?' The table laughed at this, Faulkner with them, at ease with the group now in a way he had not been before tonight.

'As I understand it, most pirates commence life as privateers, preying on their country's enemies under licence,' explained Appleby. 'Then the war ends, the licence is revoked, but now the men have acquired the taste for easy spoil, perhaps to the point of addiction much as you have described can happen with cards, Mr Faulkner.'

'You sound as if you speak from prior knowledge of such matters, Mr Appleby,' said Clay, smiling at the ship's master.

'I fear I may lack the necessary frame for such a demanding occupation, sir,' replied Appleby, stroking the front of his bulging waistcoat. 'But we from the West Country have long been close to the sea. Are we not a cradle for the Royal Navy in time of war? But then what are we to do with all of those returning tars in time of peace? A little smuggling, you may make no doubt, but hardly sufficient to occupy us all. Take this Blackbeard you speak of, he was a West Country man through and through.'

'Perhaps it is your confession we must hear when next we dine, Mr Appleby,' said Clay to general laughter. 'Still, I think tales of pirate gold need not detain us overly, although perhaps it is best if such legends are not generally known. We do not want half of the crew to run ashore with notions of buried treasure in their heads, stealing all the expedition's shovels.'

*****

The convoy had looped around the southern end of St Lucia during the night, out of sight of land, so as to approach the bay from the west at dawn. They had formed up in the dark, the bulk of St Lucia to the north of them now, the bay ahead. Captain Parker had ordered that the *Agrius* should lead the way into the bay. She was the largest warship, so best able to meet any opposition. Next came the four transporters, formed in a straggling line abreast. At the rear followed the *Rush* to guard against any interference from the open ocean. Both the warships towed their ship's boats, like ducklings behind their mother, to ensure that a minimum of time would be lost in launching them. As the sky lightened to silver in the east, the dark shape of the land grew and resolved itself before Clay's eyes where he stood in the bows of the *Rush*, his telescope in his hand.

Stretched across his front was the wide expanse of the bay, the water a mirror to the sky. The back of the bay was made up of the long peninsula, low in the centre, but rising gently towards its seaward end to the right. It was only visible as a black silhouette against the light in the east. In the middle of the peninsula the horizon was feathery with palm trees. Long lines of cooking smoke rose up into the early morning air and drifted away, showing him where the town lay on the shore of the bay. On the top of the rise to his right was the fort. The land here was kept clear of palms and the silhouette was shaped by the harsh straight lines of walls and trenches. Over all was a tall flag pole, the flag black in the grey light.

Clay looked next to the left, where the peninsula met the

land. Here a spectacular sugar loaf mountain reared up like a tower of green, the domed top gleamed as the first rays of the sun kissed it. At its feet was the beach of silver sand where they would land Colonel Gordon and his men. He could see gentle breakers there, lines of white against the grey just now becoming visible in the gloom. Behind the sugar loaf mountain rose the hills of St Lucia, the lower slopes dotted with squares of cultivation, those above wild with bushy jungle. As Clay continued to study the approaching shore, the first blinding rays of the sun spilt over the top of the peninsula, and it was day at last.

The ships stood on into the bay. In the growing light Clay began to see the detail of the land. The grey stone of the fortress walls, sharp and angled like the points of a star. A line of fishing boats was drawn up on the sand by the shore, their hulls bright colours against the white sand with heaped nets beside them. Now he could see the low buildings of the town, the walls coloured sky blue, burnt red and yellow ochre. Some houses were tiled but most had thatch. Above the roofs were lofty palm trees, bent into arcs under the burden of their fruit, and rising amongst the trees was the whitewashed tower of a church.

'Mr Sutton's compliments, sir,' said Midshipman Preston, appearing at his elbow. 'And he believes that the *Burford* may be in difficulty.' Clay glanced across at the transporters. Three had carried on towards the beach, but the fourth was stationary in the water. He could see the crew busy taking in her sails; looking closely he noticed that the angle of the motionless hull was wrong.

'Please tell Mr Sutton that I will come directly. If you please, Mr Preston,' he said, 'can you also signal the *Agrius*? Send "*Rush* to *Agrius*, *Burford* aground, submit I assist." And have the jollyboat manned ready to be row across.' It took Clay a less than a minute to reach the quarterdeck from the forecastle of the little sloop, by which time the signal had been prepared and flown.

'Signal from *Agrius*, sir,' reported Preston. 'Signal acknowledged. Join operations when able.'

'Thank you, Mr Preston,' said Clay. 'Mr Sutton, kindly close to within hailing distance of the *Burford*. Mr Preston, find Mr Carver if you please, and ask him with my compliments to rouse out a cable suitable to take one of the transporters in tow.'

While the three remaining ships sailed on towards the beach with the *Agrius*, the *Rush* bore down on the stricken brig. On board the scene appeared chaotic. The front part of the deck was full of lines of red-coated infantry, packs on their backs, muskets by their sides, ready to disembark. Further aft Clay could see frustrated army officers arguing with the seamen and gesticulating towards the growing expanse of blue water between them and the other three ships. Looking that way he saw the transporter nearest to the beach was taking in sail and preparing to drop anchor. Drifting across from the *Burford* came the sound of a sergeant bawling at his men, and officers shouting at the sailors. Clay tried to pick out from the mass of figures which was likely to be the ship's master. He settled on a balding man in a plain blue coat who stood beside the wheel. He held one hand behind his back while he mopped his brow with a large colourful handkerchief gripped in the other. He also seemed to be the recipient of most of the army officers' rage. Clay ordered the *Rush* to heave to just behind the transporter, and pointed his speaking trumpet towards the man by the wheel.

'*Burford*, ahoy,' called Clay. 'How badly are you aground?' The man by the wheel picked up his own speaking trumpet and turned away from his indignant passengers with relief.

'Barely at all, sir,' he replied. 'We have gently run up on some manner of submerged sand bar. It has done us little enough harm. If we had been less heavily laden we might well have passed right over it without touching.'

'Very well, I propose to send a boat with a line. I shall then bend a cable to that line and pass it across to your ship. Once all is made fast we can attempt to tow you off stern first,' called Clay. 'Will that answer?'

'Exceedingly well, sir,' replied the master of the *Burford*. 'You might also consid—' The rest of the message was cut off as one of the army officers seized the speaking trumpet.

'Pray let us have no more of that nonsense, young man,' bawled a gravel-voiced officer with grey side burns. 'You damned naval coves may wish to yarn all morning concerning lines across, bent on wherever, and towed astern whatnot. Fact of the matter is that there is a damned battle about to commence, and my men need to be landed on that blasted beach over yonder!' The furious officer pointed towards the end of the bay, where the first of the *Agrius*'s boats, heavy with red-coated figures, was nearing the shore.

'And who might you be, sir?' said Clay, a little frosty.

'I am Major Grafton, of the 53rd Shropshire regiment,' replied the officer.

'Well, major,' continued Clay. 'Refloating your transport ship will be the most swift way to get your men ashore, but I do comprehend how provoking this all must be. Might I propose a solution? It would aid the operation to re-float the *Burford* if her displacement could be lightened by removing some of your men. I believe we might endeavour to slay a brace of birds with one shot. If I were to allocate two of my larger ship's boats to ferry your men ashore, while we naval coves are preparing our whatnots, might that not address your chief concern? We could begin with you and your staff.'

'Upon my soul, that is more like it,' enthused the major. The ship's master behind him beamed his assent, his relief obvious even at thirty yards. 'Capital solution, what? Much obliged to you, Captain, Captain... ?'

'Commander Clay. Pleased to make your acquaintance,' Clay replied. 'I will issue the appropriate orders directly.' Clay turned away from the stricken *Burford*. 'Mr Sutton, kindly have the launch and cutter manned, and start to ferry the soldiers ashore. It's a long pull, but it will be worth it.'

'Aye aye, sir,' replied Sutton with a grin. 'Starting with the noisier cargo, I understand.'

'Quite so,' said Clay. 'Let us get the good major as far to leeward of the operation as possible. Could you also see how Mr Carver does with that cable?' While Clay waited for Sutton to return, he called over the ship's master.

'Mr Appleby,' said Clay. 'It would seem this bay of yours has more navigational hazards than we had assumed. Can you kindly take bearings to fix the exact location of this sand bank that has trapped the unfortunate *Burford*, and have it added to our chart.'

'Aye aye, sir,' replied Appleby, hurrying off to get his sextant.

Clay returned to looking across the bay towards the beach. The first parties of redcoats were ashore now. He could see where a little block of red showed clear against the white of the sand. Further up the beach individual red figures were dotted like flowers against the green foliage of the land. They must be skirmishers, Clay decided, pushed out to protect the bridgehead from any surprise attack. The ship's boats were returning to collect a fresh load of troops to reinforce those already landed. Now would be the time for the French to attack, while the numbers of men on the beach was still tiny, but looking towards the fort, he could see no sign of activity. No column of troops sallied out, hurrying forward behind a fluttering standard, their drums beating. The only flag he could see was the tricolour drifting on the breeze over the fort, the colours now obvious in the bright morning sun.

'The cable is ready, sir,' reported Sutton. 'One end is made fast to the stern bits, the other has been brought to the rear gun port, and has already been bent to a line.'

'Very good, Mr Sutton,' replied Clay. 'Kindly have the line sent across in the jollyboat, if you please.'

'Aye aye, sir,' said the lieutenant. Clay went over to the stern rail with his speaking trumpet. He looked across at the *Burford*. The cutter had just left the side of the ship, full of soldiers, including the indignant Major Grafton. On the far side of the ship Clay could see other soldiers making their way down over the side, presumably to the launch that was out of sight behind the hull.

'*Burford*, ahoy,' he called. 'Line coming across now.'

Clay leant over the side of the *Rush* and looked down. Below him he could see the end of the thick, eighteen inch cable, protruding like a snout from the gun port. A line was wound about the end, like a muzzle and then led down into the jollyboat below. As the small boat rowed across to the *Burford*, a hand in the stern paid out the line. The curve of rope rested briefly on the now blue surface of the water, and then sank beneath it. When the boat reached the stricken transporter the balance of the line was handed up, and the crew of the *Burford* began to haul the thick cable across the expanse of water between the two ships, watched by the large numbers of waiting soldiers. The cable rose up the side of the *Burford*, and disappeared through an open port. A few minutes later the ship's master waved his colourful handkerchief in Clay's direction to gain his attention, and then brought his speaking trumpet to his lips.

'*Rush*, ahoy,' he yelled. 'The cable is made fast.'

'Very well,' replied Clay. 'Prepare to be towed.' He turned back towards the quarterdeck. 'Foretopsail only, I think, Mr Sutton,' he said. 'We do not want to pull the guts of the ship out.'

'Aye aye, sir,' replied Sutton. Clay hailed the *Burford* once more.

'*Burford*, ahoy,' he called. 'I am getting under way.' He turned his attention back to the lieutenant.

'Mr Sutton! Put her before the wind.'

The *Rush* slowly gathered way and the dripping cable rose out of the sea, the arc growing ever flatter.

'Steady,' called Clay to the helmsmen. 'Here she comes.' With a volley of groans from under his feet the cable became a solid bar, water spraying from between the fibres as the strain compressed the weave of the rope. For a moment the *Rush* seemed to falter, the men at the wheel struggling to hold her to the wind, and then with a dip and a surge the *Burford* slid off the sand bank, and drifted backwards across the bay.

Chapter 11
Digging

'Dirt, Mr Preston, is shortly to become your most valued acquaintance,' said Captain Webb of the Royal Engineers, allowing a fist full of the precious substance to crumble through his outstretched hand and drift away on the gentle sea breeze.

'You don't say, captain,' said the midshipman. 'And why might that be?'

'Because it is the only thing that we have to hand that will answer to stop a cannon ball,' the engineer explained. 'For though all may seem to be quiet as we stand here now, the moment that your men start to dig, the French up there in the fortress will throw their deuced shot amongst us, and it is dirt that will save our precious hides.'

The two men were standing on a smooth field of short, scratchy grass that led up to the ditch and outer wall of the fort. It was odd to be on an area of ground that was so empty of vegetation, thought the midshipman. Every other square inch of soil he had seen on this tropical island burst with tumbling green life.

'It's because we are standing on the glacis of the fortress, Mr Preston, within range of the enemy guns,' explained

Captain Webb, noticing his puzzled look. 'The Frogs keep it nice and clear to deny us the comfort of any cover. That way they can shoot at us with much greater convenience.'

Behind them were the clustered streets of Vieux Fort town itself, now occupied by the British. Amid the trees and small fields, Preston could see lines of tents appearing like mushrooms as Colonel Gordon established his little army for the siege ahead. Just off the beach the four transporters swung at anchor with their sails furled while farther out were the warships, their black hulls picked out by a band of yellow that ran the length of each gun deck. The long hull and soaring masts of the graceful *Agrius* was easy to distinguish from the smaller, squatter *Rush*.

Preston noticed that even with all the expedition's troops now on shore, the ship's boats were still busy at work. They were rowing this way and that, crossing the calm blue water that lay between the transporters and the white sandy beach. Now they were ferrying all the masses of other items the expedition would need in the days and weeks ahead. He could see casks of beef and sacks of provisions being swung down into one of the boats. In the shallows a block and tackle had been set up, and a crowd of men were clustered around the pinnace of the *Agrius*, the largest boat available. Something of enormous weight, presumably the first of the siege guns, was being gingerly lifted out. Guns and stores, these were familiar items to Midshipman Preston. What was quite new to him was the large pile of wicker cylinders, like giant waste paper baskets, that his men had dragged up to the edge of the glacis.

'What would those strange panniers over there be all about then?' he asked.

'Those are what we engineers call gabions,' explained Captain Webb. 'They will form the principal part of the trench. Do you see the line of pegs my sergeant has placed in the ground?' Preston followed where the engineer indicated.

'The line of stakes that point across the slope,' said Preston. 'And look as if they are going to miss the fort?'

'Quite so,' said the captain. 'That shall be the line of our first trench. It will bear us closer to the enemy, but in an indirect fashion. Once we have it dug, we shall swing around and dig in the other direction. First we zig and then zag if you will, until we shall arrive nice and close to the fort.'

'Oh,' said the midshipman with sudden clarity. 'Why it is just like a ship tacking up into the wind.'

'Eh, if you say so, Mr Preston,' replied the land based engineer. 'You see a siege is a beauteous matter with a craft and science all of its own. How it proceeds is well understood by we engineers, and it all begins with a prodigious amount of digging. So, I would be obliged if your men could dig the section of trench from this peg here, to that one over there.' Preston looked at the section, about twenty yards long, and nodded.

'That seems clear enough,' he said. 'How do we set about the task?'

'Gabions, Mr Preston,' said Captain Webb. 'It is all about the gabions. Till they are in place, filled up to the brim with good honest dirt, none of us shall be safe. Place the first one by that peg, nice and upright. Then your men dig the trench behind it and use the spoil they generate to fill her up as quick as ever they can.'

'And that will protect them from a canon ball?' queried the midshipman.

'Once it is full of earth, you have my word upon it,' said the engineer.

'And when it is full?' asked Preston.

'Why you cower behind it and use its protection to fill the next one,' said Captain Webb, 'and then the next, and the next, and so by this means our trench will progress. As I said earlier, Mr Preston, your siege does involve a prodigious amount of digging.'

'We had better get started then,' said Preston. He raised his voice to the one he reserved for moderate gales, and summoned over his men.

'Right, you lot, over here with your shovels, and bring one of those big wicker baskets with you. Look lively now!'

*****

'So why did we want to volunteer for the bleeding shore party again, Sean?' asked Evans, ducking his head down as another cannon ball whistled past them. A fountain of red earth shot up farther down the glacis as the ball struck the ground and spun away onwards down the slope. O'Malley paused for a moment, leaning on his long-handled shovel, and wiped the sweat from his brow. He looked across at the tall Londoner, and then down at the broken ground at their feet. Evans followed his gaze but saw nothing beyond more of the red-coloured soil they had been frantically shovelling into the top of the gabion. He shrugged his shoulders to show his incomprehension, turning the gesture into another duck as a fresh cannon ball flew past. When he looked up O'Malley mouthed a word at him.

'Did you just say treasure?' asked Evans, speaking loud enough to be heard over the sound of the cannon fire.

'Sh Sh Shhhh,' hissed the Irishman, a finger pressed to his lips. 'Not so fecking loud!' He looked around to see if they might have been overheard.

'Can't you two be digging and talking at once, like,'

gasped Trevan. 'At least until this bugger here is filled up, like.' Sedgwick muttered his assent and the sailors set to again with a will, earth flying up as the trench they stood in grew deeper. The effort required to raise each successive shovel full of earth up to the open top of the wicker gabion became harder as they sank farther into the ground, causing even the herculean Evans to grunt. When it was full at last they settled down in the trench bottom behind it to catch their breath. The three gabions they had filled so far bulged like close packed barrels in a line behind them, and a definite trench had started to form at their feet.

All along the slope similar parties of soldiers and seamen dug away, cutting an angry red scar across the glacis. None of the sections of trenches had joined up as yet, but some were getting close to their neighbours. Each group of gabions was like a little besieged fortress, bombarded with steady deliberation from the guns of the French. But the slope was also dotted with ruined gabions, dashed away before they could be filled, while occasional bodies lay in the grass to mark where the fort's defenders had struck down one of the many diggers.

Evans peered around the edge of their shelter and up towards the fortress. He could see tendrils of gun smoke drifting across the grass. Above him the grey stone outer wall rose up proud of the glacis. Every fifteen yards or so were wide crenulations, like the gaps in the smile of a growing child. In the centre of the one immediately above him he could see the black muzzle of a cannon, its crew huddled over it. They rolled it up to the wall and pointed it straight at him. There was an orange flash and a gush of smoke as he ducked behind the gabion. A fraction of a second later he felt a solid blow against the wicker at his back. A flurry of dirt spilt down from above, but no more apparent damage had been done than that.

'Bloody hell,' he said, 'Did you all feel that? These bleeders really do work.' Evans patted the curved wicker wall with affection, and then turned towards O'Malley. 'So I know you were keen for us to volunteer to be shot at, an all,' he began, 'but I am a little unsure why. You said something about treasure?' O'Malley looked around him, and then beckoned the others closer.

'Lads, you are going to need to trust me on this, but I am after knowing that on this very spot, there is buried treasure.'

'Really?' breathed Evans, looking at the bottom of the trench with new respect. 'What right here?'

'Well, it may not be this fecking spot, like,' conceded the Irishman. 'But in this bay. I have found out that Blackbeard himself, you know, the richest fecking pirate of them all, hid his treasure here. I am telling yous, El Dorado ain't in it!'

'So have you got a map or something, Sean?' asked Trevan, his eyes alight with greed.

'Not as such, no,' said O'Malley. 'But I has it on very good authority. I can't say any more. You just need to believe me, and keep up the digging.'

'What's going on here?' said a voice. The figure of Midshipman Preston loomed up over the edge of the trench. 'Why are you lot sulking in the bottom of that hole, instead of digging?'

'That's just what I was saying to them me self, Mr Preston, sir,' replied O'Malley. 'Able, Sam, go get a fresh one of them giant lobster pots.' The two men ran off down the slope, returning shortly after dragging the bulky gabion behind them. They pushed it into place, and the labour of filling it began once more. Moments later it exploded into a mass of red earth and shattered wicker as a direct hit from the fort sent it cartwheeling down the slope.

'So off you go and get another one,' said Preston, with O'Malley nodding approvingly behind him. The midshipman waited till the next gabion was in place, and well on its way to being filled before he ran across the gap of no-man's-land between this and the next section of trench. Once he was gone, O'Malley turned back to the others.

'Now listen here,' he said. 'Anything we find, we share equal like, agreed? Dig as deep as you can, and keep your eye out for any boxes or chests. And when we gets back to the ship, you mustn't breathe a word about the treasure to anyone.'

When Evans finished his stint of trench digging, he lay down his shovel quite resolved not to mention the possibility of buried treasure to a soul. Not a soul that is, except for his particular friend Harrison, who he chanced to stand beside on the beach while they both waited to be taken back to the ship. In reality it hardly counted as an indiscretion, because before he breathed a word, he made Harrison swear on the grave of his mother that the secret would pass on no further.

Later that evening, when Harrison came to consider matters, it seemed clear to him that the binding commitment he had made on the beach could not be meant to include his tie mate O'Neil. After all, he reasoned, wasn't a tie mate virtually your own flesh and blood? O'Neil, in his turn agreed to keep the secret safe. Indeed he managed to do so for almost a full hour, right up to the moment when he found himself sitting in the heads alongside Fletcher, the cooper's mate. O'Neil was not sure what it was that had made him blurt it out. Perhaps it was a desire to interrupt the incontinent flow of shipboard gossip that Fletcher delighted in sharing. For Fletcher was the last person he should have told about the buried treasure. It was common knowledge among the crew of the *Rush* that the cooper's mate, unlike the rest of them, could not be trusted to keep a secret.

*****

'By Jove, I must say those sailors of yours are capital diggers,' exclaimed Captain Webb, brushing some reddish coloured soil from his uniform. No sooner had the offensive dirt been removed than another impact against the outer face of the trench sent a fresh plume of soil cascading over him. 'My sergeant tells me he has never seen such zeal with a shovel.'

'You don't say, captain,' said Preston. 'Even more so than the soldiers?'

'Oh, much more!' enthused the engineer officer. 'Even when off duty, many of them can be found practicing their newfound skills. He tells me they have dug trenches all over the deuced place. At this rate we should be able to start on the second parallel later today. That is a full day earlier than I thought possible.'

'Indeed, it is a little surprising,' replied the midshipman, a thoughtful expression on his young face as he watched his shore party widen the trench they stood in, flinging each shovel full of earth high in the air to fall down the outer wall.

The two officers stood in the middle of the long trench that ran like a slot across the slope. After four days of continuous work it was now wide enough for three men to walk abreast, and in places was over four feet deep. The enormous amount of earth that had been dug was heaped into a solid wall on the side that faced towards the fortress. Despite the best effort of the defenders to batter it down, and the occasional tropical shower to wash it away, it still remained, providing safe access for the attackers.

'So when must the men stop their digging for the parley you spoke of?' asked Preston. The engineer officer drew out his fob watch and flipped open the case.

'Why, it is almost time now,' he mused. 'What can be keeping them?'

'I confess to being a little puzzled by this parley,' said the midshipman. 'Are we expecting the French to simply surrender?'

'Not immediately, no,' explained the captain. 'Unless the Frogs are singularly ill prepared. But most sieges do end with some form of agreed surrender, you know. It is so much more civilised than fighting on till the inevitable, rather bloody conclusion. Today shall be more about sounding the blighters out, now that we have shown that we are in earnest.'

'How civilised it all seems compared with fights at sea,' said Preston.

'You forget that at sea, unlike a siege, the weaker party has the option to retreat,' said Webb. 'Ah, now here comes our party at last. Stop digging, you men!' Preston blew a shrill blast on his whistle, and all along the line the sailors stopped their work.

The midshipman looked down the slope at the small group of soldiers coming up the hill. The way was led by an ensign who carried a large white flag that looked suspiciously like it may have begun the day as a bed sheet. Behind him marched a drummer boy in a heavily braided tunic next to the stiff figure of Major Grafton, looking rather more pleased with himself than he had on the deck of the stricken *Burford*. Every twenty yards or so the group stopped for a moment while the ensign waved his flag, and the boy flogged away at his drum. Having established that there was no question of any attempt to surprise the French, the party advanced a further twenty yards and repeated this little performance.

Once they had climbed over the trench wall with a certain amount of difficulty, the enemy fire petered out, and an eerie calm descended. The party had not advanced very far into no-man's-land when a door swung open in the main gate of the fort, and a brisk little French officer marched out, accompanied by his own drummer.

'Ah, splendid!' exclaimed Captain Webb. 'We are to have a foot race.'

'A what?' queried Preston.

'Well, by the conventions of war the parties should meet at the midpoint between the two sides,' explained the engineer officer. 'But naturally if you can make the talks occur closer to your enemy, there is an opportunity to observe what your opponent is about. See how that French cove marches so quickly?' Captain Webb looked from one side to the other, like a spectator at a race meeting. 'Close,' he muttered. 'The Frog officer looks the quicker, but Major Grafton can be very determined.'

Preston watched with open astonishment as the scramble unfolded. Both parties were now moving forward as quickly as possible, while trying to cling to a little of the nonchalance to be expected of gentlemen. The two officers finally came together, as far as Preston could judge, in the middle of the glacis. The last few yards had been covered at a speed normally only produced by long separated lovers.

There was a few moments of pause while both sides caught their breath and adjusted their attire. Major Grafton, in particular, had come close to shedding his hat in the final surge. Then the officers saluted, shook hands, and finally got into discussions. Although they were too far away to be heard, the tone of the dialogue could be seen from their respective gestures. The Frenchman pointed at the line of trench so far constructed, his shrug of disdain clear to behold. The bristling Major pointed to the long tent lines at the bottom of the hill and to the *Rush* and the *Agrius* where they swung at anchor in the bay. He spread his arms wide, seemingly to summarise in that one gesture the hopelessness of the French position. Back came the Frenchman, waving an arm towards the untouched fort wall. He then pointed first at the sky, then at the British trench, and made a slipping gesture. Both men spoke together for a little longer, then stepped back to exchange formal salutes, and turned away towards their own sides.

'What was the outcome, sir?' asked Captain Webb when the major was back in the British trench. Grafton shook his head towards the engineer.

'Back to work, captain,' he replied. 'They say they have men and supplies enough for a long siege. He also mentioned that we had only progressed so well on account of how dry it has been. He said wait till it rains properly. Anyway, I must go and report to Colonel Gordon now on the outcome.'

'Hmm, I am not sure a bit of rain will hold us back,' mused the engineer. 'Probably just some Frog attempt to throw us off the scent. Well, Mr Preston, let us get your men started on that second parallel.'

*****

After three days of further digging, just as the French officer had predicted, the rain had come. Black clouds had loomed up out of the south in row after row of huge towering thunderheads. They looked like craggy cliffs of boiling grey with silver threads of lightening flickering beneath them.

Hissing rain had poured down, filling the trenches to the brim, and turning them into a blood red torrent. Soil had become gold panner's mud on the sailors' shovels, washed from the face long before it could reach the gaping mouth of the next gabion. The trench guards huddled in groups, knee deep in water, while the rest of the besiegers' found what shelter they could in Vieux Fort.

'When oh when will it stop fecking raining?' said O'Malley, as he stared out from beneath the eaves of the lean-to they had built on the edge of town. 'I know I am a true born Irishman an all, but even I have never seen the like before.'

'Just as we had finished that bleeding second trench, an all,' moaned Trevan. 'This rain will wash it all away.' He spat noisily out of the door, the gob of spittle rapidly flowing away down the path.

'God, it was tough, though,' said Evans. 'The closer we was getting, the harder them Frog guns was pounding us. We needed a double layer of them gabions just to keep the shot out.'

'Might it be one of them well hid blessings, Sean,' suggested Trevan, laying a finger next to his nose. 'Perhaps all this rain will wash away enough dirt to reveal some't, if you know what I mean.'

'So what progress have you lads made finding this treasure?' asked the newly arrived Rosso, part of the additional draft of seamen brought ashore to help man the siege guns. The four sailors looked at each other.

'We have found nothing, Rosie,' said Sedgwick, speaking for them all. 'Well, unless you count the belt buckle Sam came across on the first day.'

'Nice piece of brass, that,' said Evans, 'or would be, if it wasn't broken.'

'Tell me again why is it you hold there to be treasure hereabouts, Sean?' asked Rosso.

'Ah, I see how it lies,' O'Malley replied, folding his arms. 'Are we all after questioning Sean now, 'cause of a bit of disappointment? I reckon we have barely scratched the surface. The treasure could be anywhere. Why we might be sitting upon it now.' The other four looked down at the hard packed ground and mass of tree roots from the large palm tree against which their shelter had been built.

'I doubt that, Sean,' said Evans, prodding at the earth with the point of his shovel. 'Them roots look to have lain here for many an age.'

'Come on, Sean,' persisted Rosso. 'Why are you so decided in your view?'

'You know how Hart is a real good mate of mine?' began the Irishman. 'Well, the night before we arrived here, him and I were sharing a pipe in the galley, having a bit of a yarn, like. He always shares what he hears with me.' The others all nodded at this. O'Malley continued.

'"Sean," says he, "I have just been serving the Grunters their dinner, and you will never guess what they been talking about." What they been saying? says I. He looks around, all secretive like, then says, "I came into the cabin when they was all looking at the chart. 'Why is this place we're going to named Black Bay?' says the doctor to the master. 'Why, its coz Blackbeard himself buried all his treasure there,' says old Fatty Apple. Then up speaks Pipe, and he says, 'Don't go letting the hands know that.'" O'Malley looked around at the other faces. 'Now when I heard that from Hart, I am after thinking, why are they so keen on us not knowing about this treasure, unless it is true?'

'Well you can't fault his bleeding logic, Rosie,' said Evans.

'I am not sure that I agree with you there, Big Sam,' said Rosso. 'See, I have been thinking as well, Sean. It strikes me that if I was a pirate, this would be a mighty queer place for me to stash my treasure. We are in the Caribbean. There is no end of uninhabited islands to pick from. There are two just off the coast on the other side of the peninsula. So why would you chose here, with plenty of folk about who might stumble over your treasure?' The other sailors looked at one another.

'Wait a moment, Rosie,' said O'Malley. 'That may be true now, but what if this part of the island was empty back in the days when Blackbeard was doing all his buccaneering?'

'No, Sean, that will hold no water,' said Rosso. 'Blackbeard died less than eighty year ago. This fort was certainly here then. Frogs would hardly call it "Vieux Fort" if it was brand new. See, that is my other problem with all of this. The soldiers up in the fort, all the people in the town, no end of plantation owners in the hills; they've had years and years to find your treasure. Do you not think if it were here they might have turned up the odd doubloon?'

'But what if the treasure is all a great fecking secret!' said O'Malley, leaning forward to play his decisive card. 'What if nobody knows that Blackbeard ever came here?'

'If nobody knows that he came here, why is his name set down on Fatty Apple's chart?' replied Rosso. Silence descended over the group as they absorbed the remorseless logic of their friend's argument.

'Well you can't fault his bleeding logic, Sean,' said Evans.

'I think perhaps Rosie has the truth of it,' agreed Sedgwick.

'Fecking hell,' was O'Malley's more succinct summary.

Chapter 12
Siege

For three days and two nights the rain cascaded down on friend and foe alike. But at last the deluge moved away and the besiegers were able to contemplate the ravaged remains of their trenches as they steamed in the tropical sun. Some sections seemed to have been quite unaffected. Others had had much of the soil in their gabions washed through the mesh of wicker and back into the trench from whence it had come. The defenders concentrated their fire on such vulnerable targets. As each sodden gabion burst, the sight was received with a groan from the labouring British, and a faint cheer borne on the wind from behind the still untouched walls of the fortress.

Once more the British set to with a will. Fresh gabions were hauled along the parallels, and plugged into the gaps. Soil again flew into them in a frantic race to have them filled before they were dashed away. After four days of hard work, and in spite of a noticeable drop in the level of enthusiasm for the task displayed by the shore party from the *Rush*, the approach trenches were at last restored back to the state they had been in before the rains had come.

The following day saw no further extension of the British earthworks, but the French defenders still noticed a considerable amount of activity. The tops of numerous fresh gabions could be glimpsed as they were hauled along behind the parapet. The sound of coordinated heaving drifted up towards the fort, the objects in question were invisible, but the effort involved was clear to hear as heavy items were dragged forward. As night approached, the number of British in their trenches seemed to be on the increase, rather than reducing as had happened on every previous night. A worried French ensign reported all this to his captain, who in turn went to see the major, who sat down to discuss matters with the commandant of the fort.

'My sincere apologies, Claude,' said the grey-haired commander to his young subordinate. 'But I can only offer you rum. Since the English began their blockade of the island, cognac has become almost impossible to find. I do have one bottle left, but I shall keep that to toast our victory over the Roast Beefs.'

'No matter, sir,' said the major, lifting the glass to his nose. He took a cautious sip, and his face cleared. 'Actually it is very good.'

'It has been aged for ten years in the barrel. I get it from a small producer I know near Fond St Jacques,' said the commandant. 'So, mon ami, what have you to report?'

'A strange day, sir,' replied the major. 'The enemy completed all their repairs to their trenches last night, yet today they have made no further progress. Their second parallel is now close enough to the wall for them to site their siege guns, but none have appeared. There has been a lot of activity, and the trenches have many more men in them tonight than we have seen before.'

The commandant thought for a moment, and then reached towards the bookshelf that rested against the office wall behind him. He found the volume he wanted, which he pulled out and placed on the desk in front of him. From his top pocket he produced a pair of wire framed reading glasses which he hooked with care over his ears and then he opened the book.

'It is Thursday, is it not?' he asked, peering at the officer over the twin discs of silver.

'Yes, sir,' replied the major. The commandant leafed through the pages of the almanac, found the entry for that day, ran his finger along the line, and tapped the page.

'Very interesting,' he mused. 'Tonight Claude, there will be no moon,' he said. 'Do you think the English would be foolish enough to be planning a surprise attack? An assault on the walls with siege ladders maybe? Perhaps that is what you heard being dragged along behind their parapet?'

'Well, it is possible,' said the major, running a hand through his thinning hair. 'But if that is the case, they have concealed their intentions very poorly.'

'Yes they have,' said the commandant. 'In which case, let us insure they receive a nasty surprise. Have the guard doubled tonight, and arrange for the occasional flare to be tossed out into the ditch. Also make sure that at sunset you train our guns on the end of that second parallel, and that they are fired blind at intervals through the night. I am to be woken if any attack develops, and in any case an hour before dawn.' He picked up his glass and clinked it against that of the major.

'Victory to the Republic,' he toasted, and both men drained their glasses.

All through the night the French troops waited, expecting to be attacked at any moment. The darkness was full of strange sounds, overlaying the more usual rasp of tree frogs and hum of insects. There was the jink and scrape of numberless shovels and the clatter of dropped timber. Hoarse cries of 'Easy all!', 'Belay that!' and 'Handsomely there, for fuck sake!' echoed in the dark. Jumpy sentries fired their muskets into the night, but drew no return fire. When the cannons roared out, the tongue of flame caught the glint of steel, and the briefest glimpse of activity. The flash of light captured a moment of disturbed movement, like the mouth of an ants' nest, washed away by the returning night as fast as it had appeared.

As he had ordered, the commandant was woken before dawn the next day. He groaned a curse at his servant, for he had just fallen asleep, what with the night filled with trigger-prone sentries, and the periodic roar of the cannon. He washed and dressed himself and then crossed to the north wall of the fortress. There he stood near the front of the parapet and faced towards the British trenches with the major by his side. The enemy were quiet now, as if they too waited for the dawn. No surprise attack had been launched in the night, for which the commandant was grateful, but he also knew that his industrious besiegers would not have been idle either. Away to the east a tiny blush of rose showed where the sky met the ocean, but here on the walls all was still dark. A sea breeze flapped at the tail of the commandant's coat, the movement echoed by the tricolour above his head.

The commandant made small talk in the dark with the major, until a moment came when he realised it was light enough for him to be able see his face. He contemplated his subordinate's features, his tired eyes, the bristle of stubble on his chin, the silky arms of his moustache. He then broke of his conversation and both men faced towards the enemy. The morning light had just gilded the top of the sugar loaf mountain at the start of the peninsula. In the gloom at its base, where he knew the lines of his enemy's tents to be, the first of the day's cooking fires glowed red in the dark. Closer at hand were the British trenches, the line of them now clear in the grey light. He saw immediately what the British had done during the night. The second parallel now ended in a substantial gun emplacement, two gabions high, and several thick. As the light grew he could make out some of the large timbers and trunks of felled palm trees used in its construction.

'Merde!' exclaimed the commandant. 'So that is what the English have been up to. It is really quite marvellous what they have achieved in a single night. They must want to capture our fortress very much.' He looked towards the major. 'Well, Claude, can you batter it down?' he asked. The major examined the structure with care through the small spy glass he had pulled from his pocket.

'It is very well made, sir,' he replied, passing the spy glass across. 'Much too solid for the few cannon we have that will bear on it. The only weak points I can see are the gun embrasures. Of which I count three, but they have made them as narrow as possible.'

'Yes, I see them,' said the commandant. 'Two are empty, but do you see? The one on the right has a gun in it already.'

'You're right, sir,' replied the Major. 'It looks big. Twenty four pounder at least, I should say, perhaps even larger.'

The two men inspected the thick black muzzle of the siege gun, and as if in response a huge tongue of flame erupted from it. Almost before they had registered that the gun had fired, the officers felt a blow like a hammer strike the fortress beneath their feet, and fragments of broken cannon ball and stone were sent shrieking through the air. They both walked forward and leant out to look down at the base of the wall. There was enough light now to show where the stone had been struck. They could see a small blister of damage with cracks radiating out from it, and a few grey flecks of stone dotting the grass floor of the ditch below it. Both men ducked back behind the wall, and the commandant stroked his chin.

'How long do you think it will it take them to make a suitable breach in the wall?' he asked. The major shrugged his shoulders before he replied.

'If they really have three such guns, they might have a narrow breach in as little as two days, sir. It depends on how well the wall has been constructed. The outer stone appears to be good, but one can never tell what the local contractor who built it may have filled it with. Whoever he was, you can be sure he was no Vauban.'

'Alas that is true, Claude. Only two days you think?' mused the commandant. 'We will need to act soon then, before the wall is too badly damaged. For now concentrate what fire we can on the gun embrasure that is firing. It will be difficult, as you say, but we may get lucky. Meanwhile have the garrison officers join me in my office at ten. It is time for us to make the next move in this game.'

*****

'Stand clear,' yelled Rosso, as he brought the linstock down onto the touchhole. The crew around him were all within a few feet, but he still needed to shout to be heard. Like him they had their neck cloths tied in tight bandanas around their ears to protect them from the noise. The powder took, spluttered for an instant and then the cannon roared out. The recoil sent it slithering back across the floor of timber beams and the crew hurried to reload it. Evans swabbed out the barrel, steam hissing from the wet sponge, and then stood clear while a fresh charge and ball were rammed home.

'Run up,' shouted Rosso, and the sailors grabbed the wheels to roll the heavy piece back into position. He leant forward and jabbed his spike down the touchhole till he felt the barb at the end first push against and then pierce the thin canvas bag that held the charge. He filled the touchhole with a stream of fine powder from the horn around his neck, and peered down the barrel to check that the gun was run up straight. Through the thin slot in the embrasure he could see the grey wall of the fortress, pock marked now by impact craters. Cracks ran like canyons across the stone, and several large pieces had broken off the wall. Just above the point they were bombarding a pair of soldiers visible. As he looked one of them levelled his musket with care, pointed straight at him. Good luck at that range, Rosso thought. You and your mate have been trying to drill one through this gun port for the last hour. The soldier's head disappeared behind a puff of smoke as he fired, again without effect. From somewhere out of view one of the defender's cannon roared. There was a solid thud against the front of the gun emplacement to his left as the ball struck home, and a trickle of dislodged soil cascaded down onto the barrel of the gun.

'Stand clear,' he yelled again and the gun fired once more. He took a step back from the big cannon while the crew went through the routine of loading the piece, and looked around him. The gun emplacement was well built with a floor made of heavy timbers. Most had been taken from the church in Vieux Fort, supplemented by some from the ships in the bay. He stamped on it experimentally. It was far from the smooth oak deck he was used to but it was a fair surface on which to operate a gun although he could tell from the scarring beneath the iron rims of the carriage wheels that the recoil would eventually wear ruts into the wood. He looked to his left down the short second parallel of trench to where it switched back into the long first parallel. Two figures came hurrying around the corner. One carried a cannon ball, the other a fresh charge. Behind them a small group of 53rd Infantry soldiers sat with their backs in the shade of the trench wall.

He glanced back at his gun, just as O'Malley rammed the wad home with the flexible rammer. The Irishman pulled the long rod free and Rosso stepped forward once more.

'Run up,' he ordered. The gun thumped back into place and he again pricked the charge, filled the touchhole with powder and sighted down the barrel. The same view as last time, with a little more damage to the wall. No wait, thought Rosso. Something in what he was looking at was different. He looked again, grey wall damaged at its base, ditch at its feet, blue sky above. What was it? There were two guns in action in the battery now, and the third was in the process of being hauled forward. He heard the gun captain of the other piece shout a warning, and his view was obscured with dense smoke as the gun fired. He thought of waiting for the smoke to clear, but he could sense the restlessness of the gun crew behind him.

'Come on, Rosie,' urged Trevan. 'I know we ain't on the barky, but it don't seem natural not to fire as quick as we can.'

'Stand clear,' Rosso shouted, bringing down the linstock and the cannon fired once more. While the crew reloaded the gun, he stepped back again, picturing what he had seen through the narrow gap in the gun emplacement. Wall, ditch and sky. Wall, ditch and sky. What was it that was wrong? The men stepped back from the gun, and Rosso ordered it run up. He again pricked the charge, poured in the powder and sighted along the barrel. One of the dressed stones had been destroyed altogether now, revealing the softer rubble backfill that made up the central core of the fortress wall. He was about to fire again when he realised what was different.

'Mr Preston,' he called to the midshipman in charge of the battery. 'Do we have any canister for these guns, sir? I think we are about to be attacked.'

'Attacked?' said Preston, exchanging glances with Captain Webb who stood next to him. 'Why the deuce to you think that, Rosso?'

'Cause the Frogs have stopped firing at us, sir,' replied the sailor, 'and there are no soldiers in sight anymore on the top of the wall.'

The two gun crews stopped serving their guns and stood at their places. Most pulled their bandanas free from one ear to listen. It was certainly a lot quieter. For the first time in days they could hear surf as it crashed against the rocks on the Atlantic side of the peninsula. From behind them came sharp orders and the sound of grunted cries as the last of the siege guns was heaved along the trench. No cannon fire could be heard from the fort, no slap and whine of passing musket balls.

'This does seem deuced peculiar, Mr Preston,' said Captain Webb.

'Evans,' said the midshipman. 'Jump up on the gun carriage, and let us know what you can see.'

From his six and a half feet, combined with the height of the gun carriage, Evans peered towards the wall of the fort, shading his eyes with one hand and balancing with the other.

'Do Frog soldiers wear black hats with small pompoms on the top, sir?' he asked, 'because if they do, the ditch is full of the bastards.'

'Damnation!' exclaimed the engineer officer. 'They must

have a sally port in the fortress wall that opens into it. There are a few rounds of canister stored over there, but what we chiefly need is to be reinforced.'

'Sedgwick, run like the wind down the trench,' ordered Preston. 'Send every trench guard and soldier you come across up here, especially the ones shifting that last gun. When you reach camp, raise the alarm. Go man!' Sedgwick set off like a hare, and Preston turned to the waiting gun crews. 'Load with canister, lads. Ram it down on top of ball like we would on the ship, and wait on my order to fire.' He clambered up to the top of the wall of the redoubt, from where he could see the fortress ditch. With his head on one side he could just hear the sound of muted orders as the French deployed themselves for their sortie.

It took two men to lift the heavy copper cylinders and slot them into the barrels of the guns. Each made a heavy rattle as the musket balls they were packed with settled into place.

'How many balls do you reckon each of these has in it?' asked Evans, as he helped O'Malley ram the cylinder home.

'I don't know for sure,' replied the Irishman. 'I reckon hundreds from the fecking weight. This will give them Frogs something to think about.'

'Run up!' ordered Rosso. Behind him he heard the first group of the trench guard arrive, their boots clattering across the timbers.

'Right, corporal,' he heard Captain Webb say. 'The navy boys will give them a whiff of grape, and then it will be all hell. Can you post your men in a line back here ready to fire, but keep well clear of the cannons' recoil.'

As Preston watched, he heard the bark of an order from the ditch, followed by the steady rattle of a drum. He glanced back down into the emplacement to check that both guns were loaded and ready. The two gun captains held their smouldering linstocks high, eyes fixed on him as they waited for the order to fire. He thought how vulnerable the emplacement looked. There were only sixteen sailors, some with cutlasses and the odd pistol, but most would have to fight with whatever weapons they could improvise from the rammers and hand spikes they were using to serve the guns. Perhaps a dozen soldiers had arrived with muskets so far. He looked back towards the fortress ditch. A line of ladder tops appeared, followed by streams of soldiers as they came boiling out. They ran to their places, forming up in a three deep line under the urging of their officers. Christ, thought Preston, there must be at least two hundred of them.

'Ready?' he called down.

'Aye aye, sir,' shouted back the two gun captains. Preston drew his little midshipman's dirk. The shortness of the blade seemed to emphasise the weakness of their position.

The French soldiers were now a solid block of white-cross-belted figures. The sun glinted off their needle sharp bayonets. The officer in the middle of the line waved his sword, the drummer next to him began to beat his drum, and the line moved towards the gun emplacement. Preston suppressed the urge to fire straight away and forced himself to wait for the line to come within fifty yards of them. The beat of the drum and the steady tread of the advancing line seemed to mesmerise him. With a huge effort he tore his gaze from the soldiers, and instead chose to concentrate on a small patch of bare earth about the right distance away. When he saw the first French boot stamp down on it he turned to face his men.

'Fire,' he yelled. Both guns went off together, like the twin barrels of some monstrous shot gun. The cones of musket balls tore two holes in the line, each blast sweeping a dozen attackers away. The line hesitated for a moment, the soldiers shocked by the sudden onslaught, but then they surged forwards once more, closing ranks as they came. Preston dropped down into the emplacement.

'No time to reload, men,' he yelled. 'Grab what weapons you can.' From outside the emplacement a French cheer rang out as the line broke into a charge. A yelling head with a bicorn hat appeared above the parapet. The sound abruptly stopped as Evans punched the end of his rammer into the soldier's face, but no sooner had it disappeared than a dozen other heads replaced it as the attackers clambered up the wall of gabions.

*****

Lieutenant Thomas Macpherson sat in the shade under a palm tree with his hat by his side, his tunic unbuttoned and his neck cloth loose. His tree was set a little apart from those that provided shade for the combined force of forty marines drawn from both the *Rush* and the *Agrius* that he commanded. They sat around in groups and quietly chatted, their muskets leaning together in stands like a row of small wigwam frames. His little force was there to supply a reserve of men to support the trench guards, but as yet had not been called on since the siege began.

Macpherson paused to swat a small insect away with the flat of his hand, before returning to his book. He was deep into the first volume of *The Choices of Miss Amelia Grey* which he had borrowed from Sutton, and was reading the story with obvious pleasure. He had just reached the scene at the ball where Miss Amelia first danced with the dashing Mr Lavery, when a tactful cough from his sergeant drew him back into the present.

He looked up to see the figure of Sedgwick as he bounded down the line of the first parallel. He thrust the slim volume into the inside pocket of his tunic, picked up his hat and rose to his feet with a clatter of sword scabbard against palm tree.

'Thank you, sergeant,' he said. 'Have the men stand to, if you please.'

'Yes, sir,' barked the sergeant, before swivelling away towards the soldiers. Macpherson buttoned up his tunic, and placed his hat on his head as Sedgwick ran up to him.

'Mr Preston's compliments,' gasped Sedgwick, 'and the French are attacking the siege guns. Will you come as fast as may be convenient.' The Scotsman looked up towards the fortress, just in time to see the first of the French soldiers as they climbed out of the ditch.

'Corporal Patton!' he bellowed.

'Sir!' replied the corporal, striding over.

'Fly down to the camp and find Colonel Gordon,' he ordered. 'He will be near the church. Tell him that the French have made a sortie, and I have gone to assist the gunners. Request that he turns out the guard. Quickly now.' Macpherson watched the marine run down the slope, and then turned towards the sailor.

'Can you return to Mr Preston, and tell him I am on my way,' he said. Sedgwick knuckled his forehead in salute, and set off back towards the trench. Macpherson looked towards his men. 'Marines,' he ordered, 'follow me, at the double.'

The marines trotted up the now deserted first parallel behind their lieutenant, flowing past the abandoned third siege gun. The soldiers who had been pulling it must have rushed up to help at the gun emplacement, thought Macpherson. It was good fortune that the gun was being dragged forward at the time of the French assault, providing a reserve of soldiers already in the trench. His view of the action was cut off by the high wall of gabions. Occasional disembodied sounds drifted down the slope from the fight around the siege guns. He could hear the bang of muskets and the shout of orders, the shriek and clash of blade on blade and over all the cries of the wounded.

'This is bloody ridiculous,' muttered Macpherson to himself. 'How am I to know what is the right thing to do when I can see nothing?' When they reached the end of the first trench he brought his men to a halt.

'Wait here, sergeant,' he ordered. 'Keep the men closed up ready to deploy. I shall view matters for myself.' He pulled himself out of the trench, and marched around the last gabion onto the open glacis. He expected to be shot at from the fortress, but no shot came. He glanced that way but could see no defenders on the wall. Then he looked towards the gun emplacement. It seemed to heave with life as the masses of attackers struggled with those within. He tried to estimate the number of French soldiers—there were certainly far more than the forty men he had to hand. He was surprised that the French had not already overwhelmed the defenders, but then he remembered the soldiers who would have been dragging the gun forward. He forced himself to stay calm. What was the best thing for him to do? He could provide a little relief if he fed his men up the trench piecemeal, unless.... Macpherson looked back at the fortress wall as an altogether bolder idea formed in his mind. There was no one there to alert the attackers of his presence, and the troops who had sallied out all seemed to be fully engaged in their attack.

'Marines, out here,' he ordered. 'Form up between the ditch and the trench.' The men poured out and assembled into a solid block of red. 'Fix bayonets!' he ordered. Forty long blades flashed in the sunshine, and were slotted home with a collective twist and clunk.

'Marines, forward march!' The line moved towards the French infantry, boots crunching down in near perfect time on the smooth glacis of the fortress. As they neared the enemy, they began to see details of how fierce the struggle for the emplacement was. They swept past the groaning victims of the blasts of canister. Wisps of musket smoke drifted over the ground. The base of the wall of gabions was littered with fallen soldiers. Those on the top struggled with the unseen defenders within, or stood back to fire their muskets down into the redoubt. Most were either attempting to scramble up the wall, or waiting their turn at the bottom. All had their backs to the approaching body of marines as it swung around behind them.

'Shall we give them a volley, sir?' asked the sergeant.

'No shooting!' said Macpherson, 'I want to take them unawares.' He drew his own sword, and raised his voice so that all the marines could hear. 'By push of bayonets only, men. Charge!'

The men gave a cheer and broke into a shambling run, their muskets held at waist level to form a hedge of steel. At last they had been noticed. French soldiers spun round in alarm at this unexpected attack with panic on their faces. Those on top of the wall jumped back down from the gun emplacement, to join their comrades as they tried to form a line to meet the new threat, while the less resolute began to melt away towards the safety of the fortress. Before the French could organise themselves to face the attack, the marines crashed into them. Several French soldiers went down, bayoneted where they stood while others turned and fled. But some still resisted. Macpherson saw a soldier in front of him swing his musket up and take aim. He watched the barrel as it tracked round until it pointed directly towards him. The soldier steadied himself for a moment and then fired. An instant later the Scotsman felt himself knocked back by a huge blow. The ground rushed up to meet him and all went dark.

*****

Inside the gun emplacement, the defenders were fighting for their lives. They had received an initial boost when the thirty soldiers who had been hauling the siege gun forward had arrived, providing a solid body of trained men. Captain Webb had combined them with the trench guards into a firing line at the back of the redoubt to shoot over the sailors' heads at the assaulting French soldiers. They loaded and fired as fast as they could, but they were also an easy target for the French on top of the redoubt wall as they fired down into the confined space. After the first body of reinforcements only a trickle of trench guards had arrived, summoned by Sedgwick in his breathless flight towards camp. These barely served to replace the fallen. Each new arrival seemed to come just in time to take the place of a soldier who had crashed down to join the growing pile of dead and wounded on the floor of the emplacement, and now even this trickle had stopped.

In front of the soldiers were Preston's sailors, locked in battle with the French. Rosso and O'Malley were stationed at their gun embrasure, fighting to prevent the French from forcing their way through the narrow gap. A French musket, tipped with a long bayonet was thrust through the opening.

'Hit it, Sean,' yelled Rosso from his side of the embrasure. O'Malley swung a heavy crowbar down on the musket from above his head, catching it against the gun barrel with a loud clang, and Rosso darted forward with his cutlass. He thrust it hard into the now disarmed attacker. There was a cry of pain, and Rosso jumped back just as another French soldier fired his musket past his wounded comrade. The bullet whined off the barrel of the siege gun, leaving a silver smear on the metal.

'Good work, Rosie,' said O'Malley, indicating his friend's cutlass, the tip of which was now pink with blood.

'Some bleeding help back here!' shouted Evans, his voice edged with panic. He was standing beside the wheel of the gun and was using his long rammer like a spear, thrusting it at any soldier who became established on top of the emplacement wall. It was exhausting work, and as he tired he was in danger of being overwhelmed. O'Malley stepped back and saw there were now three French soldiers fighting with Evans. One was parrying the rammer, while the other two aimed their muskets at the troublesome sailor. The Irishman pulled his as yet unused pistol from his belt and fired it at one of the soldiers who was taking aim, and he tumbled backwards off the top of the embrasure, but there was little he could do about the other. The soldier Evans was fighting with now had a foot on the end of his rammer, while his colleague sighted along his musket at the disarmed sailor. O'Malley hurled his empty pistol at him, putting him off his aim, but having knocked the musket wide for a moment, the pistol dropped down outside the emplacement.

'No you fucking don't,' yelled the returning Sedgwick. He leapt past O'Malley, up onto the top of the gun carriage and swung a musket he had picked up from the ground in a wide arc through the air. It caught the soldier a savage blow to the legs, just as he pulled the trigger. The shot missed and a volley of musket fire from the back of the redoubt swept the two French soldiers away.

'Thanks, lads,' gasped Evans. 'I owe you both.'

'No worries, Sam,' replied O'Malley. 'What Irishman would not be content to be shot at for six pence a day to help the fecking English?'

'Now,' said the Londoner, 'before you start, it was your bleeding idea we should volunteer for this.'

'Sean!' shouted Rosso. 'They're coming through the embrasure again!' O'Malley spun around, to see his friend locked in battle with a soldier crouched on the barrel of the siege gun. The Frenchman thrust his musket at the sailor, and Rosso parried the blow with his cutlass. O'Malley strode across and swung his crowbar at the soldier, catching him on the arm. He crumpled under the blow and dropped his musket with a cry of pain. Rosso finished him off, and the body of the soldier slid down onto the floor of the gun emplacement. Rosso and O'Malley pushed it under the gun, and then both men resumed their places either side of the embrasure, waiting for the next assault.

No immediate attack came. The firing from the line of soldiers at the back of the redoubt petered out for want of any targets. O'Malley stepped back and looked up at the top of the wall of gabions again, now clear of attackers. Preston came over to join the two sailors.

'What's going on?' the midshipman asked. 'Did you get help, Sedgwick?'

'Yes, sir,' he replied. 'Lieutenant Macpherson should be just behind me.' He looked back down the trench, wondering where the marines could be.

'Why have the Frogs stopped their attack?' asked the teenager.

'I don't know, sir,' said Rosso. 'I can still hear them making a deal of noise, but it sounds different.' The noise of French cries drifted in through the gun embrasure, together with a more solid cheer. The men exchanged glances.

'That's our boys cheering, or I have never heard a navy huzzah before,' exclaimed Rosso.

'Evans,' said Preston. 'Can you climb back up on the gun carriage, and tell us what's happening?'

'Aye aye, sir,' said Evans, dropping his rammer and clambering up. He inched his head above the parapet, peered around with care, and then stood up straight with a grin. 'Well bugger me if it ain't the bleeding Lobsters at last!' he cried. 'They're chasing off all the Frogs, sir.'

Chapter 13
Truce

Midshipman Preston had a feeling of déjà vu. He was standing once more next to the immaculately dressed Captain Webb in the same section of trench that they had stood in over a week before. Once again they were watching the same small group of soldiers march up the main road towards the fortress gate. The same ensign led the way with his large white flag. The same drummer boy marched by his side, and behind them came Major Grafton who, if it were possible, looked even more pleased with himself than before. Just as last time the group paused every twenty yards to allow the drummer to send out his thunderous warning of their approach.

Similar, and yet not the same, thought Preston to himself. Much had changed in that time. For one thing the balance of power had swung decisively towards the attackers. Their system of trenches now came to within striking distance of the wall. The gun emplacement boasted all three siege guns, and although they had fallen silent for the period of the parley, they had been tearing steadily away at the shattered fortress wall, each impact sending a fresh fall of rubble cascading down into the ditch.

He looked much the same as he had then. Perhaps his

uniform was rather grubbier, his white breeches torn and smeared pink with soil, but inside he knew that he had changed too. The uncertain teenage midshipman he had been a week ago had matured quickly in the crucible of the redoubt on the day of the French attack. For the first time in his seventeen years he had feared that he might die. When the blasts of canister had failed to stop the French line he had felt real terror, and there had been no senior officer for him to turn to. When he looked around he had found no calm lieutenant, nor grey-haired captain. So he had done his duty and faced down his fears. He had led his men well, determined not to disgrace himself in front of them. Colonel Gordon had been full of praise for him and Captain Webb. He was to be mentioned in the Colonel's despatch home on the action, and Captain Clay had said that he would recommend him to the admiral should an opportunity come for a trial as an acting lieutenant. Inside he felt a glow of pride, but also the calm determination of one who now knows what he is capable of.

Preston looked back towards the fortress, where the party had come to a halt before the gates. They swung open at last, and the same French officer emerged as last time. Preston noticed that his left arm was now supported in a sling. The officers saluted each other, and the discussions began.

'Am I deceived, Mr Preston, or is that French officer a damn sight less cocksure?' purred Captain Webb. 'See how he has made no attempt to prevent the meeting taking place on the French side of the glacis?'

'He also seems to be inconvenienced in his discourse by only having a single arm to animate,' replied the midshipman.

'Yes, that must be vexing for him,' said the engineer. 'These Frogs do like to wave their arms about when they converse. My money is on a surrender within three days. I believe our actions in confounding their attack on the redoubt yesterday, together with the dash those marines showed, will have wholly knocked the pluck out of them.'

'We shall soon find out,' said Preston. 'They seemed to have finished their discussions already.'

The two officers shook hands, stepped smartly back from each other, and Major Grafton then swung about to set off marching down the road towards the British line, with his flag bearer and drummer trailing in his wake.

'Well, sir? What news?' asked Captain Webb when the Major was once more back in the British trench. Major Grafton beamed at them both. 'Truce for two days, and if they are not relieved by noon on the second day they will surrender the fortress, the garrison and all her contents to us. Bloody marvellous what?'

'Bloody marvellous indeed, sir,' replied the captain with a smile. 'Major, might I name Midshipman Preston to you? He was the naval officer with me in the redoubt when it was attacked.'

'Were you, by Jove? Good man,' enthused the Major, gripping the teenager's hand in his.

*****

'I am here to ascertain if the invalid will be able to attend tonight's festivities?' asked Clay, two days later, as he sat in the wardroom of the *Rush*. 'It will be a poor celebration of our most famous victory without one of the principal heroes of the hour.'

'I do have the sensation that I have been kicked in the chest by a mule, sir,' replied Macpherson. 'And I now sport a bruise on my body the size of a dinner plate, but if I might have the assurance of a comfortable seat I believe Mr Linfield will sanction my attendance.'

'Well that is splendid news,' beamed Clay. The marine officer turned stiffly round in his chair, and picked something up from the table.

'Will you also pass on my most sincere thanks to your sister for the fulsomeness of her prose?' he asked. 'If the first volume of *The Choices of Miss Amelia Grey* were but a few pages the less, I fear I might not have been here at all.'

The Scotsman passed across the small leather book, a French musket ball lodged like a plum in the centre of the cover. Clay turned the crushed novel in his hands and felt the slight dome of the ball pressed against the back.

'Upon my word, it damn nearly did go all the way through,' he exclaimed. 'I will certainly pass on your thanks to Miss Clay. Would you also like me to request a replacement volume? I am sure you would still like knowledge of how Miss Grey and Mr Lavery's relationship developed after the ball?'

'You mean after the dance, rather than the musket ball, sir?' asked Macpherson, to general laughter.

'Quite so, Mr Macpherson,' said Clay, smiling at the marine. 'It is exceedingly good to find you in such excellent spirits.'

'Why should I not be, sir?' asked the Scot. 'After such a noble victory achieved over the French.'

'Is that truly the only reason?' asked Clay. 'Surely you must have thought all was lost when the ball struck you, and yet here you still are.'

'Aye, you have the truth of it, sir,' said the marine. 'Some of my exuberance does come from finding that I yet live. It is a strange matter to be convinced one is facing death, and yet to be reprieved.'

'Well we are all thankful for that, Tom' said Clay, patting the marine on his good shoulder. 'Now, if you gentlemen are all ready, we must depart, for it is almost five bells and we should allow a little extra time for our wounded comrade. John, is the cutter ready to take us ashore?'

'Yes, sir,' replied Sutton, 'and I have had a boatswain's chair rigged for the convenience of Mr Macpherson.'

'Splendid, gentlemen,' said Clay. 'Shall we go?'

A short boat ride later the officers of the *Rush* were strolling through the streets of Vieux Fort in their best uniforms. Life had started to return to normal in the town. In the army cantonment the tents were being taken down, and the various piles of unused stores were being moved back to the beach to be returned to the waiting transporters. For the inhabitants life was beginning under their new masters. Fishing boats once more dotted the waters of Black Bay. Those that had fled to nearby plantations on the morning the British ships had arrived, now returned to see if their houses still stood and if any of their abandoned possessions remained.

The officers left the town by the road that led towards the fortress. They meandered across the glacis in no particular hurry to reach their destination. Partly they set their pace to that of the battered Macpherson, and partly to enjoy the cool of the evening. The sun drifted down towards the western horizon, throwing long shadows across the grass, and turning the tall sugar loaf mountain behind the town pink. All around them were signs that the siege was over. Emptied gabions were stacked in piles, ready to be taken away, while parties of soldiers were busy filling in the trenches dug with such effort at the start of the siege. As they approached the fortress itself, the officers from the *Agrius* came up behind them.

'Captain Clay, upon my word,' said Captain Parker, shaking his hand, 'and the victors from the *Rush*. Lieutenant Macpherson, I give you joy of your recovery. I cannot express how delighted I am to see you on your feet once more. You must surely be the most fortunate man alive!'

'Can I name Midshipman Preston to you, sir,' said Clay, drawing the teenager forward. 'He was the officer in charge of the shore party that put up such a spirited resistance until they were rescued by Lieutenant Macpherson's dashing counter attack.'

'Delighted to meet you, young man,' said Parker. 'Well done, sir, well done.'

Clay and Parker stepped away from the midshipman to allow the other officers of the *Agrius* to crowd around Preston and congratulate their former shipmate. Clay glanced across with a smile for the teenager, and noticed Windham hanging back from his fellow officers. He turned away to join Parker, and the two captains strolled along ahead of the others.

'Now here is a splendid sight, Clay,' enthused the captain, indicating the fortress when they reached the edge of the ditch and could look across the cobbled causeway which led to the main entrance. Fluttering in the breeze above the gate flew a large union flag in place of the French tricolour, while to both sides they could see the red-coated soldiers of the Shropshire regiment patrolling the walls.

'A splendid sight indeed, sir,' agreed Clay. 'But look. Direct your gaze towards the stone work above the gate? Do you see the remains of the royal arms of France cut in the stone that some zealot has chiselled off?'

'Well, that's revolutions for you,' said Parker. 'Pray God

we never see the like on our shores.'

As they went through the gate, Clay noticed a pungent aroma, which reminded him of something he had heard earlier that day.

'Colonel Gordon was telling me that when the fortress was handed over today, they discovered that the French had a secret weapon,' he said.

'Upon my word, did they really?' said Parker. 'Well, they are tricky blighters. What manner of secret weapon was that?'

'Goats, sir,' said Clay, keeping his face impassive.

'Goats!' exclaimed Parker. 'What on earth can you mean, Clay?'

'Apparently the sappers could not understand how the French had succeeded in keeping the glacis of their fortress devoid of any cover on a tropical island where everything grows so rapid,' he explained. 'The answer was found penned up inside the walls. They had a large herd of goats which are apparently the perfect creature both for eating troublesome plants while doubtless also supplying the garrison with ample milk and cheese.'

*****

The main hall of the fortress had been arranged with some style for the victory dinner. It was a large white washed room with a high ceiling, and a heavy table of tropical hard wood that ran down the centre. That had been laid with the finest silver and candles the fortress had to offer, and along each side sat the guests, the blue coats of the navy mixed among the more numerous scarlet of the army and marines. The commandant's cellar had been plundered to supply considerable amounts of wine (of his sole remaining bottle of cognac there was no sign) and this contributed to the celebratory atmosphere. The commandant's excellent chef had been persuaded to work with Captain Parker's steward Lloyd, who had been leant to Colonel Gordon for the evening. Between them they had laboured to produce as fine a banquet as possible. Clay's only contribution was that he had been asked to supply one of the *Rush*'s naval ensigns, and he was pleased to see that this was in the place of honour, crossed with the regimental colour of the Shropshire regiment and mounted on the wall above the table's head.

'I call that a very handsome gesture on the colonel's part,' he remarked to his neighbour, indicating the flags, 'to give equal prominence to both services. It is only fair in this case, but is too seldom seen.' Major Grafton followed his gaze.

'I agree, captain,' he said. 'This siege may be held as a fine example of what combined arms can achieve. On which note I believe I have not properly thanked you for the prompt way in which you landed me and my staff when that fool of a captain ran aground on that damned sand bank.'

'In fairness to the master of the *Burford,* the hazard was not set down on any of our charts, nor even on any of the French ones that were found in the fortress,' explained Clay.

'Hmm, well if you wish to defend the cove...' muttered the major. 'Still, I am very grateful. A glass of wine with you, sir?' The two men raised their glasses and the candlelight flashed off them as they were drained.

'Dashed good bishop, that,' enthused Grafton as he summoned over an orderly to refill them.

'Major, could you explain to me how the siege came to an end so abruptly after the French sortie was repulsed,' asked Clay.

'Interesting you should ask that,' said the major. 'You see, when I first had a parley with that slippery cove of theirs, they played it all superior. How the fortress was well defended with a large garrison, full with any manner of supplies and could hold out for all eternity. Turns out that was all gammon.'

'Really?' said Clay. 'I thought they acquitted themselves tolerably well.'

'Well that's the problem with your siege,' explained Grafton. 'You never truly know how many men and supplies the buggers have behind the walls till you storm the place. They can move their men about, make a deal of noise. You would be surprised how a small garrison, if well handled, can puff themselves out. It seems the Frogs were bluffing all along. In truth the garrison was quite wanting in troops. So when they attacked the redoubt all bold and full of fight, they were committing pretty much all they had in regular soldiers.'

'Ah, that explains a matter that was vexing me,' said Clay. 'When I discussed the attack with Lieutenant Macpherson, he spoke of his surprise that the French had left no troops on the fortress walls during their sortie. He thought that it was a mistake on their part, and it was the knowledge that he could approach the rear of their formation undetected that resolved him to make his attack in the open.' Clay thought about the attack for a moment and something else occurred to him.

'But tell me, major, why do you imagine that the French would hazard their whole garrison on a single sortie?' he asked. 'Does it not strike you as rather reckless and foolhardy?'

'No, not foolhardy, but certainly desperate,' said the infantry man. 'But consider how close the sortie came to success. Imagine that your midshipman did not smoke what the French were about before the attack began and so did not load the guns with canister in time, or promptly send for help? Frogs would have overwhelmed the redoubt as easy as kiss my hand. Then they might have destroyed the redoubt, perhaps set it ablaze and spiked the guns. Or imagine that the third gun was not being hauled up at the time. No gun, no extra body of troops on hand to defend the redoubt. If either of those circumstances had been otherwise, the French sortie would have succeeded. The gallant marines would then have arrived to find the Frogs snug back behind their walls, and you and I would not be sat here busy pouring the commandant's excellent claret down our gullets, what! Your good health, sir.'

'Yes, perhaps we were fortunate indeed,' mused Clay, and then he corrected himself. 'No, that is not just. The presence of the third gun was pure chance, I grant you, but the actions of Mr Preston and his men, and Captain Webb, do not fall into that category. They did smoke the French plan, and performed their duty well.'

'You have the truth of it, sir,' said the major. 'The lad is to be commended indeed.' The two men turned in their chairs and looked down the table towards where Preston sat listening to the conversation around him. The major caught his eye, and the two officers raised their glass to the midshipman, who blushed in response.

'I understand that you negotiated the truce, Major?' asked Clay.

'I had that honour, yes,' said Grafton. 'I speak tolerable French. My mother was a native of Geneva and spoke to me in that tongue from the cradle, so I have some facility with it. As a result, whenever a prisoner needs to be interrogated or a parley held Colonel Gordon will dispatch me to perform the task.'

Philip K. Allan

'Was it excessively difficult to negotiate?' continued Clay.

'Not in this case, no,' said the soldier. 'Most sieges tend to conclude in that manner. Once it is clear that the game is up, the defenders generally look for terms. It saves all the loss of life and treasure that would follow from pushing matters to a conclusion. For our part we save a fortune in shot and powder as well as having less of an inconvenient great hole in the outer wall of the fortress in need of repair as soon as we take possession of the place.'

'Sea fights are not dissimilar,' said Clay. 'They generally end in one side striking their colours to the other. When matters have reached a point when the outcome is certain, there is no disgrace in yielding to save further bloodshed.'

'Have you ever been obliged to strike, captain?' asked the soldier. Clay had enough of a sailor's superstition to place his fingers down on the wood of the table before replying.

'Thankfully I have been spared that so far,' he replied, 'although I have come decidedly close, not more than a month ago.'

'Is that so,' said Grafton. 'What were the particulars?'

'When I first took command of the *Rush* she was quite inconvenienced by a prodigious amount of weed growing on her bottom which made her decidedly sluggish,' explained Clay. 'We had the ill fortune to fall in with a Spanish ship of the line in light airs, and found ourselves being overhauled. This all happened in the waters near here. Our position was quite perilous as you can imagine, faced by such a superior ship.'

'What did you do?' asked the major.

'I negotiated no truce, you may be sure,' said Clay. 'There is no disgrace in flight from such an unequal battle. My problem was that my enemy had both overwhelming power

240

and the faster ship.' Clay paused to sip at his wine, and became aware that all at his end of the table were now listening to him.

'How did you evade such a determined foe, Captain Clay?' asked Colonel Gordon, from the head of the table.

'I used every resource at my disposal to escape, sir,' explained Clay. 'We deployed our sweeps to supplement what deficient wind we had, and my people were obliged to row with them for almost a day and a night. We also lightened the ship by throwing everything heavy we could lay hands on overboard, including our water, guns and anchors. The Dons were quite relentless in their pursuit. It was only when Bridgetown and the masts of the rest of the squadron were in sight that they gave up the chase.'

The story was met with a thunder of approval as the army officers drummed the table with their fists. When the noise had subsided, Colonel Gordon spoke up.

'Well, captain, I give you joy of your victory. I also hope that this mighty ship of yours does not turn up uninvited to spoil our little party here!'

'Amen to that,' said Captain Parker, touching the wood of the table too as he did so.

*****

The dinner ended with the guests toasting the many contributors to the victory, in such a profusion of bumpers that most of those present became quite drunk. The majority of officers left the stuffy hall to enjoy the cool of the night on the ramparts of the fortress, many with the commandant's best cigars still clamped between their teeth. Lieutenant Munro had insisted that Macpherson and Preston should walk him over the actual ground of their triumph, and some of the junior officers from the Shropshire regiment had gone with them. Charles Faulkner could hear their loud voices out on the fortress glacis below where he stood on the wall, and looking towards the noise he saw their lighted cigars dancing like fireflies in the warm air.

'Well this is an agreeable surprise, Charles old boy,' said Windham, coming up beside the purser. 'I had begun to suspect you of avoiding your old acquaintance. Have you missed my society?' Faulkner looked the younger man up and down before he replied.

'No, I have no objection to your society, Nicholas,' he replied. 'Although I will confess I do find your inclination to obsess about your uncle's death can become tiresome.'

'Not death, Charles,' corrected Windham. 'He was murdered.'

'Yes, I know, by those ne'er do wells Lieutenant Sutton, or Commander Clay, or both,' sighed the purser. He looked out into the night for a moment before turning back towards Windham. 'Of late I have found myself making the comparison between men of our station and those of the middling sort that have had to make their own way in life, like those two. It can be quite revealing, Nicholas.'

'Whatever can you mean, Charles?' said Windham. 'We were gentlemen from the cradle; they are only regarded as such in deference to their holding the King's Commission.'

'Indeed, that is my very point,' said Faulkner. 'Consider the advantages of birth and situation we had before we even took our first step. And what have we done with such blessings? Like you I am a younger son. My older brother's station in life is clear as heir to the Faulkner estate, but what was I to do? The Church held no appeal for me, nor soldiering either. I have never had much ability on the hunting field. Small wonder that I cured my ennui at the gaming table, to the detriment of my poor family.'

'At least you had the benefit of some choice in the matter,' snorted Windham. 'The Church would have suited me quite well, but oh no. Now, Nicholas, says my father, your cousin Jack has been killed on his ship in the Channel. It is your duty to the family to join the navy and so benefit from Uncle Percy's generous preferment. No question of asking me whether I actually liked the bloody sea. And now my uncle is dead, killed by that bastard Sutton, and I am left to shift for myself.' He kicked out viciously at a loose stone on the path beside them and it sailed into the dark. A few moments later it clattered in the ditch below them.

'I know you despise Clay and Sutton, Nicholas, but I believe your opinion of them both to be wrong,' resumed the purser. 'Clay's father died when he was but a boy. He was sent to sea at twelve because his mother could not keep both him and his sister. Sutton's father yet lives, but is only a naval lieutenant himself, with little enough influence to help his boy.'

'What of it?' sneered Windham. 'So they are lowly born men who have jumped up above their station?'

'That was not my point, Nicholas,' said Faulkner. 'I now find myself admiring how they have improved their situations, especially when I consider the decline in my own position.'

'Even though they are murders?' said Windham.

'As to that I am most unsure,' said the purser. 'I have tried my best to provoke an indiscretion on their part, I truly have, but without success. Lieutenant Sutton is a thoroughly amiable shipmate with what I judge to be an honest character, and the captain is one of the best commanders I have served under. In truth I start to believe that this ship's boy of yours may have made his dreadful allegation principally to gain favour with you.'

'It's not just the boy,' said Windham. 'His observations merely confirm what I already knew. I looked into their eyes, just after the deed was done, remember. I know what I saw.'

'Well, be that as it may, I can do no more to satisfy you, Nicholas,' said Faulkner. 'You must pursue your dispute with these gentlemen without me.'

'Well, this is all very vexing,' said Windham. 'I was under the impression we had an arrangement. You were resolved to find the compelling evidence that I need, and in return I would remain silent on the matter of your disreputable past.'

'I gave no such undertaking,' said Faulkner. 'My actions were motivated by the mutual regard and admiration that exists between our two families. I have done as you asked, and that is an end of the matter.'

'Not for me, Faulkner,' hissed Windham. 'There is very little regard or admiration on my part, you may be sure. Have a care. If that is truly your last word on this matter, I believe it may be time for me to have a little conversation with my old shipmate Alexander Clay, damn his eyes.'

'You must do as you see fit,' said the purser with a shrug of his shoulders. 'I believe I saw him taking the air over by the gate. Now, if you will excuse me I will rejoin those who I do regard as my friends.'

When Faulkner had left, Windham hurled his cigar to the ground and stamped on it. A trail of sparks flew up from the butt and drifted in the night air. Who did that damned fool think he was? he asked himself as he made his stumbling way along the wall. Had his family not bailed out the Faulkners when their son's foolish gambling had brought them to the edge of ruin? Had they not hushed up the scandal at the time? Well, it need be hushed up no longer. Ahead of him he saw the tall figure of Clay shaking hands with Major Grafton.

'Thank you again for a most enjoyable evening, major,' Windham heard Clay say as he approached the pair. The major raised a friendly hand, and set off towards his new quarters inside the fortress.

'Might I have a word, sir?' Windham asked.

'By all means, Mr Windham,' said Clay. 'Have you enjoyed your evening?'

'It was tolerable,' he replied. 'The society of army officers is not one I would naturally chose.'

'Indeed?' said Clay. 'I must say I found our hosts most welcoming. Major Grafton in particular was highly instructive on the science of siege warfare, and I now understand rather more about recent events than I did, but perhaps the conversation was less engaging where you were sat? Still, I digress. You wished to speak with me?'

'Yes, sir,' said Windham. 'I feel it my duty to warn you about the ill character of Mr Faulkner. The man is a notorious rake, who should certainly not be trusted with the finances of any ship.'

'I see,' said Clay. 'That is a very grave accusation. May I ask why you are able to be so decided in your view of Mr Faulkner? I thought he was a friend of yours?'

'An acquaintance certainly, sir,' corrected Windham. 'Friendship would be to overstate our relationship. He has had some dealings with my family in the past with regard to his considerable gaming debts.'

'Ah, I believe I start to see how matters stand,' said Clay. 'Tell me, are you aware of any recent actions on Mr

Faulkner's part that I should be concerned about, or do your observations relate only to events in the past?'

'They do relate to the past, sir,' conceded Windham, his face flushing with annoyance, 'but I hardly see that as a cause for you to dismiss them.'

'No, I shall not dismiss them, and I thank you for your advice, Mr Windham,' said Clay. 'But if they are of a historic nature then I am already aware of them. Mr Faulkner told me the details himself. I confess that I was concerned at first, but I have received sufficient reassurance for me to take no further action.'

'No further action!' spat Windham. 'How can that possibly be?'

'Provoking as this seems to be for you, unless you have some more current allegations about Mr Faulkner, the matter is closed,' said Clay. 'Although I am a little surprised that you have only seen fit to bring your knowledge of Mr Faulkner's past to my attention now. Surely you must have had your doubts over him for months? Or perhaps it would be for the best if we should not explore your motives too deeply? Now, if that is all, perhaps I might return to my ship?'

'I am not finished with you,' insisted Windham.

'Mr Windham!' barked Clay. 'May I remind you that I am a superior officer? You address me as sir, and you do not contradict me in such a fashion. You have obviously taken more drink than was wise and I suggest we end our discourse here.'

'Are you also aware of everything about Mr Sutton... sir?' blurted out Windham, his face contorted with fury.

'I strongly advise you to end this conversation now, Mr Windham,' said Clay, his voice ice. 'Before things are said that cannot be unsaid.'

'He murdered my uncle!' hissed Windham, past caring. 'When he fell over the side of the *Agrius*. My uncle was clinging to a line, and he took his sword and cut him free. I know he did. I have spoken to people who were there, who saw him do it.'

'Get out of here,' shouted Clay 'Go, now! That's an order!'

*****

In the main cabin of the *Rush* only two lanterns had been lit. Their light conjured dark shadows up from the furniture and objects in the room that slipped across the walls with the gentle rocking of the anchored ship. Clay sat facing the stern windows, deep in thought. He glanced across at his coat, which he had dropped over a nearby chair when he got back to the ship. The single gold epaulet flashed in the light, and he thought again about that desperate sea fight that had won him his promotion. His gaze moved from the golden epaulet to the jet black night behind the run of glass windows. As he sat, consumed with his thoughts, Hart came into the cabin.

'Has Mr Sutton returned to the ship yet?' he asked.

'Not yet, sir,' replied the steward. 'Shall I have him sent for when he does?'

'If you please,' said Clay. 'Can you also make a pot of coffee for two, and perhaps some rum as well.'

'Aye aye, sir. Rum and coffee twice it is.'

Sometime later Clay heard a hail of 'Boat ahoy' from the quarterdeck above his head, and the reply from the returning launch. A little later he heard the stamp and clatter as the marine sentry came to attention outside his door, followed by a knock.

'Come in!' he called, and Sutton came through the cabin

door with a grin.

'Where did you get to, sir?' he asked. 'One moment you were deep in conversation with Major Grafton, the next you had quite vanished.'

'John, do take a seat,' replied Clay. 'I was accosted by Mr Windham, after which I returned here. Coffee or rum?'

'Say no more, Alex,' laughed the lieutenant. 'I believe I might have flown from Mr Windham's society too. Just coffee, if you please. I have the morning watch tomorrow, or perhaps it is today now?' Clay poured out the coffee, and then sat back in his chair, wondering where to begin the conversation. Sutton stirred in his sugar, placed his spoon in the saucer, and looked at his captain.

'What did Mr Windham have to say for himself?' he asked.

'At first he wished to share his intelligence with regard to Mr Faulkner's past,' said Clay, sipping his coffee, 'which he made clear he has known about for some time, but which had become a pressing revelation only tonight.'

'He must have been sore vexed when he found that you already knew,' said Sutton with a chuckle.

'Very vexed,' said Clay. 'So angry indeed that it prompted him to share with me his view that you were responsible for the death of Captain Follett.' The cabin suddenly became very quiet.

'That blackguard has gone too far now,' Sutton eventually growled. 'How can he make such an outrageous allegation? He was not even present when the captain fell!' Clay looked at his friend before he replied.

'He is able to make such an allegation, because it is true,' he said.

'What!' exclaimed Sutton. 'Alex, you cannot possibly

believe him!'

'I am afraid that I do. The moment he said it the scales dropped from my eyes, and I realised that I have always known it to be true. John, I came up on deck just after the mast had fallen. I recall quite clearly what I saw. Everyone that was capable of action on the deck was busy striving to free the ship from the burden of the fallen mast. Everyone that is, except you. You were standing by the rail where the captain had been with your sword drawn, your attention entirely devoted to something over the side. At the time your want of animation puzzled me. You are too good an officer to have been inactive in such a crisis. The John Sutton I know would have been directing matters and issuing instructions. I did think you must have been wounded, but of course you were not. Your shock derived from a quite different source. Why did you do it, John?' Sutton stared at his friend for a long moment, his face flushing red.

'Why did I do it?' he repeated. 'Why? I did it for you, Alex, and for every other person aboard the ship. When the mast came down, and Follett was knocked over the side, I thanked God for it. I had been forced to watch the sad confusion with which he was directing the ship. We were losing the battle, and with every French broadside more shipmates were slain by his incompetence, and for what? Even if we won through he was bent on ruining the career of my closest friend in a quite unjust fashion. So when the fortune of war brought the mast down and pitched him over the side, I confess I was glad. I knew he was no swimmer. I thought, here is justice at last, all our problems solved. I ran to the side to make sure he was truly gone, and there he was, clinging on by a thread like a spider. I had ordered the crew to the far side of the deck to work on cutting the stays free from the mizzen chains, and so I finished off what the French had started.

One little cut, and one more death among so many others. I call that a fair price to pay.'

'Oh, John, what have you done?' groaned Clay.

'Alex, I killed a man who threatened my ship,' said Sutton. 'It is what the service requires of us in every action we go into. And I killed someone who threatened the person I hold to be dearer than a brother. For that I make no apology. I would gladly do it again, now, if I had to.'

'But I never required you to do this,' exclaimed Clay.

'Brothers should not need to ask,' Sutton replied. Clay ran his hand through his hair, in shock at the callous way his friend spoke.

'Windham spoke of witnesses,' he said. 'Who do you think he means?' Sutton shrugged.

'William thinks he has found a ship's boy on the *Agrius* who might have seen something, but it can be little more than speculation. If he was sure of his position, you can be certain he would have placed his allegations before the admiral by now.' Clay stared at Sutton.

'William?' he said. 'So Munro knows about this?'

'He does,' said Sutton, 'and would have acted exactly as I did if by chance our roles had been reversed. Alex, look how it has transformed your circumstances, for goodness sake. You now have a much improved chance of future happiness with Miss Browning, a command of your own and the regard of the admiral. Tell me truthfully if you are not pleased that I did what I did.'

'I will not deny that my circumstances have improved materially, but I would never have wished for such a change at such a cost! John, you do not seem to realise that your life may hang by a thread as precarious as that which Captain Follett clung too. If Windham can prove what he suspects...'

'I may be hanged for what I did,' shrugged Sutton. 'But it is unlikely. Even if Windham has his child witness, what can they have truly seen? At a time when the ship was encumbered with wreckage, I cut at some lines. No, Windham has no proof, nor will he ever have. What he does have is a most cruel and vindictive disposition. You can be sure that in making this revelation to you, his aim will have been to ruin our friendship. Please do not permit him to succeed in his design.'

Clay rose to his feet, and Sutton followed him.

'Never in life, brother,' he said, and the two men embraced. Clay looked over his friend's shoulder and out into the dark, frowning as he caught sight of something for a moment. Sutton detected his unease and released him.

'What's the matter, sir?' he asked.

'It's nothing,' said Clay. 'Probably just the reflection of the lamp upon the glass. I thought for a moment that I saw a light, far out at sea to the west.'

Chapter 14
San Felipe

'Wake up, sir,' urged Yates. 'You must wake up!' Clay came out of sleep, his senses groggy from all the wine he had drunk the previous night. From the dim light in the sleeping cabin he could tell it was just after dawn.

'All Right, boy, I am awake,' he growled, his mouth dry. He glanced beyond his servant and saw Midshipman Preston standing at the cabin door. The young officer looked as if he sported an even worse hangover than his captain.

'What is it, Mr Preston?' he said, forcing himself out of his cot.

'Mr Sutton's compliments, and there is a sail in sight bearing west by north, sir,' he said. 'The lookout reports it to be a large man-of-war, possibly the *San Felipe* again.'

'Thank you, Mr Preston,' said Clay. 'Tell Mr Sutton that I will be on deck directly. Yates, get me my coat.'

Preston barely had time to report back to the ship's lieutenant before Clay bounded up onto the quarterdeck, still buttoning his coat over his nightshirt.

'Is she visible yet, Mr Sutton?' he asked as he marched across the deck. 'A good morning to you, by the way,' he added.

'And to you too, sir,' he replied. 'Only her topgallants are in sight from here, but they do resemble those of a large ship even at this range. Ship of the line for sure, even if she is not the *San Felipe*, but the lookout is confident. It's Samuels, who is normally to be relied on.'

'Who was it that recognised her last time?' asked Clay. 'Was it Wilson?'

'Yes, sir, it was,' said Sutton. 'Shall I have him sent for?'

'If you please, Mr Sutton,' replied Clay. 'I shall go below and shift into some clothes. Have Wilson sent aloft with a glass, and let me know what he reports.'

Clay had just finished shaving, and had started to get dressed when Preston returned below once more.

'Mr Sutton's compliments, and Wilson is sure it is the Spaniard again, sir,' he reported.

'Very well, Mr Preston,' said Clay. 'Have this signal sent to the *Agrius*. "Submit unknown sail is Spanish seventy-four *San Felipe*." Then have the watch below turned up, if you please. I will be back on deck directly I am clothed.'

'Aye aye, sir,' said Preston.

*****

By the time Clay returned to the quarterdeck, the watch had been called, and an air of dread ran through the ship at the news that the Spanish vessel that had chased them so persistently on their last voyage in these waters was once more coming up over the horizon. The *San Felipe*'s top sails and topgallants were visible now, solid blocks of white on the horizon as she bore down towards them. Clay pulled his telescope out and examined the sails with care.

'*Agrius* is signalling, sir!' called Croft in a commanding tone. After weeks of unpleasant squeaking, his adolescent voice had at last broken, settling into a rich tenor. 'Captain, repair on board, sir.'

'Acknowledge, if you please, Mr Croft,' ordered Clay. 'Mr Sutton, kindly call away the jollyboat. While I am absent can you ensure that the crew are sent for an early breakfast. It may be some time before their next meal.' He thought for a moment about getting changed into his full dress uniform, but then rejected the idea. This was almost certain to be a hasty conference to decide on what to do, not a formal visit.

'The boat is ready, sir,' reported the lieutenant. Clay ran down onto the main deck and across to the entry port. In the *Rush* this was a simple ladder of slats fixed to the ship's side between two hand ropes, but it served the sloop well enough. Looking down into the jollyboat he noticed a new figure at the helm.

'Push off there,' ordered Sedgwick, the tiller of the boat tucked under one arm as Clay took his place in the stern sheets. 'Give way all.' The jollyboat gathered pace, gliding out across the sheltered waters of Black Bay and heading for the *Agrius*. Clay noted that Sedgwick steered the boat well, turning in a long gentle arc so as to minimise his use of the tiller.

'I was not aware that you were coxswain of the jollyboat now,' he said. 'When was this change made?'

'Mr Sutton was after seeing if I can hand, reef and steer, sir, with a view to rating me ordinary,' Sedgwick explained, 'and the crew of the jollyboat asked for me, on account of the boat being so small, and none of them able to swim at all.' Clay looked forward at the crew, who all listened and smiled in agreement as they swung backwards and forwards in unison. With only four oars, it was the smallest of the *Rush*'s boats, and while it was in no danger in the bay, he could see the jollyboat would have a lively ride when in open water. He remembered now that Sutton had told him he was testing Sedgwick out, but he was running a risk with the reputation of the ship. Parker would doubtless watch their approach, and even with battle at hand might remember later if the boat was poorly handled. A few minutes later they approached the tall side of the frigate.

'Larboard side, if you please, Sedgwick,' he ordered. With the *San Felipe* in the offing, there was no time for any of the naval ceremony that usually accompanied the arrival of even a lowly commander on board the deck of a warship.

'Aye aye, sir,' replied Sedgwick, watching his line into the ship's side.

'Boat ahoy!' came the hail from the *Agrius*.

'*Rush*,' shouted Sedgwick, without taking his eyes off his approach. 'Easy all! In oars!' The jollyboat swept alongside and came to a halt beneath the *Agrius*'s entry port.

'Neatly done, Sedgwick,' said Clay as he stood up in the little boat and ran up the frigate's side.

'Captain Clay, very good of you to come across,' said Parker with a smile of greeting as Clay stepped down onto the well remembered deck. He shook Parker's proffered hand and looked about him, smiling with recognition at all the familiar faces among the crew. With a pang he was also aware of the many new hands, replacements for the fallen from the last time the *Agrius* had been in action. He nodded towards Windham as he stood at his post by the guns, but received only a cold stare in return.

'I would usually avoid a council of war,' continued Parker, as he led Clay up onto the quarterdeck. 'But it would seem we do have a little time before our enemy is upon us, and in light of the disparity in our strength, I believe some agreed upon plan will be in order. My apologies, but I regret that I can offer you no refreshment, now we are cleared for action.'

The quarterdeck was as crowded as Clay remembered it had been just before they had gone into battle with the *Courageuse*. Gun crews manned the carronades that ran down each side of the deck, trails of smoke spiralled up from the gun captain's linstocks, while scarlet-coated marines lined the stretches of rail between the guns. Looking up Clay could see more marines in the rigging: sharpshooters, ready to pick off the officers on an enemy's deck spread out below them. Munro came over to him and saluted.

'Welcome aboard, sir,' he said with a grin of pleasure. Clay could tell that Munro was excited at the prospect of action, whatever the odds.

'Good to see you again, Mr Munro,' he replied, shaking the Ulsterman's hand.

'Thank you, Mr Munro,' said Parker. 'Kindly carry on. Now, captain, let us find ourselves a little privacy over by the rail here. You men, go over to the leeside of the deck, if you please.'

'Aye aye, sir,' came the replies. One side of the quarterdeck cleared, and the other became crowded. Clay noticed that the section of rail beside which he stood was quite new. This was the spot where Captain Follett had fallen. No, was killed he corrected himself. He tried to envisage how it would have happened. The shot-torn deck, strewn with the wounded and awash with the debris of the fallen mast. The survivors struggling to hack at the rigging, on the far side of the deck in an odd parallel of the situation now, he thought, glancing towards the mass of marines and gun crews gathered there. And Sutton, his closest friend, leaning over the side and cutting free a man to drown. He shuddered to think of it, unable to contort the well loved face of his friend into the mask of fury necessary to have carried out such an act. With an effort he shook himself free of the scene, and forced his thoughts back into the here and now.

'I collect from the state of the *Agrius* that you mean to fight, sir?' asked Clay, mopping a bead of sweat from his brow.

'Of course,' replied Parker. 'Your ship and mine may be able to outpace a lumbering seventy-four, but the Dons will make short work of the transporters.' He pointed to where the four troopships swung at anchor close inshore, with the looming sugar loaf mountain a dome of green immediately behind them. 'I will not abandon the shipping we were ordered to protect without even firing a shot, captain. If we are unable to devise an alternative strategy it will be our duty to fight, however slender the chance that we shall prevail.'

'I understand, sir. Might one of us keep the *San Filipe* engaged while the other brings down the main fleet from Castries?' suggested Clay, but then answered his own question. 'Except that the *San Filipe* now lies between us and them.'

'Precisely so, captain,' said Parker. 'But might you not circumnavigate the island in the other direction, and come upon the admiral from the north?' Clay looked up at the *Agrius*'s commissioning pennant and shook his head.

'That would take many hours, with the wind where she lies now, sir. Any action here would be long resolved before I could return with assistance. No, I submit we need to beat off the Dons with the resources we have to hand. What we require is a plan that will place them at a disadvantage. Could we lure them within range of the fort?'

'Regrettably there are no gunners up there yet,' said Parker. 'By the time we got them manned with gunners from our ships the Dons will have had plenty of time to finish us off. I thought that we might stand off and on the *San Filipe*, and endeavour to first cripple her at range?'

'The *Rush* is not best placed for such an action. She has just been fitted with carronades, sir,' said Clay. 'Powerful weapons, but only at close range, and at such a range even a poorly served seventy-four would still lay waste to the *Rush* with a couple of broadsides.'

He stared out over the bay seeking inspiration. He took in the calm water, the fort at the end of its narrow peninsula, the town with the transport ships in front of it, and the stubby silhouette of the *Rush*. Where was the plan they needed he thought. How could he put the elements of the puzzle together? He looked back out to sea. The *San Filipe* had grown closer since he had first seen her that morning. Her hull was now visible over the horizon. She was almost bow on to him, just as she had been for hour after long hour during that slow pursuit of the *Rush*. Those well remembered masts towered up and wide spreading yards seeming to reach out towards him once more. He looked at the Spanish ship, then back at the *Rush*, and once more at the *San Filipe* as the idea began to come to him. He turned to Captain Parker.

'Sir, do you know how much those transporters draw when fully laden?' he asked.

'I do not, but I can have them signalled to find out,' replied Parker. 'What is the significance of that?'

'Why, if it is sufficiently above twelve foot six, I believe I may have a plan that will answer, sir,' said Clay.

*****

On his return to the *Rush*, Clay's feet had barely stepped down onto the main deck before he was busy issuing orders.

'Mr Sutton!' he called.

'Sir!' came a reply from near the wheel, and he appeared, looking down at him from the quarterdeck rail.

'Can you kindly pass the word for Mr Carver and Mr Appleby to join us on the quarterdeck directly, if you please, and then let us weigh anchor as quickly as may be convenient.'

'Ah, Mr Carver,' said Clay as the boatswain ran up onto the quarterdeck with ape-like ease, coming to a halt in front of Clay and Sutton. The large figure of the master followed him, rather more slowly, his face red with the effort of keeping up with the long-limbed boatswain. 'And Mr Appleby too, that is splendid. Now gentlemen, to business. We will shortly be standing out towards the *San Filipe*, making as if we wish to pass her in order to bring down the rest of the fleet from the offing off Castries,' he explained.

'When you say "making as if", I collect that this is not what we are really about, sir?' asked Sutton.

'Quite so, Mr Sutton,' said Clay. 'The wind will not serve for such a journey. By the time we brought the admiral here, we would have lost all the transporters and perhaps the *Agrius* too. We shall make the show of being in earnest, but will actually want to be blocked in our attempt by the Dons. Our true object is to attract the attention of the *San Felipe* such that she attempts to close with us. Clear so far?'

'Aye aye, sir,' replied the officers.

'Excellent,' continued their captain. 'Now, I also need the *Rush* to seem to the *San Filipe* as if we are still encumbered with weed. We need to present ourselves as the slow moving hulk they almost caught last time we encountered them. How do you suggest we best accomplish this?' The officers thought for a moment.

Philip K. Allan

'We could set our sail in a lubberly fashion, sir,' suggested Appleby. 'Spilling the wind, and not sheeting home properly.'

'Might that not be spotted by the Dons?' said Clay. 'For my plan to work, I need them to close with the *Rush*, but not to be suspicious of us. Poorly set sails might reveal we are not in earnest?'

'Drogue, sir,' said Carver with decision. 'Get an old jib sail, and stitch it into the shape of an open cone, with a bit of chain on the bottom to hold the mouth open and to keep it below the surface. If we towed it behind us it will slow us like a sea anchor, and we can cut it free the moment we need to crack on. The Dons would need to have eyes like a hawk to spot a couple of lines running down into our wake.'

'I like it, sir,' said Sutton. 'But I would say only half a jib, else we will be too slow.'

'I believe you are right, Mr Sutton,' said Clay after a moment. 'How will we get it deployed? We will need to turn into the wind to do so.'

'Easy, sir,' said Carver. 'Do it when we tack. With the wind where it is we will be bow on to the Dons as we go about. They will not see a thing going on at our stern.'

'Very good, gentlemen; we have a plan. Mr Carver, kindly get the drogue fashioned as quickly as convenient. Tell the sail maker he may draw on as many of the crew as he wishes to help with the construction. Mr Sutton, kindly have the *Agrius* signalled. *Rush* to *Agrius*, permission to get under way.'

'*Agrius* signalling,' announced Croft. 'Proceed. Good luck.'

'Acknowledge, if you please, Mr Croft,' said Clay. 'Mr Sutton, let us weigh anchor and then stand out towards the *San Filipe*, but we must travel slowly through the water. You

260

will need to set sail poorly for now while we await the drogue, but the enemy is far enough away for that not to signify.'

He strode forward to the front of the quarterdeck. Looking down onto the main deck he could see the sail maker and the boatswain busy supervising a swarm of cross-legged seamen as they stitched away. Clay walked back to join the ship's master.

'Now for your part, Mr Appleby,' he said. 'Do you still have those bearings I asked you to take when the *Burford* ran aground?'

*****

Evans stood near the stern rail of the *Rush*, and pointed towards the Spanish ship of the line that had been looming ever closer for the last hour.

'Just so I have the plan straight like, Mr Green,' he said. 'We are to get real close to a ship as is much too big to fight, and that we spent a day and a night trying to get away from. Then when we are good and near, we shall put this here drogue in the water so as to make us sail real slow. I am certain it's bleeding genius, but I am a little unsure how?'

'Stow your noise, Evans,' rumbled the petty officer. 'You're not here to do the thinking, look you.'

'I am with Sam on this,' hissed O'Malley, glaring at the drogue as it lay under the stern rail. 'I am after thinking that Pipe has had a bit too much fecking knock me down last night with them soldiers.'

'I trusts him with my life,' announced Sedgwick, with sudden intensity. 'He took me into the bark so I didn't go back into slavery. If his plan were to voyage to the moon, I would follow him.' The others looked at the normally quiet sailor in surprise.

'I was only asking,' muttered Evans.

'Able has the truth of it lads, for shame,' said Rosso. 'Didn't he turn the tables on the Frogs back in Flanders, when we all thought it was over? Didn't he do for the *Courageuse*? He has a sound plan, I don't doubt. There are few deeper than Pipe.'

'Did he let anything slip about his plan like, when he was in the Jollyboat, Able?' asked Trevan.

'No, but on the way back I could tell he was a-pondering on something,' said Able. 'He kept looking about him, and we couldn't row quickly enough for him.'

'Well I hopes you're fecking right, and we are bound for the moon,' said O'Malley. 'For I can't see how else he means to get us out of this, trapped in this fecking bay by that hulking great ship.'

'Green, are your men ready?' called Carver, coming over to the group of men.

'Aye aye, sir,' replied the Welshman, indicating to the sailors to pick up the drogue.

'Make sure those lines aren't twisted,' said Carver. 'Tail end goes in first, that's you, Evans.'

'Aye aye, Mr Carver,' said Evans. He still looked at the bundle of canvas in his arms with a deal of suspicion.

'Wait for my signal, Mr Carver,' called Sutton. He received a nod from Clay, and put the ship on the other tack.

'Helm over!' he ordered. 'Brace the yards round! Head sails!' The *Rush* came up into the wind and turned on the spot from one tack to the other. At the moment that her bows pointed directly at the *San Felipe*, Sutton turned towards the stern of the ship.

'Now, Mr Carver!' he yelled. 'Deploy the drogue.'

'In she goes, lads,' ordered Green. The drogue slipped over the side, and sank beneath the waves.

'Neatly done, Mr Green,' said Carver. 'With all the confusion of tacking, I warrant the Dons will not have seen a thing.'

As the *Rush* gathered speed on the other tack, the twin lines rose up from the wake of the sloop and stiffened into rods as the strain came on.

'How does she feel?' asked Clay to the quartermaster at the wheel.

'Steering by the stern, sir,' he said, as he moved the wheel a little from side to side, 'and she be right sluggish, but I should be able to handle her well enough.'

'Very good,' said Clay. 'Take her as close to the wind as she will go as if we mean to slip between the Dons and the coast over there.'

The yards were braced around on the *San Felipe*, and she turned broadside on as she headed across the water towards the green coast of St Lucia. The two ships were on parallel courses now as the Spanish moved to head off the *Rush's* clumsy attempt to slip by her. Clay studied his enemy with care. Her side rose like a cliff from the sea. Each of her two long lines of gun ports was emphasised by a pale yellow strip painted the entire length of her black hull. Her masts towered up high into the blue Caribbean sky. Something in her foremast caught his attention, a spar that was out of place perhaps? He focused on it with his telescope, and realised what it was. The captain of the *San Felipe* had had a large wooden cross hauled up to the top of the mast to inspire his crew in battle.

'God, she's a big bugger,' said Sutton from beside him. 'Never mind the two rows of guns of her main batteries; she has more fire power than us just on her quarterdeck and forecastle.'

'I fear you are right,' agreed Clay. 'We are close enough now, Mr Sutton,' said Clay, still examining their opponent. 'Kindly put her on the other tack. Let us now appear to try and round her by heading out towards the open sea. You had best wear ship with that drogue on our tail.'

'Excellent point,' said Sutton, 'They would make short work of us if we were caught in irons this close to them.'

The *Rush* made a long curving turn downwind, rather than the quicker but riskier tack through the wind, and settled on her new course, heading away from land. Like an obedient dog, the *San Felipe* followed her turn and began to head reach on her once more. There was to be no escape this way either. The ships' courses converged further, and the Spanish ship grew even larger in Clay's view. He could now see individual officers on her quarterdeck watching him, and the tiny figures of crewmen in her rigging. Then the look of her changed as she opened her gun ports. All along her sides the twin lines of huge cannon were run out pointing towards the little sloop.

'That will do, Mr Sutton,' ordered Clay. 'I believe we have her attention now. Kindly bring her to the wind and head back into the bay. Once that is done you can clear the ship for action.' He next turned back towards the ship's master.

'Now, Mr Appleby, do you have the location of the *Burford*'s sand bar fixed?'

'Yes, sir, I have it to hand,' replied the master.

'Very good,' said Clay. 'I want you to lay me a course that will take the *Rush* right over the middle of that bar.'

'Right over it?' queried the master. 'But sir, if we should run aground at such a speed, it would do cruel damage to the ship.'

'But we shall not, Mr Appleby,' announced Clay. 'The *Burford* drew fifteen feet on the day she touched, and she only lightly ran aground. What does the *Rush* draw?'

'Twelve foot six at the stern, fully laden,' said Appleby.

'Exactly, so we will fly over that sand bar with two and a half feet to spare.' Clay turned to look behind them, to where the *San Felipe* charged along in their wake with all sail set.

'Tell me, Mr Appleby, how deep do you think the *San Felipe*'s hull goes? I should be very surprised if they draw an inch less than twenty feet.'

Chapter 15
Battle

The *Rush* may have been one of the Royal Navy's smaller ships, but things on board were still done correctly. Her contingent of marines, only twenty-five strong, was not large enough to have their own drummer boy, but they did have a drum. Corporal Patton, who was known to possess a little musical ability, had it hung from one of his wide leather cross belts as he marched out into the centre of the main deck. From where he stood no member of the crew could have been more than fifty feet away from him, comfortably within range of his parade ground bawl. But the preparation of a warship for battle was not called beating to quarters for nothing. He thunderously sounded his drum, and the crew of the *Rush* organised themselves for the fight ahead in a swirl of movement all around him.

Able Sedgwick ran along the main deck to his place at number five carronade. Rosso, the gun's captain, was there already, casting loose the breaching and rigging the gun tackles.

'Able, grab the other tackle and rig it to the port side, mate,' ordered Rosso. Sedgwick unhooked the heavy block and tackle and fitted one end to the ship's side and the other to the carronade. He pulled it tight to test it, and the gun

266

edged forward on its slide. While he did this Evans and O'Malley arrived. Evans untied the rammer from the underside of the gangway over his head, while O'Malley went to collect a bucket of water from those being filled at the deck pump.

Sedgwick looked up to see one of the ship's boys walking towards him, scattering handfuls of sand broadcast on the deck as if he was feeding chickens.

'Bit more of that on the deck here, lad,' called Evans. 'I don't want to fall on my arse first time we run up.'

'No, that generally only happens the second fecking time,' said O'Malley, pulling off his shirt, and putting it away. The others followed suit.

'Right, I am off to get this lit,' said Rosso, tying a length of slow match onto his linstock. He looked around him. 'Where's that lazy little nipper with the first charge?'

'It's all right, Rosie,' said Sedgwick. 'Barker will be here soon. Here come the powder monkeys now.' A line of ship's boys ran up the main ladder way from the magazine deep below the waterline, each one carrying a leather case with the cloth bag of powder for the gun they were allocated to.

When Rosso returned to the carronade with his linstock spluttering into life, the gun was rigged, the equipment all allocated out and the crew stood around it waiting for the next order.

'Is she loaded?' he asked.

'That she is,' said O'Malley, whose job this was.

'Number five gun loaded and ready, Mr Green,' he called across to the petty officer in charge of this section of guns.

'It's a funny looking bugger, ain't it,' said Evans, pointing to the shiny new carronade. 'Don't seem quite right somehow, not having no wheels an all.' The others looked at the squat mass with interest. Instead of the more normal gun carriage the barrel slid forwards and backwards on a heavy slide. This in turn was fixed by a huge bolt to the ship's side at the gun's port end. The inboard end of the slide had a roller on the bottom which rested on the deck and allowed the whole gun to be swung to the left or right.

'She's not like that pissy little cannon we used to have,' said O'Malley. 'Look at the fecking size of the barrel. She's a good honest twelve pounder like we had in the old *Agrius*,' he said, slapping the short squat gun with pride.

'Aye, and right swift to load,' said Rosso. He turned to the gun's powder monkey, and ruffled his hair. 'You're going to have to run like a rabbit to keep us fed with powder, Barker.'

'Hey I just thought,' said Evans. 'We ain't given our gun no proper name yet, her being all new like.'

'You're right there,' said Rosso. 'No time to paint a name on her proper, but we should give her one anyways. How about Spit Fire, like our old gun on the *Agrius*?'

'We have had one of them already,' said O'Malley, 'Half the ships on the list will have a Spit Fire. I am after thinking we should choose something different. What about the name of that prize fighter you bested in your last proper mill, Sam?'

'Jack Rodgers, the Southwark Butcher?' said Evans. 'Not sure that's a proper choice, Sean. For one thing he lost, and for another people may make the link to me. Remember I was paid to throw that mill. There's still some angry traps out a looking for me.'

'How about another prize fighter then?' said Rosso. 'Mendoza? Broughton?'

'Half the guns in the navy are named after those two,' protested O'Malley. 'We wants something new.'

'If it's new you're after, Sean, call the gun Shango,' suggested Sedgwick. 'He is the God of Thunder in my homeland.' The others looked at each other.

'God of Thunder, is it?' said O'Malley. 'I am fecking liking that.'

'I doubt there can be another gun so named in the whole fleet,' said Rosso.

'Done,' said Evans, patting the carronade with affection. 'Shango it is.'

*****

While number five carronade metamorphosed into a West African thunder god, Clay looked with increasing concern at the *San Felipe*. She had been growing closer as the *Rush* sailed on, filling the horizon behind them with her massive presence, much as he remembered from the last time they had met.

'We must have overdone that drogue, Mr Sutton,' said Clay. 'I should say we are almost in range of her bow chasers. If she was to shoot away an important spar too early the whole plan could fail.'

'How far have we still to go, Mr Appleby?' asked Sutton to the master, who stood by the binnacle, making sure the *Rush* was on the exact course. He glanced forward, measuring the angles in his mind's eye.

'Shade over three miles, I should say, Mr Sutton,' he replied. 'On this course we shall pass over the sandbar when that sugar loaf mountain bears exactly twelve degrees north.'

'That will be almost thirty minutes under fire at our current rate of progress, sir,' Sutton calculated.

'Too long for us, Mr Sutton,' said Clay, 'especially as the range will close during that time. Ah, the game has begun,' he added as a puff of smoke appeared on the bows of the *San Felipe*, and a line of splashes marked the passage of the cannon ball. The final splash was only twenty yards from the rear of the *Rush*.

'Hmm,' said Clay, looking at the ring of disturbed water. 'It would seem they have acquired some superior gunners. Already they make better practice than the last time they chased us. We need to find some more speed.' As he spoke the second bow chaser fired from the Spaniard, although this time the ball struck the sea off to one side of the sloop.

'We might cut free the drogue, sir,' suggested Sutton.

'We could,' agreed Clay, 'but how do we then account for our sudden increase in speed? I do not want the Dons to suspect us of making game of them till it is too late.'

'I could spill some wind from the courses once the drogue has gone,' said the lieutenant. 'That would check our progress, sir.'

'And also signal to the Dons that something is amiss,' added his captain. 'We are too close for that to answer now.'

The first bow chaser had now been reloaded and it fired again. This time the chain of splashes was much closer, the final one wetting the stern of the ship. Clay forced himself to think, groping for a solution. How might he make the drogue less effective, without losing it all together? Now the second bow chaser fired once more. The line of splashes pointed straight towards him, ending with a shuddering crash somewhere below his feet. As the need for a solution to the dilemma became critical, the answer came to him.

'We tilt the drogue,' he said to Sutton. 'Angle the mouth of it to one side so it is a little less effective, but so it shall still act to slow us.'

'That would work, sir,' said the lieutenant, 'but how do we

do that?'

'The drogue is held by two tow ropes, one line on each side of the ship, yes?' said Clay. 'If we let one out by a foot, it will tilt the mouth to that side, reducing the drag. If that doesn't answer, we let out some more, or if we find we go too fast we can pull it back some.'

'Excellent, sir!' said Sutton, 'I will do it now. Afterguard, to me!'

'Get a good body of men on that line, Mr Sutton,' advised Clay. 'The drogue will have a monstrous pull on it.'

'Just under two feet on the port side line, sir,' reported Sutton to Clay a little later. 'That's what was needed to make us a shade swifter than the *San Felipe*. It means we may have the odd ball come home for a bit, but it is worth it to keep them keen.' As he spoke there was a further crash from below the counter.

'Carpenter's crew are down there at work plugging the first hole, sir, so they should be able to fix that one too,' he added.

'Very good, Mr Sutton,' said Clay. 'Ah, and I see the *Agrius* is on the move at last.' Across the wide expanse of Black Bay, white sails appeared on the frigate as she got under way, ready to do her part in the plan. Clay moved over to the binnacle and lined himself up with the prominent dome of the sugar loaf mountain.

'Was it twelve degrees north, Mr Appleby?' he asked, sighting across the top of the compass rose.

'Yes, sir,' said Appleby, shifting from one foot to another. He drew a large red handkerchief from deep in his coat pocket and wiped the sweat from his brow. Clay looked at the master with concern.

'Are you quite sure of your calculations, Mr Appleby?' he

asked. 'You seem a little distracted.'

'Quite sure, sir,' replied the master. 'My concern is what if the *Burford* ran aground on a particular part of the sand bar that is deeper than the rest?'

'Come now, Mr Appleby,' said Clay. 'Sand bars are generally very regular features of the sea floor. Besides, the die is now cast. If your calculation is correct, we shall shortly discover all.'

Clay may have appeared calm in front of the nervous Appleby, but inside his stomach churned with anxiety. His mariner's instinct was to avoid navigational perils, yet here he was, driving his ship towards a known hazard. He could almost sense the sea bed underneath his feet as it rose up towards him, nearer and nearer. What if Appleby was right and the *Burford* had touched on a part of the sand bank that was not typical? Or what if the signal midshipman on the *Agrius* this morning had misread the *Burford*'s reply to Captain Parker's question? Did the *Burford* actually draw ten feet, not the fifteen he had reported? He looked down at his hands. His knuckles showed white under his tanned skin with the force he used to grip the binnacle, as if he was braced for an inevitable collision. Between his hands was the compass. He looked from there across to the sugar loaf mountain which now bore ten degrees from them. Almost in disbelief he realised that the *Rush* must have already sailed across the sand bar. He turned to watch the Spanish ship that followed in her wake.

She was a magnificent sight as she drove on. Her yellow and black striped hull stood high out of the water, the pronounced tumblehome of her sides obvious to him as he watched. Her bows were a mass of gilded carving, a white bow wave creamed at the foot. Her enormous masts towered up and up, the red and gold flag of Spain streamed out from the masthead a hundred and eighty feet above the surface of the sea. Every one of her spreading yards was packed with sail. The cross he had seen earlier was two bars of solid black against the white of her massive topsail. Then in a moment, everything changed.

Flowing, racing movement juddered to a halt. Her whole foremast came crashing down sheared off just above her deck, dissolving into individual sections as it fell. In its ruin it tore down her main top gallant mast with it. Clay saw a pair of tiny figures, black specks against the sky, tumble through the air and splash into the sea. Only when they had vanished did he realise they must have been the ship's lookouts, their grip wrenched free by the force of the impact. Delayed by the distance came a deep muffled rumble of noise, and the *San Felipe* settled back among her plumes of wreckage, her bow noticeable higher than her stern.

On the quarterdeck around him there was a moment of complete open-mouthed silence at the horror of what they had witnessed, followed by the wash of sound as everyone was talking at once.

'Silence!' bellowed Clay, glaring around him. When it was quiet once more he issued a series of orders. 'Afterguard! Cut free the drogue, if you please.' Two of the mizzen sail handlers rushed to the stern of the ship to release the lines and the sloop surged forwards. 'Mr Sutton, kindly reduce sail to fighting trim. Topsails only. Then have the ship put about to close with the enemy. I want her in as close as possible, within fifty yards of her bows and then hold her there.'

'Aye aye, sir,' replied Sutton.

'Mr Croft, please send this signal to the *Agrius*. I am engaging the enemy by the bow.'

'*Agrius* acknowledges the signal, sir.'

'Thank you, Mr Croft,' said Clay. He walked forward to the rail at the front of the quarterdeck. Below him the gun crews looked up expectantly, their faces alight with grins. He could feel their delight at the prospect of an easy victory over such a superior foe, mixed with respect towards their resourceful leader. Clay realised this was the moment when most captains might give a brief speech. The men wanted him to offer them some words they might cheer at, but inside he felt too flat, shocked by the devastation he had caused to that beautiful ship. In his mind's eye he could still see the little tumbling figures as they fell through the air towards the stone-hard sea far, far below.

'Mr Preston,' he ordered. 'Run out larboard side and wait for my order to fire.'

'Aye aye, sir,' said the midshipman, and Clay turned away from the rail.

*****

'Clear!' yelled Rosso before he brought down the linstock on the touch hole. The carronade belched its tongue of flame and shot back down the slide into the middle of the gun crew who leapt forward to reloaded it. Evans swabbed out the hot barrel, and twirled the rammer around, ready to ram home the next charge. O'Malley pushed in the bag of powder, followed by the ball and wad, each item forced down the short barrel by Evans. The others hauled on the tackles, and the loaded carronade slid forward up the slide. Rosso bent to spike the charge through the touchhole and insert the quill of fine powder. He glanced through the porthole at the target, but they were so close there was no need to waste time on aiming. The bows of the *San Felipe* filled his vision, an easy stone toss away, now battered and pock marked by the numerous holes torn into her by the relentless pounding of the little sloop. It was a shock to see what damage even their seven carronades could do over time at this very close range. He stepped back once more and yelled his warning to the gun crew as the carronade pumped a fresh cannon ball into the Spanish ship.

The carronade shot back down the slide again, and Evans sponged it out, steam hissing from the hot metal.

'Sorry, Rosie, I got no fecking charge to load,' said O'Malley straightening up from his place by the gun. 'Reckon we really have run that little nipper off his feet, we been working Shango that brisk.' Rosso stepped back from his place by the gun and looked around for the next powder bag, but could see no trace of Barker. Something ripped past him and he looked up. The Spanish sailors who had thronged the forecastle, battling to clear away the wreckage of the fallen mast had been replaced now by a line of marines. He could see them firing and reloading as quick as they could under the urging of their sergeant.

'Keep your heads below the gangway, lads,' he ordered his crew, ducking back into cover himself. 'The front of that ship is full of soldiers with muskets.'

'Good luck to the buggers,' grinned O'Malley. 'Muskets against cannon. I know what side of that fecking argument I wants to be on.'

'Aye,' said Rosso. 'But what about cannon with nothing to fire? Where is that bloody boy?'

'Barker may have been hit, Rosie,' said Evans. 'We're that close in now the Don's small arms fire is getting pretty warm.' Rosso glanced around to report the lack of ammunition to petty officer Green, just in time to see him being carried below clutching a wounded leg.

'Right,' he said. 'Sedgwick, go and report to the Grunters we can't fire for want of a charge. Rest of us will stay here in case Barker finally turns up.' As Sedgwick ran down the deck there came a distant roar, the sound clear even over the bang of the carronades around him.

'What was that?' asked Evans. O'Malley ducked to the next gun port and looked through. He bobbed back again with a broad grin.

'That, my shipmates, was the sweet sound of victory!' he beamed. 'The old *Agrius* has finally arrived, and just given her full measure right up her fecking arse!'

*****

In the front rank of the Spanish marines who lined the forecastle rail of the *San Felipe* stood Alvaro Gaya. He pulled another cartridge out from his ammunition pouch and lifted it up to his mouth. He ripped the top off with his teeth and felt the heavy musket ball settle on his tongue. Gunpowder peppered his lips, and he tasted once more the slight bad egg taste of the saltpetre. He took a pinch of powder from the open cartridge and stored it between his forefinger and thumb, the digits pressed into an 'O'. He then poured the balance of the powder down the barrel of his musket. Leaning forward, he spat the lead ball into the muzzle, and prodded the now empty cartridge paper in with a finger to form the wad. He banged the butt of his musket down onto the solid deck and slid the long ramrod out from its housing.

Of course the deck was solid, he fumed to himself, all too solid. Those idiot officers had rammed his beautiful ship deep onto this hidden sandbar. Now the hull lay as inert as a rock, letting the sea wash high up her sides, as if his cherished ship was already a wreck. His arm still ached from where he had fallen on it earlier. Almost the whole crew had been thrown to the deck when they had run aground, as if from an earthquake. But he was one of the lucky ones. Just beside where he had fallen had been one of the cannon. It had slewed forward against its breechings and rolled over. He had rushed to try and help lift the colossal weight from the members of the gun crew crushed beneath it, heaving at the cold metal as those trapped under it clawed at his legs, pleading for him to hurry.

Alvaro held the musket against his tunic. The butt was still on the deck and the barrel was caught against his chest by his left arm, the left hand still holding the pinch of powder. With his right hand he worked the ramrod, crushing the ball and wad of cartridge paper against the powder charge and tamping it all down firmly. He returned the ramrod to its oiled slot below the barrel and looked around him. The deck was still awash with the wreckage of the fallen mast. He shuddered at the memory of its collapse, debris raining down all around him. He had seen spars splinter and break, and shrouds part under impossible pressure in a series of whip cracks as they lashed across the deck, hissing like snakes. And then the Royal Navy ships had closed in.

That little sloop in front had spun round the moment they had struck the hidden sand bar. She had sunk her teeth into the *San Felipe*'s bows, where only her two bow chasers could return any fire. Except that both guns had been in action when they ran aground, he reminded himself. One had slammed forward into its gun port, smashing its carriage in the process. The other lay on its side near him, its crew frantically trying to get it back upright. He could hear the little ship's tiny battery of carronades as they pumped ball after ball into the bows, each one thudding home in a shower of splinters, battering through the tough curved timbers. But it was the other ship, the frigate, that was the real problem. He could see her behind him raking his beloved *San Felipe* again and again, sending broadside after broadside crashing into her unprotected stern. He felt the deck beneath his feet tremble as yet another storm of shot swept the length of the gun decks. The sound of fresh screams from the wounded drifted up through the open hatchways.

Alvaro could sense that the fight would not last much longer. He could no longer hear the noisy bravado of his shipmates. That had faded into sullen silence all around him. He understood what was happening. He knew that his fellow crew would fight bravely in an even contest, but not if they had no means of striking back. The enemy's ships had come against the *San Filipe* like jackals against a wounded lion, avoiding her still powerful jaws and claws. Down both sides of her hull were the lines of her guns, all of them silent, their crews standing mute beside them. He could feel their fighting spirit ebbing away, like children ground down by another beating from an abusive adult. His face hardened with determination. He could yet strike a blow. He rested his musket on the rail in front of him, and wiped the little pinch of powder into the firing pan. He pulled the lock back, felt the reassuring ratchet click beneath his thumb, and brought the butt up to his shoulder. Then he waited.

The marines around him banged away at the little ship, firing into the fog of gun smoke as soon as they had reloaded. It was the same little devil ship that they had met before. The one that had led them on through a day and a night, always there but ever just beyond reach. That was why the fool of a captain had been so blind to all danger, determined that they would not evade him again. The gun smoke began to thin a little, swirling in columns as the wind gusted. Alvaro saw grey figures, wraith-like, clustered on the quarterdeck below him. Which one, he thought, which one? If only the Royal Navy would wear uniforms as gaudy as that of his own officers. There could be no missing Captain Perez, gorgeous beneath his heaped braid, the Order of Santiago at his throat. A beam of sunlight cut through the smoke, and by chance found a route through the mass of rigging and sail. It glinted on the gold epaulet the tallest figure wore on his left shoulder like the flash of light from a key hole in a darkened room. Alvaro Gaya steadied his musket, settled his aim and squeezed the trigger.

Chapter 16
Departure

The impact of the bullet sounded like a hand patting the neck of a horse, hardly noticed over the thunder of the *Rush*'s carronades. Sutton looked around to trace the strange noise and saw his captain stagger backwards a step, a puzzled look on his face. He clasped his left shoulder and sank down on his knees. His drop to the deck continued as he toppled over onto his side. Sutton froze in horror for a moment, and then knelt down beside his friend. Blood spilt through Clay's fingers from the wound and dripped down onto the deck.

'They have got me, John,' he gasped. 'You must take command. Fire briskly and keep it so.'

'Oh, Alex,' said Sutton, cradling Clay's head. 'How bad do you believe it to be?'

'No good, I fear,' hissed Clay through gritted teeth. Sutton looked about him for help.

'Wilson, Brewer, yes and Sedgwick too! Over here, make haste now.' He reeled off the names of two members of the afterguard, and the sailor who had just run up from the main deck.

'Lift the captain, and take him at once down to Mr

Linfield in the cockpit,' he ordered, letting Clay's head gently back down onto the deck. He moved to one side so that the men could lift up his fallen friend. 'Handsomely now lads, he is sore hurt.'

'All Right captain, we got you,' said Sedgwick, his voice tender, and the three sailors carried the slumped figure of Clay across the quarterdeck and down the ladder way. A trail of crimson splashes on the deck marked the path they had followed. Another musket ball thudded into the planking near one of the blood stains, and Sutton turned towards the marine commander.

'Mr Macpherson, can your men not drive those damned soldiers from the enemy forecastle,' he snapped.

'Aye, in time we may, but their fire is very hot at present,' replied the Scotsman calmly. 'Might we not get one of the great guns to bear? A whiff of canister would be most helpful. Ah, now what are those tricky coves about now?' Sutton followed where Macpherson was pointing, just in time to see the last of the Spanish soldiers disappear from view. The fire of the marines around him petered out as they searched for targets through the gun smoke.

'Do you suppose that they are ready to yield?' asked Macpherson.

'Perhaps they are, Tom,' said the lieutenant. He searched the big ship's rigging for the huge yellow and red flag, but could not see it anywhere.

'I do believe the Dons may have struck their colours,' said the Scotsman. Sutton looked up at the *San Felipe* for a moment longer and then pulled out the whistle from his pocket to sound the ceasefire. One final carronade fired and the sound of the shot faded away across the bay.

'Listen, Tom,' said Sutton, his head on one side. From

somewhere beyond the rear of the *San Felipe,* where the *Agrius* lay, they could both hear the sound of cheering.

*****

'On the table, lads. Bring him closer, I pray, over here, in the light,' ordered Jacob Linfield, his arms slick to the elbows with the blood of previous patients. 'A little to the left, if you please, Sedgwick. Yes, just so.' He smiled down into Clay's face, his own only inches above it as he bent double under the low beams of the cockpit. 'Right, sir, let us see what the wicked Dons have done to you,' he said. He sliced open Clay's coat and shirt and peeled the blood-sodden cloth back to reveal the wound. He paused for a moment, his sharp scalpel glinting in the light of the single lantern that lit the space.

'Ah, yet another bullet wound,' he exclaimed, chatting towards Clay's pale face as he worked. 'What a curious action we are engaged in! Down here below the waterline it is very hard for us to judge the progress of the battle. We hear the guns rumble away above our heads for sure, but no other definite intelligence comes to us other than the flow of wounded. Lift him up for me, Webb,' he added to his assistant, and Clay felt a hand run across the back of his shoulder, the fingers probing the muscle.

'Oh, Christ that hurt!' spluttered Clay, as Linfield touched one particular point.

'Your pardon, sir, you have some broken ribs,' he said with a smile as if this was good news, before addressing his assistants. 'Back down again, if you please. Sedgwick, are you yet here? Well, if you must stay kindly tend the captain's head. Cut away the rest of the coat and shirt if you please, Web, and prepare the gag and straps.' Clay felt himself settled back down and his head being cradled. He glanced backwards and saw the anxious face of Sedgwick. He found his look of concern comforting, and tried to smile through his pain at the sailor. From elsewhere he felt a tugging as his clothes were stripped away, while Linfield continued his chatter.

'Ah, do you hear, sir?' he exclaimed. 'The guns have ceased to fire at last. Let us hope it may signify a victory.' Clay felt Linfield's hands on his shoulder again, this time accompanied by his breath as he examined the wound. 'So what are we to make of the battle from the wounds we have treated?' he asked. Clay was groggy with lack of blood now and close to passing out, but fortunately Linfield seemed happy to answer his own question. 'Why, that it is barely a naval action at all! No splinter wounds, no great traumas from the impact of cannon balls, just a steady progression of musket wounds. I might think myself the surgeon of an infantry regiment, were it not for the anchors on the buttons of my coat.' Clay sensed him turn away from him to address his assistants again. 'Strap down an arm each and get some rum. Large probe and extractor if you please, Webb. You may stay if you wish, Sedgwick, but be warned that matters may become lively.'

'Now to your wound, sir,' said Linfield. 'In one sense you are very fortunate. You have been struck in the left shoulder in a down ways fashion, and yet the ball has somehow contrived to miss your lung, heart and all of the great blood vessels, for which you may heartily thank your Maker. However, the ball is still lodged deep within the wound, and must come out. I will extract it now, but I must warn you that it will not cooperate at all in its removal, yet emerge it must. Webb here has rum for your present relief. I would urge you to take as much as you are able, after which he will gag you for the preservation of your tongue.'

Once Clay had choked down a few mouthfuls of the fiery spirit, he felt the wet leather gag pushed into his mouth, and firm hands pressed him back down onto the canvas-covered top of the operating table. Next a belt tightened across his chest, and straps closed about his arms. He tried to force himself to relax, hoping that this might help the surgeon in his task. He focused on Sedgwick's anxious face, reading the concern in his eyes. He felt Linfield's hand near to the wound and wondered why the surgeon had stopped talking. Moments later his shoulder was a mass of searing pain the like of which he had not imagined possible.

*****

Clay walked along a cobbled road under a low dark sky, heavy with the threat of rain. The land around him was barren and seemed to be composed of grey ash. Stare as he might he could not see any trace of green. A chill wind blew, raising dust devils from the road surface near his feet. He trudged along with little idea where he was going, driven onwards by the feeling that there was somewhere ahead he should be. His shoulder throbbed with pain and his left arm hung useless by his side.

A bell tolled from somewhere close at hand, and looking towards the sound he saw a grey stone church with blank, dark windows by the side of the road. He hurried towards it, and came to the lichgate where a sailor stood. He recognised the man, although he thought that he had died, struck down by a cannon ball when the *Agrius* had fought the *Courageuse*.

'Afternoon, captain,' said the sailor, knuckling his forehead in salute.

'It is Drinkwater, is it not? Gun captain on the *Agrius*?' Clay heard himself ask.

'Late of the *Agrius*, that's right, sir,' smiled the sailor.

'Tell me, shipmate, am I late for the funeral?' continued Clay.

'No, eight bells it is,' said Drinkwater. 'You're right on time, sir, but it be no funeral, it be a wedding.'

'A wedding?' muttered Clay as he made his way to the entrance. He pushed the heavy oak doors apart. Inside the church was empty, save for the priest, and the couple who were to be married.

'Ah, the guest of honour at long last!' exclaimed the priest, with a wave in Clay's direction, 'We can proceed with the ceremony.' The groom turned towards Clay.

'Good day, old boy,' he said with a smile.

'Windham!' exclaimed Clay.

'*Captain* Windham, if you please,' said the groom, indicating the gold epaulet on his left shoulder. 'Pretty, isn't it? It was yours once, but now that your shoulder is no more, they gave it to me.' Clay looked at his shoulder and noticed for the first time it was little more than a gaping wound. The lips of pale skin hung open and the inside brimmed with blood.

'Oh,' he said in surprise.

'You call me sir!' yelled Windham. 'You must say, "Oh, sir", not just Oh!'

'Aye aye, sir,' said Clay.

'Yes, they have promoted me in your place, at last,' continued Windham. 'They gave me this wench to marry too,' he added, giving his bride a hefty wallop on her backside. She stumbled forward under the blow, her veil sliding open as she tripped to reveal the beautiful but tear-stained face of Lydia Browning.

'No!' yelled Clay, striding down the aisle towards them. He tried to run, but each successive step seemed harder to take than the last. He was sinking lower and lower. Increasingly he had to crane his neck upwards to see Lydia and Windham. He was aware of a chill that had spread up his legs and looked down to find he was sinking into jade green water. He glanced up in despair towards Lydia and the water closed over his head. Down he sunk, deeper and deeper. He could still see the surface above him, but struggle as he might he could not swim towards it. His leg seemed to be caught. He looked down, and saw that Captain Follett, his eyes vacant and dead in his pale face, had a firm grip on his leg, and was pulling him ever deeper. Clay opened his mouth to cry out, and the greedy water flowed in.

*****

The *Rush* was at sea, running across the channel of deep blue ocean that lay between St Lucia and Barbados once more. To leeward of her were three of the troop transporters that had carried the successful expedition to Vieux Fort and were now returning to Barbados full of Spanish and French prisoners of war from the *San Felipe* and the captured fortress. Sutton examined them with care through his glass to make sure all was well. On the deck of each ship he could see a cluster of red-coated figures standing guard around the battened down hatchways, members of the detachment from the Shropshire regiment detailed to see the prisoners taken safely to Bridgetown.

'All appears to be as it should be, Mr Appleby,' he said as he turned from the rail.

'Indeed, Mr Sutton,' said the master. 'In fact the situation has not changed this past three hours. I assure you all will be fine, John. Even if the Dons and Frogs did managed to break free and capture one of the transporters, we would be able to very swiftly run down on them.'

'Doubtless that is so,' said Sutton, still glancing across at the cluster of ships. 'Oh, I know you think I am fussing like a brood hen with her chicks, Joseph, but this is effectively my first independent command. I cannot but be a little anxious that all should go well.' He started to open his telescope to look at the transporters once more. Appleby noticed the movement and caught his arm. He gently drew him away from the rail and made him pace up and down the deck beside him.

'Do you think they will ever get the *San Felipe* off that sand bank?' he asked. 'She still seemed to be most stubbornly wedged when we left.'

'I am sure Captain Parker and the crew of the *Agrius* will do their upmost to get her re-floated, even if they have to empty her of every gun, spar and barrel,' said Sutton. 'If she cannot be brought home to Bridgetown, there will be no prize money, and they are due the same share as us.'

'I hope they do not have to remove her ballast,' said Appleby, screwing up his face. 'Nasty job that on a Spanish ship.'

'Really?' asked Sutton. 'Why so?'

'Do you not know?' queried the master. 'Why it is because of their religion. Being fervent papists to a man means they will not commit their dead to the sea as we do. No, the bodies have to be interred on land, ready for their resurrection on the last day. So they bury them in the ballast until they can be transferred to graves ashore. Even without the hazards of war, a big crew like that of a seventy-four might expect at least one fatality each ten days or so. You can well imagine that on a cruise of a few months, in this Caribbean heat.... As I say, Mr Sutton, nasty job that, digging out her ballast.'

'You amaze me, Mr Appleby,' said Sutton, shaking his head. 'But surely they must store their water and vittles as we do, just on top of the ballast?'

'Indeed they do,' said the master with satisfaction. 'Don't bear thinking upon, do it?'

From the forecastle came the sound of five clear bell strokes.

'Ah, that is my summons,' said Sutton. 'I am to meet with the surgeon for a report on the captain's progress. Keep a steady eye upon the transporters, if you please, Mr Appleby. Pass the word for me if you see anything suspicious.'

'Aye aye, Mr Sutton,' replied Appleby, rolling a weary eye towards Preston. The midshipman of the watch adopted a fixed expression to stifle the laugh rising in his chest.

In the captain's quarters Sutton saw that all had been done that could be to make the patient comfortable. Most of the cabin lights had been screened to block out the bright sun, and a wind scoop had been rigged on the deck above to bring some of the cool ocean breeze into the cabin where he lay. Despite this his sheets were still clammy with sweat.

Linfield held a hand to Clay's burning forehead, and the patient writhed away from the touch, muttering to himself. He ran his hands down onto the bandaged shoulder, and felt the furnace heat just beneath the dressing.

'The fever approaches its crisis, Mr Sutton,' said the surgeon, his face grim, 'and he is ill equipped to battle it. In the normal course of events I would combat the fever by taking several ounces of blood, but the captain has lost so much already I fear the vital functions of his great organs may be harmed if he were to lose any more.'

'How long has he been like this?' asked Sutton, his face shocked at the change in his friend.

'The fever has been building since last night,' said Linfield. 'The delirium has been quite pronounced for the last few hours. Partly it is the laudanum I have administered to control his pain, but much stems from his fever. He is relatively calm now. Earlier he was fair ranting. Calling out and shouting for someone called Lydia, among others.'

'Why should it be him? It is so unfair,' said Sutton. 'The fight was all but over with the Dons when he fell. This should have been his victory.' Sutton glanced away from the bed as he felt tears moisten his eyes. 'Do you believe he will live?' he asked. Linfield took his arm and led him away from the bed.

'There is always a little hope, John, but you must prepare yourself for the worst,' he said. 'In some regards it is remarkable that he yet lives. The normal course with such cases is that the patient will often be fortunate enough to survive the trauma of the initial wound, especially if they are young and fit like the captain. It is only later that they succumb to the corruption that always follows such injuries. I have extracted the bullet and cleaned the wound, to be sure, but there is always something left behind, a fragment of coat borne in by the bullet, a little dirt. If the wound was lower on his arm I could have amputated the limb and stopped the putrefaction in that way.'

'What odds will you give me that he will live?' muttered Sutton.

'John, please do not ask me to reduce his life chances to such terms,' said Linfield.

'Give me the damned odds,' snapped Sutton. Linfield stared at him for a moment before he replied.

'If he lives till Bridgetown, and can be transferred to a hospital on shore, perhaps one in ten, God willing.'

'Thank you, Mr Linfield,' said Sutton. 'I will take such odds, for I believe they will answer very well. Many would have rated a sloop and a twelve pounder frigate's chances against a seventy-four at longer than that, and yet the captain won through to win us our victory none the less. I will sit by him for a while. Do you think if I was to speak to him, he might hear me?'

'Yes, it is probable that he might,' lied the surgeon. 'It can certainly do no harm. Now, if you will excuse me I must attend to my other patients.'

*****

The sun shone down on the back of Jacob Linfield's best uniform coat as he bumped up the road that wound out of Bridgetown towards Melverton and the Robertson's plantation. He rode on a borrowed horse, and the elderly mare was making heavy weather of the climb. She needed considerable urging from the surgeon's knees and heels to move forward at all. When at last they reached the summit, he brought her to a halt to recover her wind, and looked back down the slope at the view.

Carlisle Bay was a splendid sight, packed with shipping once more. The squadron had returned victorious from their capture of St Lucia the day after the *Rush* had arrived with her prisoners. Castries, the capital, had surrendered to General Abercromby the day that Vieux Fort had fallen, completing the expedition's victory. Clustered near the shore were all the transporters, while farther out he could see the row of stately warships at their moorings, laid out like models on a bright blue cloth. The admiral's massive flagship was easy enough to pick out, but it took him some time to locate the stubby little *Rush* towards the far end of the line. When his mare was breathing a little easier, he turned his back on Bridgetown and with some further urging managed to prod his horse into a shambling trot.

It was a hot and dusty road, and Linfield found himself regretting his choice of clothing. The dark blue of his full dress coat was near perfect for absorbing the heat from the sun's rays, while the thick wool of its material retained that warmth with equal efficiency. His ancient horse needed constant encouragement to move at all, and this was slowly destroying his best stockings and white woollen breaches. The shiny black leather of the shoes that his servant had worked on most of the morning could only now be guessed at through a thick layer of dust and horse hair. It was a hot and dishevelled figure who arrived at last at the front door of Spring Hill plantation.

'Miss Emma?' queried the black maid who opened the door. 'No master, she not here, so sorry.'

'Oh, really?' said Linfield, 'Will she be back soon?'

'Perhaps,' conceded the maid, eyeing the filthy rider with a jaundiced eye. She saw the look of disappointment spread on the young man's face, and added, 'Mr Robertson, he here.'

'Yes, I would very much like to pay my respects to him,' said the surgeon. 'Could you tell him that Mr Linfield is here to see him.'

'My dear Mr Linfield, how delighted I am to see you again,' said Robertson, as he bustled into Spring Hill's second best drawing room, his arms wide in welcome. 'I had heard that Admiral Caldwell's armada had returned triumphant from its descent on St Lucia, and was wondering when I might see you. What wonderful news of their victory,

Philip K. Allan

in which doubtless you played a full part? But Mr Linfield, are you quite well? Have you fallen from your horse?'

'Quite well, I thank you Mr Robertson,' said the young man. 'It was a rather hot and dusty journey.'

'So I see,' said his host, peering at his guest's clothes. 'Is that your full dress uniform beneath all that filth? There was no need to don such formal attire to come and see us here, unless of course you were planning to ask for my daughter's hand, eh?' Robertson broke into gales of laughter at his own wit, which faded as he realised that his guest had not joined in.

'My dear sir, I am so terribly sorry,' he said, ringing the hand bell that stood on the table. 'That was quite unforgivable of me, to make light of such matters. Let me first summon the assistance in which you stand in such sore need, and then perhaps we can discuss this all properly. Ah, Mary, kindly show Mr Linfield to where he can reorder his attire. Get George to assist him, and arrange some refreshment for his return. In the best drawing room if you please.'

Once Linfield had washed his face and body clean, and the efficient George had beat and sponged the worst of the dust from his clothes, he felt a new man. A large glass of Madeira and some cold beef sandwiches completed his recovery.

'Now, sir, that is better,' said Robertson, 'You are once more the elegant naval officer I first met in Milton's all those months ago. May I get you anything else?'

'Nothing further, I thank you, Mr Robertson,' said the surgeon. 'I am quite restored.'

'Capital,' said his host. 'So I collect you have been involved in yet more victories over the base French?'

'Yes, sir,' said Linfield. 'I believe the *Rush* can be said to have played her full part. We were sent against the lesser stronghold of Vieux Fort, at the southern end of St Lucia, which we reduced in creditable style. Our Mr Preston and Lieutenant Macpherson of the marines played a prominent part in that victory. Then to crown that we bested a Spanish seventy-four that arrived in the bay to create mischief. Together with the *Agrius* we defeated her, a victory that is rightly the talk of the fleet.'

'By Jove, that is a notable action,' exclaimed Robertson. 'Pray, how was it achieved?'

'Captain Clay lured the Spaniard onto a sand bank,' explained Linfield. 'We then caught him between our two fires while he was unable to manoeuvre.'

'How deuced cunning of him!' chuckled his host. 'I trust it came at a modest cost in our brave men?'

'In overall numbers yes, but I fear Captain Clay paid a heavy price for his victory,' said Linfield, his face clouding. 'He was struck in the shoulder towards the end of the action, and at one moment I did despair for him. The worst is now past, but he is very weak, and will need a considerable convalescence. I have given him over to the care of the naval hospital here in Bridgetown, if you wish to see him.'

'Indeed I shall, poor man,' said Robertson. 'My daughters will certainly want to visit him.'

'Ah yes,' said the young surgeon, 'your daughters.' A silence descended over the pair. Linfield looked towards the handsome case clock that stood behind his host's back, aware in the sudden quiet of the room of the dry click of its mechanism. Robertson shuffled his feet, and cleared his throat. When this failed to draw any more from his guest, he felt compelled to fill the gap.

'Mr Linfield, may I make a request?' he asked. 'Can I prevail on your better nature to excuse my disgraceful behaviour earlier? I should never have made light of such a grave matter as a proposal of marriage.'

'Of course, Mr Robertson,' said Linfield. 'Let us consider that it never happened.'

'That is very obliging of you,' said his host, making a steeple of his fingers and addressing his next remark towards the open window. 'Because I would not want you to form the impression that I would find a suitable approach to be unwelcome.' He returned his gaze to his guest and smiled. 'Both my daughters are at present away visiting friends, from which you will collect that our reintegration into Barbadian society that began after the governor's ball has continued in a modest way. We can now number perhaps a dozen houses on the island where our presence is no longer regarded as abhorrent.'

'I am very pleased to hear it, Mr Robertson,' said the surgeon, 'Although I must confess to be a little vexed that Miss Emma is not here. Do you expect her to return soon?'

'Soon for certain, I make no doubt,' said Robertson. 'You will pardon my impertinence, but I take it the purpose of your visit was not just to pay your respects to me, welcome as your attention is. You are here to solicit the hand of my youngest daughter, are you not?'

'It might be thought strange to discuss such matters with the father in advance of the subject of such a proposal, but you have guessed correctly, sir,' said Linfield. 'Having gained her acceptance, I would naturally have asked for an interview with you next, to seek your consent.'

'Quite so,' said the planter. 'I wondered perhaps, in the absence of my daughter, we might not use the time we have to discuss some of the particulars that I would want clarified before such a union could have my blessing?'

'It seems a little irregular,' said Linfield, 'but I have no objection. What would you like to know?'

'Once married, will you continue with your career as a naval surgeon, Mr Linfield?' asked Robertson.

'If Miss Emma were to do me the honour of accepting me,' said the surgeon, 'I would resign my warrant as surgeon and set up in practice onshore as a doctor. I hold that the lengthy absences of a naval officer are likely to be injurious to Emma's happiness.'

'An interesting plan, Mr Linfield,' said Robertson. 'Did you have any notion of where you might set up your practice?'

'Why, back in England, in a rural area close to London,' replied Linfield.

'I see,' said the plantation owner. 'And what can you do to reassure me that you will be able to maintain my daughter in the style to which she is accustomed here in Barbados? Servants, a carriage, some horses to ride for her leisure, and so forth?'

'I am not wholly without financial resource,' said Linfield. 'I have some of my service pay that I have saved, and prize money that I have received or am due, but I will not deny that it would not be adequate to fund such levels of expenditure.'

'That is disappointing to hear, Mr Linfield,' said Robertson.

'But let me reassure you that I am not without prospects,' said the surgeon. 'There will naturally be a period while I establish my reputation and connections as a doctor when we will be under some financial constraint, but after that I am sure matters will improve. I speak only of my own resources. If Miss Emma's dowry was sufficiently generous to fund such luxury, matters might lie differently?'

'Aye, I am sure they might,' said Robertson, appraising his guest from under his bushy eye brows. 'Look, sir, I am a man of business. As such, may I offer you a little advice, examining your situation as I might a business proposition with regard to your future happiness?'

'By all means, sir,' said Linfield.

'Miss Emma was born on Barbados, and has only known an upbringing of ease in the warmth of the tropics,' began Robertson. 'I well remember the climate of our home island. I was brought up in Dundee, you will collect. I make no doubt that Emma would endure whatever she must to be with the man she loves. But in time might not some understandable resentment accrue against the person who had taken her from her life here in Barbados to be the wife of a struggling rural doctor in the midst of an English winter?'

'Well, I would need to explain to her how matters lie before she made her final commitment,' said Linfield, his brow furrowed. Robertson looked at the young man for a moment, not unkindly.

'May I lay out an alternate proposal, Mr Linfield?' he asked. 'Set up your practice here in Barbados. There is a shortage of good medical care for the white population, and none at all for the black. As part of Emma's dowry I can fund you while you become established in your career and set up your home together, and I will also be your first client. I will pay you to look after the medical needs of my plantation workers. How does that sound?'

'If I was here on the island, I would still agitate for the abolition of slavery,' warned Linfield.

'I didn't doubt it for a moment,' said Robertson.

'Well it rather puts the cart before the horse since I have yet to speak to your daughter,' said the surgeon, 'but if it would truly make Emma happy, I will gladly accept.'

'Well that is resolved then,' said Robertson, clasping Linfield's hand, 'for I know for certain she will have you. She has spoken of little else since the night of the ball.'

'Is that so?' laughed Linfield in relief.

'You need not take my word for it much longer, for if I am not very much mistaken that is the sound of the returning carriage,' said Robertson, rising from his chair and cocking an ear towards the hall. 'I will take Elizabeth for a turn in the garden, while you speak with Emma in here. Will that answer?' He slipped from the room, and Linfield heard his booming voice in the hall.

'Emma, my dear, you have a visitor in the drawing room. Off you go now, child.'

*****

Clay heard the sound of water as it tinkled into a bowl and opened his eyes. He was in a small whitewashed room in the naval hospital in Bridgetown. The door stood open, allowing him to see out onto a shaded veranda and beyond that the flowers and trees of a small sunlit garden. From the length of the shadows he could tell that evening approached. He tried to push himself up in his bed, but then winced at the hot pain in his shoulder.

'Easy there, sir,' said the sailor who had been mixing the water. He hurried over to lift Clay up in bed, and to adjust his pillows.

'I am Wheeler, sir,' explained the man, 'I am here to give you a shave and a bit of a wash. The admiral is on his way to see you, and I am quite sure you would not wish to present yourself to him looking as you do, begging your pardon like.'

'Can you pass me the glass, Wheeler,' he asked. The sailor held the small mirror up in front of him and Clay examined the strange face that looked back at him from the square frame. For all his life at sea his skin had been tanned from long exposure to sun and wind, yet the Clay in the mirror appeared pale and anaemic. He ran his hand over the unfamiliar stubble that covered his lower face. Even his calm grey eyes looked a little different, as if still haunted by the pain he had gone through.

'Let's get that filthy beard away, sir,' urged Wheeler. 'You will feel better with that off.' He placed a towel around Clay's neck, and tilted his head back. As he worked up a lather of soap he chatted to the patient.

'So the little old *Rush* has done for a mighty Spanish galleon, they tell me,' he said. 'Have you ever heard tell of such a victory? You're going to be right famous after this, sir. General Abercromby is quite put out, they say, him having captured the whole of Old Saint Lucy, and yet returns to find everyone talking only of this ship you bested. The *Saint Paul* wasn't it?'

'*San Felipe*, and she was only a seventy-four,' corrected Clay, wisely saying no more as he felt the edge of Wheeler's razor running over his throat.

'Aye, the *San Philip*, that's the one. Only a seventy-four, you says, sir!' marvelled Wheeler, working his way across Clay's face. 'Still not exactly a fair fight, was it? Done with a very creditable butcher's bill I hear too. Hardly a man lost on the *Agrius*, and only a few on the *Rush*. Oh!' he paused, the razor hovering above Clay's face.

'What have you done man?' asked Clay, reaching for the

mirror.

'No, I ain't nicked you, sir,' continued Wheeler. 'Just realised how stupid I have been, talking of butcher's bills with you being injured an' all. Right, let's rinse you off. There, don't that feel more like it?'

As Clay wiped his face clean he heard a commotion on the veranda.

'Yes, yes,' said the voice of Admiral Caldwell. 'Of course I will not over tax your damned patient, who, may I remind you, is also one of my captains. Now, kindly step aside, young man and let me through.' Wheeler gathered up his bowl and towel, and slipped from the room, just as the jaunty figure of the admiral bustled in.

'Ah, Clay, my dear sir,' he said. 'Good to see you awake at last.' Clay tried to pull himself out of bed, but was stopped by his visitor.

'No, none of that, captain. Back into bed, if you please. That is an order.' Admiral Caldwell pulled up a chair, and sat down next to the bed. He fixed Clay with the same kindly brown eyes he remembered so well.

'I trust I find you on the mend, my dear sir?' he asked.

'Yes, thank you, sir,' replied Clay. 'I am still rather weak, but I was able to walk a little on the veranda earlier, and I have had some portable soup. My wound still troubles me, but I am told that will pass. The surgeons say that it may never be wholly restored, but I am fortunate that it is my left arm. I can still use my right to wield a sword or a pen.'

'Well, that is excellent news,' said Caldwell. 'We did fear we had lost you when you first arrived. A musket ball can be a most unwelcome visitor.'

The admiral studied Clay's face, and thought how thin and gaunt he looked. No question of him resuming duty for many months, he said to himself. Still, I have a plan for that.

'Yes, you really do look much improved,' he continued. 'Now, have you heard much intelligence of the expedition? I am sure you have been told that the attack on St Lucia was a great success, and the whole island is now under our control. Once the army has it quite pacified we shall move on to take Martinique from the Frogs. Your prize is still stuck on that infernal sand bank, by the way, but Captain Parker is confident he will get it afloat soon. Apparently the hull is not too badly damaged. Upon my word Clay, you're making a fine reputation for yourself as a fighting captain. Is there any size of enemy you are not prepared to take on, what?'

'We did have them at a disadvantage, sir,' said Clay.

'Yes you did,' said Caldwell, 'but isn't that the essence of the thing? I have plenty of captains who can fight the enemy broadside to broadside. Every one of them is a capital fellow, sound as a bell. None of them want for pluck and all can spill an ocean of gore when required. But I know of far fewer captains who can consider first how they might place their enemy at a disadvantage, and I know less still who would have thought to have sprung a trick such as the one you did. Captain Parker, who let me tell you, Clay, is not an easy man to impress, has been most fulsome in his praise of you. Gushing like a virgin bride almost, if you can imagine that.'

'That is very handsome of him, sir,' said the patient. 'He played his part too, accepting my suggestion to lure the San Felipe on, and delivering the coup de grace to finish the Dons. The credit should be shared, by rights.'

'Well, that is very handsomely said too, Clay,' said the admiral. 'Now, before I fall foul of the sawbones for keeping you up too long, and aggravating your damned humours, or whatever, I need to tell you what will be happening next. The fleet will be departing again soon for the attack on

Martinique, but you shall not be coming with us this time.'

'But sir,' protested Clay. Caldwell held up a restraining hand.

'You have been very gravely wounded, and have frankly confounded the surgeons by being alive at all,' he explained. 'You stand in need of a considerable period of convalescence, for which I will be sending you home as soon as you are fit to travel. Besides, I no longer have a suitable vacancy for you.'

'I don't understand, sir,' said Clay. 'Why would I not resume the command of the *Rush*?' Deep in Caldwell's eyes the kindly twinkle returned.

'Because, my dear Clay, a sloop of war is much too small a ship for a post captain to command.' Clay stared at the admiral for a moment as what he had said sunk in.

'You are promoting me, sir?' he said, almost to himself.

'Yes I am,' smiled Caldwell. 'You know, Clay, now that you have made post at a relatively young age, it is most probable that, should you live long enough, you too will one day be an admiral. When that should happen you may be favoured with the command of a foreign station, as I have been privileged to have. One of the perquisites that come with that role is the ability to promote without reference to London in time of war. More often than not it is used to reward followers and repay favours. But it can also be used for the good of the service, to elevate an outstanding individual who lacks the connections to advance in any other way. It is for this reason that I am promoting you now. Well, that, and also the knowledge that anything less would provoke a mutiny in my squadron after your recent heroics.'

'I don't know how to begin to thank you for this, sir,' said Clay.

'No need for thanks,' said Caldwell. 'As I have explained,

my motives are quite selfish really. But now that you are one of my post captains, however briefly, perhaps you might give me some advice. Who do you hold should replace you as commander of the *Rush*? I was thinking about Lieutenant Windham? He comes from a long established naval family.'

'I do not think Mr Windham is quite ready for that step yet, sir,' said Clay. 'I would say he lacks the experience for an independent command at this time.'

'No?' said the admiral. 'Who would you suggest then?' Clay thought for a moment. This was heady stuff indeed. For years he had been without any influence in the service, and now he found he had the power to make someone's career, and perhaps to pay back a debt. There was only one name he could choose.

'I believe that Lieutenant John Sutton would make an excellent Master and Commander, sir,' said Clay.

'Sutton, you say?' said Caldwell. 'Very well, let us make it so. Now I must leave you, before I am set upon by a battalion of furious naval surgeons. Goodbye for now, Clay, and good luck to you.' He rose to his feet and turned to leave, but then paused at the door.

'I almost forgot,' he said. 'As a post captain you will be entitled to followers to return home with you. Your own coxswain for example. No need to decide immediately, but let me have the names before the squadron departs. Now kindly get some rest, Clay. That is an order.'

Once the admiral had left, rest was the last thing on Clay's mind. He found himself chuckling at the evening's turn of events. His entire naval career had seemed to be a long battle against the iniquities of patronage in the service, as he had witnessed others favoured around him. But now it was he who had been favoured, and he had been able to promote his friend too. He thought about who he would choose as his followers. He had no doubts now about the person he wanted as his coxswain, the only question was what the reaction would be in his sleepy home village when Sedgwick stepped down from the coach. He stared out of the door into the darkening garden, and his thoughts turned to Lydia, somewhere on the other side of the world. In miles she was impossibly distant still, but she was now much closer in terms of eligibility. He had been deemed unsuitable by her guardian when he was penniless Lieutenant Alexander Clay, but perhaps Captain Alexander Clay RN could expect a more favourable reception when he came to ask for Lydia's hand. He smiled to himself at the prospect.

'Yes', he said out loud. 'I am ready to go home.'

*****

The sun that had slipped below the western horizon in Barbados was already staining the eastern sky in far off Bengal with a blush of lemon. From a nearby mosque the muezzin started his call to prayers, the sound flowing across the city's roof tops like a disembodied spirit. It drifted through the curtains of Lydia Browning's bedroom and eased her awake. Her head turned on the pillow towards the sound and with blue eyes still vacant from sleep she stared at the slot of light where the curtains met. The muezzin finished his call and the birds in the garden below her balcony replaced him, the gentle coo of the green pigeons punctuated by the strident call of a Tailorbird.

She felt languid contentment as she first stretched out beneath the sheets, and then folded her slender limbs back into the warm nest close about her body. For a moment she puzzled over this feeling of joy that had replaced so much recent pain, and then in a rush she remembered. There had been a letter that had arrived yesterday from darling, darling Betsey Clay. When she held the package it had felt oddly stiff, but when she opened it she had immediately seen why. Within the folded sheets in Betsey's rounded hand had been the second letter, the writing unknown, but obviously masculine. Daring to hope what it might be, she had taken it out into the garden to find her favourite bower in which to read it in private. Her heart had leapt as she saw who it was from. *Commander Alexander Clay, at sea on board His Majesty's Sloop of War* Rush. It had travelled for over four months, across the wide Atlantic, around the Cape of Good Hope to Bombay, and then over the dusty Indian plains to find her here, in her garden, just as he had imagined in his final paragraph.

She pulled the folded sheets from beneath her pillow, and angled them towards the slither of light that came from the window. She read the end of the letter, warmed once more by the serendipity of where she had first read it.

I shall imagine you reading this letter in some private situation all of your own, in the oriental garden that surrounds your house. It will be quite full of exotic flowers, huge colourful butterflies and strange birds. The garden I hold before my mind's eye is walled in red sandstone, with palm trees framing the tops of the temples visible in the distance. You will read this letter, and I hope smile with pleasure, sure in your heart that though I am far away, my love is all about you. I can picture you now, in a sky blue riding habit. You will put away my letter, and go off on your ride, preferably upon an elephant!

A Sloop of War

Until we are together once more, believe in me.

Alexander Clay

'Oh, I do believe in you, my darling Alexander,' she whispered, as if the well remembered head of chestnut curls rested next to her on her pillow, the steel grey eyes gazing back at her. The description of the garden was as if he had been there with her, almost every detail correct. What he could not know was that her morning rides had been cancelled for weeks now, and that her dress was not blue but black out of respect for her uncle, struck down by cholera.

Lydia slid the letter back under her pillow as the door creaked open. From the lightness of the step she guessed it was her maid, and she looked round to see her place a jug of steaming water and a towel by the wash stand. When she had done so, she turned to see if her mistress was awake.

'Thank you, Talika,' said Lydia with a smile. 'I believe I will stay abed a little longer this morning. Will you return in half an hour?' In response Talika brought her hands together and lowered her eyes as if in prayer for a moment, and then slipped from the room. Lydia relaxed back into her bed, and continued to gaze towards the silver line of daylight, her thoughts far away, until she sensed someone was looking at her. She glanced around and saw her aunt stood at the door.

'Aunt, have you been there long?' Lydia asked, sitting up in bed and patting the covers in invitation. The older woman came over and sat down next to her, running a hand over her niece's hair as she did so.

'You are so beautiful, my child, and so very brave,' she said. 'To have lost your parents at such a tender age, and now your darling Uncle Francis too....' Her words were cut off as she turned her face away, her shoulders heaving with grief. Lydia enfolded an arm around her aunt and drew her sobbing face into the cradle between her shoulder and neck.

'It will be all right,' she whispered, her own eyes brimming with tears. After a while she felt her aunt stiffen a little in her arms, and she let her sit back upright.

'Thank you, Lydia,' she said. 'I have regained my composure now. The reason I came to see you so early in the morning is to tell you that I have come to a decision. Raw as the loss of dear Francis still is, I believe it is time for us to return to England. India can have no hold on us, now that the chief reason for our being here is no more. Are you ready to undertake such a journey?'

'Yes, aunt,' smiled Lydia, 'I am ready with all my heart. It is time to go home.'

The End

Author's Note

Historical fiction is by its very nature a blend of truth and the made up, and *A Sloop of War* is no exception. For those who would like to understand where that boundary is, the ships *Rush*, *Agrius* and *San Felipe* are fictitious, as are the characters that make up their crews. That said, I have matched them, and the lives of their sailors, as closely as I can to ships and practices of the time. Those with an exceptional knowledge of the period may have noticed that I have added gangways to the Swan class sloop *Rush*, which is not accurate, but helps the purposes of the plot. All other errors are my own.

Historical figures, such as Sir Richard Nugent and Admiral Caldwell, are accurate. St Lucia was captured from the French, although I have moved the campaign a little in time. Details of the landing and the action ashore is wholly my own creation. The area around Vieux Fort in particular is hard to re-imagine, as it is now the site of St Lucia's main international airport. Similarly the details of plantation life on Barbados are also fictitious.

Those with an interest in 18th century medicine may find the treatment that Clay undergoes all too convincing for a period before anaesthetic or modern anti-bacterial practices. If anything I have toned down the Goyan horror of that scene.

The role of black sailors in the 18th century navy has been sadly neglected, often because one of the prime sources, muster books, give no clues to ethnicity. But other evidence exists of the significant role they played in the navy, perhaps most strikingly in the bronze plaques that decorate the base of Nelson's column in London. The one that depicts Trafalgar shows a black sailor in a prominent position. I will hope to address this under representation in a small way through the medium of Able Sedgwick in future novels in this series.

About The Author

Philip K. Allan

Philip K. Allan comes from Watford in the United Kingdom. He still lives in Hertfordshire with his wife and his two teenage daughters. He has spent most of his working life to date as a senior manager in the motor industry. It was only in the last few years that he has given that up to concentrate on his novels full time.

He has a good knowledge of the ships of the 18th century navy, having studied them as part of his history degree at London University, which awoke a lifelong passion for the period. He is a member of the Society for Nautical Research and a keen sailor. He believes the period has unrivalled potential for a writer, stretching from the age of piracy via the voyages of Cook to the battles and campaigns of Nelson.

Philip K. Allan

From a creative point of view he finds it offers him a wonderful platform for his work. On the one hand there is the strange, claustrophobic wooden world of the period's ships; and on the other hand there is the boundless freedom to move those ships around the globe wherever the narrative takes them. All these possibilities are fully exploited in the Alexander Clay series of novels.

His inspiration for the series was to build on the works of novelists like C.S. Forester and in particular Patrick O'Brian. His prose is heavily influenced by O'Brian's immersive style. He too uses meticulously researched period language and authentic nautical detail to draw the reader into a different world. But the Alexander Clay books also bring something fresh to the genre, with a cast of fully formed lower deck characters with their own back histories and plot lines in addition to the officers. Think *Downton Abbey* on a ship, with the lower deck as the below stairs servants.

If You Enjoyed This Book Visit

PENMORE PRESS

www.penmorepress.com

All Penmore Press books are available directly through our website, amazon.com, Barnes and Noble and Nook, Sony Reader, Apple iTunes, Kobo books and via leading bookshops across the United States, Canada, the UK, Australia and Europe.

The Captain's Nephew

by

Philip K. Allan

After a century of war, revolutions, and Imperial conquests, 179
Europe is still embroiled in a battle for control of the sea a
colonies. Tall ships navigate familiar and foreign waters, a
ambitious young men without rank or status seek their futures
Naval commands. First Lieutenant Alexander Clay of HMS Agrius
self-made, clever, and ready for the new age. But the old wor
dominated by patronage, retains a tight hold on advanceme
Though Clay has proven himself many times over, Captain Per
Follett is determined to promote his own nephew.

Before Clay finds a way to receive due credit for his exploits, he
first need to survive them. Ill-conceived expeditions ashore, hur
for privateers in treacherous fog, and a desperate chase across t
Atlantic are only some of the challenges he faces. He must endeav
to bring his ship and crew through a series of adventures stretchi
from the bleak coast of Flanders to the warm waters of t
Caribbean. Only then might high society recognize his achievemen
—and allow him to ask for the hand of Lydia Browning, the wom
who loves him regardless of his station.

PENMORE PRESS
www.penmorepress.com

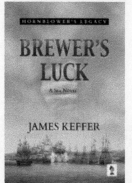

BREWER'S LUCK

BY

JAMES KEFFER

After gaining valuable experience as an aide to Governor Lord Horatio Hornblower, William Brewer is rewarded with a posting as first lieutenant on the frigate HMS *Defiant*, bound for American waters. Early in their travels, it seems as though Brewer's greatest challenge will be evading the wrath of a tyrannical captain who has taken an active dislike to him. But when a hurricane sweeps away the captain, the young lieutenant is forced to assume command of the damaged ship, and a crew suffering from low morale.

Brewer reports their condition to Admiral Hornblower, who orders them into the Caribbean to destroy a nest of pirates hidden among the numerous islands. Luring the pirates out of their coastal lairs will be difficult enough; fighting them at sea could bring disaster to the entire operation. For the *Defiant* to succeed, Brewer must rely on his wits, his training, and his ability to shape a once-ragged crew into a coherent fighting force.

PENMORE PRESS
www.penmorepress.com

Fortune's Whelp
by
Benerson Little

Privateer, Swordsman, and Rake:

Set in the 17th century during the heyday of privateering and the decline of buccaneering, *Fortune's Whelp* is a brash, swords-out sea-going adventure. Scotsman Edward MacNaughton, a former privateer captain, twice accused and acquitted of piracy and currently seeking a commission, is ensnared in the intrigue associated with the attempt to assassinate King William III in 1696. Who plots to kill the king, who will rise in rebellion—and which of three women in his life, the dangerous smuggler, the wealthy widow with a dark past, or the former lover seeking independence—might kill to further political ends? Variously wooing and defying Fortune, Captain MacNaughton approaches life in the same way he wields a sword or commands a fighting ship: with the heart of a lion and the craft of a fox.

PENMORE PRESS
www.penmorepress.com

MIDSHIPMAN GRAHAM AND THE
BATTLE OF
ABUKIR

BY

JAMES BOSCHERT

It is midsummer of 1799 and the British Navy in the Mediterranean Theater of operations. Napoleon has brought the best soldiers and scientists from France to claim Egypt and replace the Turkish empire with one of his own making, but the debacle at Acre has caused the brilliant general to retreat to Cairo.

Commodore Sir Sidney Smith and the Turkish army land at the strategically critical fortress of Abukir, on the northern coast of Egypt. Here Smith plans to further the reversal of Napoleon's fortunes. Unfortunately, the Turks badly underestimate the speed, strength, and resolve of the French Army, and the ensuing battle becomes one of the worst defeats in Arab history.

Young Midshipman Duncan Graham is anxious to get ahead in the British Navy, but has many hurdles to overcome. Without any familial privileges to smooth his way, he can only advance through merit. The fires of war prove his mettle, but during an expedition to obtain desperately needed fresh water – and an illegal duel – a French patrol drives off the boats, and Graham is left stranded on shore. It now becomes a question of evasion and survival with the help of a British spy. Graham has to become very adaptable in order to avoid detection by the French police, and he must help the spy facilitate a daring escape by sea in order to get back to the British squadron.

"Midshipman Graham and The Battle of Abukir is both a rousing Napoleonic naval yarn and a convincing coming of age story. The battle scenes are riveting and powerful, the exotic Egyptian locales colorfully rendered." – John Danielski, author of *Capital's Punishment*

PENMORE PRESS
www.penmorepress.com

KING'S SCARLET

BY

JOHN DANIELSKI

Chivalry comes naturally to Royal Marine captain Thomas Pennywhistle, but in the savage Peninsular War, it's a luxury he can ill afford. Trapped behind enemy lines with vital dispatches for Lord Wellington, Pennywhistle violates orders when he saves a beautiful stranger, setting off a sequence of events that jeopardize his mission. The French launch a massive manhunt to capture him. His Spanish allies prove less than reliable. The woman he rescued has an agenda of her own that might help him along, if it doesn't get them all killed.

A time will come when, outmaneuvered, captured, and stripped of everything, he must stand alone before his enemies. But Pennywhistle is a hard man to kill and too bloody obstinate to concede defeat.

PENMORE PRESS
www.penmorepress.com

Penmore Press
Challenging, Intriguing, Adventurous, Historical and Imaginative

www.penmorepress.com